A SHOT AT JUSTICE

— Karla M. Jay —

This is a work of fiction. All the characters, organizations, and events portrayed in the novel are either products of the author's imagination or used fictitiously. (except for those mentioned in the Author's Note)

Printed in the United States of America
Book Circle Press

Cover designed by Emma Faith Mayo

ISBN: 9798985322224

This book is dedicated to every person or organization who rescues children or animals from abuse and neglect

Other books by Karla M. Jay

When We Were Brave

It Happened in Silence

The Puppet Maker's Daughter

"Injustice remains injustice even if everyone participates."
~ Magnus Schwantje

– 1 –

May 18, 1998

E ach part of the weapon is in place, like a deadly table setting, but instead of crystal goblets, I see a thing that kills.

Killed.

I blink away the memories and attach a brush head soaked in bore cleanser to the cleaning rod and run it through the barrel of my grandfather's disassembled Winchester 30-30. Next, I run several cloth patches through, then a final one with oil.

I woke this morning feeling the need to pull out the old thing. Something in my dreams maybe, something itching at my past. I couldn't shake it, so I skipped breakfast, instead filling the table with the stripped pieces of Gramps's gun.

Why I chose this gun, I can't say. I still have the Glock I used during my time in Intelligence in a locker under my bed, where I keep my old badge and Nicaraguan ID from when I started out as a bridge agent. While passing on a message to an undercover officer, my cover was blown. Fucking Latin American language with the same pronunciation of *votar* and *botar*. My "vote for" a grenade instead of "throw" a grenade nearly got us killed.

I got promoted. The "guy in chair" life served me better. High-stress, fast moving, real impact. My brain's need to organize and order information, people, and tasks kept me well suited to the office atmosphere. But the Glock came with the badge, something I strapped to myself the few times I went out into the field with an agent, a thing I never fired outside of my proficiency testing.

I finish wiping the rifle barrel and place it on the worn wooden table in the same kitchen my grandmother used when she'd scramble eggs and kiss me on the forehead. But instead of her homemade meals, this kitchen is filled with the rank aromas of metal and grease.

I'd forgotten how much I hated the scent of gun oil. It's like a distasteful relative showing up, uninvited. The scent is suddenly too heavy, weighing me down with darker recollections. That day in the woods when I was eleven and everything went sideways.

A premonition of danger tickles at my neck like loose spiderwebs. My shitty upbringing has given me a skewed sixth sense that if all is well, soon the other shoe is going to kick me in the ass. Or maybe because life isn't trying to completely fuck me over, I believe some terrible event must be imminent, shaking itself into life just beyond the edge of tomorrow.

Probably the imminent danger idea.

I readjust the disassembled pieces, admiring the order of each. Barrel, slide, guide rod, frame, and magazine. In perfect order. One by one I wipe them down and replace each to its spot on the table.

I left the CIA after six years and, at age twenty-eight, returned to rural Ohio where I'd built a small community of friends, even more so after my grandparents died three years ago. They raised me here from age eleven until I left seven years later for college and then my "supply job" with the military. My life now is in direct contrast to the isolated childhood I had in Bitterroot National Forest with my father. If you pointed it out on a map, your finger would land on the bottom left corner of Montana.

So why can't I shake away the ominous feeling? Maybe it's the season, the end of spring warming into summer. The sweet bloom of fully green leaves, mixed with the pungent tang of iron filling the air. I shut my eyes at the memory of the barrel flash, the weight of the gun. The blood.

Again, I resist being pulled into the past and check the cleanliness of each part on the table.

My father and I never had many good moments. He'd been a forest ranger, often trailing the scents of pine needles and whiskey off him, especially during the deep folds of winter nights. But our last day in the woods, that day had been a life changer. For both of us.

I can't reassemble the gun fast enough before I return it to the gun cabinet, a piece of locked furniture I've been able to ignore these past three years.

Three clucks of my tongue and my Dobermans, Florence and Rome, jump up from where they're curled on the kitchen floor, their nails clicking on the linoleum as they approach me.

"Hey you two." I rub their heads, relishing the sensation of their warm bodies under my hands. They lean against me on either side. "Daddy's off to teach for a few hours."

I acquired the dogs after my grandparents died, when the house echoed grief over their deaths. The pups were barely eight weeks old, and I got them in a trade. A local Doberman breeder, one of the world's top producers of best-in-show winners, commissioned a Doberman sculpture from me for three thousand dollars. While they were both the smallest in the litter, I saw how tiny Rome propped up little Florence. As they cuddled in their box to keep each other warm, the tenderness I saw there was foreign to my own childhood. I asked for them in lieu of payment for the Doberman sculpture. The owner laughed at my choice, but now they're massive, healthy, and beautiful. The breeder offered six thousand dollars to buy them back a year ago.

As if.

Florence and Rome follow at my heels, their stump tails wagging. Some things don't have a price.

Yet, there's no remedy for what happened to my first dog in Montana. Again, that memory tries to push into my mind. That fucking smug face—dad's face. Heat warms my neck. No. I can't let that image back in. Keesha's furry body, and the gun still in my father's shaking hand.

Sick of these memories, I head outside and scan the property and massive junkyard I inherited when my grandparents died. Of course, it's been my home too since I moved here after my dad's death.

Belton, Ohio has an isolation that feels more friendly than the lonely mountains of Montana. It offers its own form of companionship.

The sun is well into the sky as I cross the flat yard that separates the house from the store. As a child, this area was a curious labyrinth of strewn cars and rusted junk. After my grandfather died, I organized the vehicles in the junkyard that extends for acres to the side of the house, leaving a path to the small country store my grandpa opened with my grandma in the '40s.

I've had enough shocks in my thirty-five years on earth. The traumatic past, the high-stress career. I can't imagine I'll ever leave here now that I've arranged my life where I can indulge the artistic side I'd used as an escape as a kid. Few interruptions and limited surprises.

I shake away the musings of the past—it's time to get going.

"Snuggle up," I say to the dogs. They disappear through the doorway of their doghouse as I close the gate in the fencing surrounding it. Their mini house is climate-controlled and the size of a large shed, with room for my repurposed childhood bed, complete with their favorite blankets and pillows, a braided rug on the hardwood floor, and an outside covered patio where they always have fresh water and food.

I'm accused of liking my dogs more than people. And it's true. They're my sounding board most days when no one is around.

My girlfriend, Victoria, loves my dogs. So far, our on-again, off-again relationship has worked for us, although the last time we talked I got the feeling she wants something deeper. She mentioned spending more nights over, having space for some clothes, a toothbrush. Her pretty brown eyes drilled into mine as she suggested it two days ago, and I kept it cool. I want her around. I like having her around. But does she deserve to be with a guy who keeps her at arm's length because the secrets from his past can't be shared?

No. Breathe deep and shut these memories the fuck up.

I follow the dirt driveway to the store and try to avoid the standing puddles. It's mid-May, and although spring has been unseasonably warm, this morning's rain leaves fingers of cold trailing across the surrounding woods and fields from Lake Erie.

I squint as the sun glints off the various old signs attached to the front wall of the store, named On the Rustic Side. For sale inside are old-timey items like apple butter, whisk brooms decorated in aprons, and bibs embroidered with bunnies.

Grandpa Dardin collected the signs. It was basically an obsession. I run my fingers along the raised metal on two of my favorites, *Old Gold Cigarettes—not a cough in a carload* and *Pepsi Cola—A nickel drink worth a dime.*

Finding places for the signs was easy. Grandpa built the house behind the store that sits up front along the road, giving plenty of space on the front walls for the décor. Grandma added to it with a giant sunflower clock with a bent minute hand that makes a tiny screech when it passes the nine. Not much has changed in either building since the '40s.

I push through the front door.

"How's it going, Greta?" I lift the lid of the pop cooler and take out an Orange Crush.

Greta sits on a stool behind the counter, reading a paperback. She sets the book down; her smile is generous and welcoming. "Hiya, Wyatt. It's been slow today."

"So the usual, right?" I chuckle. The store is not a moneymaker, but it's a great tax write-off. It's just off Route 59, making it a good location for road trippers looking for a quick stop on their way to Akron or locals who love to stop for a beer and a chat.

Greta shrugs. "There's a chill out. Might keep people home." Her knuckles are swollen, and I know the cold bothers her, but she never complains. She works the store most days, allowing me time with junk sales, the time I volunteer at the club, or even my own budding hobby in painting frescoes using slack-lime putty, like the old Italian masters made. Outside is a shack where I hold the white, high-calcium, liquid lime putty that matures over a few weeks so that I can then slap it onto a wooden plank and begin sculpting figures and shapes. It gives me a sense of control, I think. The commissioned scenery piece I finished that covered the side of a nursery was an exciting challenge. And lucrative.

She runs her fingers through her short white hair. It's combed off to one side, in almost a manly way, but she likes it like that. When she has her monthly hair appointments in Geigerton, a nearby town, I always drive her because we catch lunch after. The beautician tries to convince her to grow it out, but Greta refuses.

"Where are you off to today?" She pulls her blue cardigan tighter. She lives a half mile down the road in a double-wide next to a much larger maple syrup production shack. Her husband, Meryl, died twenty-four years ago. She never remarried.

"Back to the Boys and Girls Club. I'm teaching watercolor this time." I shake my head. "Learned my lesson with pastel crayons and beginners last week."

She chuckles. "I imagine that was a mess."

"Ten minutes to get going and an hour to clean up the kids' hands."

"Well, you best get on. I'm good to stay and lock up if you don't want to hurry back." She straightens a few of the maple syrup bottles lined up by the register. Each spring, Greta taps the trees and produces quart jugs of syrup she sells in the store. I have a few locals bring their goods for consignment, and I almost always sign them up, but I had to tell old man Sprague out on Highway 94 that I wasn't interested in deer antler wine stoppers. No one says, "I wish this wine bottle looked more like a deer," unless they've downed too much wine to begin with. I've also said no to AstroTurf flip-flops—*you'll feel like you're walking on grass everywhere*—and miniature toilet bowl necklaces.

I retrace my steps to the side of the house making my way to the junk-yard, as most people would call it. I refer to the expansive acres of rusted metal as treasures, all carefully lined up in twenty or more rows. Like the '84 Oldsmobile Firenza station wagon I'm currently driving. I have my pick from a lot of old cars Gramps collected, some all the way back to the '30s. Most are more corroded metal husks than actual cars, but there are many that still run.

I tap the Firenza's roof, satisfied at the hollow sound that answers. It's square, compact, with a ludicrous number of headlights, as if the designers wanted to show the world this was their version of a "bright idea."

Ha.

Corny jokes aside, it runs well, never lets me down, and has a "Sorry for Driving So Close in Front of You" bumper sticker that makes me smile when big ol' trucks ride my tail.

I drop into the seat and roll down the window. In the distance, one of my favorite sounds is coming out of hibernation. The buzz of a distant chainsaw signals that spring is here and the woods are warm enough to clear away the winter's deadfall. Spring was my mother's favorite time of year too. "You smell like dirt," she'd say, pulling me close after a busy day playing around our cabin in Montana. "It must be spring."

Damn, today is just sucking me backward in time. I push away the deep ache that surfaces when I think of my mom and try to remember the good times. There were smiles and laughter, those years before I turned nine, when she left Dad and me.

The hot flush is back, and I roll down a window to let in some of the spring air. If she hadn't left, I wouldn't have been stuck with the drunk, and my dog Keesha would have been safe from him. He would have been safe from me.

I stick to the less traveled back roads as I near Akron, trying to weed through the shitstorm of my past, trying to grasp something warm and fuzzy, but it takes an energy I'm not quite willing to spend.

The sun highlights the spider pattern running through the tarmac, where road crews filled its cracked face with tar. This is a land of barbed wire fences, cow pastures, and ofttimes a wind feathering through the grasses along the ditch. If I currently painted landscapes, I could throw up an easel anywhere along here. The setting is the balm I need to pull away from the mixed torture this morning's memories have stirred up in me.

Painting, sculpting, the frescoes. It's all an escape and I know it. When I left the CIA, I went from having two dozen action items—weeks spent prepping and planning for an agent to go into the field under extremely dangerous circumstances—to a simpler life in rural Ohio. Any screwup here didn't lead to the death of team members or more civilians. I'd only been back four years when my grandparents died. Their deaths narrowed my world even more and I've been happy to create order on a smaller scale. An individual one. Art allows me to mix a meaningful combination of colors and add the strokes to create an image so inviting, a person would want to step inside.

I never thought artist was a word I'd be known by. Or two words, responsible adult. Perhaps I subconsciously needed to be the opposite of what my old man was, and art was my way to do that.

A hawk circles over a cornfield of last year's stalks, hunting for lunch. I steer around broken glass in the road. Car shrapnel is a telltale sign somebody recently hit something. Most likely a deer got clipped, one of the main reasons cars end up in my junkyard.

And there it is off to the side of the road—a mangled pile of tan fur and legs pointing in four directions.

The foreboding creates a tight place behind my eyes. Twenty-four years ago. An ordinary day like today, in the Montana forest, when I raised the gun like the one I had so carefully cleaned this morning and quickly aimed it at a bear charging alongside my father. After I pulled the trigger and unloaded all six shots, they both were dead.

I punch on the radio to a hard rock station, spin the volume, and let Steven Tyler drown out the bloody images, looking forward to spending my afternoon with a group of kids whose lives are a little less fucked-up than my own.

– 2 –

The thirty-minute drive to Akron flies by as I organize my thoughts for today's project with the kids. We'll focus on perspective with lighter images in the background and darker up front. I can feel the weight of the morning's apprehension begin to melt away as my car navigates the open freeway. Not much traffic late afternoon on a Monday, although getting back home will be a different story.

After moving in with my grandparents, I spent a fair number of weekdays after school and during summer afternoons at the Boys and Girls Club. It's what introduced me to art, letting me express some of my trauma through color and medium. This last year or so volunteering at the club is the least I could do to give a little back.

The kids that show up range from age nine to fourteen so it's tricky teaching new concepts, but I usually let the younger kids free paint, exploring the medium in their own way, while walking the older kids step-by-step through some of the basics of art theory.

I pull into the parking lot and back into a space, hood of the car toward the exit. Military habits die hard. Never put your back toward trouble. Have an escape plan. I grab my art bag from the backseat and push through the front door. Today the kitchen pushes out smells that signify it's a pigs-in-a-blanket kind of day.

"Hiya, Wyatt." Yvonne works the front desk, and nobody gets in unless she approves. She's in her forties, wiry, and her calm exterior hides a tiger. I've seen her push through a group of fighting boys and never flinch as blows landed on her.

"Hey, Yvonne." I set my bag down and hitch my shoulders a tad to unzip my outer jacket. "How was your weekend?"

"Went to my sister's up in Cleveland." She crosses her arms. "I still want to set you two up. She's pretty but shy, like you."

"You're always looking out for me." I want to add that I'm not shy—I just don't like people all that much. And things are going great with Victoria. Instead, I say, "I finished off your rhubarb jam. You know, it would sell real well at my store."

"You're frittering your life away out at that junkyard." She raises her hands. "I'm just saying. Whenever you're ready."

"I'll let you know when I'm tired of frittering." I smile and grab my supplies and head to the arts and crafts room.

A small group of boys are shooting hoops across the gym floor, sneakers squeaking in time with their hurried movements. Twenty years ago, this gym had wooden bleachers that gave you a splinter when you sat on them—at least that's been upgraded. I've seen other changes like carpet and paint through the years, but the kids are the same, coming from families with problems, or parents who both work more than one job. Everyone here has a story.

I set up the painting stuff in the middle of a long table and fill up the water jars while I wait for the kids to join me.

As the youngsters clamor in, I note the regulars. Kendra who always wears basketball shorts and is funny as hell sits at the first table, checking out the paint sets. Ike, who has a bit of a limp and a shy smile, likes to let the others settle before finding a place to sit, so I don't rush him. Soon, the clatter calms and most everyone has found a seat.

Denny has already begun dipping his brush in the water and messing with the paints. The tablecloth around him and the old T-shirts I brought to protect the kids' clothes are splattered with a pretty good imitation of a Jackson Pollock.

"Hold up, Denny. You're gonna be out of paint before we all get started."

He grins, his top two teeth missing, the side ones filled with silver.

Just as I finish explaining our project for the day and hold up the simple monochrome landscape we're going to create together, one of my favorite students shuffles in, his head hung low. My eyes go straight to the cast covering his right forearm and hand.

Shit.

I look away, letting him find a place near Kendra while I try to keep calm. I've met his mom several times when she comes to pick him up. She works hard, is raising two kids, and puts up with a giant asshole of a husband. I hear he's a drunk, but as far as I know, he's never been violent before. The prickling sensation on my neck and arms, however, recognizes the look of a kid who's been smacked by his shithole father.

I walk down the long table, looking over shoulders as they all paint the first layer of the landscape—a light-colored mountain range in a single color. Once that dries, we'll add the next layer on top in a slightly darker shade of the same color, creating the feeling of depth and perspective.

Kendra chooses a periwinkle blue. Ike is working in lilac. A boy with a mop of blond hair who've I've only seen here once before uses orange, which is looking Mars-planet cool.

I make it to Jasper, who is staring at his blank page, his paint brush still dry. I kneel next to him. His eyes are puffy and a little red and he sniffs and wipes at his nose with his non-cast-covered hand. Seeing him hurt stokes that deep, achy rage inside me, but I swallow it down and lean in.

"Jasper. Hey, buddy." I'm careful not to touch him. Not only does the club have strict rules, but I also know that touch can feel overstimulating when you're going through a lot. I sit there, letting him know I'm close, and speak quietly as the others keep forming their mountain ranges.

I nod to the cast. "Does your arm hurt?"

He shakes his head and keeps it covered with his other arm.

My stomach contracts. I hate when there's nothing I can do. And I know that if I try and ask him what happened, he'll feel the need to lie.

How many times did I tell my mom I fell out of a tree or ran into a lodgepole? I was just a clumsy kid, and to keep the peace, I let my dad remain a damn saint before she left.

He finally looks up. "I can't paint." He swings his cast back and forth on the desk, tearing the paper I've laid there and nearly knocking the water to the floor. I grab the jar before it topples.

"You know what, Jasper, my man? Watercolors are meant to look abstract." I reach for another sheet on a nearby empty desk and place it in front of him. "I'll bet your left hand is just as creative as your right."

I point to the other kids' work. Jasper's mood lightens when he sees most everyone has what looks like spikey blobs filling the bottom three-quarters of their page. With a few more layers and details they might start looking like mountains.

He swipes his arm under his nose, and the move leaves a snail's trail of snot. He looks at the other kids and takes in a shuddering breath.

"Okay," he whispers.

I give him an encouraging nod and stand up. Before I reach the front of the table, I can see he's picked a deep green and begun spreading the color over his page. Kendra, who was already done with this first part, helps him hold his page in place. These are great kids. Rome and Florence are at the top of my best friend list, but these kids are there too. And even though I'm probably biased and seeing a lot of my own self in him, Jasper has become a kid I really care about.

When I first met him, he seemed like he might be trouble. He had a scowl that spoke louder than the ill-fitting clothes he wore. His name only proved his right to be angry—Xsess Randall. Only a drunk or a jerk names their kid "excess." He perked up when the staff decided to call him Jasper, a name he picked out for himself.

I keep an eye on him as I introduce the second layer while pointing to my example. More mountains painted a little lower and a little darker than the first set.

"Layers create the feeling of depth." I see a few skeptical faces. "Just give it a try. Even weird looking blobs will start to look like a landscape. Just wait until we get to the trees."

The kids dive in, dipping paintbrushes and chattering quietly. I start my rounds again.

"We're keeping the paint on the paper." I tap the page in front of Luisa who is brushing red on her fingernails.

"Okay." Her small cheeks dimple as she gives me a big smile and holds her hand up as a translucent stream of the color runs down her fingers.

I reach for one of the wet rags I brought. "Use this—"

Too late. She's wiped her hands on her white shirt, leaving a red smear across the front. I should have insisted all the kids wear the paint shirts I brought. I'll probably hear about this, although the paint is washable.

"Alrighty,"—I point at the bit of paint that has made it on the page—"I like the lollipop you're painting."

Her forehead bunches. "It's a tree when the leaves get changed."

"I see that now." I give her a big smile, which she happily returns. "Very nice."

I circle back to Jasper. He has calmed down as the thirty minutes have passed. He's not doing a half-bad job with his left hand, something I could never pull off.

I lean close to him. He's decided to paint his own version of today's project. In front of his first layer of paint, he's outlined a house with four windows. In it are three people, clearly a woman with curly hair and two smaller stick people looking out—him and his brother maybe? The fourth window showcases a dog. They're all smiling. "I knew you could do it."

He offers a tiny grin.

I circle the table again as I move us into the final layer. Details like long tree trunks in the darkest shade available that go all the way to the top of the page. It gives the illusion that you are looking through the trees to the mountain scene beyond. The kids love dragging their paint-loaded brushes up to the top of the page. The plastic tablecloths become stripes as the landscapes take form.

Ike has added a sun or moon to the sky, Kendra some small flying birds. And Jasper isn't the only one to add a happy family scene to their page. Stick figures abound.

I return to the front of the room. "Alright, guys. We're done for today. Wash your hands at the sink and I'll clean the brushes and trays." Once I gather the tablecloths, cleanup shouldn't take too long.

"I'll tape your paintings up on the wall to dry and you can take them home next time."

As the kids grab their bags and leave, I see Jasper is still seated and tearful again.

I wipe my hands on an old paint shirt and bend down. "Do you want to go to the office for a while and sit with Miss Yvonne?"

"I want my puppy back."

The flash of matted fur, the smoking gun. I blink away this morning's memories. "What's your puppy's name?" I'm curious of the breed too. A small dog? A large one? I see a malamute, but I know I'm projecting my dog into his life.

"Millie." He wipes away tears. "We just got her a few weeks ago."

Millie. Cute. I see a small dog, maybe with curly hair? Soft ears? But it's silly to imagine a breed just from a name. Really, I'm afraid to ask what happened. "Did she run away?" I swallow, trying to put the pieces together. A new dog. A broken arm. A hateful dad.

"My dad took my dog when my mom made him leave."

His mom, curly red hair, tired eyes. I only see her through the window of their dark-blue Honda Civic when she pulls up in front of the building and Jasper hops in. She kicked the dad out. Good for her. But I know how torn in half this kid feels. "I'm sorry. That's hard." Visitation, weekend schedules. It's a mess, but maybe I'm wrong. Maybe Jasper's arm really is an accident, and having some separation from his dad is the best thing for the family. Except for the dog. Of course, the bastard took the dog. Using it as leverage. "But you'll get to see Millie when you visit your dad, right?"

"He said he's going to kill Millie if he doesn't get to come home soon." His chin judders. Tears run down his face, unresponsive to his efforts to calm himself.

A high-pitched ringing fills my ears, and I'm a kid back in the Montana wilds and my father is threatening my mother, his voice like sandpaper, *If you leave, you'll be responsible for what happens to Wyatt and the dog.*

"He kicked her," Jasper whispers, bringing me back to the present.

"He kicked your mom?" Jasper has my full attention now. The room has emptied out—the kids are getting their backpacks to meet their parents at pickup.

He drops his head. "I'm not supposed to say."

I lean in and catch his eyes. "If you want to tell me, I promise it's our secret."

He pauses, then nods. "He hits my mom." His voice is tiny, and tears prick the corners of his eyes as he admits this. I never told anyone what my dad did to us. But then again, there was no one around in the backwoods to ever ask.

I pull in a breath to raise the question again about his arm, but Jasper continues.

"He kicked Millie. When I tried to stop him, he pushed me." He points to the cast. I can see that Kendra signed it before leaving, as did a couple of the other kids.

It's all I can do to keep my face calm as my emotions roil inside. I fight to offer comforting words. "Parents say awful things when they're mad at each other. I'm sure your dad won't hurt your puppy." But my heart isn't in it. I know what an angry, selfish man can do to an innocent animal. And an innocent boy.

"I hope not." He cries harder, sobs shaking his body. "She's my best friend."

I relate to that too.

"Come here." I pull him out of his chair and into a hug. Screw the club's rules of not touching a child. I get it, but this is not what they're worried about. I needed a thousand hugs after my mom left but I got the opposite many days.

"Hey. Is your mom picking you up today?"

He nods. "But she'll be late. She told me."

I take his hand. "Let's go talk to Miss Yvonne."

When we reach the office, she listens to my story, keeping her face set in a neutral gaze as her nails dig into the palm of her other hand. "Y'all can just hang here for a minute. Okay?"

I've never seen this softer side of Yvonne. She gestures to me while Jasper looks out a window, probably hoping his mom won't be too late. She pulls a file from the metal cabinet and opens it on the desk.

"Jasper's file says he's in Sagerton. Mom works at the FedEx there, and she let me know she'll be here about fifteen minutes late." We both look at our watches. It's already seven minutes past regular four thirty pickup time. Out the window, I see the line of cars from other parents has mostly dwindled.

I nod. Sagerton is about eleven miles away, southeast of Geigerton where Greta and I eat Serbian chicken on her hair appointment days, so she's probably left work on her way here by now. No need to call her; I'll talk to her when she arrives.

Yvonne crosses the room, and when her back is to me, I glance at the intake sheet for Jasper and memorize the address. This hearkens back to my days organizing rescue missions, although I have no plans to visit their house.

I sit next to Jasper in the poorly padded office chairs. "Did it hurt much when the doctor fixed your arm?"

His face is pointed to the window, watching the last few kids climb into minivans and cars. "It was so fast. The doctor gave me a pill before to help."

"That's good." I ponder what I should say to his mom when she arrives. She's not the bad guy here. But if anyone even insinuated a husband was hurting their child, a woman might get defensive because it reflects on her. At least Jasper's mom wasn't hiding it—she'd kicked him out. That took a strength I guess my mom never found in herself. Instead, she'd run away.

"Hey. Where's your dad staying when he's not home?" I try not to sound as if I'm too nosy, but I want more information, and his mom may shut me out.

"You know the water tower?" Jasper pushes his hair out of his eyes with his uninjured hand. "Um, it has woods and swamp and then the tower. My dad sometimes stays in Grandma's trailer there."

I nod, letting some silence fill the space as we wait.

"I'm sorry you have to see them fight," I say quietly, my mouth set in a grim line. "My parents did the same when I was your age."

"Did you live with your mom?" His voice says this is his wish.

"Nah." Can't tell the kid my mother left me behind. "I moved here to live with my grandparents." Which was true two years later. I glance at my watch. Four forty p.m. I decide to get his mind off his home life. "Have you always liked drawing?"

He nods. "Sometimes my mom takes me to Nell's Art Store so I can buy a colored pencil with my allowance."

His face lit right up, so I continue, "Ah, a career guy. How do you earn your allowance?"

"My little brother and me pull weeds or sometimes shovel snow off the roof..."

The roof? What the hell? "Dang! That seems dangerous. Hope you're getting hazard pay." I try to make light of it but my hands tighten, imaging a couple of little kids on a sloping roof, shoving snow off.

"We get a quarter a week." His smile is hopeful. "I have four pencils now and almost enough to buy another one next week."

Yvonne is back and gestures to the window. She must have been watching for Jasper's mom. Sure enough, a dark-blue Honda Civic pulls up.

"Alright, kid. Your ride's here."

Jasper nods and grabs his backpack as I stand and lead him out the big front doors of the club.

"Mrs. Randall?" I ask, raising my hand in greeting as we approach the car.

She steps half out of her driver's side and looks over the car's roof at me. "Maybe not a missus for long." She shakes her head. "But, yeah, I'm Xsess's mom."

It takes me a second to understand who she's talking about. Ah yes. The kid's fucked-up name.

"I'm Wyatt. You have a very talented young man here." I ruffle the boy's hair. "Sorry he's going through some hard times right now."

"What do you mean by that?" Her words are bullets, but I can't blame her for reacting to a stranger knowing about her life.

"I'm sorry. It was rude of me to pry but he was upset about your dog." I step back. "Your son's a delight at the club. I hope he'll be back soon." I turn to leave.

"Okay." She pauses and rubs her forehead. "Sorry I snapped. I don't trust men in general but his father's getting worse." She speaks over the car still. Jasper, possibly trying to avoid the conversation, is already in the backseat.

I turn back and move closer. "Can I talk to you alone for a moment?" I try to keep my tone neutral. I don't want to put her on the defense, but I know if I don't try to understand the situation, I'll toss all night wishing I'd done more. No one did anything for me back then. I have to step up if there's a way for me to help.

She studies me then ducks inside the car to talk to Jasper. She straightens, closing the driver's door, and walks toward me. The day is cool, so he should be fine waiting there for a few minutes. I'm relieved she's willing to talk.

As she gets near, I note her chipped blue nail polish.

I gesture for her to join me closer to the building. The rest of the kids are gone by now, and Yvonne is back in the office, but I feel the need to make this conversation feel private. I lower my voice. "Are you and the boys safe?"

She raises her chin and stares me down. "Why is it any of your business?"

"You're right." I pause and shove my hands in my pockets. There are no right words for this kind of conversation. Just honesty. I look over her head a bit, no longer able to look her in the eyes, as I tell her how I was raised with a shitty dad, how I had days where I was bruised and bandaged and tried to hide the injuries from the rare visitors to our remote cabin. The scent of thick pine on crisp Montana air comes out of nowhere. I shove the olfactory memory away.

I glance at her and she's hearing me, looking at me as if deciding whether I'm telling the truth, her stiff shoulders relaxing a bit.

"I understand how trapped you might feel. I'm mostly just here to listen," I finish.

She absently picks at something on her arm, but her eyes study me. "We're safe. I threw Randy out."

I nod at the car. Toward Jasper and his broken arm. "He sounds like a jerk."

"He wants back in the house." She scrapes her sandal over something invisible on the sidewalk. "You know he kicked that puppy right in front of my boys. Busted Jasper's arm trying to get my baby to shut up."

My gut instinct was right.

I nod, relieved that she's willing to talk. "Was he arrested?" The question leaves my mouth before I can stop it, but I've already passed the too nosy line.

She shrugs, then deflates like all the fight in her drains out. "He told the cops the kid tripped. He threatened to hurt my younger boy if I said any different."

I nod, afraid if I speak that she'll stop.

She lets out a long sigh. "Randy's up at The Green Roof bragging how he got off with a warning and a fifty-buck fine." She swipes a tear that spills down her cheek, leaving a wet line that shines in the afternoon sun. "I hope my boys aren't scarred for life."

"Hey, my mom up and left." I raise my hands before she can say the "I'm so sorry" I usually get when I share stuff about Mom. "At least you've stuck around. They won't forget that."

"Thanks," she said, palming sticky hair away from her wet cheeks. "I'm glad we found the club for Jasper. Everyone here is so nice, and he's talking more, leaving his room. He draws all the time." She laughs a bit through her tears.

I smile, imagining Jasper at home, bent over a sketchpad with his new pencils, drawing his feelings, his fantasies.

"He really is a great kid."

Her eyebrows scrunch together. "Well, I appreciate you…"—she looks up at me—"saying something. We'll be all right. But if Randy hears I've been blabbing…well, keep this to yourself, okay?" Her smile fades as she turns back to the car, her beat leather sandals making a dry scraping sound on the cement.

After locking things up in the multipurpose room and saying good-bye to Yvonne, I ease into my car, letting the interior swallow me whole. I'm glad I met Jasper's mom, proud of myself for saying something. She's clearly a caring mom and that gives me hope, but will that protect them from a father that treats children and animals like punching bags?

Circling the town, I pass layered project housing and blackened smoke-stacks on a long line of factories. Akron was first a canal town until the turn of the century when it became "The Rubber Capital of the World," famous for all the car tire brands slapped onto every car in America. Schools and parks here carry the names Goodyear and Firestone.

Soon I'm back in the countryside, but I'm antsy and my fingers drum the steering wheel. A guy like her husband doesn't change. He gets away with his mean outbursts and they only escalate. Obviously, he's conned the police into not worrying about his abuse. And there are no laws that say you can't kick your own dog around. Hell, even if he killed the pup, he wouldn't be charged with anything.

I fight the memories that now resurface.

My father's drunken words tumble out of the recess from where I trapped them. *You spend too much time with that dog, Wyatt. I'm here too.*

Keesha lying on the ground, her fur matted in dark blood as thick as mud. She isn't moving. Dad's gun hangs limp in his hand.

The sky is cocktail blue, and puffy clouds are latched to an unending sky. A deep call to action bubbles inside me, releasing a cavernous hurt I don't often allow myself to feel. No one saved me. No one saved my dog. But who the hell am I to take on someone else's problems?

I should let it go. Teresa is strong enough to throw Randy out. She isn't going to be easily talked into more of the same abuse.

But as I reach my small city and finally pull onto my property, my mind takes each piece of the situation out like a chess piece, and they stand before me. Randall thinks he's the one with the most power, the queen with every move available to him, but he isn't. He's a damn rook stuck in a corner, doomed to freeze or repeat a decision that will end the game. And he'll take as many other pieces with him as he can.

But I can see the whole board. He spends his time at a bar, The Green Roof. He lives in an old trailer by a water tower. He has Jasper's dog.

I wave to Greta, who's chatting with a man in front of the store, but I don't stop to talk. I'll pop by to say goodbye before the place closes in an hour.

Without meaning to, a plan is already forming, and every nerve in my body is charged into acting on it.

– 3 –

Florence and Rome rush at me as soon as I open the door, tongues wagging and eyes shining, delighted I've returned. I scratch their ears and give them each a good rub. They are ready for our daily outing, but before that, I need some time before I head to the Akron Library and a computer.

They follow me into the sitting room which holds a '70s style couch and bookshelves of old, dusty novels my grandparents collected, facing a sturdy wooden desk Gramps fashioned from some found wood. Several decades ago, Gramps had a craftsman buddy help him prop up the wood with solidly carved legs to create a truly unique piece of furniture that weighs about five hundred pounds. I'd never be able to move with it, but its wide surface is a great place to sort mail or to spread out invoices and type those accounts into my Dell.

But my search in an hour won't go through my Internet Explorer. I learned enough at Langley and what happens to ex-CIA officers who use their computers at home to search for information that later can incriminate them. I search for cars that I'm interested in, and I follow auctions and ads for a wreck to haul away, but that's it.

I move the mouse and it wakes up my computer as I settle into the chair. I smile at my screen picture of me crouched between Florence and Rome. They're actually looking at the camera, and the angle perfectly captures open mouths and pink tongues, all of us smiling. Damn, I love those two.

They've already taken up their usual space around my feet, so I toss my sneakers into the corner of the room and rub a foot across their backs. Flo is already snoozing.

I grab a notepad and tear off the top sheet and place it in front of me. Old habits die hard. Never write on top of a pad that leaves your words invisible, but discoverable, on the stack below.

I make a list of searches I need to make on the library's computer. They shouldn't take long. I'll get onto AOL again. I used CompuServe in the CIA but I like this new server better.

I fold the paper and put it in my back pocket.

I rub the dogs' heads one more time. "I'll be back soon and we'll hit the trails."

The Akron-Summit County Library has served the area since 1874. I park my car to the side of the brick building and walk through the front doors.

Victoria's parents said there was talk of a new library proposal, something phallic, erected in steel and glass, with ten times the space. This dream in the minds of the Akron city fathers seems a bit far-fetched, but maybe not if enough people got motivated. The mustiness of century-old air inside welcomes me, and I breathe deeply. I hope they never get their funding.

I choose the computer farthest from the check-in desk and where I'm facing the front doors. *Never turn your back to foot traffic.*

I wait for the Internet to connect and open MapQuest and begin searching, starting with The Green Roof Bar. I switch to a map of the area and plot a route from my house—no more than a half hour it looks like.

Time to find the tower. A quick search gives me few places to start, but water towers are ordinary sights in most small towns, and some are even old, rusted things that have been abandoned.

I scan the map for towns nearest to Sagerton, surmising Jasper has been there before so it's not out of state and probably not out of the county. A familiar ache starts in my neck and shoulders. Hours at a desk with rustic computers during my years in Operations and Support— tracking agents and monitoring missions—was the start of the chronic tightness, but the work there lit my whole brain up with a satisfying control I never had growing up over dangerous situations.

It doesn't take long to find the correct water tower. It stands along a secondary road, and there's a small body of water next to it. A tiny road leads into the woods. I'm betting that's where the grandmother's trailer sits.

Bingo.

I memorize the maps, sign off, and soon am back on the road toward home. This was a productive task and easier than I thought. Now for my next steps.

"You guys ready for a run?" Both dogs jump up as I enter the kitchen, catching big air between their paws and the floor.

The sun is disappearing behind the trees, so I grab a headlamp and pull on my shoes. The dogs stay at my heels as I push off away from the house and wind through junk cars toward the paths in the woods.

In my mind, I'm mapping out my route to the bar. I also need to determine the best time to avoid too much traffic, but hit the bar at a time when there's enough business that two men arguing won't cause a huge scene.

I don't know Jasper's dad, and I'm not blind to the fact that I'm clearly projecting my own father's issues onto this man, but as I rehearse scenarios of confrontation, I begin to wonder if even speaking to the man is worth it. All I want is the dog, really.

Still, every scenario I consider—where that piece is removed from the game—opens up Jasper and his family to this man's rage. They will take the brunt of it when he discovers the dog is back with them.

The headlamp illuminates the rough terrain in front of me, and I focus on it as I turn up the pace, needing my stride to match the rapid-fire thoughts ricocheting around inside.

If I confront Randall, he can put a face to the dognapper. Dog-returner, really. I need to let him see me. Blame *me*.

And after taking too many punches from my own dad, not to mention years of my own training per CIA requirements in case I ever needed it in the field, I should be able to hold my own. Maybe even teach him to think before using his fists to express his *feelings*.

My footsteps dig in, beating against the ground in a pace I can't continue, but the punishment feels right. I'm beginning to wheeze, but the dogs have no trouble keeping up and streak along with me. Memories of Dad are really screwing with me today.

We are deep among the trees now, where Gramps's older cars once sat in the clear. Fifty years on, they're now entombed in the woods. Trees grow through floorboards and protrude through empty window eye sockets, as they push their way to the sky. It's eerie yet immortal.

I slow and stop for a rest. The dogs begin to sniff around while I regain my breath. My favorite hideaway is here. A 1963 Volkswagen 15-Window Microbus. It was a common sight back in the '70s at music festivals and civil rights protests—the days of *McHale's Navy*, President Kennedy's assassination, and the year I was born.

The thirty-five-year-old bus still holds most of its turquoise-and-white paint, but brown cancer spots are taking over its shell year by year. Soon after I moved in with my grandparents, I discovered it. It became my escape whenever reality was too harsh.

I run a hand along its textured paint, remembering the make-believe world I created for myself here. Living in this van, traveling across the world—I didn't fully understand geography back then—as an international spy, solving crimes, or some shit like that. If my grandparents knew where I disappeared to for hours on end, they never said. I guess they understood the healing properties of silence. Pain can't always be tamed, but silence often suppresses it.

Those were the days I hoped to find my mother. I dreamed she'd read that my father was dead and come looking for me or I'd take this old bus and drive until I found her.

I don't know if she's even alive now, but the banged-up child inside me still has those hopeful daydreams. There'd be a phone call, her voice would sound huskier, but I'd recognize it. She'd come to Ohio and we would embrace, years of "I love yous" and "look at yous!" exchanged at the same time.

I call Florence and Rome back from where they're wandering into some of the rougher patches where rusted pieces could cut them. They trot to me, and I greet them with open hands and scratches behind their ears.

I've tried to imagine Mom's face at age fifty-six. She was barely thirty when she left us, so that's the image I still hold of her. And where my mother went has always been a kaleidoscope of half-guessed possibilities. Maybe she started over, has a new husband and new son. Maybe she changed her name, moved to another country. I loved her, yet a deep, painful heat always fills me when I think of her not coming back for me.

My father seemed to pick up on the idea that he should be a dad after she was gone. True to his cold nature, he never came looking for me on the day she left when I ran away into the deeper folds of the forest. Or the next. When I finally staggered from the trees two days later, famished and wiped out from crying, he said, "You missed a great game last night. Vancouver stomped Calgary, four to zip."

Fuck him.

For nearly two years my father tried to be a tough role model, to make me want to be with him as much as I was with my dog, Keesha. Shooting her taught my eleven-year-old mind the meaning of raw hate.

Another layer of trust ripped away.

I shake my head, cold now from the sheen of sweat. The fact is, I may never know what happened to Mom. And maybe it's better that way.

Back at the house, the satisfaction of returning with the dogs, my sides heaving from exertion, has cleared my head. Thoreau wrote something about being able to find eternity in the woods and how the deep pulse of greenness healed all wounds. With the runner's high and the grip of sweat-soaked clothes sticking to me—I'll take that any day.

My mother thought Thoreau was God. She left two books behind when she fled my father's abuse—*Walden* and *Civil Disobedience*. They were my reading options whenever I escaped into the trees with Keesha back then. The forest is still my favorite place to be with heavenly scents of wood and new greenery. And I still have dogs.

I shower then check inventory at the store and write out product orders for Greta to call in. Tomorrow is Tuesday. The Green Roof Bar will have its regulars, but not its weekend patrons, ready to forget the long week.

I set up and rearrange the pieces in my head as I pull out the leftovers of some beef stew and reheat it. I feed the dogs and brush their black and tan coats.

If I go to The Green Roof first, I can time it around sundown. Go in and ask for Randall. He's a regular so they'll know him, but I'm a stranger, so they'll be suspicious. I found a mugshot of him from my research. Three years ago, he was pulled over for a DUI. Probably not his first, but his license was revoked, and he hasn't bothered to renew it since. People rarely looked like their drunk mugshots, but maybe I'd be able to make an ID.

I still don't completely like it. Too many variables.

Next scenario is to go to The Green Roof tomorrow, and again the next day. Talk and chat, say I've been looking for a new local bar and this one fits the bill. It will be a larger crowd than it would be on a Monday, and maybe the extra bodies are a good cover." And more people to ask about Randall. The extra day might be enough to make me seem less suspicious, and I can make some excuse about how we ran into each other, and he recommended this place.

Is Randall the kind of guy to recommend a place to a near stranger? The regulars may see through that and warn him. Two days would be lost, the dog still separated from Jasper, probably poorly cared for.

I rinse my empty bowl, and the dogs follow me to the bedroom. They sleep here most nights, but they're comfortable in their outside doggy apartment on rare evenings I'm away.

My night routine is a simple one, and as I brush my teeth, I consider a different tactic. I'll take the old Firenza wagon, the one I use for slack lime runs to keep the shed full for my ongoing mural relief project. That car will blend in when I'm looking for Randall at the bar.

No not the bar. I'll head straight to the mobile home tucked in the woods. Park and walk around the trailer until…what? I find a dog tied up? Or hear a dog barking? Randall's mother may be there and have the dog locked inside.

I take my frustration out on the faucet as I shut the water off after cleaning my hands, change into a pair of boxer shorts, and join the dogs in my king-sized bed. When Victoria stays over, the four of us are quite cozy, but that's a rare event. I usually go to her house, then leave to come home rather than staying over."

Rome nuzzles up to me as I climb under the covers, but I'm not ready to turn the bedside lamp out. I stare at the bland ceiling and work out my plan one more time.

Decision made. I click off the light and roll to my side. The dogs adjust their warm bodies around me, and I run a hand along Rome's smooth coat.

Tomorrow. I'll drive to The Green Roof. I'll get there a bit early, enough time to buy a beer or two, get friendly. Chat up the Joes and the Sharons and the whoever-the-fucks. Tell them how I met this guy Randall and he said The Green Roof was the absolute shit. Maybe even buy the group a round.

I'll get eyes on him, buy him a drink if he isn't too messed-up already. Ask him if he knows anyone selling a dog, my nephew wants one for his birthday.

I'm drifting off before I finish the imagined conversation, but it feels right. Pick the carrot over the stick. Bribe the guy with more drinking money, and he'll think he landed on top. I get the dog and before I leave with it, maybe I'll look that fucker in the eye and tell him if he hits or harms another person or animal, I'll come after him.

The dogs are snoring now and with the semblance of a fair plan in place, I join them in the depths of a much-needed sleep.

— 4 —

I slowly trawl the narrow streets of Sagerton. Trees tower both sides of the roads, modest homes built after WWII filling in the blocks.

The blinking bar sign for The Green Roof shines ahead of me just past the unassertive business district of a bank, a pawn shop with an attached diner, and a fabric shop. I'd spent all day anticipating this moment, trying to stay busy at the store until Greta told me my pacing was driving her to madness. My salary at Langley was a generous one for a single guy, and Gramps outright owned his property. There was a wrongful-death settlement from the drunk's insurance company who hit my grandparents head-on, killing them four years earlier. Also, the junkyard brings in six figures every year, so with my expenses low, I have a healthy savings account.

But I also have a brain that needs to keep busy, so I filled the afternoon working on the mural relief. It's physical work to slap the lime mixture onto the board, then more finite focus to begin molding and sculpting the individual figures. This one featured a line of cows against a backdrop of fields and fences. It was good work that kept my hands busy while I reviewed my plan for the evening too many times to count.

I drive past the bar sign for about two blocks and pull into the parking lot of a motel I'd located yesterday. This afternoon, hand wet with lime putty, I decided against arriving early. If I waited around for Randall, that would look more suspicious. Better to join the bar crowd with the high probability that Randall was already among them and take it from there. Best-case scenario is I recognize him quickly, offer him the drink and to pay for the dog, scare the shit out of him with a word of warning to stay away from his kids, his wife, and the puppy, then be on my way.

It's nearly ten p.m. and most of the lights are out behind the motel rooms' curtains. I lock the car and walk toward the main drag. The inky night that I always find calming is suddenly gone, held hostage somewhere above the yellow streetlights.

I keep hearing the fear in Teresa's voice. "If Randall hears I've been blabbing…"

I tamp down the hot coals broiling inside me as I walk closer to the front door. Years behind a computer—sending files to decision makers above me—isn't the best preparation for what I'm about to do. But I've been smart, thought through the parameters. I'd left Gramps's gun in the closet, my old piece in the locker. Get the dog, scare the man. Leave.

I approach the appropriately colored green door, walking around two drunk guys who are urinating on the building, hands against the wall, legs splayed, heads down. A neon sign in the window says The Green Roof is OPEN and the noise coming through the walls tells me this is clearly a local favorite.

One of the men zips up and walks to the door and starts to go back inside. The boozy noises push out into the night as he calls over his shoulder, "Randall! Get your ass back in here and buy the next round."

Holy shit.

I do an about-face to look at the man.

The drunk's head snaps up. "Fuck you. I ain't buying a damn thing." His words slur. "I'm still celebrating my legal victory."

Laughter disappears as the bar door closes.

Holy fucking shit.

In the deep shadows I try to make out the man's features, matching them with the mug shot. It could be him. But *could* isn't good enough. Alarms sound in my head. It's a trap. Back off. Pull back.

Out in the field, it would be a sure sign that some information had leaked, and we were about to get ambushed if we didn't retreat. Not a common circumstance, but one I'd recommended a few times around a conference table of very serious looking officers.

But this isn't a month-long operation with multisided factors. Even if Jasper or his mom contacted Randall, there is no way for him to guess that I was coming here.

The inebriated man wavers below the electric glow of the neon bar sign and returns to his sporadic urinating.

Jasper's mom's voice rings in my mind. *He's up at The Green Roof bragging how he got off with a fifty-buck fine.* At some subconscious level, I'm happy he's here and that he's drunk. He'll be less inhibited, more honest. It feels like fate. Like the universe has granted its approval for being here.

I fight the emotion, deep and primal, that boils inside me. He kicked a puppy and hurt his own kid.

I move behind him in ten steps as he zips up and steps from the wall. I block his way back to the door. "Hey, are you *the* Randy Randall?" My jaw is tight, the words squeezing between my lips.

He steadies himself on a metal railing under an overhanging light. He's a scrawny man, with a scruffy goatee and greasy hair tied back at the nape of his neck. I have about three inches on him, but the black look in his eye is bigger than any anger I've ever owned.

He slurs, "The fuck are you?" He pushes off the rail and takes two steps toward me.

I almost see the hate moving in the wash of booze in his head. I take two steps back. "I wanted to meet you," I shrug, cocking my head to emphasize my scrutiny. "Have a little talk."

"About what?" His stare is now intense, fevered.

"I heard about your trouble at home." I raise my hands. "Is it true you busted your kid's arm, hurt the puppy?" What the fuck am I doing? The carrot—offer him the cash in my pocket, wave it in front of him to lead me to the dog—has disappeared. But seeing his puffy face, his small eyes—my brain is blue screening. I needed to get a grip and go with my plans.

"None of your damn business." An ugly sneer fills his stubbly face. His T-shirt is stained, his jacket ripped. The look of a drunk out of control. A drunk that won't stop himself.

"I disagree." I straighten my shoulders. "If you are scum as the police report on you describes, then yeah, I might make this my business."

I underestimate his ability to function. He's on me in seconds, pummeling my back as I protect my head with my arms.

Spinning away, I get out from under him, then grab his shirt and pull him close enough to slam my fist into his nose. I shove him backward and shake out the pain spiking through my hand as he drops to his knees. I'm out of practice, but it feels good to do something. To make a point he won't forget.

He growls as he cups his face, and blood drips between his fingers.

Although the crunch of bones under my fist was satisfying, I'm as surprised as Randall looks. My father would be so proud of me at this moment. His stories of barrack brawls and barroom fights always animated him when he retold them.

I look around. Thankfully nothing moves on the street, and no one pours out of the bar. I might be able to knock down one drunk guy, but I'd bet my left nut against my ability to fight a group.

My breath is coming in slowly timed inhalations. All my scenarios crumble around me. I stumbled on Randall too quickly, he is too drunk, and not enough other people are around to keep things from getting out of control. I should leave. He's so wasted, he may not even remember me. I can try again another night.

But when Randall smiles up at me with blood-stained smoker's teeth, I see the future of everyone around him. More injury to Jasper. More lives destroyed.

"I will kill you," he snarls, each word laid out like a land mine.

I keep the muscles in my face still though inside I'm a stoked fire, ready to erupt.

"You're just a stupid shit who beats up innocent kids and dogs."

"That mutt." Randall scoffs and even though I know I can't let my own past color this moment, I can't help it. I hear my father's scratchy voice as Randall says, "The kids like him more than me." He sloppily smacks a fist into his other hand. "I'm their damn father."

I slam right into him.

Randall falls backward, moaning, then crawls until he rights himself against the wall of the bar. We are moving into some trees, the sounds of the bar already dimming as we fall back to the rear of the place.

"That fucking bitch called the police…"

He keeps talking, as if he can't help himself from spewing more crap. I'm stalking him through the shadows as he stumbles into the scraggly trees.

"...and my kids are whiny little pricks. Paycheck suckers." He spits off to the side. "Now Teresa's really gonna wish she hadn't brought that fucking dog home."

He *is* going to kill Jasper's puppy. He's no different than my own dad from hell. My shoulders tighten. Every slurred word is another hate-filled reason to keep this bastard far from his family. Run him out of town. Give him no reasons to stay.

A smile twists his mouth. "Who are you? Are you screwing her?" He blows out a guffaw.

He must be talking about his wife, but I know that he's beyond being reasonable, so I maintain the distance between us, keeping my mind clear enough to create my next plan, but every word fills me with rising heat.

"You're one unlucky bastard," he says, stumbling again among the weeds. The last word came out "bashtard," his slurred speech conjuring a budget version of Sean Connery.

All my scenarios have failed, and my mind is in tangles. If I walk away now, I've failed. I still don't know where the dog is, and even if Randall remembers my face, he seems more concerned with punishing Jasper and his mom than me. I could go back, wait in the car. Maybe follow him once he stumbles home. Or maybe it is time to call it and try again another time.

"You've made your point," I say, raising both hands. "I'm leaving."

"No, you're not." He spits at me, an angry ghoul in the depleting light behind the bar. "You're gonna be real sorry you ever touched me."

I stare through the gloom. Olive-green shadows cover him, but the knife that appears in his hand is clearly silver and holds a mean glint.

I think of Florence and Rome. Jasper and his family. Victoria.

My last option is to stay and fight. I'd packed those skills away years earlier when I left the CIA. Fuck me for leaving the gun at home. Now, I kick open my imaginary footlocker and don that old fighting persona. I push up both sleeves and hold a defensive stance, trying to remember my rusty training for how to disarm an enemy with a knife.

He growls and launches toward me, slashing at me.

Shit. I'm in no mood to stitch myself up.

I turn and run. Weeds whip against my legs until I reach the crumbled blacktop of the parking lot. Looking over my shoulder, I see Randall still bumbling toward me. I could run into the bar, but he's the favorite there, so I doubt they'd recognize what a loose screw he is and help me. That variable is too uncomfortable to try, so I turn away from the building and run along the park strip connecting The Green Roof to the motel. I'm faster than he is. I can make it to my car. Once I'm on the road, I'll make a new plan.

Randall's strangled yell fades behind me as, out of breath, I reach my car, and it's a relief to climb in and shut the door. Without turning on my lights, I spin out of the motel, hoping he's too drunk to notice or remember my license plate. What cop would believe a clear drunk like him, anyway?

I roll my neck from side to side and rub my injured hand. Then I hit the two-lane road and flip on my lights. Traffic is light at this hour, but I don't think my nerves will settle until I reach the interstate. I haven't hit anyone in seven years since I left the CIA. My first successful punch came long ago when I was in junior high school, during my loner years. I got tired of getting picked on by the local bully during my first year in Ohio. Kids had howled behind my back—mocking the new kid from the forest who had been cabin-schooled, who had no parents, and who lived at a junkyard. I walked up to the bigger guy, grabbed his ears, pulled him down hard, and kneed him in the sternum. I'd been suspended, sure, and was still a loner when I finally returned to school, but I'd done something. I'd had the power to do something.

I'm not done with Randall. Things went sideways this time, but I still have the power to help Jasper, to return his puppy.

As I merge onto a quieter highway, I begin forming Plan B.

-5-

I'm five miles into my trip home and it's nearly midnight when Jasper's words play through my mind. *He stays at my grandmother's trailer.*

Since I'd memorized where this is on a map, it just doesn't feel right to go home. Leaving this alone is maybe the smarter call, the safest. But how would I face Jasper at the club with the repercussions the dog might face because of my failed attempt to intimidate Randall tonight?

I turn the car around and head toward the country road where the trailer most likely is. Ten minutes later, I hunch over the steering wheel and scan the darkened sky. Most towers have some kind of lighting to warn pilots from flying too close.

The trees are a dark silhouette against the ebony sky, and there, to my left is the stilted base holding the round tower. The only one in the area. So if Jasper was coming here to visit his grandmother, he'd see only this one.

I take the chipped tarmac road and follow the cylinder-style tower that stands on stilts in the near distance.

I drive slowly because there are more deer warning signs than houses.

Before long, I pass a swampy area, and when I cross a dilapidated bridge, I slow to a crawl. In the dim light from a half moon, almost directly in the tower's shadow, I nearly miss the only dwelling along here, a double-wide trailer tucked up against the trees across an unused field.

I ease down the dirt path toward it. My tires drop into ruts, and the scrubby grass in the center softly tickles the car's undercarriage.

There are no lights on in the trailer. Randall is probably still at the bar. Or drooling, passed out in the parking lot.

I never clarified with Jasper if his grandma still lives here. Even if she lets Randall stay here, she might flip out if she sees me sneaking around the property in search of the puppy. If she's here at all.

It's too late now. I'm here and I'm not gonna leave until I've tried everything to bring this puppy home to his kid.

I flip off my headlights and park near the trailer. The night is filled with the chirp of crickets in the otherwise deep silence.

I step into the grassy field, still soggy from last night's rain. The trailer extends the long way away from me about twenty yards ahead. Still no sign of movement or life. No sign of a dog either.

The trailer is the lone structure, but as I approach, I see shadowy mounds of junk, oil barrels, and broken lawn chairs. A burn barrel sits removed from the trailer, and after meeting Randall, I imagine him using it to roast hot dogs. I crouch and move forward as quietly as possible to the trailer's side, raising a hand to feel the thin siding.

No sounds come from inside.

I move around to the front, ducking beneath the windows, and lift a leg to quietly climb the wooden steps when a high-pitched yapping freezes my movement.

The dog's barks are coming from behind the trailer. I sag in relief. The puppy *is* here and she's alive.

I hurry around to the other side, dodging a busted sawhorse, old tires, and rusted buckets, but the continuing yips lead me to my left, away from the trailer and into the woods. The pup sounds young, and I congratulate myself for listening to whatever voice kept me from going home. Randall wasn't even decent enough to keep the dog in a safe area. Hidden in trees meant vulnerable to animals that could maul a puppy, no problem. That familiar hatred of this horrible little man rises through me as I follow the puppy's increasingly frantic barks.

I swipe away brush and find a trail in the dim light and follow the sounds. I spot the pup, a golden retriever mix, jumping as she sees me, straining against a rope tied to a tree. She can't be more than three months old.

Her barks fill the night, and if anyone is in that trailer, no doubt they'll be wondering what is making the dog go crazy.

I shush the poor thing, then hold out a hand to let her sniff me. Amazingly, she shows little fear, nuzzling immediately into my palm.

Squirmy and desperate for some tender attention, her little body moves under my crouched legs as she licks and paws at me.

"It's okay, girl," I whisper, reaching around her side to see how hard it will be to loosen the rope tied to her collar. My jaw tightens. That prick. He tied the puppy out here, left it alone. The knot has been tugged tight and it will take some doing to get it loose. I pull out my keys and open the small pocketknife attached and begin working against the tough rope.

This guy is worse than Teresa portrayed, meaner than I imagined. No matter how I try to get my head around it, I could never kick a puppy and then leave it to slowly die in the woods. Not to mention what the guy did to his kid.

"Don't worry, Millie. I'm gonna get you home." I cut through the last fibers of the rope and as soon as she's freed, she jumps up at me. She licks my face and whimpers, but these are the sounds of joy and not pain. When I pick her up, she snuggles into my chest, her body quaking.

"You're going to be fine," I say into her ear.

Ten feet away, along a cleared path, sit two bowls. At least he thought of feeding her. But as I walk to them I can see one is empty and other is full of untouched, soggy food.

My eyesight blurs for a moment. I hate this guy more and more. There's no way Millie could reach either bowl. And by the looks of her, she spent last night out here in the rain.

I picture my dogs' warm shed with their bed and blankets. The loving home every pet deserves—

The air tightens around me as something plows into me.

Millie yips as I drop her and try to brace myself as I hit the ground. The force nearly jars my teeth loose.

What the fuck?

The puppy rolls away. I immediately scramble to my feet, raising my hands, preparing for a second blow.

Randall looms over me, waving his knife at me. "You're not taking my dog anywhere, fucker."

Fear, raw and primal, flashes through me. My pocketknife can't defend against that, and I'm no more motivated to get into it with him here than I was back at the bar. I'd taken too long to come here, too long to find her.

But I'm not ready to back down.

"I'm getting my kids a real dog, not this whiney thing." He moves toward the puppy who is cowering nearby. Before she can run, he grabs her by the scruff of her neck, and she yips. Every squeal sends an electric shock down my spine, pulling me back. *You need a real dog, Wyatt. Not this half wolf.*

I push away the memories of the shot as it fires, the sound of Keesha's pain-filled howl. Fear chokes me and I charge Randy, knife and all.

He swipes with his blade. A sting ripens on my left forearm, and my sleeve grows wet.

"Fucker." I pull away and spin, avoiding a deeper slash. Blood begins to drip off the ends of my elbow as I keep that arm raised.

"Get off my property." Randall tucks Millie under his arm like a quarterback cradling a football. Her whimpers rip through my chest.

My eyes have adjusted to the dark, and I quickly scan the area, seeing only dark shadows of thick trees behind him.

Randall heads to the trailer, the weak moonlight glinting off the knife's blade, the dog still tucked beneath his other arm. He seems more sober than he was an hour ago.

I turn after him and match his steps, keeping my distance. *A guy with a knife can't kill you unless you're stupid enough to get too close or the guy's a knife thrower by trade.* Past training advice that I decide to use now.

I scan the ground as I follow him around the side of the trailer to the front. The windows are still dark. It must be empty, or Grandma sleeps really heavy.

"I'll pay you two hundred dollars for the pup," I call.

"Screw you."

I need to knock Randall down long enough so I can grab Millie and get out of here.

There. The trash heap near the junk pile between the trailer and the woods.

I sprint ahead, passing Randall. Then in one smooth movement, I grab a two-by-four from the pile of rubbish and swing like Jim Thome in the World Series.

I aim for Randall's arm to knock the knife far enough away to get another hit or two into his busted nose. Instead, I catch him squarely on the side of his head. A sound akin to a sharp cry escapes Randall's lips right before he buckles. Millie drops to the ground and runs my way.

My arms tremble, and I try to calm my ragged breath as I scoop her up.

Randall lies on his back, his legs twisted to one side, his arms pointing in the other direction in a human S shape. His eyes are open, startled but empty, his stained teeth showing in his slack mouth, his chest unmoving.

"Oh, shit!" I whisper as I slowly rise. I will my mind to stay clear around flickering feelings, but I know before I study him that he's dead.

My eyes trace the outline of his body. Move, dammit! I've seen men die fast before, but this is a record. No wiggling around, no twitching, just a sharp cry then flat-out, stone-cold dead.

Still no lights flip on. The night is the same, punctuated with insects and the rustle of a gentle wind.

There should be sirens, or a dark whisper in the breeze, but the silence looms large, and unbelievably, nothing seems to have changed in the world.

Opposing thoughts zing back and forth in my adrenaline-charged mind.

I'll call the police.

I'll take the pup and drive home.

I just killed a man.

The knife wound proves self-defense. I check on the cut in the moonlight and see a dark line in my skin that screams when I touch it. It's still bleeding, so I rip my sleeve and use my teeth and right hand to tie the tattered sleeve around the wound, ignoring the singing pain this causes.

My blood. I look down, and behind me, see small dark drops leading back to where Millie was kept.

Not good.

I need time to think, to put the foggy events in the correct order.

Millie licks my chin, her warm tongue reminding me why I'm here. I accomplished what I came for.

I saved her. And maybe that's all that matters.

−6−

My car feels unfamiliar on the way home, and several times I startle as I hear sounds coming from behind me. I half expect a set of cold hands to wrap around my neck, but a glance over my shoulder says Randy hasn't moved.

I turn the radio on to a pop hits station to drown out any invented noises. It's past midnight. The roads are empty.

I snort. There's a dead guy in my car. The reality doesn't fit, doesn't feel right. But it's true. I'm a hearse driver.

My brain reaches for the parameters. The data. The specifics I need in order to construct a plan. How long until Randall will be missed? Did he have a job that will call looking for him? How close was he to the people at the bar, and will they wonder about him?

Something tells me that if he follows the patterns of many alcoholics, missing work, not showing up, is probably normal for him. But even that will only buy a few days, maybe a week.

Small dirt lanes leading off into thick woods call to me, and I resist the overwhelming desire to turn down one, dump his body, and drive home.

The view from the side mirror is my constant go-to. I've traveled close to fifteen miles, covering fourteen of them while studying the road shrinking behind me. I've waited to be followed, to see a roadblock, to see rotating lights slashing the night.

But why would any of that happen? No one knows Randall is missing.

The *thud* of the board connecting with the side of his head plays over and over in my brain, reminding me of a floppy tire. And the sharp cry he made? I hear that too.

The stars that prick the black sky overhead are too bright, accusatory. "Christ! I know. I killed a guy!" I yell, causing Millie to lift her head and look at me before curling back into a sleeping ball.

I can't actually run from this. I'll have to let someone know that Randall and I got into a fight. I slap my forehead. Why did I move him? It was just a fight that got out of control. I supply an argument like I'm in court. "He broke his kid's arm, hurt the dog in front of the boys, and was willing to kill it."

In my mind I see the faces of the jury nod in understanding as they stare at pictures of Millie, of Jasper in his cast. Everyone hates people who hurt animals and kids. He had to be stopped. Anyone would do what I just did.

I push the station wagon along a nondescript strip of pavement with random patches of lights near houses, farms, and trailers on either side of the road. To help clear the feces smell out of the car, I crank the window lower and breathe in the clean scents of wetlands and raw air.

The road is invisible outside the wash of my headlights, but now I come upon a milk delivery truck that slows and signals to turn down a lane. The driver looks my way.

I put myself in the driver's place and imagine what he sees as I pass him. Is he thinking *there goes a prudent young man, driving a fifteen-year-old car, minding the speed limit, coming home from his night job?* He has no way of knowing that the tarp on the floor in the back covers a board, a knife, and a body.

I keep the speedometer pegged at fifty and try to stay between the lines and not set off any impaired-driver vibes, knowing that if I'm pulled over, there is no adequate explanation for the smell, let alone the stiff body behind me.

I take the turn onto my back road outside Belton, letting the midnight air drift through the open windows of the car. If today wasn't the second worst day of my life, this drive would be peaceful.

I've had two chapters in my life—the one chronicling my time before my father's death, and this longer section after. My adult years are working out fine. My time in Nicaragua in the '80s taught me control over my feelings. I'd successfully locked the old hate and rage from my childhood away. For the most part, anyway. This deal with Randall is a midlife accident. My stomach churns at the possible repercussions if I'm found out.

Accident. I'm sticking with that word. No body, no crime.

Killing my father was called an accident too. That guilt had picked at me like a dedicated vulture for years until counselors rammed home what the word accident meant.

"You tried to save your father," they told me during those long sessions. "You fired because you had to." This gave me the mantra, "I had to." It works now, as well.

That old flutter of something nibbling at me is back. Had it only been forty-eight hours since I'd felt the need to clean Gramps's gun. Prepare myself for something coming. I shake away the needle pricks along my arms and concentrate on the road.

Ahead, the highway dips beneath a train trestle, and I take the smaller road that veers to the right. I'm lightheaded with the realization I'm almost home. There I'll be able to think clearly, make a true plan for what to do next.

I pass the darkened store then pull through the junkyard's front gate and follow the gravel drive around the house to the back of the property.

I park beside the slack-lime putty shed and shut off the car.

Millie spent the drive sleeping, curled in the blanket I placed around her, but feeling the car stop, she lifts her head, her soft ears perking as she gets up to look out the window. I smile at her curiosity. She'd been kept from food and warmth for at least two days. She is the priority now.

I carry Millie into the house and set her on the floor where she stays nestled in the blanket. Rome and Florence are still in their cushy doghouse. I'll check in on them in a bit, but Millie needs food and rest before she'll be ready to meet the big dogs.

I get out two bowls and open a can of dog food, scooping half the can into one and filling the other with water. As soon as I place them in front of her, Millie's nose twitches and she struggles to stand. I lift and hold her as she eats.

She finishes the food in no time then laps the water and sits on her own looking up at me. I'm relieved she was able to eat—hopefully that means she was dehydrated and starving but not seriously ill.

"That better?" I bend down and pet her. She leans into my touch. A surge of relief moves through me and my mood lifts. "We need to get you healthy…then…well, we'll figure something out."

I imagine bringing her to Jasper and seeing his big brown eyes light up. The joy of a boy with his puppy. This image helps push back the heaviness that plagued me during the ride home. But this—a healthy dog, the promise of a future reconciliation with an owner who will love and care for her— this puts everything into perspective.

Doing wrong is about malicious intent. If prison and the police's role is to keep people who mean to harm and hurt away from the rest of us, what about people who harm and hurt animals? Who is protecting them? And what should the rest of us do when the police fail?

I wrap Millie up again and carry her to one of the dog beds on the screened-in porch at the front of the house. Here, she's out of the line of sight of my dogs, who might get agitated at the tiny interloper. And if she goes to the bathroom on the linoleum floor, I won't care.

"I'll be back in a while." I pet her soft fur and scratch around her fluffy ears. She's finally stopped trembling and curls into the blanket.

Randall needed to be stopped. I'm the one who stepped up and did it. No need for elaborate plans on this one. The police had their chance to stop a man—a father and husband—who clearly had the intent to harm and was going to keep doing so. I was the one who did what they should have.

I'm not proud that it ended Randall's life. I'll have to bear that weight next to the one I hold for my father's death. But both men slid through the system. Kept hurting others and they weren't going to stop.

It's an ugly truth and not one I would brag about, but it quiets the spinning unease and confusion in my head. When a plan really comes together there is a sharp sense of clarity, and all the pieces work together and point to a single goal. That's how I feel as I head back out into the cool night.

Under the glowing light of the half moon, I return to the car and open the rear hatch of the station wagon. The stink of Randall's dead body hits me, but the anguish and fear is gone. No one will ever need to be protected from this man again. I did that.

I grab the tarp and let the weight of the body fall as I pull him across the gravel yard to the slack-lime shed.

The stainless steel lime troughs are empty and due for a cleaning before I make my next batch of slack-lime putty.

Instead of diluting the hydrochloric acid, this time I'll use it full strength. Twenty hours ought to liquidate Randall, or at least that's what the CIA field reports crossing my desk noted as the time period it took to have "no longer any trace of target subject."

– 7 –

A *thwang* resounds in the stillness of the day. I'm in row nineteen of the junkyard, among the husks of trucks from the fifties, chucking rocks at a blue Ford. With Millie inside the house, my dogs explore other parts of the yard. They've seen my thinking process before and know forty or fifty rocks takes a long time to wait out. The satisfying crash of glass takes my blood pressure down a few notches. Good thing too. I need to stay calm for my night with Victoria and her parents. I promised I'd be her date tonight at some swanky outing. It's the first time I'll meet her parents, something I've pushed off for far too long.

I have no idea how I'll look by then, or how I'll contribute anything meaningful to a conversation, but it's happening anyway. I can't get out of it now.

I had five solid hours of sleep but awoke to flashes of Randall's ghostly face, Dad aiming a rifle at me, and Mom playing hide-and-seek in the junk-yard. *Come out, come out wherever you are.*

When I finally peeled myself from my bed, I spent the rest of the morning doing a few chores, saying my usual hello to Greta at the store. Following routine.

I throw another rock. It bounces off a rusty blue hatchback.

I expect waves of emotion to hit me today, but the peace that settles on me now feels like it will stick around. I try not to let my eyes glance over at the lime shed. Let dust return to dust. Or in his case, let flesh and bone dissolve down the drain. Justice served. Goodness restored.

I never was what my father wanted me to be, and maybe he was right about that. I was athletic enough and could upright a flipped kayak in a churning river with one stroke, climb most trees without spiked-logger shoes, and I had the strength at nine to drag a deer home that my father shot—just one of his many tests to see what I was made of. My reticence while hunting was what pissed him off. I was a crack shot when it came to picking cans off rocks, milk jugs out of tree crotches, all the while running a zigzag path through the woods. But animals? I learned to shoot a hair to the side and to act disappointed when I missed.

I throw two more rocks.

My dad was large and raw and cruelly effective, the kind that gets asked to leave the army after two years. How out of control do you have to be to have the army send you packing? Oddly enough, I never observed any of these cruel characteristics in my grandparents who ended up raising me. Wouldn't some things, like blue-green algae, stay in the genetic pool and resurface from time to time? Maybe I want my father to be completely different from his parents. And different from me.

My dad called me flawed, too sensitive to be any good. I've proven him wrong. I can kill when provoked. Another rock pings against a rusted-out Jeep.

When I reflect on my younger years, pain emerges, both physical and emotional. I'd controlled it for years until last night.

The man who wore wool shirts, drank too much, and carried a gun—that man I hated and treated as if he was a kidnapper to fear. When my father spoke of my mother during the years between her leaving us and his own end, he used words like "abandoned us" and "too wild for these woods" after too much Johnny Walker Red in the bleak depths of a blizzard when we were both trapped inside.

"We don't need her," he'd say. The sentence was always laid out slowly, the four syllables like an ax chopping into wood.

I was a bewildered kid who couldn't believe his mom abandoned him. She must have loved me, right?

Another few stones leave my hand. *Bam. Bam Bam.*

The night before my father's death, he took a stab at an apology. We'd finished restacking the loose wood in the shed, another winter gone, making room for new cords that fall. Hix Dardin was not much of a hugger, so when he pulled me close that evening, it got my attention.

"Let's get you a real good dog," he said.

Caught up in his embrace, I didn't respond, but my eleven-year-old mind screamed, *I had a real good dog until two days ago. And I had a real good mother, you bastard.*

To this day, I can recall the brush of his bristled cheek against mine, and my anger resurfaces from that unsaid apology of killing Keesha.

I throw another rock. A soft *whump* of bent metal, more calmness.

Don't show a kid a dream life with a mom and dad, a forest for a backyard, a pet dog, and then punch holes in it. Reprogramming happens—that kid doesn't believe anything will be safe again. My grandparents didn't understand this at first. Seven years in, when I hit eighteen, and the world thought I was "back to normal," they still didn't know what I was thinking most of the time.

One thing Victoria says she likes about me is the way I think. I'm organized and methodical for good reason—it controls the pissed-off man that lives inside. It served me well in the CIA.

But today, my thoughts aren't good. Not just because Randall is cooking away in the lime shed. But because it has opened something inside me. A need to do more. Stories on the news haunt me. People hurting each other. Hurting animals. All I could do as a kid was picture myself getting revenge for the victims. I'd be a Marvel comic character like Deadpool, who walked that fine line between moral and unhinged, but he was the guy to call when no one else would do. Deadpool with his wicked sense of humor right before the kill.

But this is real life, not the comics. Did I have the right to step in, create justice, if not punishment?

Ready to leave the junkyard, I take three steps to the dog run, and once loose, the dogs follow me to the porch.

"Setz," I say at the doorway. Both dogs sit obediently.

Millie warily lifts her head then crawls out of the dog bed, stretching each back leg, one at a time. Adorable. I pick her up. "Look who's here to meet you." I kiss her head.

I let them sniff her. She licks at their noses and when Florence licks back, I know there won't be any problem. My dogs look ferocious, thanks to a dozen movies that have misrepresented Dobermans, but they're loving and will only attack on my command. Rome once chased a squirrel around the yard, clearly not trying to catch it but enjoying the game.

I carry Millie inside as the dogs follow. I make ham omelets for the three of us, a real treat for my dogs. "Don't think this is going to be every day, you two. It's because we have a guest with us." I rub a hand along their sleek backs as they eat.

Millie digs into another half can of wet dog food, and I'm pleased her appetite seems to be a healthy one.

I wash their bowls and laugh as Florence nuzzles Millie, her long nose lifting the puppy nearly off the floor. Rome rolls on his back and lets the puppy crawl all over him as he playfully growls and uses his paws to gently move her around. I'd like to keep Millie here longer, but I know the pain Jasper and his brother are feeling at her absence. The pup already seems more energetic with no sign of lasting injuries or illness. I'll take her back tomorrow.

Checking my watch, I find I only have three hours to finish errands before driving to Victoria's. One big errand looms the largest.

I lock the dogs up, this time letting Millie stay in the big dog pen. She curls up on one of the beds, and Florence circles and finally drops down next to her, creating a moon shape of protection around her.

Ten minutes later, I drive the station wagon to the interior of the car yard, row thirteen, section eight. The scrapyard might look haphazard to a casual observer, but it's logically laid out, so car parts are easier to find. Buses in one area, trucks in a larger section, and cars worth picking parked side by side in long rows, looking like a giant car dealership after a corrosive bomb exploded overhead. For the most part, I keep to the same plan my grandfather used. Newer cars up front, similar makes together, and huge piles of scrap metal in another section.

I nudge a station wagon by its bumper out of its resting place and push it along the row, then park the Oldsmobile Firenza between two similar Oldsmobiles from 1980. I already removed the license plates and sprayed the car's interior with water from a garden hose before pulling away from the house. When I dust Quicklime around the insides of the vehicle, I get the sizzling reaction that will kill all bacteria.

"Sorry to do this, old gal."

I check the time. Two hours. Enough time to start up the crane and get the car into one of the stacks.

I pop the hood and remove the starter and then walk back to the large metal shop. A string of bare light bulbs hangs from the crossbeams in the ceiling, one at each wooden intersection. I cut the starter to bits with an acetylene torch, the final death of that car, then I throw the pieces into a barrel of scrap metal.

Heading to the crane, I cross the large building and climb up on the big machine. My grandfather never wanted a fancy recycling plant or a wrecking yard, so we have no crushers or giant metal cutters with which to destroy a vehicle, but I bought the crane with his death benefits so I can stack more cars in the yard.

When the tall machine exits the building, the round magnet hanging out in front bounces up and down like the thin plume on a quail's head. I bump along the ruts in the dirt-packed aisles, jarring the cut on my arm as I hold on to the track controls.

I stop alongside the station wagon I'd pushed out of its row. With the crane's large iron disk hovering over its roof, I flip the switch to let the electricity flow and lift the car as easily as a kid picking up a Hot Wheels car.

Over and over again, I let it drop hard on top of my Oldsmobile Firenza. Lift. Drop. Lift. Drop. Homemade crusher.

I'm not worried about the noise. People bring me old cars all the time and my neighbor, Lloyd, a wheat field away, hears me stacking them several times a month.

I manage the controls as one of my favorite rides is flattened lower and lower, until on the last plummet, I leave the top car resting there. With several rows of double-deck stacks, this two-car pileup looks no different from many other heaps on the lot.

Regret is an emotion I rarely indulge in, but as I return the crane to the shop, I recognize the heaviness in my arms as just that. I'd hoped to keep that Firenza in my rotating set of drivable cars. But it was the cost of saving Millie and helping Jasper and his family. Stopping a monster. The regret blows away, and peace reinstates itself, centering me once again in the firm knowledge that what happened last night was more than happenstance. Perhaps, as crazy as it might be, it could end up my first acceptance of a new calling.

Task complete, I let the dogs loose and we remain in the backyard, away from the road.

I chuck balls to them to reward their patience. I laugh at Millie as she tries her stumbling best to keep up. My Dobermans' sleek-muscled bodies tear across the yard then dash back, breathing hard, smiling around the rubber balls. Millie's tiny tail swishes back and forth. My dogs, like other guard breeds, have docked tails to not broadcast their emotions. I smile at the obvious message Millie sends out.

While they're playing, I add scrap wood into the burn barrel on top of the daily newspaper and my bloody shirt, the board, and tarp from last night. I pour gas around the stack and toss in a match. The fire burns tall and hot.

I get out a wrench and cross to the small pile of rocks behind the dogs' pen. All the rocks are real except for the artificial one in the middle that Gramps bought to cover the metal cap to the well, an eyesore as Gramps called it. I loosen the bolts and drop Randall's knife down the center of the ten-inch-wide casing. With the well's hundred and twenty-foot depth, the knife will never be seen again. With every rock back in place, I return to play with the dogs.

Soon they drop to the ground, and I return the balls to the shed. By nature, Dobermans are leaners, and as I cradle Millie and take in the dreary gray sky, they flank me, pressing against my legs, completely comfortable to stay that way for as long as I allow.

Millie looks exhausted. "It's hard work keeping up with the big kids, huh, baby girl?" I pet her head. "You get to go home soon because that mean man is dead."

I need to hear these words again. Let the good that I've done resonate, stoking the peaceful assurance that I was choosing the best path.

Studying a line of usable cars, I decide to take a Porsche tonight. Although I don't really care if I impress Victoria's parents, she might like a special car for the evening. Her parents climbed their way to the upper rungs of society when she was a kid, though she seems content having never stepped near the ladder.

It's one of the things I admire—she's anti-bling.

In the closest area of the junkyard, I park vehicles with off-road certificates. The certificate means I don't pay taxes because they're certified
as "not for public road use" but with a little work, they'll all run. I pull out
a look-alike Firenza, nearly identical brown color and year as the one I
smashed.

Victoria is used to me switching cars out on a whim. After I show off
the Porsche tonight, this Firenza wagon will be the one I use for every day.
Almost no one will notice that it's a different car.

I shrug. Part of me wonders if she'll notice that I'm a different me.

− 8 −

The Monaco Hotel's white stone exterior has a turn-of-the-century style with at least fifteen floors. The night is clear, and I keep an eye out for the SUV her parents will drive up in to join us for the evening's fundraiser event.

I flinch as Victoria slips her arm across the bandage she doesn't know is on my arm.

Her olive eyes look up at me sharply, then back to my arm in question.

"I cut it on a piece of metal in the workshop." The lie is easy and one I hope everyone will believe.

Victoria looks sexy but sophisticated in a white lacy blouse, a black miniskirt, and heels that make her legs appear long and amazing. Granted she looks just as good in the Birkenstocks she wears most days.

She warned me the fundraiser will be a blowout event with perfect tans, champagne, a celebrity chef, and a silent auction. I hope I'm presentable enough in my suit and fresh shave to make her proud.

She shakes her head, her long dark hair swishing side to side. She claims she's Scottish but all I see is Italian. "I keep telling you, sooner or later you're gonna get killed at that junkyard." Her hands speak for her; she is not happy I've gotten hurt.

I offer the laugh I know she hopes for, but my heart stutters a few beats. Do I look different to her? Part of me hopes I look more confident, like a man who feels unfettered for the first time since childhood.

I check the time. The event will start in fifteen minutes, and Victoria is bouncing anxiously next to me, clearly hoping her parents will arrive soon.

Unbelievably, Victoria says she's the black sheep of her family, refusing to finish a college degree in lieu of starting the non-profit For Art's Sake. She organizes the yearly arts fair in Belton where I first met her eighteen months ago. She stopped by my display booth and asked about my fresco paintings. Something in our equally empty souls connected.

Between watching the parking entrance and looking back at me, I can tell she's still concerned about my injured arm. I pat her hand. "If only there was a woman who liked staying out in junkyards, I might be safer." This is a standing joke.

"Ha." She nestles close under my arm. "Fat chance."

Victoria's father was an early investor in a company making car air-bags, and now he's a multimillionaire. Her parents turned out to be over-achievers, taking their civic-mindedness to a whole new level of charity. This dinner is to honor them for the new homeless shelter in central-city Akron, almost the only brick building that doesn't yet have their name stuck on it.

"Here they are," Victoria says, as a black Mercedes pulls up and stops in front of the revolving doors. Her father hops out and hands the keys to a valet. He opens the door for his wife and turns to speak to the kid. "Don't do anything in this car that a monk wouldn't do." They both laugh.

I bet a hundred bucks he's got a dozen more knee-slapping lines like that. I need to behave myself. He's already rubbing me the wrong way.

"Wyatt," Victoria says, leading me to them. "This is my mother, Henrietta."

"Nice to meet you," I say and give Henrietta a quick hug. Dozens of exotic flowers died to create her perfume.

"And my father, Ben." Victoria is less animated now, their strained relationship dampening her excitement.

I accept a crushing handshake from him but I come from decent people, handshake people, so I return the favor and smile. "It's nice to meet you, Mr. Montrose."

"Same here, Wyatt. But call me Ben." He drops my hand. "I let my banker call me Mister."

Wrong line to influence me, Bucko. But I keep my face frozen in a good-natured smile and nod. "Ben, it is."

Victoria's mom gushes about her daughter's outfit as we head inside.

"Did you hear about the origami company that went out of business?" Ben is at my side, a wide grin on his face.

"No," I say, drawing out the word and keeping an eye on Victoria's face. Her mother's words can carry a double-edged sword, so I ready my-self to step in if I see Victoria's smile drop even a millimeter.

"Yeah, that's because it folded." He guffaws.

I offer a lighthearted snort that I hope sounds like a chuckle. This cannot be how the night will go or I'll have to visit the cash bar frequently.

We're seated at a table for six, and the waiters in black tie attentively pour water and offer drinks.

"Do you have Blanton's?" I ask.

The waiter nods.

"I'll have a double with a twist," I say, watching Victoria nod at her mother pointing out the table layout and centerpieces. Henrietta looks approving enough, but I can see nervousness in Victoria's eyes as she follows her mother's observations.

"Ah, a man after my tastes, Wyatt." Ben holds up two fingers to the waiter. "I'll have the same."

I order Victoria some champagne and Henrietta accepts an offer of the same.

The ballroom is gorgeous, and I find myself ignoring the table for a moment to take in the details. The interior shows off its art deco influence and I'm tempted to ask the waiter if he knows when the hotel was built. The graphic lines of the long pillars continue up across the ceiling in gold striping that is stunning against the darker backdrop. My plaster reliefs stay mostly in the nouveau-classical space, but I find myself intrigued in the geometric symmetry I see here. Perhaps they have a pamphlet I can request with pictures of these details.

Our drinks arrive, and Ben calls for a toast. "To finally meeting someone that Victoria thinks highly of." He takes a slug of his drink then adds. "What's it been, two years?"

"Eighteen months, Dad." Her voice warns him, but he plows ahead.

"And perhaps we will have occasion to toast something more serious in the future."

I nearly choke on my drink. I know Victoria is more serious about our relationship than I am, but we've never talked about marriage.

Victoria covers her reaction with a quick sip of her champagne.

"Just saying." He shrugs and then takes a swallow from his drink.

I love Victoria. And the way things are now is the perfect blend of time together while maintaining what makes us individuals. She knows I can never leave Gramps's shop and junkyard or the house I grew up in with much happier memories than the decade that came before them when I was stuck out in the Bitterroot Forest.

And I don't expect her to give up her nice house in Ovid, nor the style of living she's used to.

We are good for each other. Good together. But I don't know what a full-time committed relationship between the two of us would look like.

The last open seats at our table are filled by a sparkly couple with very white teeth. Victoria listens as her mom greets them, and they launch into a conversation about a Greek restaurant in Akron.

I throw back a large gulp from my glass.

"You doing okay? Not in a hurry, are you?" Ben asks, dropping a hand on my arm. "The bar will be open all night."

Something in his voice triggers tension in me and my muscles contract. Does he know I come from alcoholic genes and he is worried it's my path too? Maybe Victoria told them about my past, although it doesn't seem likely since she rarely sees them. "Yeah. Yes." I clear my throat. "I'm fine."

"Good. Need you clear enough to drive my beautiful girl home later." He flashes an expensive smile and waves at the waiter for another drink. I guess he isn't planning on driving himself home.

Hypocrisy in fathers is a familiar look, and in some way it relaxes me. Ben doesn't seem like a bad man, in the "kick the shit out of his kid" way, but he is clearly a man who is used to being in control. Being heard.

I shrug. "I'll be fine. Bit tired, I guess. I've put in some long hours in my studio. Got a big show in Cleveland coming up soon."

"That's right. Victoria mentioned it." He nods. "Hopefully the show pays off. Far too many starving artists like you trying to make it work."

A snort escapes me and I try to cover it up by wiping my mouth.

Two years ago, Thomas J. Stanley wrote the book, *The Millionaire Next Door,* about people like me. My lifestyle isn't much to envy—old house, old cars, simple tastes—but I have a big bank account that tells the history of a six-figure income year after year.

"Guess I'll just stay hungry until I get my big break."

"Hey, did you hear about the guy who quit his job at the helium factory?" Ben's talking louder to corral the attention of the whole table. Good Lord, can't aliens invade and zap this guy?

Victoria rolls her eyes my way and mouths, "I'm sorry."

"Yeah, he didn't like being spoken to in that *tone*." Ben takes a sitting bow as the guests laugh.

The shrimp appetizer arrives and saves us all.

The evening trudges forward, maddeningly slow. Forced conversations, extra-loud laughter. I barely recognize my own pretending-I'm-having-a-good-time voice in the mix of the cocktail chatter.

Her parents take to the stage after dinner, the spotlight favoring them. They champion the need for raising money to build a teen homeless shelter—the high incidence of alcohol and drug usage, sexual assault, the school dropout rate with teens on the street.

I'm usually on board with any proposal for saving youth. I was once saved myself by my grandparents, the Boys and Girls Club, and other great community programs. It wasn't until I reached adulthood that I truly saw how incredible it was that my grandparents cared, and in a minute's notice, drove to Montana to claim me after I accidently shot their only son dead.

The front-page headlines in the Missoula rag that day stated, "Son Fires Wildly as Grizzly Charges." Then the smaller print detailed, "Local forest ranger, Hix Dardin, dies in the forest he fought to protect."

Those words still tickertape around in my head if I let them get loose.

Control is the key to keeping all that shit stuffed in the dark creases of my mind.

The charity gig morphs into background noise, and I find I can plant a neutral look on my face while I'm tuned out.

After my dad died, I was known as "The Kid Who Shot His Dad." The sudden silence when I walked into a room was excruciating, and I sagged under the weight of words unsaid.

A therapist once told me to stop looking over my shoulder at the past.

I learned to think of it as no longer dragging around an old corpse. Killing Randall stirred my memory pot, and I don't like tasting the old shame stored there.

Ben and Henrietta stop speaking, and I applaud along with everyone else. Victoria looks proud, beaming up at them as she stands to clap. I stand with her and kiss her on the cheek to let her know I'm proud to be by her side.

The lights come back up, and Victoria takes my arm and leads me to stand off to the side as her parents finish their society-page pose with three adults from the hard-knock side of the city.

"Wyatt," Ben approaches me, the crowd of enthusiastic supporters diminishing behind him. "Don't keep yourself scarce." We shake hands, and I hug Henrietta goodbye.

The valet returns their car, and they wave as they motor to their massive house on the more well-mannered side of Cleveland.

When we head for the door, Victoria leans into my side, my arm around her back. Two glasses of champagne and her heels make her unsafe to navigate on her own.

"Let me get you home," I say, forcing lightheartedness into my voice.

She must hear something there. She pulls back, studying me. "You aren't staying for a while?"

I managed to suppress my exhaustion during the dinner and the speech, but my ruse is failing from the late night, the stress of worry, the cognitive shifts between shame and certainty.

"I ate something bad last night." I pat my middle as if this proves it's true. "My stomach is a bit off." The lie feels tolerable because my stomach has been twitchy for hours. I kiss her on the forehead. "Tomorrow night, I promise."

She nods, eyes down. I hate that she's disappointed, but I truly would be bad company tonight.

"I wouldn't have missed this evening. And I really enjoyed meeting your parents." I pull her close and when she looks up at me, I see her soft smile there.

"My dad likes you; I can tell." Her hands are against my chest as my arms wrap around her, and it would be fine if the valet never delivers my car. Holding her like this is nearly enough to change my mind. "He's a complete dork, so thanks for putting up with him."

"Not a problem." I press my forehead against hers. "He reminds me of my grandpa with all those cornponey jokes."

The Porsche pulls up with its quiet purr. I kind of hate separating from her as I help her into the passenger side. Once we buckle up and pull away, she lets her head drop back against the headrest before asking, "Why aren't you driving your other car?"

I hope my shrug looks casual. "You're beautiful and should be seen in a nice car. Besides, that car was acting up."

My mind flashes to the slack-lime troughs. Randall should be reduced to slurry by now.

She seems to accept this answer, reaching an arm to punch the radio on, landing on KCAL, Ohio's link to the latest country hits.

We're quiet on the drive. I think she even nods off a bit. Shania Twain is singing "You're Still the One" as we reach her cottage-style home. Two weeping willow trees flank either side of the house and hang over the roofline, like green lacy umbrellas, softening the hard pitch of the roof.

"You're still my one," I say and lean across the seat to kiss her.

"Mine too." She touches my face then opens her door. "Maybe more so than when I first met you."

I lift my eyebrows. "That much, huh? What if I start changing things up a bit, you know, become more spontaneous?" This question wasn't one I'd planned on asking but it felt important. As if somehow I knew that as soon as she left, I'd turn the radio to the news, scouting for stories about animal abuse and where next to enact justice. I've had it with the system failing these beautiful animals we humans should care for.

She shrugs and sends me a flirty smile. "I wouldn't mind testing that hypothesis."

Victoria is the spur-of-the-moment one and a charming chameleon to match any situation. Like tonight. She dresses up because that's what's called for, but I've also seen her in hayseed casual when she's speaking at the local FFA. Her speech pattern changes, word usage, delivery speed of the information about her non-profit. She says my personality evens her out. Calm, rule bound and organized.

She tilts her head for a kiss, and I lean in, grateful for the sweetness on her soft lips. Again, I'm tempted to stay for an hour or so, but this other part of me calls. A pent-up heat that's been building all day. Randall was not the only one out there who was harming kids or family pets. He wasn't the only one slipping through the laws meant to protect the vulnerable. More need to be stopped.

I work the car through Ovid, heading home, passing glassy-eyed store-fronts, columned mansions, and the park-like town square with its canopy of oaks and graying statues.

The night air is full of damp fog and carries a green taste of midsummer. As the pavement hums under my tires, I flip through radio stations, listening for reports of dog rings, missing kids, or anything else that hits the same nerve Jasper's sad story did. My shoulders tighten as I take the scenic route home, waiting for a story to pique my interest. But the local stations focus on relationship advice, an ad from a new drug promising to end erectile dysfunction, and a story from Rome of art thieves getting away with two Van Goghs and one Cézanne.

Always a stupid move—you'd never be able to sell them with the art world watching.

Frustrated, I flip the radio off. Tomorrow, I'm going to find a police scanner.

– 9 –

The next morning, I call around to the local Radio Shacks to look for a police scanner in stock. By the third store, I finally get them to put one on hold for me. The itch to do more gnaws at me, but I can't stop the violence and hurt until I first learn who is doling it out.

I spend an hour or so playing with the dogs and can't stop smiling to see that Millie is happy and healthy, running between the big dogs' legs, nipping and jumping at them to try and keep up. I need to take her back to Jasper sooner than later. If anyone has noticed Randall missing, it hasn't made the six o'clock news. Will it look suspicious for Millie to show up at Jasper's house? How many people even knew Randall took the dog? He'd practically hidden her in the woods, and he lived alone it seemed.

I review the options as I get my mail, sorting it by envelope size, then by importance.

I flip through the newspaper and stall on the words "mother" and "California" in a headline. Apparently, upset over a pending custody hearing, a woman gassed her four daughters to death in their small kitchen, having surprised them with a special pizza party. The police found them snuggled in sleeping bags on the floor with the gas stove still running. My fingers curl into the paper, warping the story, but I can't stand to read more.

What's the correct punishment in this situation? Clearly this woman wasn't tracking along healthy lines and she'll relive her deed for the rest of her life. That's punishment enough. But those four children's lives were snuffed out while she lives on.

A girlfriend once labeled me cruel for bringing up the eye-for-an-eye theory. But really. How long can injustice go on until you say something? To speak out against it. It seems to me that an unjust law is no law at all. Like giving Randy Randall a fifty-dollar fine for child and pet abuse.

I throw the paper in the wastebasket and check the answering machine connected to the junkyard's phone line. I have three lines—one for the store, which doesn't connect here but I pay for it. The other two connect to phones in the office, an old rotary for the junkyard and a cordless for my personal line.

The messages play back and I jot down the information with a pad and pencil I keep by the phone. A local artist needs more scrap metal. He was commissioned to build a giant fork for a new pie eatery outside of Cincinnati.

Another man needs a A/C compressor for his '72 Dodge Demon. I have a couple of Demons in the yard, pretty smashed up. But I call them back and arrange for both to come by tomorrow. I'll let them cherry-pick with a thirty-dollar charge to walk in and grab whatever they want, minimum supervision.

On occasion, I pick up abandoned cars that don't sell at police auctions, or I pull in junkers disintegrating in someone's field they've grown tired of mowing around. Running the junkyard takes up about thirty percent of my week, leaving me free to paint, teach, and run errands.

I still need to get to Radio Shack for the scanner, but right now, I want to clear my brain and concentrate on finishing the frescoes for the upcoming exhibit.

I promised the Cleveland Art Center six pieces in the collection I'm calling *Fresh Air*. Two months ago, getting six paintings done seemed like a snap, but now with two paintings to go, I have no time to waste.

I enter my studio, on the east side of the house. Morning light pours in from behind, casting my silhouette across the white-tiled floor of the bright studio. My sanctuary. Its layers of paint fumes, earthy clay, and slack-lime putty on fresco boards is where I disappear, a place to slather over unwanted memories.

My grandparents, Thomas and Harriet Dardin, bought the two-story Marion model when they caught the Sears Roebuck house-kit craze that swept the nation in the '30s. I've since learned that Ohio has more Sears kit homes than any other state.

The original five rooms with an indoor bath were luxurious at the end of the Depression years and set my grandparents back $1,537. I haven't updated anything since taking ownership four years ago, and I won't. I love the creaking hardwood floors, the glass door knobs, and curved staircase. Why ruin a structure with good bones?

The twenty-by-fifteen-foot space was added at the back of the house in the '70s as a sunroom. When I expressed an interest in painting in high school, my grandparents added electric wallboard heaters for year-round use and window shades so I could adjust the lighting. They'd have built a second house for me if I'd asked since this was my first request of them, the first glimmer that I wouldn't remain morose forever.

Who knew that an average sixteen-year-old, raised in the uncultured wilds of Montana, when given brushes and paint, would be able to create something halfway decent on canvas? That interest took me to Ohio State, where I majored in art and minored in business.

Both of my degrees came in handy, although initially the business degree was all about running a potential art studio and not a junkyard.

Planning on opening a studio and actually doing it brought the truth home. I don't want people wandering in and out of my creative space.

I check on the dogs on my way to the studio. They are practically piled on top of each other, napping together on the porch. My dogs will miss Millie when I take her back, but maybe we could arrange some play dates between them. I smile at the thoughts of meeting up with Jasper and his family at a park and watching the three pups bounce and play together.

In the sun-filled studio, I look at the *Fresh Air* grouping of paintings set up against one wall. They celebrate nature and the fact that so many people no longer take the time to enjoy it. The idea must have resurfaced from my years of reading Thoreau and his belief about nature's healing properties.

Number four in the series shows the raised form of two children playing video games, intent on the TV and Nintendo equipment in front of them. The 3D element and monochrome paint I washed over the dried plaster places the figures in shades of gray, while behind them spans a sweeping, colorful panorama of the Grand Canyon painted in reddish hues.

An unfinished canvas set on an easel shows the sketches of a man and woman sagged into leather recliners in front of a TV. I'm still building up the layers of dimension for their forms, but I will paint them also in gray tones with the green and purple Grand Tetons their backdrop. The woman's face will be in a half-turn, as if she's starting to notice the beauty she's ignoring, that side of her face flesh colored.

My plan for painting six is a businessman in a cubicle, but that one is still just a pencil drawing in my sketchbook. The subject will be intent on the work piled on his desk, perched on a cliff, with Hawaii as the siren of nature around him.

I settle in and work for an hour, laying down 3D contours, layer after layer, building the outline of the woman's face. Once I get the shapes right, I'll paint on top of the dried putty to add dimension and the contrast between monotone and full color.

The scent of wet putty helps soothe my mind, and I fall into a comfortable rhythm. I imagine a future trip to Rome and Florence with Victoria, to see where the great fresco painters started.

Florence and Rome. I was bringing future hopes into the present by giving those names to my pups four years ago.

I breathe deeply but worry still surfaces. Randall might not be missed at work right off but his buddies at the bar will wonder why his ass isn't attached to his barstool. Teresa will say he's been out at his mother's trailer but when pressed further, she may remember I asked about her safety. Although she didn't tell me about the trailer, Jasper did. The boy might try to be helpful and tell his mom what he told me.

And the puppy. I'll sneak Millie back to their house tonight. I hope they have fencing around their yard that is intact and safe to leave her inside. If not, I'll figure something else out. Those kids are probably still crying in their beds, worried about her. I need to take her back tonight.

I'm jumpy again, like I have a belly full of grasshoppers. I lose concentration on the relief panel and quit. I cover it with a piece of cloth and clean the tools and brushes, then leave the studio.

The cordless phone is ringing in the office. I grab it before the answering machine kicks in.

"Are you feeling better?" Victoria's voice always makes me happy, although it takes a moment to remember I complained about being sick the night before at the gala.

"Much better. I had a pretty good night's sleep." A ceiling fan churns warm air above the scratched wooden desk. It's covered with dog-eared ledgers that log everything in the junkyard that comes and goes. I return a question. "What are you doing today?"

"Just finished a class on making waxed linen figures. Had eight women from the Catholic Charity House. A couple of them were quite good at it."

"That's a drug recovery program, right?" I can't keep up with all the charities she helps.

"Well, mainly. Lots of tough-luck stories before they tried on drugs as a solution."

Teresa pops in my head. Hopefully she is at the end of her tough-luck days. I imagine their family reunion with Millie and it keeps me centered. "You're doing them all good."

"I'll never be rich, but I like what this place has become." She pauses. "Just wondering if you're coming over tonight?"

Dammit. That *is* what I told her last night. I need to make sure Randall has disappeared and clear the trough out and then stop by Teresa's first to leave Millie after dark, but that won't be until almost nine.

"I've thrown myself into these paintings so I can get them done."

"That's great." She means it but her voice says she's disappointed. "I can't wait to see the new ones."

I draw in a silent breath then speak. "I can pop by late…say 10-ish?"

"Works for me." I hear a smile in her answer.

"Want me to pick up any food?" Often, I arrive with Pad Thai or Tom Yong Goong from Tongue Thai'd near her house.

"Probably not tonight. Just bring you."

We say goodbye and hang up. I smile, aware what a great deal I got when I met her. A lot of other women would be suspicious or clingy. Victoria knew who she was and trusted me. I don't know how she might take knowing what happened with Randall, but I do know that her deep sense of empathy would be on the side of reuniting a boy with his dog and protecting children and animals from a monster.

I wander to the living room, and I drop into a plaid chair. This out-of-date space is one of my favorites, with its adhesive wood paneling, wall-to-wall green shag, and bird collector plates. On some days I swear my grandfather's spicy aftershave hangs in the air, and the click of Gram's knitting needles turns my attention to an empty corner of the couch. My grandparents never completely left, and I'm fine with that.

I don't have to wonder how they would react to what happened with Randall. After my dad's death, they supported and loved me. Heard my side of the story. Trusted my judgment. Encouraged me to not blame myself. They understood me better than I even understood myself.

I head to the lime shed and don the respirator with full face piece and synthetic rubber Butyl gloves before I approach the trough. Pieces of cloth and bones remain in the goo in the bottom. I pull the plug in the center of the channel and the liquid washes down the wide drain. I scrape the remaining bits out with a small shovel, drop them into a bucket, and splash more hydrochloric acid along the trough's length for good measure. It guggles its way down the drain.

The drain system here does not connect to the house or store. An underground leach field with four arms of perforated drainpipes runs below the shack through layers of gravel completely on the opposite side of the property from the well and fifteen feet below ground instead of one-twenty. I give opposing arms a rest every two months with a shut-off valve to make sure the leach field has a chance to do its magic of filtering away the slack-lime putty. Today I leave all four arms open, spreading Randall to the four points on a compass.

I dump the cloth and small bone bits into the burn barrel outside and rinse the bucket with more acid before pouring that down the trough's drain. I spray out the trough and bucket with water and return to build a gas fire in the burn barrel, jumping back as the first *whoomph* of flames licks the wood on top.

The heat flickers off my face and I relax. This ended up nice and tidy after all.

-10-

Like an artist, as this evening's sun lowers to the horizon, it paints the sky in long strokes of vibrant red and orange, as if this is its last chance to create fleeting beauty before dying.

The dogs surround my lawn chair in the backyard, chasing after bubbles I blow from the plastic wand. Rome is good at snapping them out of the air while Florence pops more with her nose. Millie is still in the mystified stage and offers high yipping sounds at the bubbles that land near her.

After a trip into the city to pick up the scanner, the big dogs and I did a five-mile run today. We pushed hard and returned with our tongues hanging out.

Burning off the pent-up anxiety was liberating.

I left Millie inside the porch, chewing on a ham bone, wearing her new pink collar. I bought it today at Kmart while I was out, that amazing wonderland where you can get pretty much any item you never knew you needed or desired. There's still a kid in me because I always take a lap through the toy section. I almost bought the Magic 8 Ball which could "make all life's hard decisions" for me. That clairvoyant plastic orb has twenty possible answers, but in the store, all I got was, "Cannot Predict Now" and "Don't Count on It" to my silent question about being linked to Randall's disappearance. I left it there.

The scanner has been uneventful over the past two hours. It came with a Call Frequency Guide that listed the codes police used over their radios. It was an education in itself to begin to translate the codes, but with the guide on my lap I tuned my ears for the 10-11s that warned of an animal problem and the 10-16s that meant domestic issues. But the chatter turns to mundane issues like two cows out for a stroll along a county road and an ambulance called for a man suffering a dizzy spell. The most exciting report ends up being a 10-55 drunk driver.

It's getting too dark to see, so I click off the scanner and fold the chair and lean it against the back wall. I pause for a moment, listening to the end of the day—night sounds sifting from the woods, floating across the junk cars. Almost like a warm sigh.

The dogs follow me inside.

I cuddle Millie again. I'll miss the little fur ball, and I know my dogs had fun with her. I keep my dogs inside as I prep to go Teresa's house and then Victoria's. I'll be back before midnight.

I don a black cap to go with my dark coat and pants. If I'm going to disappear into the night, I ought to match the darkness as best I can. Victoria has justifiably never been impressed with my fashion sense, so I'm sure she won't notice the outfit.

Millie licks my face when I carry her to the Porsche. Along with the new collar, I bought a leash, a bag of puppy food, and some chew toys. The envelope in my shirt pocket has five hundred in cash. Whether or not the guy was planning to pay alimony, Randall's days of punching a time clock are over, so this money should help pay another month's rent.

When I reach Sagerton, I park the car one block away from the address I memorized as Teresa's house. I gather Millie and the brown paper bag with the other purchases. Her house sits in deep shadows from the trees along the street, and no front light blazes by the steps. Relief moves through me at the lack of adequate streetlights. Darkness is an equalizer, disguising who by day is struggling and who has time and money for yard beautification.

I walk past Teresa's house to check out the front yard's fencing. It looks complete with no way for Millie to escape.

The street is deserted, so I slowly lift the latch on the metal gate.

Millie starts to whimper as I approach the house. Does she remember this as a bad place?

"Shh," I whisper into her ear. "You're safe now."

I set her and the bag in front of the door, drop a handful of treats at her feet, then press the doorbell.

I take off and am out the gate and have it locked behind me when I hear the click of the door bolt. I dash in the opposite direction than my car and cross the street, keeping to the shadows and stopping behind the trunk of an oak tree.

Seconds later, I hear the joyful words I hoped for. "Millie!"

I peek around the tree. The light from the house's interior illuminates the front steps. The boys are on their knees petting the wiggly puppy.

Teresa looks through the bag and stands with the envelope, opens it and freezes, then quickly looks around.

"Bring her inside, boys." She waits on the porch a moment longer, studying the street before following them and closing the door.

The heavy weight that I'd been carrying for the past two days lifts, transforming into wings. I haven't been this light or fulfilled in ages. Winning art awards doesn't do it. Making more money never motivated me. But offering happiness? Booyah. The smile on my face will be there for a long while.

In case Teresa has a curtain parted, I wait fifteen minutes more before circling the block. I eventually slip inside the Porsche and quietly close the door and head out of town.

I imagine this as "The Magical Night Millie Came Home" and will be most likely the best moment of their lives but probably raises some questions for them. The puppy is here but not their father.

For Teresa, it has only been two days since she last heard from Randy. The steel company will come asking where he is if they haven't already. Is she worried about what he's up to? He could be drunk someplace, lying low, or planning a nasty payback. I wanted to give her peace of mind and a feeling of safety, but maybe I've only done the opposite. A mystery person delivered their dog with some supplies and cash. I wish I could tell her he is most definitely lying low but not in the way she might be thinking. Unfortunately, there's no safe way for me to do that.

How long before she can relax and not worry about him? This isn't the quick closure I'd hoped for her. She'll be looking over her shoulder for a long time.

A star-flooded night greets me on the drive to Victoria's. I tap out the beat on the steering wheel, agreeing with Elton John that I'm still standing and feeling like a little kid.

I arrive at her house, and she greets me in a fuzzy blue bathrobe. I know what awaits underneath.

"You look happy." She cocks her head and steps back to let me in. When her parents upscaled to a finer home, she accepted all their cast-off furniture which, even as used, is ten times nicer than anything I own.

I try to tone down my glee, but my insides feel like I've chugged a fizzy tonic. "I had a very productive day."

She nods. "That makes sense. I know how you love checking things off a list."

"I do." I take her in my arms and kiss her. "But, I have one more mission to accomplish tonight."

We head into the bedroom and as always, the next thirty minutes are an amazing workout, culminating in an even more spectacular release. It's a good thing her neighbor to one side is nearly deaf and the other is a night-shift nurse.

"Well, that was worth waiting for." She slings a bare leg across my waist. "You seemed extra, uh, how should I phrase this? Extra *ready* tonight."

Some people smoke after sex, but this position, of her leg wrapped across me, is much more satisfying.

I smile. "Just pent-up, I guess."

She rakes her nails lightly down my chest, playing with a small patch of hair in the center. "Do me a favor then—whatever you've been doing, keep it up."

I play with a long tendril of her hair and chuckle inside. She has no idea what she has just requested. Today *was* an A-okay day and I plan to have many more just like this one.

-11-

"How was bridge last night?" I hand Greta a ham-and-cheese sandwich on a plate and take a seat in an old rocking chair in the store to eat mine.

"It was fine. Ruby made her version of chili, and we all tolerated it."

"No noodles?" I chew around my words. Ohio chili is a meaty, rich red sauce served over spaghetti.

"Not a one. I don't get why the woman has to mess up a good recipe." Greta moves a plaid stuffed bunny and settles into a matching rocker across from me.

It's the Friday late-morning lull at the shop, and as we often do, Greta and I share a simple lunch. Those times when I've been in the city running errands, I bring back food for us to share.

"Dessert was better. Lemon chiffon pie," Greta says around a mouthful of sandwich.

"Ah, your favorite." I rock back and forth, sipping a soda. Best thing about owning a shop is the discount.

"Got a bit loud at one point. We debated if *Friends* or *Home Improvement* were the best shows out."

"Haven't seen either." Usually when I want company in my studio, I turn on the radio, although lately I spend most of my free time listening to the scanner. No 10-11s yet, a few 10-16s but it was hard to know if children were involved in those disputes and it was probably best to let the police handle those, though I've begun to make a list of addresses in case there are multiple calls. Abusers don't stop unless stopped.

"Which one did you pick?" I take another sip of the cola.

"I said *Home Improvement*. Tim Taylor reminds me of my husband." She wipes her mouth with a napkin and drops it onto the plate. "Handsome devil." She shakes her head. "Then we talked about *Friends* and everybody got busy with the act of complaining about TV and its immoral behavior."

I laugh at the image of her bridge club clucking away at the television's secret corruption agenda.

"Martha is collecting clothes for The Women's Assistance League." She raises her eyebrows. "You ready to donate your grandmother's things yet?"

I haven't been able to bring myself to empty out their closet. Being surrounded by their home, the life they built, should be enough to keep their memory alive, but there is something too permanent about removing any of their personal things from the home they built together. "I suppose it's about time."

"It's a good cause," she says, finishing the sandwich and brushing the crumbs from her sweater. "I'll pack up her clothes if you don't feel up to it."

"Let's do it together."

"Good deal."

On the wall above Greta's head, the door of a cuckoo clock flies open, and the wooden bird appears and rasps out twelve calls. One of the bellows in the old clock has a hole in it so he sounds like a three-pack-a-day smoker. This is my reminder to get going to run one more errand before getting to the Boys and Girls Club. "I've gotta skeedaddle." I cross the room and give her a quick hug. "Be back in a few hours."

"See ya, hon." She picks up a paperback and returns to the chair behind the counter to wait for possible customers.

Today I'm driving the Firenza that's a good copy of the car I flattened. This one's a chocolate-brown color instead of a nearly identical ultra-brown. I put the old license plates from the destroyed Firenza on this one, and thanks to my Statutory Off-Road Notification form, I don't need to worry about insurance issues and VIN numbers.

I motor under a wide sky pleated with a lattice of clouds. A darker huddle of aimless clouds is in the distance, threatening a rain shower. The day is pink and fragrant, full of lilac and mock orange bushes giving it their all.

I drive to the small art store in Belton. The store is narrow and limited in shelving space, but the owner has enough to supply the amateur artist. I wander the aisles, feasting on the possibilities of so many ways to create. Money can't buy happiness, but it can buy art supplies, and that's the same thing in my mind. I grab several boxes of colored pencils and a pack of loose sketch paper. Colored pencils are a great medium for learning about value. Push hard and get opaque values, blend lightly for lighter values that can overlap and mix on the page. The kids are going to have fun experimenting with them.

I bring everything to the counter where Frank, the rotund, ruby-cheeked owner, rings up my items. "Anything new out your way, Wyatt?"

My shoulders stiffen, wondering for a moment if he sees some change in me, some subtle hints that I've added a new hobby to my life. But Frank's face shows its usually friendliness, so I force my shoulders to drop as I hand him a few bills. "No change, Frank. Still selling old metal to new people." I accept the change and receipt. "Everything good around here?"

"Fine, fine." He wags a finger in my direction. "I'm still waiting on the pictures you promised to show me of your work. You've got that show coming up, don't you?"

I nod, relieved that Frank only sees an artist under a deadline in front of him. Nothing more. I promise to be better prepared next time and wave a goodbye, then head to the club to teach another art class to the kids.

I wave to Yvonne as I walk through the glass doors. She's crouched, talking to a crying girl. With one hundred plus kids here, there's always someone who needs a hug.

Once in the craft room, I open my bag and place a new box of twenty Crayola colored pencils on each desk and then return with blank paper.

I'm extra excited to see Jasper. His puppy is home, and I'll tell him to take home a batch of colored pencils that would have taken him into adulthood to earn at the rate he was going.

The kids wander in and Jasper waves to me, a wide smile on his face. A chorus of exclamations fills the air over the new pencils. Their cheers only increase when I tell them they get to keep them. Jasper opens his and studies the rows of pencils like they're sticks of gold.

Warmth spreads through me. I've never seen him smile like this. I put that smile there. I made that happen.

"Draw anything you want," I say, walking around the room. "I'd like to see your use of shading that we learned a few weeks ago with regular pencils."

Denny and Luisa resort to the standard sunshine or clouds, grinding the pencils into a nub. I help Denny resharpen his yellow and orange pencils and wish I'd bought an electric sharpener. Kendra sits at the end of the table, and I can see her sketching out a few ideas, not ready to commit to any. Trent is experimenting with drawing a tree, then using the shading technique to fill in different hues of green for the leaves. I don't recall him being here at our last class, so I'm impressed at the depth he's creating in his landscape.

One girl, Mattie, draws a horse. She was absent last class, which wasn't unusual—kids come and go—but it's nice to see her again and see her engaging in the activity. "Impressive," I say, kneeling next to her desk. She smells like woodsmoke. "Do you own a horse?"

"My grandpa had three." She outlines a saddle above four very long, thin legs. "But he died, and Grandma can't feed them, so she gave them away."

"I'm sorry." I stand. "That happens sometimes. But I'm sure they are very happy at their new home." It's the nice thing to say, but in reality, a lot of horses bought through quick sales were purchased by the worst owners who overworked, underfed, or outright abused them.

Mattie keeps her eye on her drawing, but nods.

I stand and make my way around the table. I can see Jasper is listening from a few feet away, so I go and stand behind him, looking over his shoulder. He's drawn a good depiction of his dog using his left hand. I feign ignorance. "What do we have here?"

He nods. "It's my puppy, Millie." He looks up at me, grinning. "She came home."

"Wow, Jasper! That's great news." I press on, acting like I don't know the circumstances. "Did your dad bring her back?"

He pauses and his eyebrows knit together. "No. Mom said it was someone dressed in black."

I cringe. She spotted me. My mind flips through what this could mean.

Then I conclude she saw me from the back as I jogged away. No way to identify me. I clear my throat. "Well, however your puppy got home, I'll bet you're happy."

"She sleeps with my brother and me now." He draws whiskers around her muzzle. Her ears are the right floppy shape. It isn't a bad likeness and I find myself missing her a little. My dogs roamed the yard the day after I returned her to Jasper, searching everywhere for their new little friend.

"I'll bet that's nice."

"It is." He pauses, then turns to look up at me. "Thank you for the pencils, Mr. Wyatt." His brown eyes, flecked in gold, open wide in appreciation. "Now I'm going to save my allowance for a bike."

At twenty-five cents a week? I caution myself, *Don't even think about it*, as I picture taking two brand-spanking-new bikes to their house. Which I can't do. Maybe I can start a free bike program. That way there's no direct connection to Jasper's family. Instead I nod. "That's a good plan, kiddo."

The kids finish up and call out thank yous again as they put their pencil boxes in their backpacks. Jasper gives me another wave as he leaves the gym, and part of me wants to follow, catch a glimpse of his mom driving up in her Honda Civic. Maybe Millie will be in the backseat, tongue hanging out with her head stuck out the window.

I shake the image away and instead wipe down the tables and pick up papers from the floor. From another room, I hear high-pitched voices singing "If You're Happy and You Know It."

During my summers at this club, I learned flag football and how to play basketball without punching out the opposing scorers. And I discovered the thrill of running. Mr. Fieldcrest let me train with the local cross-country high school team when I was thirteen. I tried sprints but soon discovered long distance meant hours of no talking as I took the coach's words to heart, "stay focused on only your body, your machine, finely tuned with all pistons firing." Mr. Fieldcrest also taught auto mechanics at the school. He might have influenced me there too.

I notice that Yvonne doesn't look too busy at the registration desk as I walk toward the exit. I head over for a chat. "How are you?"

"Good, Wyatt." She wears a lanyard that holds the keys to the whole club. Without her this place would be utter chaos. "Thanks again for staying with Jasper the other day."

I nod, glancing out the window, but it looks like Teresa has already come and gone. "He seems happier today."

She looks around to see if we're alone. "Did you hear about his father?"

I shrug, ignoring the chill that crawls along my neck. "No. What about him?"

"He's missing. The police think someone killed him."

I freeze every muscle in my face, determined to keep my expression neutral. "What makes them think that?" Surely the front of my shirt is visibly moving with the uptick in my heart rate, like a frightened baby bird.

"I guess he hangs out at this one bar all the time. His friends said he left a few nights ago but hasn't come back. And there's blood on the sidewalk. They're testing it to see if it's his."

It's his, alright.

I want to say, "That's shocking!"—especially the part where she said he has friends. Instead, I go with a sad shake of the head and say, "Wow. When was this?"

"Three nights ago." She offers a crooked smile. She lowers her voice. "I hear he was a mean prick."

"So good riddance to bad rubbish, you're thinking?" Someone else verifying that he won't be missed feels good.

She laughs. "I'm just saying." Then her face falls and her brows knit together. "Well, that's not all. There's a bad part to the rumor too."

I nod slowly, trying to stave off what might be coming.

"I heard from a waitress at the diner that the police think Teresa had something to do with it."

I groan inside. Shit.

"Jasper's mom? That's crazy." More vigorous head shaking, but in my mind I'm trying to determine if I should admit what I talked to her about in the front of the club that day.

Yvonne raises her hands. "I'm just the messenger. I've met the woman, and all I know is she works two jobs because that man is no good and a drunk. And you know Jasper is in a cast..." Her eyebrow raises, communicating that I should know the obvious. Know what everyone else knows. Jasper's dad hurt him.

This triggers a flush of hurt and anger in me. People suspected Randall hurt Jasper but no one did anything.

Well, I did.

I look at my watch as if I need to get going. "Let me know if you hear anything else," I manage to say, and Yvonne gives me a wave, then turns back to a stack of papers at her desk she's probably been avoiding.

My legs are wooden as I exit the building. I sit in the car and mull over the information.

Randall will become another cold case with enough time. Teresa has nothing to add to solve his disappearance, and I'm sure she can prove she was home the night he went missing. Even if she mentions a secretive person returning the dog, she never saw my face. Maybe she'll think the money I left was a bribe to keep her quiet. Maybe she won't connect the return of Millie with the missing husband.

I need to figure out a way to get her off the hook without indicting myself.

My earlier upbeat mood is gone as I turn the engine and begin my journey home.

-12-

Early the next morning, Chris Bain, the guy building the giant fork, pulls away, his trailer full of corrugated sheet metal, old tire rims, and rusted gas stove burners. He promises to send pictures of the final product.

The man wanting the part for the Dodge Demon comes prepared with a diagram and the tools he needs to pull the A/C compressor. I let him have it for a tenth of what a new part would cost, then listen for ten minutes about how the rebuild is going, before he pays me cash and leaves.

Last night, rain dropped in for a brief visit but quit at some point before morning. Puddles sit in low spots in the gravel drive and around the yard. Nevertheless, the dogs and I need to go for a run.

In the thick fog, a stray goose complains about something, and its empty grievance is lost in the mist. I sound like Thoreau.

We take off and fifteen minutes later cross a small wooden bridge that arches over the shallow creek. Bumping up a weed-choked trail, I turn a hard left up a rise to where my father and grandparents are buried.

The old cemetery opens up thirty feet into the woods to reveal two dozen headstones, eerie in the deep forest shadows. Fingers of fog twist around the granite slabs, a horror movie in the making. Many of the stones near the back have fallen over or are sunken into the soft ground, with dates as far back as 1789. The oldest granite faces are etched with nonfamilial names like Slaymaker or O'Shea. Previous landowners before Gramps bought the place.

My grandparents' monument stands closest to the drive, neat and new. Behind them is my father's grave, a three-foot square marble stone with a symbol etched on either side of his name—a forest ranger badge and an American flag with "Army" written below it. I rarely visit my dad's grave. Although I remember the creaking sound of the rope around the casket as it was lowered into ground, this burial spot feels cold and empty. A closed casket was the only option at his funeral, and with no visual memory of him outlined in the silky quilted coffin, it hadn't seemed real.

It's different with my grandparents' grave. I talk to them whenever I stop by on my runs with the dogs. I don't know what I would say to them today.

In the far back section of the headstones is the older, moldering area.

Ernest Slaymaker was laid to rest two hundred and ten years ago. His wife, Willomina, joined him twelve years later. Woodchucks have burrowed behind their head stones, and both plots are soft and spongy underfoot.

The trees surround me, a childhood comfort, and the soft ground absorbs my footfalls as I leave the cemetery and head deeper into the woods. Sunshine drops a kaleidoscope of slotted yellow and gold on the trail. I swat my way through a sheer netting of gnats hanging in the air. The dogs run figure eights off the trail and then back on, never far away, their noses flaring wide with a banquet of smells. Dobermans hold the world record for tracking a human being's scent—over a hundred miles across a portion of Italy. This isn't a breed a person wants to try to hide from.

What Yvonne told me still plagues my mind. I considered that Teresa would be questioned once Randall was reported missing—they always talk to the spouse first—but for it to go so quickly to suspicion as Yvonne seemed to suggest has me worried.

A half an hour later, the combined aromas of pine resin and the wet greenery put me straight. My head is clearer, and my thoughts sorted themselves into nice stacks of events to prioritize, like keeping Teresa from going to jail versus fewer pressing ones like what I should make for supper.

By the time I'm out of the shower, the only solution I've figured out is to write a letter to throw the cops off Teresa's track. Give them someone else to look for.

I pull rubber gloves from under the sink. With a pad of paper and a pen, I sit at the desk. My untrained left hand forms letters that feel foreign as I write out the words.

Dear Akron Monitor News Editor,

Better them than the police. If Randall's disappearance hits the news, the newspaper won't hold back publishing this letter.

When people and animals are abused, justice needs to be served. In the case of the man in Sagerton, the court records show he paid too little a price. No worries, we've handled that now.

VAPPA
Vigilantes Against People & Pet Abuse

If the news people hadn't heard about Randall before this, they would definitely look into it now.

I reread the note and chuckle at the group I concocted. Better than my first idea—CHAPS-Children's Health and Pet Safety.

I fold and slide it into an envelope while still wearing the gloves. No prints. Then I seal the letter with a bit of water on a rag. No DNA even though the FBI has just barely started a national database. Probably have a measly hundred or so samples in there so far. I'll take the letter with me on my regular errands and find a place to post it.

My quicklime supply is from a guy in northwestern Ohio, a two-hour drive in the truck. A Toledo postal code from there will hopefully detour the police out of this county.

Before I leave, I drop the writing pad and gloves in a burn barrel and soak the contents with gasoline. The soft *whumpfff* precedes the flames that shoot from the top of the metal container.

I watch as the items darken and curl in the heat of the flame.

As the items crumble to ash, I let the fire die on its own and head out to the truck to begin my trip, setting the scanner on the dashboard. With the dogs in their pen, I leave food and water then pull away, clicking on the chatter of the police scanner as I go.

A new supply of lime fills the truck bed and I'm whistling to an Eagles song, feeling a sense of relief over sending the VAPPA letter. Maybe it will solve the problem, ease up their suspicion of Teresa, or just confuse the hell out of the police. Either way, to my bones it feels like the right move.

I'm just outside Parks when the police scanner crackles to life. I turn up the volume.

"10-35 all units in the area of Parks and Route 176, requesting backup to 1893 Hillock Rd. Repeat, 1893 Hillock Rd. Please advise of 10-61 and DEA."

I lean back, disappointed. The DEA? I was in the area, but I wasn't interested in drug busts. I lean forward to turn the volume back down when another voice comes on.

"10-4 Dispatch. This is Unit 7331, we are en route. I'm hearing chatter about dog fighting. Are the dogs still loose? My partner is deathly afraid of mutts and needs to know—"

The sound cuts off with a mic scuffle, and I have a feeling the officer was just ragging on his partner. But the mention of a possible dog-fighting ring has my interest. I pull off onto the grass strip and lean in for the details. My heart is pumping as I wait for more.

"Carl, don't be an ass and get off the comm. Yes, there's dogs. Animal rescue is on their way but they are still ten minutes out. We picked up one poor dog. I mean holy shit, who does this?"

I lean forward again, my heart pounding.

"They nailed the dog's paw to the porch or the floor or something. It's pretty bad. It's full-on rabid and won't let them into the house so officers are on hold, waiting for Animal Rescue."

A quiet 10-4 responds, then the radio goes silent.

Fucking monsters. I see red imagining the pain the wounded dog must be in. Ten minutes? They might just decide to shoot the dog in order to get into the house. Meanwhile, how many other dogs are in terrible condition wherever this asshole is keeping them?

The police will often take the dogs in as evidence of dog fighting and then euthanize them. The trauma they endure to become fighters, killers really, is so hard to train back out of them. But not impossible. I need to see if they're still there.

I don't remember the number of the address, but the name of the road was Hill-something. Hillhouse? Hill—

I pull the map from the glove compartment and open to this county. Parks is small, but it still takes me fifteen minutes of running my fingers down road names looking for H's and Hill-somethings 'til I finally find the small print of Hillock Rd.

I pull back onto the road and wind into small, overgrown neighborhoods with backyards that extend into fields and barns. I have to backtrack at least twice, and when another thirty minutes tick away, I'm sure that by the time I get there, Animal Control will have scooped up all the dogs and left. At least the asshole was going to be arrested. I hope he will be charged heavily for animal abuse and illegal gambling along with the drug charges. Fucker deserves to stay in prison for life.

Finally, Hillock Rd. shines on a reflective sign and I turn down it, looking for police cruisers and DEA vans in the too bright afternoon sun. I pass a claptrap house with chain link fencing along the road. Yellow police tape crisscrosses the front door.

No police cars are around. Sure enough, I'm too late to do much for the dogs, but I'm still compelled to look around, see if they missed anything, maybe. Or find evidence of others who supported the dog ring. If I'm lucky, that will lead me to freeing other abused dogs.

Not far down the road, I pull into a cornfield following tractor ruts and park the truck. I don't have a plan, which leaves me deeply unsettled. Normally I would have researched the area, looked into past dog ring busts, brought at least one weapon…

I listen but hear nothing except a light wind sighing along the tops of the green corn leaves.

I do at least have some dog treats in the car, just in case they've left a pup behind. I put a handful in my jeans pocket and cross through the field until I reach the backyard of the house and wait to listen again. Nothing. The poor dogs have probably all been taken away. My ears ring as I imagine what these animals went through before they were killed in the ring or made to fight again.

I know how they are kept in cages and starved, hit, repeatedly overstimulated by banging on the bars to trigger their fight response and turn them into killers.

It's unforgivable, and a heated rage begins to fill me as I step into the open fence of the backyard.

I reach a chicken coop with weathered wood framing surrounded by bare earth, pockmarked with holes. I see paw prints here, along with shoe prints.

I ease open the door, and the scent of dusty feed and chicken crap greet me. But no chickens.

They must have learned that selling eggs and chickens isn't as lucrative as dog fighting. Or sacrificed all the chickens to the dogs.

I close that door then hear a scrambling behind me. My heart jumps in my chest as I slowly turn, not sure what my excuse will be if the police find me here. I relax when I see the rear of a dog as it limps behind the coop.

I slowly round the corner to find a white pitbull cowering against the wall, ribs showing, covered in wounds, and obviously in pain.

"Hi, sweetie." I slowly crouch down and duck walk closer, but very slowly. These animals are abused and know only fear. Rehabilitation is long and slow.

As I get nearer, I can see some of her face is bumpy, pink skin, no fur. It must have been torn away in the past but healed. And she's shaking and whining. Her head is ducked low, no eye contact.

I stop. This isn't the look of a fighting dog.

Shit.

She's the bait dog. She must have hidden when the police were here rounding up the other dogs that were all kept in cages somewhere else on the property. No one thought to check the chicken coop, I guess.

I keep my distance, knowing that though she won't attack me, she will be very scared of me. Back when they were training her to fight, she must have been too timid. When they banged on her cage and tried to get her to strike and bite and attack, she backed off. But instead of saving her from the ring, her fate is almost worse. She gets used for practice on the dogs who are willing to tear one another apart. She's the punching bag.

I reach into my pocket and pull out two dog treats and toss them at her feet. She flinches, then within seconds, sniffs and gobbles them up from the patchy grass. Damn. She's probably starving.

I move closer. I'm ten feet from her now. I make soft sounds. She gives me a tiny glance then looks back down.

I toss another treat which she eats quickly.

I make it three feet more and she doesn't run off, so I sit with my legs crossed and set more treats in front of me. Then I wait, not making eye contact and relaxing every part of my body. I'm not a threat. I won't hurt you.

It takes her a couple of minutes, but slowly she crawls my way and eats them and doesn't leave. I extend my hand under her head. She sniffs the air, then my fingers, then offers a tiny lick.

I begin to pet her, around her ears first—I've never met a dog who doesn't like that, then under her chin, another favorite. As my hand reaches her head she flinches and pulls back. It's where her fur is missing. She must remember the injury.

No head pats, got it.

Five minutes later, I've found her favorite place for scratches is down her spine, and once her tail is wagging happily, I feel she's ready for me to carry her to the car and settle her on the passenger seat. She's still shaking, but when she turns her eyes my way, I swear I see tears.

I fight my own.

God, I hate the men who did this for sport.

Leaving her in the car, I do a quick second look at the property but it seems any other dogs that were here have been cleared out. I see empty and upturned bowls and stakes with chains attached spread throughout the yard. There's a barn in the back left of the property, and that's where all the cages are. I count at least a dozen, now empty.

I shudder at the things hanging on nails—harnesses and muzzles, animal pelts, whips, a stick that looks like it can deliver an electric shock, and pots and pans I assume are used to make noise to overstimulate and confuse the dogs into aggressive behavior.

Cages are stained dark with blood, either from injured dogs or more likely the small rabbits or chickens the trainers stick in the cage with an enraged dog to encourage it to kill.

Acid coats the back of my tongue. This was happening so close to me and I couldn't do anything. How do I help these animals before the police finally come? How do I stop things exactly like this?

The pitbull is staring out the window as I come back. She'll have some anxious attachment issues for a while. I keep my actions slow and steady as I join her in the car and get us on the road. Her head swivels around as if it's her first car ride. It's possible that it is.

I pull up to a phone booth near a 7-Eleven to call information for the nearest animal shelter and get the address of a nearby Cuyahoga Humane Society. I call to confirm that they are a no-kill shelter and can take in an animal. Fifteen minutes later, I carry the dog inside. "I called earlier? I found this dog along the road, and as you can see she needs lots of help and a good family."

The young man at the desk nods and pulls out a form for me to fill out. Since I don't know much about the dog, I leave most of it blank and fill in a fake name and number for myself.

Another man with curly red hair comes through a set of plastic saloon-style doors. He's wearing scrubs and has a badge that says Wayne Droubay, DVM. I slowly transfer the dog into the vet's arms.

The dog must sense she's safe because she doesn't even try to squirm away.

I reach into my wallet and hand the guy at the desk a hundred-dollar bill. "Make sure she gets an amazing home."

The receptionist stares at the bill in my hand, eyebrow raised. "The surrendering fee is only twenty-five bucks, and since you found the dog, we can even waive that."

I slap the bill on the desk and push it toward him. "Then consider it a donation. Please, just make sure she gets some good care." I nod at her starved and scarred body. "And make sure people know that she doesn't like her head to be touched." I point at the old injury and the vet puts her down and begins to look it over.

"Yeah, cool. We definitely will." The receptionist opens a cash box and fills out yet another form to go with it.

I nod and prepare to leave. I couldn't save the other dogs, but this one was well worth the search.

"Do you live around here?" asks the vet. He's petting the dog's neck, staying away from her head. These are good people. They'll care for her.

"Naw." The truck currently has Wyoming plates. "Way out west. Was just dropping down from a great-aunt's house in Cleveland to catch route 80 back that way."

I need to get out of here before they decide to take my picture and put me in the Good Neighbor section of the local paper.

I raise a hand in farewell as I leave. The drive home is a blink, and all I can think is that if it feels this good to save another animal, how will it feel to do more? I have to figure out a way to be alerted when more of these abuse cases come up.

-13-

B ack home finally, I let the dogs out and unload the bags in the shed and lock it. I'll prepare more troughs full of slack lime for my next project. It's easy to forget that under this shed, Randall has oozed through the leach fields and completely disappeared. But none of that matters anymore. I mailed the letter; I saved another animal. If Karma is real, it's proof that my actions with Randy were justified.

I envision how the next week will go. I'll spend two days and finish a fresco, maybe hang out with Victoria again. At the Boys and Girls Club I'll act the regular amount of interested in what is happening with Teresa Randall. Between keeping an ear on the scanner, I'll run with my dogs, sell junk, check in on the store, and enjoy the great weather predicted for the next few weeks. Part of me is relieved that I haven't heard any reports of harm to animals or children. Another part feels tightly coiled, like everything that's happened so far, even the letter I mailed today, is all meant for something. Again, I can sense a call to do more about those who cannot speak for themselves, and every cell inside me is brimming with a pent-up energy to get to work.

Rome starts barking, and I glance up from locking the shed. Florence joins in, so I remove my lime-crusted gloves, dust off my clothing, and get back to the house as a police cruiser pulls into the drive and parks. I have a pretty good idea they aren't here looking for scrap metal. My heart kicks up but I shake away the wave of vertigo and smooth my face. Did a neighbor call on me while I was snooping around the dog fighter's yard? Even if they had, my plates are bogus and wouldn't lead to here. This has to be about Randall.

The two state troopers hover near the cruiser, their hands on their holstered guns. The looks on their faces when they spot Rome and Florence behind me say they respect the message on the large sign at the entrance, "The dogs are not friendly. Don't lose a hand testing their mood."

"Platz," I say to the dogs as I approach them. They are on full alert and bristled. I drop my hands on their backs and use the German word for "lie down" again. They comply.

The cop car says, *Ohio State Highway Patrol* on its doors. I know some of the local policemen because I tow wrecks for them. These two guys, I haven't seen before.

The cops are still eyeing my dogs, seemingly ready to pull their weapons. Their ignorance stokes something dangerous inside. Clearly, I've killed a person for less. Harming my dogs would unleash a side of me I wouldn't be able to stop.

"How are you today?" I keep my voice calm and strong. I've heard it said guilty people can't make eye contact, so I zone in on them, giving them both a good long look, and add a dose of guarded suspicion that most people approach cops with.

The taller guy is about my height, five foot ten, and is the crisper looking of the two. Pressed pants, jaunty brimmed hat perfectly placed, extra shiny badge. The shorter cop has a belly battling the buttons on his shirt, and I bet he can't outrun a kid on a pogo stick.

The fat one speaks first. "We're looking for Wyatt Dardin."

"You found him." I walk the short distance to the men and shake their hands. "What can I do for you?" I pretend casualness although something feels as if it's swimming circles in my stomach. I keep pressing the eye contact.

Tall Guy speaks, "I'm Deputy Bobby Smith with criminal investigations." He hands me a card. "We have a few questions. Been investigating a disappearance east of here, and your name came up."

Teresa must have mentioned me. I crook an eyebrow just as anyone would if they heard their name connected to a criminal investigation.

"I'm happy to cooperate, but could you give me an idea of what this is about?" If I'm too eager, they will be as suspicious as if I chased them off and started yelling. Anyone would get a little freaked if cops showed up and suggested you were involved in something.

"That might be a conversation better had inside, if you don't mind," Bobby says, nodding to my house.

I hold a neutral face. "Give me a second, then we can head that way." I say, trying to sound a little put out but willing to comply.

I direct the dogs into their enclosure and latch the fencing. Then I gesture to the cops. "C'mon in." I lead them through the back door.

"Have a seat." I motion to the dining room and quickly stuff my shaking hands in my pocket. "Coffee? Cream, sugar?"

They both nod. "Just black for me," Bobby says.

I slow down and take my time getting the cups and carrying them to where the cops are sitting at the formal table. Then return to the kitchen to babysit the brewing coffee. If Yvonne gave them my name, then this was about the club connection. Easy to explain and let them know I only see Jasper once or twice a week and his mother even less.

But if Teresa mentioned my name, that's trickier. I had little to nothing to do with Randall before that night, so that doesn't really make sense. The real danger will be if she put together that someone returned her dog and Jasper told me about the dog... That will be much harder to explain and shrug off as mere coincidence.

I return with the pot of coffee and the cream and a sugar bowl. The teapot clock ticking on the wall is the only sound for a few moments after I take the chair facing them. I busy myself with pouring coffee then offering them the pot, then stir in some sugar and try to sit normally. I catch myself tilting away from them. Nothing like bad body language. I put my elbows on the table and lean closer to the men. "So...criminal investigation. Should I be worried?" I raise my eyebrows, then take a sip to cover any further chance my face will give away my racing thoughts.

Short Stuff pulls out his business card and hands it to me.

Doug Poole. Too close of a name to "Dog Poo" to get any respect. I bet he was the kid who got beat up beside the bike racks every day after school.

"Doug." I nod. "Good name."

Next, he opens a file and slides a mug shot of Randall across the table. In it he's looking rough, the same arrest photo I saw from before. Messy hair, graying stubble, flushed cheeks. Classic DUI or Domestic Disturbance energy.

Doug keeps his fingers on the edge of the photo, as if afraid he won't get it back. "Do you know this guy?"

I shrug and say, "No." Technically, I don't. Have I seen this guy? Well, that's a different question. "Not very photogenic, is he?"

Doug smirks, but Bobby is all business, sending his partner a hard stare.

Bobby turns to me, tapping on the photo. "He's missing. From Sagerton. You heard of it?"

I squint hard and let some time roll back and forth between us. Then I lean forward. "I think I've gone out there a few times." I shrug and sit back, acting like I don't know why they're asking me this.

"His name is Randy Randall. Maybe you've heard the name?" Doug asks.

I put down my coffee midsip, as if I'm worried I'll do a spit-take. "Randy Randall?" I smile big, offering them the opportunity to acknowledge the ridiculous name that sounds like a comic book character.

They remain stoic. I don't think Bobby has even touched his coffee. And Doug might drop his because his thick fingers barely fit through the coffee mug's handle.

I clear my throat. "Okay, no. I don't think I know that name."

"But you know his family." He leaves that statement floating between us as if it will suddenly jog my memory.

I return with a blank stare, giving him nothing.

Bobby's stare back is contest worthy, and soon it gets awkward. I look to Doug, who is shoveling another spoonful of sugar into his coffee and stirring.

"I seriously don't know who this guy is. Why would I know his family?" I put a little skepticism in my voice, hitching it up by a half octave so it's clear that I'm getting frustrated by their questions.

Bobby finally relents, pulling something else from his file. It's a photo. Not a professional one, just a candid shot. Its glossy surface shows Jasper bent down petting a smaller, fluffier Millie, his face beaming. Next to him is his little brother, eyes squinted in laughter. Teresa must be taking the picture. Randy, the "Father of the Year," is nowhere to be seen.

"*This* is Randy Randall's family." Bobby stabs at the picture.

I push my coffee cup to the side and lean in, as if I'm trying to identify the boys in the photo, then straighten quickly to show my sudden understanding. "That's Jasper." I point to the photo and reestablish eye contact. "He's one of the kids I teach at the Boys and Girls Club."

I let a beat pass, then breathe in a quick gasp as if I've finally put the pieces together. "His dad is missing? For how long?"

Bobby keeps a calculating eye on me as he answers. "He's missed work, and although his truck is at the place he's staying, he's not around."

Their eyes are tearing holes in me, but I keep my face steady. I reach for the picture and pull it closer. "Poor Jasper. That's what he asked us to call him. He's such a great kid. A little shy, but he told me all about his puppy. He was at my class yesterday. Was his dad missing then?"

The ceiling fan slowly chops the air above us as they study me over their cups. We sit quietly, like uncomfortable relatives who've exhausted all the family gossip. The less I say the better.

Bobby takes the topic in another direction. "You met Mrs. Randall. Do you think she could have done something to him?"

I jerk back to show my shock at the question. Then shake my head with raised hands. "Not for a minute. I mean, I've only met her a couple of times when she comes to pick up Jasper. He's a good kid, like I said, so I didn't really need to talk to her about his behavior or anything." I stop, another little gasp as if I just remembered something. "His arm!"

"What's that?" Bobby asks.

I gesture to my own arm as I tell them about Jasper's broken arm and how I talked to Teresa that day, meeting her out at her car, asking if she was safe or needed any help. That I had a feeling Jasper wasn't telling me the whole story and might be getting hurt at home. I look at Randall's photo as I say this, trying to match up the sightless eyes and bloody face I dissolved in my shed with the man in the picture.

They listen without interrupting, then Doug pipes in, "You fancy yourself a social worker?" He drains the last of the coffee.

I let my face drop, show my displeasure. "Not a social worker...just a good observer." This is exactly why I had to step in. These morons were just told a kid had a broken arm and they didn't bat an eye.

They exchange a look. And for a moment I worry I've said too much, shown too much that I care about this family. But a volunteer at the club would care, right? Would take notice.

"Did she act unusual when you spoke to her that day?"

I rub my forehead, as if I'm trying to remember. How can I shift the focus away from her? But the only thing that comes to mind is the truth. "No, but like I said, I've only met her a couple of times. I mean, it was a tricky conversation, but she said that she'd kicked her husband out and they would be fine."

Bobby stands and his partner follows. "That's all the questions we have for now." He gathers the photos and places them back in the file, tucking it under an arm. He points to his partner's business card. "You have our number. If the boy says anything at the club about his mom or dad, we want to know."

I stand as well. It's an odd request and such a general one. Did that mean they don't have a lot to go on? Not one mention of a dog, or the bar, or the trailer. Did they run forensics? Find blood?

Doug drops his hand to his large belt, and the leather creaks under the additional weight. He studies me a long moment before they turn to leave, and I follow them out the door.

When the officers pass the dog pen, the animals lift their noses, sniffing the air trailing off the men.

Doug slides into the patrol car's passenger side while Bobby opens his door and waits a moment before firing a question across the hood. "How many vehicles you got here?"

I look up, doing a quick tally in my head. "The logbooks put inventory up around 3,750."

His eyebrows bunch together. "Logbook? Why not use the computer?"

His casualness doesn't fool me. He's fishing, wondering what a guy like me does way out here by myself.

"The logbook worked for my grandfather, and I keep the inventory up-to-date with it." I shove my hands in my pockets. "I've been forced to get a computer for billing and receipts though. I admit it's easier around tax time."

His eyes sweep over the newly rehabbed station wagon. Even if someone saw the one I was driving the night I went to the bar, they'll never find a trace of Randall in this one if they decide to search it.

I flick my head toward the rows of vehicles. "You ever want a project car, I'm the guy you need to see."

He indicates the Firenza. "This the vehicle you drive?" He closes his car door and walks to it.

I follow, and a wave of relief washes through me that I already destroyed the other one.

He leans in, and his eyes sweep the interior. "Mint condition. What year is it?"

"An '84. Best station wagon Oldsmobile ever made."

He steps away and walks to the front as his gaze falls to the license plate. He runs a hand along the grille, distracted for a few seconds as he studies the plate number. "It's in good shape."

I nod. "Don't make them this sturdy anymore." If the sheriff gets interested in the VIN number and whether it lines up with the registration or not, our conversation will take a different turn.

I point to the white Porsche. "I drive that in nice weather. Just had it out a couple of days ago." I move into guy banter, conjuring the way my grandfather used to talk to other men. "Got it from a guy who super-charged it. It'll part your hair a different way on a racetrack."

"I imagine," he says. He heads back to his car and offers a wave. "Thanks for the coffee."

"I hope Jasper's dad is okay. I'll give you a holler if I hear anything."

He gets in the car, and they pull away.

I let the dogs free, and they sniff the men's tracks before we return to the house. The cops came here on the thinnest of leads. I hope this will turn out to be another dead end in their search. I'm proud of how I answered their questions. As I review the conversation and their reactions, everything seems like they came out here to cross off a task for their investigation to-do list. There was no indication they found me suspicious. And though I'm not sure if I helped Teresa with my answers, I don't think I made anything worse.

I walk back out into the yard to complete a few more chores before I lose the light, my dogs at my heels. It will be interesting to see if the VAPPA letter does anything to change their investigation.

Time will tell.

-14-

Last night, Victoria and I attended an outdoor concert of a local cover band. We got home after midnight, so I'm staying at her place for the night. Again, she hinted at maybe moving in together, but when I bring up the junkyard and the store that I can't abandon and would feel wrong to sell, she nods sadly. Her work is a five-minute commute from her house, which is much newer and nicer than my grandparents' home and much more to her taste. We drop it, and she falls asleep in my arms while I lie staring at the ceiling thinking of the ease of making a body disappear that also comes with my property.

I haven't heard from the cops since they came by a week ago, and Jasper was back to being a normal, happy kid last time I saw him at the club. Maybe everything is finally blowing over.

The police scanner doesn't lead me to any more clues, and I'm sick of flipping pages of the newspaper to look for terrible words like "animal found beaten" or "child locked in closet, parents remain uncharged." It isn't great for my mental or emotional health, and that tight anxiety that has been building since I disposed of Randall has no place for release.

My completed frescoes all sold yesterday at the Padileski Art Gallery in Cleveland. The local paper ran a story on my work and Victoria's parents came as promised. Her father didn't disappoint with his corny sayings. "Looks like you've had a *stroke* of luck here. Can't *brush* off how good you are now!"

Vic and I groaned in unison.

Her mother nodded at the frescoes. "I can tell you're an optimistic person by your work."

"People are more likely to say they're sarcastic," I shrug. "But I like your assessment." I could add that most art never comes from a place of happiness. Ask Van Gogh. Then her parents rushed off to a brighter lime-light somewhere in Chicago for a few days away.

Victoria is snoring softly under my embrace, so I gently slide my arm from beneath her head. She rolls deeper into the pillow, and I shift to my own side of the bed. Sleeping side by side is supposed to be a euphemism for love. I do care for Victoria. A lot. But I can't see the shape of our future, and the answer doesn't come to me before I finally drift off.

I don't sleep well, although Victoria looks refreshed in the morning. Over coffee at her kitchen table, she reads the newspaper, which is a little wet with morning dew. At least my paperboy covers the paper with a plastic sleeve.

As I sip a very good cup of French-pressed coffee, I look out the patio doors to the deck, a small, grassy yard, and the back fence butting up against her neighbor's back yard filled with yard-sale gnomes and tinkling windchimes. I find myself missing the view of the woods from my own back porch.

The sun is boasting its late-spring trajectory across the sky. This time of year holds that familiar conviction that life is beginning over again—a trembling butterfly emerging from a cocoon, an unexplored life full of possibilities.

May is nearly over, and the coming summer always depresses me. I arrived at my grandparents' house in early June all those years ago and spent the next three summer months in a white-hot blur of too few trees—compared to the forested Montana—and more open space than I'd ever seen in my life. I had about as much energy in me during those months as the husks of cars stacked in the long rows of the junkyard.

I would walk for hours among the trees, have a daily cry in the woods, then do what my grandparents asked, which wasn't much. Get good grades when school starts back up, help Gramps in the junkyard, help Gram with dishes and taking out the garbage.

Despite falling into a sort of routine with Gram and Gramps after three months of living with them, I look back and admit my attitude was sullen. I went about my chores like a robot, I didn't talk to them, and whenever I could make an excuse, I just stayed in my room. They tried to be patient, to understand—I know they did. They never asked me to "hurry up and get over what happened," but their worried looks and their short but calm words gave me the impression they wished I could move on faster. Once they even suggested getting me a dog, but the memory of Keesha's dead body and what happened next was still too fresh for me. It would take me another two decades before I was ready to surround myself with dogs again, when Rome and Florence came into my life.

So, come August of that year, I decided to find my mother, deluding myself that life would be better anywhere but in Ohio, especially with the looming threat of starting a new school with hundreds of strangers. It was a big school, so maybe I could just disappear among the other kids, but still, the idea of putting effort into anything, be it homework or studying, or even getting dressed and showering regularly, was more than I could handle.

"I was going to head into the city today. Do some shopping," Victoria says, turning another page of the newspaper. "Want to join me? We could grab lunch at the little café we like."

I don't mind spending the day with her, and that café makes a damn fine two-inch-thick pastrami on rye. But while Sundays are her weekend, it's a day when the store tends to be a bit busier and people call to come by the junkyard.

And if I'm really being honest, all I really want to do right now is see my dogs.

I stand and give her a kiss, thanking her for the invite but saying there are some tasks I need to get back to the junkyard for.

She nods, going back to her newspaper. She isn't angry. Not even super disappointed. Victoria likes her independence and likes that I have my own life. She's complained in the past of needy boyfriends, and worse, ones who leech from her while fulfilling none of their own aspirations. It's why we work.

But as I put my coffee cup in the sink, grab my things, and give her another kiss, I get the sense that the thing that works so well for both of us is also the thing that keeps it from progressing.

The drive home is uneventful. I can see a couple of trucks and a motorcycle parked in front of the store as I pull in and park the Firenza by the junkyard. I let the dogs loose and let them jump all over me, as excited to see them as they are to see me. I spend a good amount of time scratching under chins and over wiggly bodies.

Inside the house, I drop into the office chair to check the junkyard messages. The light is blinking, so there's at least one. I reach for the writing pad as a tail of a memory drags me to an August day, twenty-three years earlier, when I left for California to find my mom.

I'd taken a couple hundred dollars from a cigar box Grandpa kept above the canning shelves in the basement, a backpack, and an old envelope addressed to my father, the return address in my mother's handwriting. According to the postmark, she'd written this letter six months after she'd left Montana, when I was nine. The correspondence inside was long gone, but I'd studied my mother's penmanship for hours in my "hut," that old, discarded VW bus in the trees. It still smelled of pot, vegetables, and rebellion. I imagined incorrectly that if I focused on my mother's handwriting long enough, it would connect her to me.

Under normal circumstances, a kid who just turned twelve would know that California was an unreachable goal. But I wasn't raised under normal circumstances, and I trusted I was tougher than I actually was. I ran away with the backpack Gram had bought me for the first day of school happening in two weeks, packed with three boxers, two T-shirts, and a second pair of jeans. I'd snuck in a box of Pop-Tarts from the pantry as well. In the very early sunrise, before Gramps would be up and the store would open, I walked down the gravel drive to the two-lane road that led to the freeway if you turn left, or the shopping center of our small town if you go right. I decided to stay off the freeways—cars going too fast, semis barreling down on me. No. So I turned right and walked along the grassy bit near the road, sticking my thumb out every time a vehicle passed.

A lady in a white car stopped and asked if I was okay, but I refused to speak to her, so she finally drove off. I got farther down the road when a man who looked about the same age as my Gramps slowed and agreed to take me as far as Columbus. I told him I wanted to visit my mom in California, but my grandparents were too sick or old to take me, so I was going to get myself there. There was enough pitiful truth in my story that he agreed.

The whole way there he talked about growing up by Lake Erie, fishing, boating, and camping on the beach. He made it sound so amazing that in my mind, I imagined setting up my own camp by the lake, fishing for food—I knew how to make a fire and cook, and I had the utmost confidence that living off the land wouldn't be a problem. I didn't realize, of course, that we were heading southwest, which would get me slightly closer to California, but Lake Erie was north and he was merely sharing his memories. I also didn't realize that he'd been pulling information from me throughout the drive, and halfway to Columbus when we pulled over for gas and a bathroom break, he used a pay phone to find my grandparents' number through information and arranged for them to come get me.

They met us at a diner, walking in as I was only halfway through the burger and chocolate shake the man had gotten me. At the time, I was furious at this old man, who lied to me like every adult in my life had lied. Now I look back and realize how lucky I was that he'd been the one to find me, rather than some freak or pedophile.

Leaving the blinking light of the answering machine for now, I lean back against the office chair and open the bottom drawer, the keepsake compartment. I haul up the Dardin family Bible, letting my fingers linger on the smooth leather and raised words on the cover. The good book traces births and deaths, marriages and divorces, from 1878 to 1994, stopping the year my grandparents died.

My Dardin family tree looks like an upright maple, the names in my grandfather's line converging from plentiful boughs at the top, down to one name—mine.

This must be the genealogical end of the line. I have no marriage prospect in my future, and as much as I enjoy kids, I like raising dogs better. True love is like the idea of ghosts—plenty of people believe in them but few are ever seen.

When my grandparents drove me back home, they told me they'd reached out to my mother when I came to live with them. Phone calls were never answered, and a written letter came back from California as undeliverable with no forwarding address.

They told me I could ask them anything about my mother and father and they wouldn't lie or cover things up. We spent the rest of the trip home with me asking questions from the backseat while Gramps and Gram took turns replying.

Dad joined the army the day after he graduated from high school. He came home a changed person after his time in the army, and Gram got quiet when Gramps talked about how angry and different he was when he got back. No way was he going to work a scrapyard the rest of his life. So he left for California where he met Patty Powell, my mom. She was working in a bar, and when she got pregnant with me, they married in a courthouse in Fresno. They didn't invite Gramps or Gram, who found out about the marriage in a letter two weeks after the fact.

Dad took a job with the forestry service in Montana because apparently the pay got better the more remote the forest ranger's post, and amazingly, Mom came with him, and that's where I was born.

Gram told me about finally meeting Mom on a visit to Montana when I was one. They liked her, but Dad told them, almost out of the blue, that she had some dark history that made her unsettled and, at times, unhappy.

Eight years later, when my mom left, my dad told them Montana was too confining for her, that our homestead in the backwoods was too secluded and she couldn't breathe. She was going to California but promised to come back, a promise she never kept.

Our drive passed quickly as they shared their memories with me, letting me ask about details like what did they first think of me when they met me—cute, with a head of dark curly hair and big blue eyes. I also asked what Mom looked like back then—long, brown hair, small face, nice laugh.

It was dark when Gramps pulled onto the gravel driveway that led to the junkyard. We stayed in the truck in silence, in the dark, and for the first time, I started to really talk to them.

They were surprised when I told them I remembered fights, with lots of screaming and no shy amount of beating on each other. They nodded and listened instead of pulling back from hearing this about their own son. But of course, they had seen how the army had changed him, and maybe they'd seen how much he liked to drink. It must have been hard to be so far from him, from their young grandson, knowing things weren't going well.

They let me talk about getting Keesha, meeting her for the first time. Raising her from a pup, half wolf, half malamute. We ran the woods together. On summer nights she and I slept in a tent staked in the trees, the evenings full of bug symphonies and Keesha's furry aroma. She was my best friend—my only friend, really. I let her sleep in my bed, eat off my plate.

They were patient as my words got swallowed up in my tears as I told them how Dad started hurting her. Kicking her, yelling at her. When he came home, she would hide behind me.

They were true to their word, and from then up to their death, they answered me when I wondered about Dad's first girlfriend, or how old he was when he got his driver's license. Or when he started drinking. It was the turning point we needed to settle into a normal life together in Ohio. And what my broken spirit needed to heal. What I learned didn't make me any happier, but I better understood my parents after that. I also learned what it was like to trust and feel safe and loved.

They'd given up trying to track Mom down, and I accepted that they had exhausted all avenues. The pain was palpable that August, and I hated the long fingers of the sun touching everything with the truth that my mom was never going to come get me.

From outside the window, a chorus of birdsong drifts in and the occasional barking of faraway dogs breaks the silence.

A new thought takes hold. Maybe I should try to find my mother, but this time as an adult, not as a needy twelve-year-old. Mature and wiser, I'll be able to put the nagging question to rest as to why she left. And why she hadn't taken me with her. That question bothers me the most when I dig through my past.

More importantly, I'd find out if she's still alive. That question aches like a bruise.

In the bottom of the drawer are pictures of my father.

An army buddy sent a letter to me one day in the late '70s. The faded picture shows a band of suntanned men, all sporting buzz cuts, kneeling, dogs tags gleaming on their naked chests. My father's smirk is neither a smile nor a frown.

His face is uncomfortably familiar. Each morning the mirror reflects it back as I shave those similar slopes. My grandparents raved about how much I look like him, until one day I asked them to stop. And they did.

Things from photographs, whether bad or good, follow a person. I'm certain of that. Like genetics, they trickle down to who you become and often they don't let go. The picture of my father takes me back to what I became after that early June morning when my father died. Life as I knew it changed immediately. The scent of pine and moss still clung to my belongings the day my grandparents came for me and drove me to Ohio, to their world of open spaces, twisted metal, and acres and acres of blighted cars and trucks.

Shaking my head, I return to now, to 1998.

"I'm nothing like you," I say to my father's photo as I slide it back and place the Bible on top. "You were abusive for years, even before Mom left."

Mining through these old memories brings me to a decision. I have the resources of the Internet now, and with a CIA background and some discretionary funds, it's time to find my mom.

~15~

The next day, I drive out near Randolph to pick up two wrecks—both Mustangs, both popular for parts. I'm hauling them on a long trailer behind my truck, and on the way back I spot a farm with a For Sale sign in the front yard. The place looks abandoned except for a pen next to a barn with blistering paint, where several animals stare through the wooden fencing like POWs waiting for an incoming chopper to rescue them.

My newfound animal-abuse sense tugs at me. This is just the kind of place where profits are put before animal care. I pull into the circular drive that goes past the barn, and I park. A bleating sheep, a heartbreaking sound, draws me to the pen.

"Fucking farmer." There are three emaciated pigs and two listless sheep standing side by side with huge pleading eyes. The body of a lamb and an older sheep lie in the dirt that's depleted of all vegetation. Except for water that may puddle in small muddy areas after a rain, there's no fresh water or feed trough in sight. "You poor babies."

There's no shade here and the door to the barn is closed. How long have they been out here? One day without water and food is too long.

I walk to the barn door and roll it open, relieved it's not locked. I rummage around, and near the closed door to the animals' pen, some creep dragged the water and feed troughs inside. God, I hate this guy. I hope he comes back and finds me here.

I open the door and the animals stumble inside. As I fill the water trough from a hose, the animals line the lip and begin drinking. Then I grab a bag of corn feed and fill the next trough with that and some dried alfalfa.

I've heard of an animal sanctuary perhaps twenty miles south of here. Just east of Canton. The trick will be getting the animals in the back of my pickup truck and safely transporting them. there. I check around for other animals, but these seem to be the only sacrificial ones.

After they've finished eating and drinking, I try the oldest sheep first. She easily tags along on the rope lead I found in the barn. "Stay here, sweetie. I'm going back for the other hostages."

All of them come with me, obviously recognizing freedom when they see it.

I think about covering them with a cargo net but they might freak out and hurt each other. I have to believe in their exhausted state, they'll lie down and not jump out.

I drive slowly with my flashers on, and a half hour later, two women help me unload the animals at The Good Place Sanctuary.

"Where'd you pick them up?" the one with curly red hair sticking out of an IFA cap asks.

"Just this side of hell." I shrug. "Thanks for creating your little piece of heaven."

"Our pleasure." This woman is older, her overalls unable to hide her fitness.

The two women barely wave to me as they lead the animals inside their new home.

Still high on the buzz of helping a few more animals in this godforsaken world, I reach my final destination before heading home. The Akron-Summit County Library is becoming my unwitting accomplice on my mission to hunt down abusers.

A fortyish woman named Pamela, with a blonde ball of hair on top of her round face, takes me on as her personal project once I ask her how to search for a person on the Internet. She stays just long enough to wish me luck after to make sure I get connected in a search engine.

I type in "Patricia Powell Dardin Fresno" to see if something of value shows up on the screen.

I'll be damned. It does work. Within minutes, my parents' marriage information appears in a newspaper, a sterile record with a date and courthouse filing in Fresno. I click on a few more links but find no record of my mom's death.

Good news so far.

I click onto another search engine and find a story about a Patricia

Powell in a small-town newspaper near Pueblo, Colorado, dated when she was seventeen, almost eighteen, two years before she married my dad. The article says the police are searching for her, an underage runaway.

My grandparents said there was a Powell family secret. It seems my mother left it behind in Colorado as soon as she got a chance. She barely had a driver's license. Did she even finish high school? I hate that I have no one to ask.

No other newspaper articles follow from Pueblo. This could mean my mom let them know she was married and not coming back.

I sit back in the chair and stretch a kink out of my neck. There are other sites I can pay to search—one genealogy database in Salt Lake City looks promising.

What if I head to Colorado and ask around? There must be relatives somewhere there. My maternal grandparents might still live in the area. I can make a run to Colorado to pick up a new car, and Greta will take the dogs home each night for as long as I'm away. She treats them even better than I do and that takes some doing.

I've made up my mind. The plan is doable. I'd be there and back in four days tops.

While I have access to a computer, I type in Randall's name to see if any new information has surfaced. A short article mentions nothing about Teresa being a suspect, and it ends with a suspicion that there may be foul play since Randall's case was listed on one of the anti-animal-abuse websites.

Three websites are listed. I type in one, and within seconds case after case of animal atrocities show up. From hoarders to the worst offenders, all of them fall into the category of animal abuser. My leg jumps up and down, and the images turn my stomach.

I can't take any more, so I log out. I shouldn't have gone looking. These pictures will haunt me for a long time, and there's just too many for me to deal with on my own.

I push those killing thoughts away and focus on a new plan. In Colorado, I may solve a mystery that's haunted me for decades—what happened to my mother?

Back home, Greta asks what took me so long.

"I rescued some pigs and sheep and talked myself out of burning the asshole's house and barn down." I shrug. "At least for now."

She laughs but has no idea that I'm serious. Nor that I'm planning another trip very soon. One to search for my mother.

-16-

I pour coffee into a cup and add a shot of Bailey's Irish Cream. I'm still processing the information I learned last week about my mother's hometown near Pueblo.

I feed Rome and Florence breakfast, then wash the dishes and put them in their correct places on the shelves. I'd found no record of my mom's death.

That was the good news.

I finish my morning cleanup by wiping down the appliances then re-folding the dishtowels over the oven handle.

Outside the kitchen window, the morning sun flows over the east hills like soft yellow lava.

So Mom isn't dead, or at least there's no record of it.

I glance at the clock. Greta will be here sometime later today after an AA meeting. Her son, David, is taking a new stab at sobriety, hoping the next decades of his adulthood are more sober than the last thirty years. Courage in Vietnam came in the forms of heroin or opium. Once stateside, David dulled his days with amphetamines and alcohol.

I take my second cup of coffee out to the porch with me. My dogs dutifully follow and settle themselves beside the Adirondack chair I often sit in, enjoying the crisp morning air and nature's beautiful sounds as they stir under the morning sun.

This search for mom was disappointing. Maybe this world wide web stuff isn't all it's cracked up to be. Or it's because I don't know enough about what I'm doing and should just hire myself a PI.

But I don't want anyone learning about my mom before I do. I've already made up my mind—it's now or never.

Now that I've lit the fuse, I'm antsy to get going.

I'm driving a white truck from the off-road group that I can use without getting registered. It's a '71 Ford F-150 with a cranky engine, Wyoming plates, and a great CB radio.

The alternator fights the idea of turning, but once it gets going, it's Old Reliable. I spray a bit of ether on the carburetor, and it usually fires up after a dance of sputtering and stalling.

I've been on the road for almost eleven hours; it's after midnight and I've downed at least three of these Red Bull drinks the gas station guy said were all the rage with the long haulers. I welcome the soothing darkness of night after passing through each city and town.

It's silly, but I'm already imagining meeting Mom's side of the family. I know I'm getting my hopes up, and it sounds like Mom left some bad situation. Was her dad a drunk and an alcoholic too? The cycle repeats so often in families.

I rarely drink at home. Not out of some self-righteous attitude that I'm better than my dad or others, but in fact, I think it's the opposite. I'm almost sure that if I like beer too much or keep a bottle of whiskey in my house, I'll start getting too familiar with making it part of my life. Then letting it take over, just like it did to Dad.

To keep from dozing off, I turn my CB radio to a popular channel, hoping to catch some skip. I'm a little burned out by the police scanner right now. Sure, I helped one animal, but with better information, I could have done so much more. It's a problem I haven't discovered how to fix, so I left it behind. Besides, nothing passes a long road trip better than hearing the gossip over the CB.

Skip is a rare atmospheric condition, allowing radio transmissions to travel long distances. These conditions send signals from state to state or even country to country. Once, I talked to a guy in Dublin for ten minutes. The problem is, if skip is happening, operators broadcast the event and soon, thousands tune their radios and try to make contact with other far-away stations and it ruins the moment.

I don't find any, so I listen in on a conversation going on between two truckers. My handle is DobieDad, but I rarely key in and add to a conversation. It's called sandbagging, and is acceptable CB protocol. Never had anyone tell me to get off yet.

"Break 17 for Godzilla. Are you out there, Godzilla?"

The man's voice is deep. I try to imagine what a person drives just by their voice. I give this guy a coal truck, coming out of Kentucky.

There's dead space. Godzilla must be out of range, so he opens it up to anyone.

"Break 17 for anyone on the West Big Road 70 near Odessa."

I'm running twenty miles in front of this guy, also westbound on Interstate 70 heading to Kansas City. I remain silent to see who answers. I don't have long to wait.

"10-4. You've got Stumper ten miles at your backdoor."

Stumper's voice is phlegmy. Must have started smoking in third grade. I'm giving him a milk truck.

"Stumper, this here's Night Hawk. Where you heading? Over."

"I'm doing a flip flop out to Shaky. Dragging wiggle wagons full of tooth-picks. You? Over."

Damn I was wrong on the milk truck. CB lingo was confusing when I first got the radio. Before Victoria, I used to spend most evenings listening to the truckers passing through Ohio, trying to figure out what the hell they were saying. This guy, Stumper, is heading to California and doing a turn-around trip after he drops off his triple-trailer load of logs. Should have figured he was hauling logs by his handle.

Night Hawk again. "Branson. Loaded with iron. Wanted to warn you there's full grown bear taking pictures just past Milkweed."

"Thanks, good buddy." Stumper clears his throat. "Don't need no driving award."

That means a speeding ticket. And the bear is a cop who is hunkered down in a known speed trap.

"Keep your shiny side, Stumper." Nighthawk chuckles. "Catch you another night."

I switch to a new frequency, but there's gas price talk over there, no fun CB lingo to puzzle through.

Do the police check in and listen to conversations? Like any system that started out as a helpful way to communicate, a darker side develops. Does the law try to intervene when they hear the words "lot lizard" or "sleeper creeper"—code for prostitutes who work the truck stops? In Ohio, the nine young women killed by a Dr. No were all known to solicit truckers before they were raped and killed. He's never been caught.

A person can change their handle without registering a new name. Dr. No could be Night Hawk or Stumper as far as anyone would know.

I turn off the radio. As I study the night sky and pick out constellations, I try again to picture my mother's relatives. Do they even know I exist? Maybe not.

The stars seem to vibrate, and there's an eternal message there, I know it, whispering in a way the ears can't perceive. The vastness above takes me closer to the truth of who I am. A two-time accidental killer. There's no lying out here. The stars have seen it all. But not just a killer, a savior too. Did two dogs and a little boy balance the scales? A few starving farm animals? Maybe not. But saving that pitbull only made me crave another opportunity to right the wrongs enacted on innocents. Right now, I am taking a spontaneous trip to find a mother who probably forgot she even had a son. Where had the careful planner gone? I was the desk guy at the CIA who made even his equally plan-obsessed coworkers roll their eyes when he'd create yet another layer of safeguards for the field officers on a new mission.

Normally I would have spent two weeks planning this road trip, coinciding it with pickups and deliveries for the yard or the store. But no, something is changing in me, the need to answer these pulls me toward something I can't quite name.

Forty minutes later, my eyelids are drooping, so I swing into a small truck stop and park near the back. I've passed Kansas City and am near Topeka. I'll sleep for an hour and then if I keep pushing, I can make the border of Colorado just after dawn.

I lean the seat back and settle in for some shut-eye.

-17-

My eyes fly open at three thirty a.m. It takes me a minute to register where I am. I raise the seat back and look at my watch. I've slept an hour longer than planned.

I exit the truck and stretch; the parking lot is empty, other than the line of eighteen-wheelers along the side of the facility.

I fill up with gas then go inside to hit the can. I pay for the fuel, a large coffee, and an apple fritter with cash, then carry those to a red Formica table and sit down to polish both off. My neck aches from the discomfort of sleeping in the truck. Maybe on the way back I'll splurge for a cheap motel.

A folded newspaper is pushed off to the side of the table, so instead of returning the stare of the blonde seated at the counter whose T-shirt looks small enough for a toddler, I flip it open and read. It's a local paper, the *Topeka Capital-Journal*.

I scan the local stories, expecting things like Senator McDowell to visit, or summer fairground news, and a large obituary section. Instead, an electric spike runs up my spine at a story on page two.

Local Rancher Charged for Dragging Colt
The fritter sits like a rock in my stomach as I study the photo of a bandaged colt, no more than two maybe three years old.

The rancher, Mark Foster, from around here, tried running a young colt to death behind his truck. Foster received one-year probation and a public nuisance charge after police received a call from the parents of three neighborhood children who witnessed the whole thing.

A roaring in my ears blocks out everything else.

Foster's mug shot reveals a full head of thick hair, a drinker's nose—large and bulbous with a road map of veins. The article says he's forty, yet he's weathered beyond those decades. Married, two kids. He was hauled in last year with suspected spousal abuse, but she dropped the charges.

My leg jumps up and down under the table. I'm wide awake now.

Damn it all. The photo of the colt will plague me all day, probably forever.

His address is a ranch south of here on Route 4 near Halsom. I study my truck through the window. This is the call. Maybe I was meant to come out here more for this moment than even to find Mom or her family.

To meet Foster and ask him why he did it.

But is it possible an abuser can explain where his cruelty comes from? If I'm honest with myself, I don't care. No amount of reasons are good enough. Breaking a horse is not the same as torturing it. Foster clearly has more property, which means he most likely has more horses. Does he treat the other animals any better than this young one? Worse perhaps?

I check the sky. I need to check a map to confirm, but Halsom is probably forty-five minutes away. Back at the counter, I buy a state map, and in the truck's cab, confirm that if I drop off I-70 to Route 4 and stay on it, I'll see the signs.

I return to the truck and fire it up.

When viewed as a whole, it doesn't make much sense for me to meet Foster—I already dislike everything about him. But I'm hungry for this confrontation, and a part of me hopes he's proud of what he did and is willing to argue the logic he went through before hurting the horse.

I want to knock a few of his teeth out.

I can feel the old rage fire up in my chest, the tensing in my shoulders, the grip on the steering wheel. Keesha lying too still, her blood-stained fur moving in the breeze. *Calm down, Wyatt.*

I'm going for the horses. I couldn't save all those dogs; they are probably gone now. People don't want to take the time to help rehab them and help them get loving homes.

I don't have proof that Foster's other animals are being poorly cared for, but people follow patterns and habits, and dragging the colt was not the first savage thing this man's done to an animal. There will be more.

I focus on the road, turn on the radio, and let Willie Nelson's guitar strums distract the disturbing images my brain is producing. Horses starved thin, whipped and kicked, forced to race or run or some other stupid thing humans do out of greed at the expense of an animal's right to proper care.

But how the hell am I going to rescue horses? I have no idea how many he owns. I might need to do some reconnaissance first, make a plan.

Just the idea of a strategy calms me, and I enjoy the next five country songs, even belting out a few as I follow Route 4.

I'll do what needs to be done at Foster's place, then drop southwest to Route 50 which will take me straight into Lamar, Colorado.

-18-

A sign reads Halsom – 6. Somewhere around here is Foster's ranch. The newspaper showed the front gate and an arch over the drive with his last name spelled out in ironwork. No need to stop and ask directions when there's signage pointing the way.

Sprawling ranches dominate the sides of the road. Huge barns and fencing are the norm. My eyes ache from studying the roadsides for his place, for the image from the newspaper. I'm like a marooned survivor searching for a plane on the horizon.

Disappointment settles into my chest. Did I miss it? Maybe Foster's ranch was on the other side of town.

Halsom consists of a hammered-looking hardware building stuck between faded-brick storefronts from the turn of the century. Signs promoting saddles, beef jerky, and beer blink by my windshield as I force my mind to stay sharp. I keep an eye out for a motel where I can sleep for a few more hours. Although it might be smarter to just sleep in my truck again. My neck hates that idea, but I don't want to leave any trail of my being here if I can help it.

I'll do the reconnaissance today, get a count of the horses and their state, find a horse trailer somehow… Yes, my plan is contingent on a lot of factors still, but this is horse country and I brought a lot of cash with me. I will need to ask around about who can take in the horses. I have a good amount of property, yes, but I am not prepared to make an eight-hundred-mile trip with a trailer of horses. Certainly, there is a local rancher or nonprofit that can take on the animals.

Three miles south of town I finally spot his gate. It's open. I take note. Does he always keep it open during the day? Or only recently because of the news article? Although, wouldn't most people leave it locked to keep out the busybodies and any other reporters that pick up the story? If he doesn't lock it for them, he must never lock it. That will make things easier when I come back.

I turn down the long two-lane gravel and dirt road. It's five a.m. and dawn waits just below the horizon.

Ranchers get up early, so I keep an eye out for any movement.

Long stretches of grass extend on both sides of rail fencing. Two brown horses have their muzzles in the grass. I keep my eye on them as I approach the first building I see. They seem healthy enough. I'm a good ten feet away, but I don't see ribs poking through dull coats. If I can see them walk, I'll know if they are getting shoed often enough, but I don't see crusted eyes or any other evidence of illness. Maybe I was wrong, wasting my time coming here.

The dirt road becomes a cement lot connecting to a long, low home to my right and a large stable to the left. I'm immediately nervous that I've gotten too close to things, but my truck isn't the only vehicle here. Two other trucks are parked along with a two-bay horse trailer.

I pull in and turn around, parking between an old green Ford and the horse trailer. The nose of my truck faces away from the barn and corral in case I need a quick getaway. Through my window, a symphony of warm grasses and ripe manure is the first scent to reach me. It's not bad.

I've barely taken in the layout of his property when I hear the slap of work boots against cement.

I exit the truck as the barn sensor light suddenly breaks into pieces as a man crosses below it on the pad by the barn. The hair rises on my arms, and I move into defensive mode when I register his size. Randall was a scrawny drunk. I pictured Mark Foster the same way, but with the drinker's face I saw in the paper. This guy has me by two inches and possibly a hundred pounds. An image of him punching me in the face pops in my head. I need to make sure it's the other way around.

I speak first, forcing casual, cool, and what I hope sounds collected in my words. "Are you Mark Foster?"

"Who the fuck wants to know?" he says. His voice is rough, a twinge of battery acid in his words. He wears jeans, cuffed above his work boots, a white T-shirt, and a ball cap. He holds a cup in his left hand.

When he comes closer, I see his mouth is set in a tight line and his eyes hold a hard squint.

"Wy…." No reason to give him my name. "Why…now that you've asked, it's John."

My heart thumps against my breastbone. What am I doing here? I can leave right now.

He studies my truck. "You from Wyoming?"

"My truck is," I say. "You got a nice place here. Quiet."

"Huhn," is all he says, but his voice is full of suspicion. The raised hair on my forearms agrees.

I'd hoped for an easier time in checking out the place. And if I ran into him like this I imagined we'd be two guys jawing about horses and the beauty of living in a rural place and then I'd slide into the personal questions. Instead, there's danger here and I have to be careful.

I might as well do what I came for. "So, you got a pretty bum deal with all the bad press."

He nods and tips his cup over, emptying the short splash of brown onto the ground.

I indicate the road. "Is this where it happened?"

He nods but doesn't answer.

I push on, biting back the heat rising in me, the image of the colt and the details about its skin nearly torn off. "From what I read, you were taking the colt to another pasture when it tripped and was dragged by mistake?"

"Naw, but that's the story I told." He straightens his back. "It was lame, born with a short leg, so I was gonna shoot it over there." He waves a hand toward a far field. "I was considering the other horses, you know. I've learned that they get nervous when they see one of their own takes a bullet to the head."

Bastard. I'd like to put a bullet in *his* head, but I have no gun. My apple fritter and stale coffee reach the back of my throat, and I swallow to keep the mess down.

He keeps talking, seeming to enjoy the soapbox.

"Animal-rights pussies. I should be able to do whatever the hell I want out here, but these pricks from the city got all interested in my business."

His fists clench and unclench as he speaks. "I'm a damn rancher. I can kill anything I want when I want."

My friendly face slides away and I can't stop it. He's a horrible human being. To regain my composure, I study the horizon. The day will be muggy and overcast, with a slight chance of a fight breaking out.

Am I contemplating that? This guy is huge. And I'll never understand an abuser's side of the story, so why let him blab on? He's just making me see red.

I turn my gaze to Foster. "Does it bother you that you're known as a fucking prick?"

His hard stare is full of hate.

I stare back.

"Who the hell are you to come here and talk to me like this?" He moves a step toward me. "My land, my rules."

"I don't give a shit what a loser like you has to say, you don't get to torture animals."

"Really, asshole." He rushes me and shoves me against the back of my truck, his hands squeezing my neck.

I pull at his hands, but he doesn't let go, and I'm not strong enough to pry him free. Panic rips through me. I'm going to die here.

Spots fill my vision. I have to do something fast, or this is it.

I kick him in the shins, glad I'm wearing steel-toed boots. His hands loosen for a moment, and I spin away and put distance between us as I suck in air.

"You prick!" I croak. "What the hell was that for?"

"You do not get to tell me what to do." He takes ten steps to the barn and turns around holding a rifle. "Watch this."

Fear spikes my blood pressure as he heads to the nearest pasture. Three horses have come to the fence as we've talked.

"Don't do that!" I call. Panic seizes my throat. "I'm leaving."

He points the rifle at a black horse, and this time I charge him and knock him down.

He loses his grip on the gun as I scramble to my feet.

"You don't want to do this!" I have to stop him from killing one of these beautiful animals just to prove he can. "I'll go right now. I will."

I head to the truck as he picks himself up. I scramble inside, but my wallet falls out of my back pocket and drops to the ground. I step down and get it as a shot rings out and a horse screams.

Fucker! The remaining horses scatter and frantically run around in their enclosure as he raises the gun again.

I jump in the cab, snap the door shut, and throw the truck into reverse, heading straight for him.

He barely yells, "Hey," as the vehicle jerks when I knock him down. The rear axle bucks upward as I run him over.

I squeeze the gearshift, kick in the clutch again, and find first gear. The truck's rear axle jumps again as it clears Foster's body. Is he dead? In the rearview mirror he's an unmoving heap. Can a guy, even a big one, survive two tons of weight driving over him? Twice?

He must be dead.

The dying cries from the horse have stopped, but tears wet my cheeks. I caused this—an innocent animal's death.

The sun's head creeps up to the edge of the world, as if checking to see if it's safe to launch a new day.

I don't wait around to find out what happens next. I can't leave the horses here. His wife let him mistreat the animals, and there's no telling if she will be any better with them if he's dead.

I back up to the horse trailer and connect. Then I lead the two horses inside, where they come with little resistance.

Why no one has poured from the house after hearing the shot, I can't fathom. I close the trailer's door and don't wait around one minute longer. I go.

At the end of his long drive, I stop and exit the truck. I pick up a large piece of gravel and scratch letters into the side of his metal gate.

I kick away my footsteps in the dirt and crunch my way back to the truck, taking the stone with me.

That should send a message.

-19-

Forty minutes later after heading west, I stop at a wide river alongside the road. It's swollen to a summer high watermark, and its edges are choked with dead trees, tumbleweed exoskeletons, and sporadic piles of trash. I toss the rock from Foster's into the middle of the river then check on the horses, ensuring they have enough food and water. They are calm and dipping their heads into the oat bag, which was a bonus find in a storage box at the front of the trailer.

Now that I see the animals in broad daylight, they are too skinny and have scars across their flanks. Yes, I've stolen them and the trailer, but this is the only way they'll get a shot at a good life.

Back in the cab, I continue our journey. My heart stops banging once I'm on Route 50, a busier highway. Back on the smaller roads, I was a lone beacon with a horse trailer attached, so if anyone was looking for someone who was recently at Foster's, I may as well be wearing a fucking neon sign that says, "it was me."

I drive on as music crackles through the truck's speakers, every song twanging out a story of despair and loss. LeAnn Rimes begs me to look at the sky and tell her what I see, a song appropriately titled "Looking Through Your Eyes."

And just what am I seeing with these eyes?

Randall's death seemed otherworldly, a one-off, but here I am again, another dead guy, another chance to be discovered and sent to prison. But I caught Foster in the act. There was no second-guessing what he was willing to do, continuing until he'd shot all three horses dead.

An hour later at a pay phone, I call information and ask for horse adoption or horse rescue programs in Colorado. The operator keeps me on hold for a while before coming back on to say the nearest horse rescue is Red

Rose Ranch south of Lamar, just across the Colorado border and not too far from my original plans of grabbing a hotel in the area.

The horses snuffle and snort in the trailer behind me. They must be afraid of the bumpy ride, but they don't know it's very well the price I just paid to get them to a happier, healthier life.

The morning air is as calm and peaceful as it was when I first arrived as I breeze toward the sanctuary and their new future and Pueblo, Colorado, where I hope to get answers about my past.

I shake away murderous thoughts and focus on my day. I need to call Greta to check on the dogs because she'll be expecting that. I'm not in any shape to do it just yet. I replay the reasons I came west—to find out more about my mother's family, to pick up another car.

Fear ripples through me. I move my jaw from side to side, loosening up the clenched muscles. Exhaustion and worry eat at my ability to stay focused on my speed. But what if Foster isn't dead? He saw my truck, noticed the Wyoming plate.

I push the truck westward. The sooner I put Kansas in the rearview mirror, the better.

He's dead, I reason. The weight of the truck would have crushed him.

He almost killed me, wanted to kill the horses. I had to do something.

I turn the music up and force myself to stay awake. When I spot a large Travel Plaza Center, I signal and exit and pull into the busy lot.

My energy is fading fast, but I need to reach Colorado sometime today. More than anything, I want a scalding shower. I check on the horses again, promising they can have some time out of the trailer when I get back. I carry fresh clothes in a duffle bag into the locker area, and for nine bucks, I get a clean but thin towel and washcloth, a miniature bar of soap, and a hot, private ten-minute shower. The caustic-smelling soap all but abrades my arms and hands as I scrub, but it isn't entirely unpleasant. If there was any speck of Foster on me, it's gone now.

The Travel Plaza has the forward-thinking slogan of, "Your Home Away from Home," offering among other conveniences, a two-hour laundry service. After I'm dry, I dress and bundle my dirty clothes in the provided laundry bag, scribbling the name Bob Smathers on the card and attaching a twenty-dollar bill. I drop it into the laundry chute with a one-day turnaround request, to be picked up at the folding area tomorrow. I'll be long gone by the time my old clothes are clean and left unclaimed, and if somehow a description of a man seen at Foster's is linked to these clothes, they'll be looking for a bogus Bob and not me.

In front of the mirror, I push my hair into an orderly style, but I still look like hell. I notice bruises on my neck from when Foster tackled me. "Shit," I draw out the whispered word. The marks are dark and bluing-up into a nice set of fingerprints. I'll need to hide them until they're gone. Which will be almost impossible in summer clothes.

After a trip through the attached sundries store, I leave the service plaza wearing a red bandanna around my neck. I return to the truck carrying a triangular package of prefab cheese sandwiches, chips, and an extra-large black coffee.

I lead the two horses out by their reins and tie them to a pole two feet from the trailer near a patch of tall sweetgrass. They immediately begin sniffing and munching the fresh vegetation. I fill the pail with fresh water from an outside spigot and they drink deeply.

The food and coffee barely go down as I watch over the two horses. I'm sure they'd love to be let free to run along the pastures here. Two hundred or so more miles and they'll be able to do just that. I breathe in the smell of dusty cement and diesel fumes from the big rigs coming and going. This is no place for them.

The food eventually works like it's supposed to and my strength returns. I load the horses back up without any issues, lock the trailer, then cross the lot to a pay phone, open a new roll of quarters, and feed the device. It clicks and beeps and finally grants me a dial tone.

I force energy into my voice when Greta answers. "I'm almost to Colorado. Just wanted to check on you and the kids."

"We're great, Wyatt." She pauses. "Did you know they love sausage for breakfast?"

I groan. "I did not." I open the folding door in the booth to let out the stagnant air smelling of old cigarettes and desperation. "They'll never want to come home if you keep doing that."

"It's a nice kielbasa. High-end like you would expect them to have."

"Thank you, but I expect them to enjoy the expensive dog food I buy." I chuckle. "I like it when you baby them, so no further lecture from me. When are you heading into the store today?"

"I'm leaving soon. And I'll put the dogs in their pen while I'm working."

"Good plan. Florence has a delicate stomach. Dobie diarrhea is not fun to clean up, believe me."

"I'll remember that." She chuckles. "Oh, and a guy called and wants to know if we can sell a couple of things for him."

"God, what is it this time, dried kitten fetuses?"

She laughs. "Not quite that bad. One is a jump rope made of licorice, comes in three flavors."

"And we eat it after it drags along the ground?" I snort. Do people think these ideas through? "Good way to get the health department hanging around."

"Right?" It sounds like she's shuffling papers. "I have a picture of the other one. It's literally a teddy bear dipped in wax called the Teddy Candle."

"The hell?" Sounds like a joke skit from *Saturday Night Live* where Dan Ackroyd promoted a Bag-O-Glass for creative kids.

"It's dipped in cinnamon-scented wax, but the tiny tag reminds you not to burn it. It's for your table to provide a festive holiday aroma."

"You know someone's gonna light it," I say. "Should inform Don Bradley over at the fire department this is selling out there."

"Yeah, it's creepy too. The eyes look all crusty with that waxy hair going in all directions."

"Send them both our polite letter saying no thank you."

"Already done. How's your trip going? You must be getting excited now that you're closer."

"I'm getting nervous. But all's good." I hold off saying I'm making good time because if Foster is alive, I'll be *doing* time. "Oh, I saw a funny bumper sticker."

"Tell me."

She loves this kind of thing. "It said, 'I've been dieting for a week and all I've lost is seven days.'"

"That's a good one." She laughs. "Oh, may I lock up the store an hour early? I have dinner plans with Marla and Fred." They are her sister and brother-in-law.

"Of course." The store barely hauls in enough to pay her salary and cover property taxes, which I'm fine with. I keep it open mostly in my Gramps's memory and because the locals and tourists like it. "And if it's slow, knock off even earlier."

"Great. You still planning on being back Thursday night?"

Not with the strangle marks on my neck. "I'll try but it might be later. The dogs will be great in their house if you don't want to keep them that long." That's where they are supposed to stay, honestly, but I know she takes them home with her and spoils them rotten.

"No way. They're with Aunty Greta until you get back."

"Okay, thanks."

"Happy hunting," she says.

Paranoia dies harder than old habits, especially when it's grounded in reality. She knows me better than anyone else alive. Has she guessed what I've left behind on a dusty lane?

I shake my head. C'mon, Wyatt. She's talking about finding your mother.

"Yes. Wish me luck," I say, trying to work the pitchiness out of my voice.

"And I know you like the open road. Enjoy your time away."

"You do know me well." The phone gives me the one-minute warning. I either have to pay up or shut up. "I'll call you later to check in. Hug those dogs for me."

"I will."

She's gone before my time runs out.

Those words circle back as I cross to the truck. In all likelihood, she will pass away before me. Losing her will be devastating. But then again, if I keep acting on these vigilante impulses, who's to say I'll last the next month.

$-20-$

O n the road far too many hours with little sleep, I've wilted in the hard press of the June sun. After chasing wavering tarmac mirages all morning, I'm flirting at some level with killing myself on the road—I'm that tired and barely cognizant of the other vehicles on the speeding black-top. Everything blurs around the edges as I cross the Colorado state line, but the horses have endured this long trip, and so can I.

Another hour floats by in a haze of energy drinks, bad coffee, and more Slim Jims than one man can handle, but I finally pull up to the Red Rose Sanctuary. When I called them from the pay phone, a woman explained they take in horses with little-to-no questions and use them as rehabilitation for the inmates of the Colorado Department of Corrections. It's a fantastic program that allows for people to gain a skill and receive the healing and rejuvenation that only comes from animals.

It's a nonprofit, no money is exchanged, and they'll care for the animals fully. They have a large-animal vet that comes by once a week to check in on the animals, so these skinny horses will get the attention they need.

I park a quarter of a mile away and search the fence line for a way to let the animals inside without me being seen. There's no gate for as far as I can see. I have no choice but to rock two fence posts out of the ground and lay them flat. I lead the horses one at a time over the horizontal wires.

"Enjoy your freedom," I say as they watch me replant the fence posts. I stay long enough to watch them trot off toward a line of shade trees where I imagine a creek flows.

I hope they'll have long, happy lives with lots of free runs, open sky, and the opportunity to feel the love of many.

I drive back in the direction I came and when I find a decrepit barn off to the side of the road, I pull in, unhitch the trailer behind the abandoned structure, and leave it.

I feel better having it off my hands. It's a tractor beam that would connect me to Foster.

He sure as hell could identify it if he's still alive, although his wife and kids might not be that interested in getting it back.

I'm so tired, I'm almost to the blackout stage when I pull into a Travel Lodge parking lot in Lamar, the place I planned to stay all along. I've arrived five hours past the schedule I'd laid out before I left Ohio. I'm back on track and can forget what happened in Kansas and focus again on what brought me out here—looking for my mother or her people.

The scents of warm sagebrush and dry grass hit me when I slide the truck into a parking spot near the back. The engine stutters a few times after I turn it off, and I sit there for five minutes, willing my eyes to focus. Other than my short nap in the truck near Topeka, I've been awake for thirty-one hours and have driven this last hour with nothing but sheer luck and my gaze fixed on the painted lines. They kept my truck moving along with other vehicles, like rabid explorers heading west.

Once I extricate myself from the truck, I do a good job of walking a straight line to the lobby.

A girl with a dark ponytail, a white halter top, and a denim mini-skirt checks me in with only a cursory glance. She pops her gum as she watches a shoebox-sized television with giant rabbit ears on one end of the counter.

I fill out the papers and write down random numbers and letters for my license plate. With over forty cars in the Travel Lodge parking lot, I doubt the girl is going to turn off *Days of Our Lives* to wander the parking lot and match up numbers on the forms with the vehicles parked there.

"Thank you." I accept the room key.

"Yup."

I appreciate the lack of interest.

My room tries for an upscale Native American theme, but there's too much emphasis on arrowheads and buffalo to be anything but insulting. I strip to my boxers and study the bruises on my neck, then sag against the bathroom wall and curse. Of course, no miracle has happened—they're still there. And they'll still be there Thursday, a day and a half away.

Sitting on the end of the bed, I eat a bag of pretzels. The act of chewing is automatic, the paste in my mouth tasteless.

My body literally thrums with exhaustion. With every beat of my heart, the buffalo on the wallpaper pulse in and out, on the verge of stampeding.

I swallow four aspirin with Sprite. The muscles in my arms and shoulders ache, not only from wrestling with Foster, but from driving the entire day under stress. But through all the aching and fatigue, something inside me thrums with a deep warmth. A feeling of satisfaction, of making a difference. Sure it was just two horses, like it was just one dog, and the sheep and pigs, and one little boy and his puppy. But the numbers are adding up. I am helping. Saving. Making the world a better place, not to mention ridding it from monsters that like nothing more than to hurt, and cheat, and cause pain.

I stretch out on the bed, reaching for the hotel phone to call Greta and check on the dogs. I'd be lying if I said I wasn't relieved when I reach Greta's answering machine instead of her chipper voice. I have no energy left to talk to anyone. I leave a message that I made it to Colorado and would call tomorrow.

Propped up against the pillows, I go through my wallet, satisfied all my cards are there. That a card might have fallen out in the chaotic moments when I scrambled to collect my wallet from the ground has haunted me all day. There would be no explaining away the discovery of a card with my name on it near Foster's home. Bobby and Doug would be waiting for me at the junkyard, and I'd be on my way to the Ohio State Penitentiary.

Instead of Foster, I focus on my mother—memories of her smile, timid but wide, her wavy brown hair pulled back in a clip. These images are stored in a soft sepia color, that comforting hue of faded photographs. Maybe one day, I'll view her in living color again.

A black wave of exhaustion finally shuts everything off.

-21-

I slept through the afternoon and night, sixteen hours straight instead of my usual seven. I wander to the breakfast room off the main lobby with plastic chairs parked around square tables. They're packed so closely together, whispering would be the only way to have a private conversation. It's a terrible setup, as if eating in public is a shameful thing, forcing people to hunch over their plates, elbows tucked close to their sides, praying-mantis mode, the sibilance of hushed speech competing with the clatter of silverware against plates.

I swallow my last bite of a Denver omelet while the wall-mounted TV reviews the news.

I'm stirring cream into my fourth cup of weak coffee when a word from the announcer stops me. I set the spoon aside, afraid it might start knocking against the cup, as if I have an announcement to make, which is the last thing I intend.

"VAPPA," the male news anchor says again, then raises his eyebrows before going on. He knows when he has a good story to milk.

I don't know why I feel surprised as this inevitable thing happens. Of course this story would eventually make headlines—it was the plan all along. Still, disbelief surges through my body, alerting my whole vascular and nervous systems to pay attention.

"Has a vigilante group killed a rancher in Kansas early yesterday morning?"

Foster *is* dead. Relief surges through me, and I want to yell halle-fuck-ing-lujah. I waited twenty-four long hours for that answer. Now I know there is no witness to me, my truck, or the missing horses and trailer. Any of it. And the man was too cheap or stupid to have any surveillance or security at the ranch. I was scot-free.

The announcer continues, "A group that calls itself Vigilantes Against People and Pet Abusers may be responsible for the death of another person."

The Internet photo I first saw of Foster appears on the television. "Mark Foster was found dead by his barn, according to the sheriff department near Halsom. The police say his death does not seem accidental. And a message was left near the scene."

They found my scrawling on the metal gate. Abusers Beware ~ VAPPA.

A woman at my right says, "That's terrible." Her hair is pulled back into a messy bun, and her feathered bangs start from the middle of her crown and spring out all over. She looks like a Polish Frizzle Chicken my neighbors once raised.

The news continues. "With no witnesses, the police have linked this case to the disappearance of a man in Ohio last month because of a message left on Foster's front gate. A group by this same name claims they killed him, although no body has been found."

I try to look casual and sip my coffee, but the movement feels foreign, so I set my cup back on the table without taking my eyes off the broadcaster.

Will the police reveal the message I scratched into the gate?

"In the Ohio case, a note from VAPPA explained that the group had taken action against a man there who hurt one of his children while harming the family pet." The newscaster turns a sheet of paper. "Foster was given probation for nearly dragging a colt to death." He sets his mouth in a grim line. "Authorities ask for anyone to come forward who may have information in this case."

From another table to my left, a teenager speaks up, "I'd join that group. This guy tried to kill a baby horse. He deserves it."

A woman's reproach follows. "You sound just like your father. That was a living person this crazy group killed. The name sounds like auto parts for vampires."

I had just managed to take the last swallow of my coffee and then I choke on it. That's a good one.

The TV story finishes with a statement that Foster left behind a wife and two teens. I bet the new widow, abused herself according to the newspaper article, has been celebrating with Jack on the rocks since yesterday.

The teenager hisses, "I know you don't think so, Mom, but animals are living things too."

Their conversation disintegrates into him wanting to live with his father and have a dog.

I stand and drop three bucks on the table. I hope the kid gets his wish. Sounds like he has a good dad.

I tune them out but not before my thoughts jump to my father and why he killed my dog, Keesha. He knew I loved that dog, and I'm sure he knew I didn't care much for his abusive words and drunken nights.

I push those thoughts away. I need to quit picking at old scabs. Right now, I relish the sense of relief after hearing Foster is dead. He'll never hurt another animal. Or his family.

And I may have escaped the hangman's noose once again.

I hear VAPPA again, this time in a conversation between two women working the front desk when I check out. They're discussing the news story when I slide my key across the green marbled counter.

"VAPPA's got to be from these parts," the older woman says to the younger.

The older woman's dark makeup stops at her jawline and looks garish against her otherwise pale skin. Obviously a lover of rings, each finger sports one.

The younger woman is her opposite—clean face, no jewelry, modest clothes, could be running for Demure Girl of the month.

"No, really." This time the woman is speaking to me. My silence must mean I'm involved in this conversation.

I meet her gaze. "Are you talking about the guy in Kansas?"

"Yeah. Somebody killed him for almost dragging a colt to death."

No, I killed him for his being an asshole and shooting his horse.

She taps a long fingernail on the counter. "It's a group of people who hate abuse, for both people and animals."

These two are referring to VAPPA as a group which is helpful. I nod. "Could be. Just wondering why you say they're from around here?" The fact the acronym is moving into everyday conversation will only increase the confusion of who killed Foster. Rumors have a great way of muddying investigative waters, and I'm fine with the murky infiltration.

"This is horse country." She smiles, and the lines on her face speak of long days in the sun and wind. "We name our kids things like Cutter, Roper, and Brander."

The meeker woman—Darla according to her nametag—nods. "My son leaves from school midday and gets on home and feeds the horses. Horses come first, English class second."

"Hardworking people is what I hear you saying." I twirl the truck's keyring around my index finger. "Nothing wrong with that. But killing a guy?"

The older woman pushes poofy bangs off to the side. "We got a few guys around that might be willing to do the job. Jeb McGruber." She looks at Darla. "Right?"

They laugh and Darla nods. "He *could* do it."

I smile as if I know all about old Jeb and his crazy antics. "Do tell." I want to hear more about the man they feel could do what I'd done. They comply, talking over each other.

"He's a wild one," Darla says. "Lights a fire down a rattlesnake hole and when the snake comes up—"

"He thumps it on the head with a shovel," says the older woman with all the makeup. No nametag so I'm calling her Mary Kay. She adds, "Nothing scares him. He's got no thumbs, you know." She says it casually as if stating, *he just got a new Ford, you know.*

No thumbs? This conversation is all over the place, but I take the bait. "Why's that?" I raise my eyebrows and wait.

"He was a big stud on the rodeo circuit," Darla says. "Most cowboys in that league lose a left thumb after a while. Jeb just thought he was ambidextral, or whatever the word is, and he kept riding."

I tilt my head trying to connect seemingly unrelated facts—snakes to no thumbs to vigilantism? "Mangled hands makes him a killer?"

The phone rings and Mary Kay turns to answer it, her rings clicking on the receiver as she lifts it.

"In the right circumstance." Darla rolls a pen back and forth on the counter. Somehow it feels flirtatious. "Can't rope no more so he trains horses now, and he'd go after anyone that would hurt his animals. Course he ain't shooting any guns either, so maybe it wasn't him."

Her statement makes me realize the news report didn't say *how* Foster died. This woman assumes he was shot. Another plus.

"We may never know." I tap the counter and then raise my hands. "Gotta get. Thanks for the chat." And I mean it. Relief washes through me with the misconceptions of what's happened.

I hit the road and take Rt. 50 through Swink, a town once situated in Mexican territory, still holding on to that south-of-the-border feel. One thing about the people in these small towns—they come from hardy stock. This whole area would have been scoured out during the Great Dust Bowl tragedy in the 1930s. *The Grapes of Wrath* depicted the hell—the simplest acts of life, like breathing, eating a meal, taking a walk, were no longer simple.

It still looks listless and parched, although moments ago I saw a sign proclaiming World's Best Watermelons Grown Here. Sagebrush and tan dirt hills run in every direction, but someone persuaded large juicy fruit to grow out of the barrenness.

Hardy people, hardy crops.

I drive, and although I should feel relieved, I'm short-tempered. It must come from this kind of wide-open land, with no stopping places in any direction. It makes me nervous. Raised in a thick forest, I like edges, borders, something to part the wind. My place in Ohio has that bind-me-together feel with my acres of cars surrounded on three sides by woods.

My mother came from this flattened area, but now that I'm here, I don't sense a connection. Everything is too vulnerable, the ground looks chafed, scarred over in some spots, yet farm after farm along the main road seem ripe and operational.

I head west, carrying the threadlike hope of finding more about my relatives. According to the newspaper article in the library about my mother, the Powell family lived on a farm outside of a town called Manzanola. I hope to find a clerk in charge of the county records.

My mother would only be fifty-six now. It's hard to imagine she died, yet it would explain why I've had no contact from her. The other explanation is that she never tried, which is far less appealing.

A hawk swoops low over a bristly field, searching. I've never believed that my mom is dead. Wouldn't I have a sixth sense about that at some level? Genetic radar that warns you when the last of your bloodline dies, alerting you to start procreating, to keep the DNA torch burning and moving along lineage paths? I haven't felt even a flicker or a blip on my radar.

There are stories of families reuniting all the time, later in life, with silly circumstances having kept them apart. That's my hope. Some relative must know her whereabouts. I can't imagine my mom hasn't contacted anyone in her family after she left Montana. There must be someone who has communicated with her over the years.

By the end of today, I should have the answer to that and hopefully more.

$-22-$

My stops so far on the Powell family quest have led me almost no-where and it's almost two in the afternoon. The day is rolling on and I have no new information about my family. I was all the way to Manzanola when I realized that I'd passed the county courthouse twenty miles back. Rather than backtracking right away, I decided to stop and ask a local. A fruit stand vendor was a hundred percent certain I'd find everything I'm looking for at the Olney Springs City Government Building.

I spent an hour in Olney Springs looking through cemetery records before a rotund man with feminine features redirected me to the Crowley City Hall.

At the Crowley City Hall, Harold, a man with petrified wood for skin, handed me a map of the area and sent me to Manzanola. I've been turned away so many times today I might as well be an armful of zucchini no one wants at harvest time.

The Manzanola Town Hall on Main Street has an old western look—a narrow brick structure up front with a peaked facade, yet it has three times that in length behind the front doors, running on about a third of a block.

The high metal ceiling inside the Manzanola Town Hall is stamped with an intricate pattern evoking images of men in smoking jackets and women in matching heels and hats. The historical plaque in the parking lot explains the brick building's rich history as the Santa Fe Railway Depot in the early 1900s. Manzanola was an important stop for passenger and freight trains, a city whose name meant "large apple" in Spanish. Nothing apple-ish is evident as I motor through the listless town.

Evelyn, a woman of about forty, with reddish hair and freckles splashed around her face and arms, is finally my saving grace. The town clerk leads me down the long corridor of the town hall, through descending decades of census records, to those from 1942 to 1960—my mother's birth year through the time she supposedly left the area.

My guide talks nonstop from the moment I explained I'm on a genealogy journey, a near East Coaster searching for my Western heritage.

"The Dust Bowl made bad people worse and good people hard." Evelyn tightens the belt on her green flowered dress. "My grandparents stuck it out here, but tens of thousands headed to completely different terrain."

I nod. "Steinbeck said it quite well, didn't he?"

"Sure did. You know, it takes a special person to be a flatlander." She raises her eyebrows, giving her a semi-startled look, mainly because she's sketched them in so they're higher than her natural brows. "Out here, it's so wide open you can watch your dog run away for two weeks."

I laugh again. That sparks a memory. The most memorable element for me in *The Grapes of Wrath* was when the family abandoned their dog along the road, on the way to California.

I hated Steinbeck and his fictional family for that.

Evelyn points me toward a wide desk while she pulls boxes from the shelves. As the town clerk and the keeper of vital records, the lady is efficient and quick.

"Here's some." She drops a box on the table and turns to another shelf. "And you'll want these." She tugs her belt again and leaves.

The lacquered wood on the long desk is so sleek it shines, begging to have a hand run over it. I comply, lost in thought. Gram would have loved leaving the junkyard, exploring this area of the country with me. She called our trips "voyages." Off we'd go to an old, abandoned farm, to swap meets, or auctions. I miss her. She had a quick giggle and always seemed upbeat. And I know she wanted the same answers I'm now looking for—what happened to her daughter-in-law, my mother?

Sun pours in through the western-facing windows, and dust dances up and down in the warm beam touching the corner of the large desk. Foster and the fear of being arrested seem a million miles away. But once I learn information about my mother, I need to call Greta and Victoria to share the news with them. I never told Victoria I was leaving, not that we check in daily with each other. But if she's called the house, she might be worried when she can't reach me for days. After all, she believes the junkyard is dangerous, with all the sharp metal and my car smasher.

A month ago, I couldn't have foreseen where I am today. This is something I should have done years ago. Trying to guess where I'll be in a month from now would be like predicting where the next tornado will touch down.

Evelyn startles me by dropping stacks of files and a pad of paper and a pen next to me.

"This should do it," she chimes. Her belt must be fine now because she walks away without touching it.

In front of me are stacks of land deeds, county censuses for fifty years, water rights, and certificates of births, marriages, and deaths. I dig in and lose track of the next hour, caught up in the facts, knowing these records have probably not seen the light of day in decades.

I read through the papers and study an area census. My mother, Patricia Ann Powell, was born to Ralph and Cleone in 1942. Ralph was from the Oklahoma panhandle while Cleone Harper was born in Lamar, in Eastern Colorado. They were young teens during the Depression and the Dust Bowl years.

I jot down her parents' last known address, a farm outside of Manzanola, along County Rd. 11. This is the same address I found for my mother at the Akron library. Her parents would be in their eighties now, so there is a good chance they're still alive.

The sun is picking its way across my desk when I come across the name "Wyatt" in print. My heart stutters and I lean closer to read it again. The shock lingers as I realize it's not me referenced in the papers, but an uncle, Wyatt Powell, someone I never knew existed. My mom's brother, her only sibling, according to the records, three years younger than she was. The form holds no clue to his cause of death, but it's recorded in 1960, right around the time my mother ran away and eventually ended up in California.

A smile grows on my lips. My mother named me after her brother who died at age fourteen, someone she must have cared deeply for.

I need to find out what happened to Wyatt. Mom left home soon after he died. There must be a connection to his death and her running away.

I cross the musty room to the microfiche machine Evelyn showed me. She left the square plastic films for the time periods I requested piled beside the machine. These are archives of Manzanola and the other local towns' newspapers. I slide in the Manzanola papers first, lean into the eye piece, and let time spin backward, a history of the area told in reverse, one head-line at a time.

A frustrating forty-five minutes later filled with news stories of sto-len cows, grain prices, and vandalism of the popcorn maker at the local movie theater, I find a reference to my uncle, Wyatt Powell. He died in an explosion on the family farm, in the barn. My mother, almost eighteen at the time, was near the barn but escaped the ensuing flames. Two horses, a calf, and a loft full of kittens perished, according to the blurry story from thirty-eight years earlier. In the papers from a week after Wyatt died, I find the story I first read at the Akron library. My mother had run away, and al-though there were pleas from her now-childless parents for her return, the search tapered off just like the story in the newspapers did.

Patricia had vanished.

My grandparents said she eventually met Dad in California, got preg-nant, married him, moved to the backwoods of Montana and, by age thirty, disappeared again.

I'm only five years older than she was when she left me behind in Montana. When I was a kid, she was a full-fledged adult to me, but she was barely out of her twenties the last time I saw her. My chest constricts. What mom doesn't want her child with her, no matter how young she is? Who runs off and leaves their kid in the fucking trees with a mean drunk?

I stretch back in the chair and let my spine crack. I roll a kink out of my neck, digesting the scant details of my mother's childhood. She'd known tragedy, pain that hurt so much it must have defined the rest of her life. She ran away after her brother died and then again, after years of feeling trapped in the forest with my abusive dad.

I fold my note paper and stuff it in my back pocket. I head down the long center hall, find Evelyn and thank her, saying I might be back.

She's in one of the newer sections. "Did you find anything interesting?" She uses her index finger to push up her orange-framed glasses.

I pause before answering. "I discovered my relatives had a run of bad luck, but they seem to be a whole lot tougher than I am."

She nods. "My parents used to say some folks are so unlucky, they could buy a cemetery just as people would discover immortality." The crinkles at the edges of her eyes say she smiles more often than not.

I laugh. "Or their guardian angel took up drinking when the chips were down." That's a Greta saying.

"I'm gonna use that one if you don't mind," she says.

"It's yours for the keeping. I was just borrowing it." I thank her again and leave.

The inside of the town hall was cool, so I'm not prepared for the ninety-plus degrees that envelops me on the front steps. The afternoon sun blazes down, and the sky is a fierce blue looking for a fight with any cloud that dares show up.

Fatigue hits me then, with the intensity of the last two days catching up to me. My plan was to drive to the Powell homestead today, but now I want some distance, some time to process what I learned before I face my past.

In search of a motel, I drive aimlessly for a half hour thinking about what I know about the Powells. My uncle's death must be the dark secret my grandparents talked about after I tried to run away and find Mom in California. But an explosion on a farm couldn't have been unusual, so why not talk about it? Gasoline, fertilizers, and other accelerants blow up all the time. This might be one answer I learn tomorrow.

Driving toward Main Street, I'm irritable again. The empty skies feel too raw, too honest, but above all, the openness leaves no place to hide.

And I've spent a great deal of my life hiding. In the forest, in my art studio, behind my artist facade and the notion I need to be alone to create, even from Victoria and her desire to progress in our relationship. I'm the only person I can't run from no matter how small I try to keep my world.

Back in Manzanola, I park in front of a listless ochre-colored motel with signage almost as big as the building. It brags of clean rooms, low prices, and free cable. It fits my cranky mood perfectly.

I grab my bag and check in with a gaunt man, who takes fifty-nine dollars in cash. He hands me a silver-colored key on a giant wooden key fob.

"Hefty." I pat the piece of wood.

"If you lose it, it's ten bucks to replace." He turns my registration papers around. "Only staying the one night?"

"Yep."

The lobby is musty. The air conditioner in the window pushes semicool air around, but it has a death rattle that says it might not be long for this world.

"Is the diner next door any good?"

"If you aren't too worried about life expectancy and you don't mind everything tasting like bacon, it's as good as any." This time his mouth does a weird movement and I assume he's smiling.

"Good enough." I head outside, find my room along the broken cement sidewalk, and try to hold the tiny key with its two-pound anchor in place to turn the lock. I toss my bag inside. Later, I'll deal with what might await me in there.

In the diner beside the motel, I slide into a red Naugahyde booth and order a patty melt and a Coors, a beer that had finally migrated from Colorado to Ohio only a decade earlier.

Three beers later, and with no bacon aftertaste, I leave a hefty tip for Tamara—pronounced Ta-MAR-a as in *tamara I'll be long gone*. Her double Ds are busting out of the top of her red-and-white-striped uniform and reach my table seconds before the rest of her arrives. She's been overly attentive so we've become well acquainted. I say goodbye to all three of them and head for the pay phone.

Time to call Victoria.

"I'm going to get you a mobile phone," she says within seconds of answering. "I've been trying to reach you."

At the sound of her voice, I realize how much I miss her. Her hand locked in mine, the feel of one smooth leg thrown over me as we lie in bed watching TV or just talking.

I sigh. "I'm out of town for a few days, and it's been almost impossible to find a phone out here. I'm sorry."

"Really? You must be staying at hotels. They've had them since the 1950s." She sounds angry, but even more confused. "I found out from Greta you'd left here Monday."

Two days ago. It seems like a month.

"I should have called you. But I was pressured to get moving since I wanted to drive through the night to avoid traffic."

She doesn't reply.

"And you're right. I need to get a mobile phone." I shift the stale-smelling receiver to my other ear so I can turn my back against the sun. Even with no door, the glass phone booth is heating up fast. "But now that I have you, I have some exciting news."

"Hey. I do too. You go first." She's upbeat again, interested in my story. I don't deserve this nice of a person.

"Before I left, I looked through some records at the Akron library and found out my mom's family is from a small town in Colorado. Manzanola. I'm near there right now. The old homestead is about twenty minutes away."

"What? Wyatt, that's great."

"I read an article that said she ran away when she was seventeen. That must be when she ended up in California, met my dad, and married him." I pause. "And I had an uncle I'm named after."

"This is way more than you've ever found out before." She laughs. "Did you happen to find any of this on that evil Internet?"

I had called it evil in the beginning knowing that CIA secrets might one day be exposed there. Seems a bit more innocent than I first thought. "Yes, I might have dabbled. But most of the information was on old records and microfiche." I fan the stale air in front of my face. "I'm dying in this hot telephone booth." I'm sorry I say those words the minute they leave my mouth. It feels like a confession. Dying, dead, murdered should never leave my lips again. "And, yes, I know! If only I had a mobile phone."

She chuckles. "Why did you say you *had* an uncle? Is he dead?"

"Yeah. He blew up in a barn." I laugh when I hear her gasp.

"God. Really? That's tragic."

"I should have said he died in a barn explosion, not that it sounds much better." I pause. "I'm going to the old homestead *tamara*." I chuckle at my own inside joke.

"Why are you talking so weird? Are you drunk?" Now she seems concerned although she's never seen me drunk.

"Just talkin' like the locals. Tomorrow, *tamara*. All the same." I pause. "Anyway, maybe someone there will remember my mom's family."

"You should go out today. How can you stand to wait now that you're so close?

Exactly what she would have done—no plans, just wing it.

"I don't even know if anyone is living there." The excuse sounds flimsy to my own ears so I add, "And my eyes are about out of my head from reading through the papers and films all day. Tomorrow, first thing."

"Stop at the post office. They'll tell you if anyone is there or not."

Now there's a simple solution. "Remind me never to try to hide from you."

She snorts. "I'd find you so fast. And then I'd do wicked things to you."

"I like the way you think." The phone gives me the one-minute warning, and I push another quarter through the metal slot. When the beeps stop, I ask her about her good news.

"The Women's Assistance League heard about my nonprofit, and they're helping me with a fundraiser on Saturday. I signed us up for the 5K run. How cool is that?"

"That's fantastic news." I pause. "But not this Saturday, right?" No way my neck will be healed, and what dork runs with a bandanna around his neck?

"Yeah, this one." She sighs. "I thought you'd be back."

"I may be here longer. I'm so close to answers now, and I don't want to cut it short."

She's quiet for several beats. "You're right. This is too important. But I want to hear all about it, and not next week."

"I'll call you tomorrow night to fill you in."

The one-minute warning is back, but I don't feed the machine. "Gotta go. Thanks for understanding."

"Always." She hangs up.

I hope she means that. I'm not an easy man to be with.

I gotta get out of this blasted heat, but I have one more call.

Another forty cents disappears into the phone slots and I've got Greta on the line. She reassures me the dogs are great and are sleeping off their steak dinner. I explain that my plans have changed.

"I'll be back in three days, definitely no later than Saturday night." I tell her what I hope to find outside of town.

She's not nearly as excited as Victoria was. "Wyatt. Please protect your heart. I don't want to see it broken again."

"I will." I know full well how the tug-of-war between hope and disappointment will break a kid. In my rebellious teen years, I lived by the mantra *expect nothing and you'll never be disappointed.* "I've toughened up. And it's been enough years that I'm ready for whatever."

"I'm sending good thoughts then."

After we hang up, I check my watch. It's too late for the post office I spotted on the main drag. I'll be there at nine in the morning and at least find out if any of Mom's family is still in the area.

The local phone book, anorexically thin, swings from a chain inside the booth. On a whim, I thumb through it. There are two Powell listings, a T. Powell and a Sam Powell. Neither were in my family records. Then I try searching for Dardin. No hits there, not that I expected any.

Too full to go for a run, I walk the circumference of the downtown and return to Main Street in less than half an hour. I step into a shed-like bar called Saddle Up, and once my eyes adjust to the smoky gloom, I take an empty bar stool halfway down the room. For a Wednesday night, the place is full. The bartender and I are the only ones not wearing a cowboy hat or a cap with a logo, but I think the bandanna gives me some clout.

A guy built like a bulldog raises a beer my way, and I return an upward chin flick, a standard country greeting back in Ohio. It seems to work here too.

I drink another Coors and watch the Angels stomp the Diamondbacks 10-5 on one television while the national news plays on the other. Just as the crowd erupts as the pitcher strikes out a batter, I hear the words, "Halsom, Kansas" from the dueling TV to my right.

My full attention goes there.

"...with no leads except for a message connecting the two, police are now hopeful this new bit of information will get them one step closer to what group is behind the killing in this remote part of the state."

The announcer's mouth keeps moving but a high-pitched sound fills my head, blocking out every noise except my banging heart.

What have they found? I want to immediately yank out my wallet and check my cards again, make sure I left no evidence behind, but I restrain myself. I replay what happened at the ranch. I'm positive I didn't leave anything. So, if I didn't drop anything, then someone must have seen me or described the truck.

Fear rakes its fingers down my spine as I picture my arrest and imprisonment. What cuts through me the most is picturing Victoria's and Greta's reactions. Their absolute shock when they hear the man they believe to be kind and artistic could kill someone. Would they understand the reason behind what I've done—the need for justice due to the lack of sentencing for abuse? I envision my dead grandparents shaking their heads and my dogs dragged away yelping, forever wondering why I abandoned them. That image gets to me the most. I take the last pull from my glass, drop a five on the bar and push toward the door.

The sky is performing a slow burn from yellow to orange as I cross to the motel.

In the last few weeks, I believed I was bad to the bone, killing losers and getting away with it, when the truth is, I'm more likely a royal screwup.

As has always been true, the last witness in any event gets to tell the story. Yesterday, I was that guy, the only witness, but apparently now this is no longer true.

-23-

Two hours later, I give up flipping through the five TV channels trying to find a news station rebroadcasting Foster's story. I'll have to wait for the late report.

I call Victoria back. I didn't give her enough time earlier to let her know how excited I am about her news. Her answering machine picks up, so I leave the motel's phone number and my room information.

Ten minutes later, the phone blares so loud that I jump. I'm sure people across the street heard it too. I lift the handset.

"Hi, sexy." Victoria clears her throat as if preparing for a speech. "What are you wearing?" she whispers.

I whisper back, "The Van Halen T-shirt you hate and some old jeans."

"Wyatt!" She lets fly an exasperated sigh. "You're really bad at this game."

I chuckle. "I play better in person, I guess." I take a moment to savor the memory of the curve of her hip, the weight of one breast cupped in my hand, the fall of her hair over her shoulder.

"You do." She clears her throat and I know the sex talk is over. "Did you get to the post office?"

"I missed getting there by five minutes, but I'll go first thing." I offer a shrug she can't see. "It may be there's no one living out at that old house anyway."

"I have a good hunch about this. I really do."

Something about her voice—the ring of certainty in it—gives me a bad feeling. "What have you been doing, Victoria?" I sit up straighter on the bed, bunching the mauve comforter under me. I don't want her discovering the Powell family's dark secret before I do. Or ever, if it's too awful. She comes from fairly normal stock. Who knows what tangled roots I've sprung from?

The silence on the line crawls slowly from Ohio to Colorado, fighting its way to me over each mile of that distance. She finally answers, "Don't be mad."

Then she's talking fast, and I know I'm about to hear something that could very well make me angry.

"I wanted to help speed up your search and you were doing it in such an old-fashioned way. Microfiche, some lady, old dusty ledgers. That could take forever—"

I interrupt, trying to keep the irritation out of my voice. "I saw no dust. Besides, I'm making great progress." Victoria loves research; I just didn't expect it would involve me and my family. "You know I like to do things my way. Orderly. Not too many changes."

With a heavy truck and trailer, the devil's advocate whispers in my head. *Not much planning there, Bucko.*

She pushes ahead, "You're going to be excited. I promise. I searched for your mom's parents and found out they're still listed as owning the house outside of Manzanola. Wyatt, tomorrow you'll get to meet them."

A tickle of excitement raises its head and pushes past the wall of irritation I'm pounding into place. It really could happen.

I jump to a vision of wary embraces from people who have my mother's green eyes and maybe resemble her. There'll be backslapping, stacks of photos sifted from old shoeboxes showing my mother as a little girl, then coming of age with a barren landscape expanding behind her. A camera will come out, and new pictures will be snapped and addresses exchanged.

Victoria said something with the word mansion, but I missed it. "I'm sorry. What was that?"

"One report says they live in an old house, called The Collyer's Mansion. That's kind of cool, don't you think?"

"Wow. That is." My voice softens. "Sorry I got irritated. I wanted to surprise you with what I found out on my own, and you beat me to it."

"Are you mad?"

I take inventory of my emotions. "No, of course not. I need your spontaneous ways to even out my slow-poke investigations." I mean it as a joke but she doesn't laugh.

After a pause, she says, "Wyatt, I won't interfere again unless you ask me. Deal?"

I know she pays a price for a statement like that since hunting down information on the Internet is her new passion. "I appreciate your help, I do. But I want to be the person with the big scoop tomorrow."

"Fine. When do you pick up that car?"

"What car?" The words exit my mouth before my brain reminds me I told Greta I was also picking up a car while I'm out here. I scrape my fingers through my hair. What an idiot.

Her tongue click hangs in the air, drawing out her surprise.

"Oh, God. You can tell I'm tired." I *tssk.* "I was still picturing my family reunion." I wait and so does she. I break the silence. "It's north of Denver, outside of Ft. Collins. I should be there sometime tomorrow afternoon." Then I'll create a new delay since I can't head home even then.

"Call me after you meet your grandparents and pick up the mystery car." Her voice holds a trickle of suspicion.

I suddenly feel naked, as if she understands all too well what I've been doing, what I've become. This may happen if the new information in Kansas nails me. A shiver of worry runs down my spine. "Of course I will. I know I've been awful about staying in touch. What's your day like tomorrow?"

"I'm meeting with the race organizers to check all the final deatils."

"You know I'm super happy for you. I didn't say that enough earlier today. This will really launch your nonprofit like nothing else."

"The local news is doing a story too." Her happy tone is back.

"Even better. I am sorry I'll miss it."

"I'll manage, you know me. Just thought it would be fun to run the race together."

"Set up another one and I'll be there." *If I'm not in an orange jumpsuit.*

We say our goodbyes. "I miss you" comes from me and "I love you" from her.

I punch the pile of pillows into compliance and lie back, studying the plaster swirls on the ceiling. I've spent most of my life in a prison I built, blocking out thoughts of my mother abandoning me, of my father and his cruelty. I played by the rules after I reached adulthood, safe rules to not allow bad things to happen. My flaws aren't lost on me. I'm finally chipping away at the emotional ramparts I hammered in place. The thin drifts of fresh air leaking in over the last six weeks since I killed Randall have been somewhat refreshing.

The late news finally comes on, and within five minutes, I have my answer about the developing story in Halsom. A gas receipt was found near Foster's barn. Wide tire tracks and the amount of fuel listed on the sales receipt has led the police to say the killer was driving a truck. They didn't mention a missing horse trailer and two wide-eyed escapees.

A truck isn't much of a clue in cattle country. Who doesn't own a truck in Kansas? But I know tires can be traced by the tread on them. I let out the breath I didn't realize I was holding. This isn't bad news for me. I paid cash when I filled up the truck at the small truck stop, and I'm driving on not-so-new tires.

Orderly. Organized. Maybe I'll keep those old habits around.

I turn out the bedside lamp, but the room doesn't go entirely black as the giant motel sign pushes light around the edges of the heavy, gold-tone drapes. I lie awake for over an hour, thinking of how I've turned off the straight and narrow path I centered my life around, onto a winding course with no definite destination.

Will I kill someone else? I can't say I won't. It's hard to guess what circumstances will cross my path. If I'm attacked. Or someone or something I love is in danger.

As the night moves time ahead, I wear myself out trying to picture what the next bend in the road will bring after I meet the Powell family. Answers are one thing, but happiness is another. I'll know soon enough tomorrow if I'll find both.

-24-

"Only the old lady still lives out there," the wrinkled postmaster says, from the other side of the Dutch door. He was reticent to open the top part after I crossed the small interior and knocked several times. The ancient linoleum floor crackles, an eerie sound in the small space. "Not that she's actually spoken to anyone in decades. You'll find her in the enclosed porch at the front of the old place."

I love small towns. No different from in my rural town, there are few subjects that residents won't share about the other folks in the area.

"Is that the Collyer's Mansion?" My hands are stuffed in the back pockets of my jeans, my dress shirt freshly pressed, light blue. It matches the sky hanging overhead in the morning light. My bandanna still hides the bruises on my neck. It seems impossible but they've darkened overnight. I hate the scarf, but my other choices are to start wearing turtlenecks in the summer like an Alaskan fisherman or to just say screw it and show off Mark Foster's fingerprints.

Maybe I'm branded for life. A Scarlet M for murderer.

"Some people might call it a mansion." The postman's right eyebrow shoots up in a question, but it appears the other brow isn't as curious because it doesn't even twitch. He chuckles and shakes his head. Then he studies me. "I don't know who you hope to see out there, but she won't come to the door. Only way we know she's still alive is the mail is missing when the driver brings more."

This lonely and reclusive image doesn't match the cheery picture I built of my grandmother. I want knitted doilies, fresh bread, potted Christmas cacti that bloom whenever they damn well pleased. And it appears no man lives there. My grandfather must have died.

I push a smile on my face. "I'll give it a try."

"You with the law?" All the strained friendliness has vanished, as if we're suddenly in the middle of an argument.

I step back as if I've taken a punch. "No. Why would you think that?"

He shrugs. "Something came up about that house a while back. Could have been a rumor, they get going faster than brushfires out here." He raises a hand signaling he's done with me. "Let me know if you find anything interesting."

I thank him and exit the pony-express-era building. I hop into the cab and hand crank the truck window lower. The hairs inside my nose are brittle from the dry heat. How does anyone run in this oven?

I fire up the truck after three tries and point it in the direction the postmaster provided.

The fence posts indicate the way as I head into farmland. I pass the nearest huddle of houses. A hive of tractors and hay-baling equipment is buzzing through the fields around the homes, worker bees everywhere, early hay bales stacked high on the wagon following behind.

I'm surprised at how calm I feel. Shouldn't my mind be telling my body to prepare itself? Adrenaline should be flooding my bloodstream; my hands should be sweating. Probably impossible with the hot air blowing in on me.

The scent of manure off a horse pasture envelops me. The smell transports me back to the Foster place, to the feeling of hate boiling to the surface when he aimed at the horses.

I know I've arrived when a disheveled house floats into view at the end of the long, sloping lane, just as the postman described. The large house is brown, most of its paint long gone, worn down to sporadic spots of yellow. It looks to be held in place by two scarred oak trees on either side. The fields along the drive are peppered with dead cherry trees, twisted and black, like groping hands reaching up through the dried weeds.

The house is a far cry from any distorted definition of mansion and even further from the label of inhabitable. It's the opposite of what I thought I'd find. No restored brick exterior, no statues of lions flanking an ornate door, no bay windows or peaked roofline. Just a jumbo-sized house, fallen to ruin after years of neglect.

Although I want it to be the wrong address, I know deep down it isn't. The postmaster described the dead trees out front as an abandoned orchard. I wrestle with my rising disappointment. I imagined Mom came from awful circumstances, but this was the home of a family that meant something to their community once. Had the orchard thrived when she was young? Had this house been the pride of the town as she grew up?

I stall, cracking my knuckles and sitting back in the seat as the truck idles at the top of the dirt drive. I don't have to go any farther. I can turn around, head straight to Ft. Collins to find some old car to buy, and not investigate where this weed-choked path may take me. I can run away just as my mother did.

Everything fades given enough years. I certainly know that to be true. Except for self-deception. Self-deception helped me cover painful truths and made my childhood opaque, less transparent. Tolerable for the most part. I count it as a friend.

But regret? I've carried regret around my whole life. Why didn't I tell Mom I'd go with her instead of begging her to stay in her abusive marriage? Crying and holding on to her, I never told her I loved her. It was all about not leaving me behind. Why hadn't I slugged my dad? It had been at dinner when he said, "Wyatt, your mom won't be back," around a mouthful of barbecued elk.

Regret has its own weight and heft. Do I really need more family angst to carry around?

I study the house and make the decision. I drop the truck's stick shift into first and pop the clutch and head forward. I'll regret not trying if I leave right now.

Parking off to the side of the building, I stop under one of the gnarled oaks by the rusted mailbox. The name "Powell" must have been on the side of the letterbox at one time. The stick-on letters are long gone, but the ghostly outline spells out the family name.

Closing the truck door, I weigh the options of whether to tell my grandmother that I'm her grandson or to say something vague about looking for the family who lived here.

The introduction debate ends the second I reach the front of the house.

The postman said that my grandmother, Cleone, spends her days inside the attached porch. The room is connected to the rest of the house to the right of the tall front door. At one time it probably was a woodshed, but now most likely affords the best breeze on a hot day. One window faces the road, and I see movement inside and a head of gray hair. My heart rate kicks up a notch, banging out a faster beat now that I realize what's about to happen.

I'm finally here to meet my mother's family. I have a connection.

I walk the few yards to the weathered porch's door and knock. My cool facade is gone, and I wipe my hands down the sides of my jeans. Dry heat or not, my hands are damp.

Seconds drag into minutes. Clearly someone is inside because I see movement. In a few more steps, I peek in the porch window.

"Hello?" The outline of a person is fuzzy through the filthy window.

My heart rate doubles again. My earlier life was defined by headlines in small-town papers, and now I've created a new one. Man Locates Grandmother—Ten Minutes After Her Death.

Shaking away the dismal words, I speak louder, "I'm looking for Mrs. Powell?"

The woman stands, and something soft thumps to the floor. She moves toward the porch door. I lose sight of her as I return to the door where flowered curtains, now graying with age, cover the window.

I catch a flash of pallid skin when she pulls the cloth aside for a moment. The door opens an inch, and she says from behind it, "Leave the groceries on the step." Her voice is rough. Either she's a smoker or she hardly ever speaks. She starts to push the door shut but I stop it from closing.

"I don't have groceries, but I'd like to talk to you for a few minutes."

She pushes harder, but I hold it in place with my foot. Am I being too aggressive? She's only trying to protect herself from a stranger. "Please, Mrs. Powell. I think you'll be surprised."

There's a pause, then, "I don't like surprises."

You and me both.

The door moves in a few inches as she lets go. I ease my next words forward like a special offering. "Give me five minutes." My reflection in the glass shows a scowling man so I work my face into something more pleasant, just as the door opens all the way.

The brain can process dozens of images and sensations within milliseconds and still make sense of them all. The first thing my brain seizes on is the smell pushing from the room—something simmering in ketchup is barely found above the stink of cat urine. I wince and force my legs not to backpedal out of the room.

Second, the room is beyond cluttered. The wooden floor is roughhewn, sparsely covered with old, braided rugs, and the couches and chairs sit at haphazard angles, the once-colorful quilts on them worn out and covered with cat fur.

As if on cue, three cats run from the room, brushing my legs on the way out. The soft thump I heard earlier must have been one of them jumping to the floor.

I catalog my grandmother. Her face is broad, like her body, sagged into rolls that speak of inactivity and aging. Her eyes are flat green and now, face-to-face with her, I have no sense of a connection, no instinctual bond I expect might exist between two people who are related.

A new stab of regret to add to a lifetime—I should have looked for her years ago. Maybe I could have kept her from this physical decline. My hands hang limp at my side, accepting what has become of Cleone.

"I got rid of some of them, like you said." Her eyes are anxious under nonexistent brows. Her haircut looks to be one she gave herself without the benefit of a mirror. She wears a pink housedress and short white socks in her stained pink house slippers.

My brain is recalculating, trying to make sense of everything at once, trying to reconcile this woman and her living conditions with what I imagined.

I forget for a moment why I've come, replaying the postal worker's words, his half smile. *"Let me know if you find anything interesting."* He knew what I'd encounter.

I finally speak, "I haven't asked you to get rid of anything. We haven't met before."

She walks back to her chair and two more cats dash for the door. I move inside a few more steps. My eyes sting from ammonia. How can she breathe in this stifling room?

She drops into a chair as I look around. The room's interior is three unfinished walls of coarse wood, with the window to my right that I'd peered through. Bare light bulbs are in two ceiling fixtures, and a tiny TV sits on a folding metal tray in the center of the room. The walls are unadorned, no paintings, no family photos, no clock. The rest of the room holds stacked packing boxes. Clothes spill over the tops of some, others contain books, and one has six bags of cat food in it. I don't have to search far for the main source of the stench. Four litter boxes line the floorboards to the left, like train cars, lumpy, clay-covered cat crap spilling onto the floor.

"I've gotten rid of some of them, like you said." I'm putting it together. The mailman asked if I was the law. "You've been in trouble, haven't you?"

Her head drops and she studies her chapped hands, then the cat food, then gazes somewhere over my head.

"Dad always said, 'We live life one step from hell,' and he was right." Her voice is barely audible.

Everything about her screams that she's beaten down, depressed.

Nodding, wanting to keep her talking, I say, "Your father grew up in tough times, didn't he?"

She raises her eyes just enough to meet mine. A childish look crosses her face. "He did. The Depression rolled right on into those dust-twister years. All bad news for his family."

A memory fights for my attention. Something that I should be questioning about what she just said. Nothing comes to me.

"And your mom?" I step another foot into the room, trying to breathe through my mouth. "She must have been a strong woman too."

Cleone perks up at the mention of her mother, like someone is working a foot pedal connected to an air pump. "Oh, she was. She worked hard around here. Went to raising two kids for all she was worth. Didn't do her much good in the end it seems."

There's something important in her words I should be catching, but it eludes me. If I take a seat, will she feel uncomfortable? The couch has a free place to sit, but the layers of cat hair change my mind. I squat so we are closer to eye level.

I want to move a generation closer, to ask about my mother. I need to know if Cleone still has contact with her, to discover where Mom lives.

"Why did things end so badly for your mom?" I say, tagging on to her last statement.

Her face bunches and there's dislike written across her forehead. A black-and-white cat crawls out from under the skirt of the decomposing chair and jumps onto her lap. It's skinny and missing some neck hair. She pulls it close to her chest and kisses its head.

I fight a surge of revulsion and force a kinder smile onto my face. Disgusting or not, these animals are all she has.

"My father was so poor in the thirties, always dirty or hungry. What little he had, he fiercely protected. He booby-trapped the house, in every door, window. Out in the barn."

I nod. "He was protecting his possessions and raising a family while everything turned to dust around him."

She pauses then her face turns angry. "Not the dust storms. He was a collector. Didn't want to lose the things he found."

I'm intrigued. What could he have been stockpiling when everyone in a four-state area had nothing left during those Dust Bowl years?

"What did your mother think about all of his collecting?"

Her face darkens. Her gaze remains unfixed and she absently runs her hands over the compliant cat. Her eyes snap back to today, as alertness fills them. "None of us minded any of it until the explosion."

Ah, when my uncle Wyatt died. I cross my arms, trying to look comfortable while standing.

"Did they lose everything then?" My words tiptoe around her mood.

She leans forward in her chair, smashing the cat flatter on her lap, and looks directly at me. "Didn't lose none of the collection." She waves her hand toward the big house. "It's all safe in there."

I turn my head as if I can see through the walls. "You live there alone now?"

Fear crosses her face. "I stay out here mostly."

I ask on impulse. "Can I tour the house?" I wait. "I like antiques."

Her expression tightens. She wants to fight me on this. Who wouldn't? A stranger shows up and asks to go into her residence.

"Only with your permission, of course," I add. "I'd want you to show me around."

She rises from the seat and drops the cat to the floor. It returns to the underbelly of the chair.

I step outside and pull in long breaths of air, trying to cleanse my nostrils without being obvious.

She moves fast for an old woman, and I let her lead the way. She pulls out a handful of keys from her housedress pocket and fiddles with the skeleton key lock.

Why would she need to keep the house locked when she's right there on the porch? I don't ask.

The large wooden door swings inward, and I follow her over the stoop into the dimly lit interior. We stand in a high-ceilinged entryway. A dizzying amount of patterned wallpaper covers the walls. Stairs run up to the right, a living room is off to the left, and a hallway disappears deeper into the house.

How is it possible that the scent in here is even worse than in her small porch? Here it's overlaid with something decaying.

The rooms are cluttered with boxes, wooden bureaus, floor lamps, and furniture from decades long gone. A narrow path runs between the stacks, but it looks like a precarious route with teetering piles on the verge of collapse.

"Do you ever come in here?" I can't imagine how she moves around. Even the stairs are loaded with stacks of books, more boxes, and newspaper piles. She's a hoarder. Or her father was.

"You *said* you have a surprise for me." Her voice is challenging. "Why are you here?"

What should I tell her? Would knowing that her grandson is standing in front of her be a good surprise or an unwelcome shock? "I wanted to meet you. We both know your daughter."

She squints hard at me. "Are you that mean Johnson boy that used to throw rocks at my cats?"

I hold up my hands. "No, I wouldn't do that."

"He's why I keep my babies locked up in here." She points to the dark interior. "So nobody can hurt them."

A prickle on the back of my neck is so real it could have been a hand laid there. It isn't. Animal hoarders are classified as pet abusers. And these poor cats. Clearly she loves them but is perhaps not able to truly take care of them. Still, what a terrible existence for the animals. This explains the terrible smell on the porch. The cats weren't being given access to regularly changed litter boxes, and if I checked would I find they are getting adequate food and water?

I'm at a loss for words. With my logic about abusers, that means she should be arrested and serve time for what she's done here. Sure, the cat she'd been petting looked fairly healthy, but there could be dozens of cats hidden around here, some even sick and dying, and she would have no idea. I'm conflicted. This is my grandmother, and she's not doing this out of cruelty, but that feeling begins to bubble up inside me—the need to right a wrong, stop an injustice. Do something to better the lives of these cats, and also this woman who has clearly been forgotten by the people around her.

"And I don't have a daughter," she snaps.

I slide out the next words. "Someone in town said you did."

"I don't!" Her eyes flash and her mouth sets in a hard line.

I leave the daughter subject alone. She probably wrote my mother off long ago; she clearly didn't leave under positive circumstances.

I walk along the narrow passages. Cats are everywhere, and while some are as spry and bright-eyed as the black-and-white one from the porch, I see the true evidence of neglect here. Many have matted fur, some torn ears and scars as if fights have broken out among them. I see ribs poking through the fur of a few others with threadbare tails that hang low, and these are just the ones willing to show themselves or follow their curiosity to investigate the sound of our voices. Cats that are sick or injured stay hidden. Who knows how many of them could be found under these stacks?

"You've gotten in trouble for having so many cats, haven't you?" I turn back and walk toward her. "How did this happen?"

Backlit by the open doorway, she drops her head and studies her hands again. Finally, she speaks, "A small problem that mushroomed. I took in a few cats, and they all had babies." Her voice cracks. "Can't give them away because people mistreat them." She swipes at a nonexistent eyebrow. "Some agency came out here a month ago and said I had to clean up or they'll take all this away." She meets my eyes. "Can they really do that? This is my house. My parents' possessions."

"I'm sorry, but they can." I point to the boxes. "For starters, this house is a fire hazard. What's in all these cartons?"

"Pictures. Thousands of photos my daddy had."

That number stops me. "Really?"

She shuffles, her slippers rasping on the wooden floors until she reaches a dresser near the entrance to the living room. The top drawer has fallen out of its tracks, but she tugs it open. Inside is a mound of photos.

I pick up a handful. They're black and white, many from the days of rudimentary photography. Some show windmills, river scenes, skinny horses, used-up people standing against a small lean-to house. Blighted landscapes in all of them.

"Your dad took these?" I flip through some more. An unsmiling woman rocks a baby, a man by a barn with tattered coveralls, a wagon loaded with household items.

"No. My father collected them after everybody left for the West Coast."

I let the pictures slide back into the drawer and rock it back and forth and manage to push it shut. The other two drawers below hold the same slippery piles of fading memories. I turn to another cardboard box and pull open the flaps. Dust floats upward, and I cough and wave it away. The box contains more of the same.

She has a museum's worth of photos and furniture from an era gone by. She most certainly could use the financial help if these have any worth. "Do you know any of the people or places in the pictures?"

Wisps of gray hair move across her cheek as she shakes her head.

Why keep them then? The prospects for a Powell family reunion are on hold. I decide in that moment that here is my way to rally around one member of my family. "I can help you get cleaned up. Organize all of this. Find homes for the cats." Everyone deserves help. Animals. People. Especially those who have been left and forgotten.

Her eyes fly open, startled. "I won't have anything left if you take them away."

When I reach for her arm, it isn't as soft and fleshy as I imagined. Under the veneer of wrinkled flesh is a strength and stubbornness I'll have to work around.

"Not all the cats. You can keep some. Just as many as you can take care of. It looks like some need to be checked out by a vet."

She starts to cry, a high keening sound. Something shifts in me, something that evokes the same emotion as the sound of a far-off train whistle in the night, an echo of despair.

She lets me lead her outside and back to her safe room at the front of the house. Once she's in her chair, she blows her nose and shakes her head. "I can't lose anything else."

"I understand." I kneel in front of her. "I heard about your son."

"Wyatt?" Her gaze travels off into the distance.

A chill races up my back even as stifling heat fills the room. All sound evaporates for a moment. The shock comes from how she says my name. The room blurs because for a split second, I hear my mother's voice in hers, my yearning for the past to come alive.

I fight to clear my vision and put the next words together. "Yes, Wyatt." I clear my throat. "I read that he died here on the farm. That's terrible."

She scrutinizes my face, as if refuting my kindness. Her next words leave her mouth, jerky and unstable. "You're confusing me." Tears run from the edges of her eyes. "I should have been with him. He was so young."

I know that pressing her more about these events makes me heartless, but I sense my time here is about up, and I can't leave until I discover something about my mom. "And your daughter? She left home and never came back?"

"Why are you here? Are you the law?" she suddenly snaps at me.

"No. I wanted to meet you." I take a chance with my next words. "I'm your grandson. And I can help you."

She waves me away. "I don't have any grandsons. And I don't need your help. I'm just fine."

Delusion is a powerful antidote. She's probably been self-medicating with it for years. And she might not know I exist. Maybe Mom never came back here. Otherwise, wouldn't she have mentioned she had a son named after her only brother?

I let out a long exhale. My mother is most likely dead.

"I'm going to check into how we can clean up your place," I say, standing and dusting off my knees. "So you don't get in any more trouble."

She flies into a rage. "Go away!" She picks up a plastic coffee mug and throws it at me.

I duck even though it wouldn't have hurt if it connected. It lands short and rolls to the side of the room.

"I'm fine here with my babies." Her voice escalates. "I don't need anybody, 'specially not a fake grandson. Go away!" She closes her eyes, a childish dismissal, but it's clear she's done with me.

After shutting the door, I stand in the festering heat and time presses down. The situation is maddening. My grandmother needs help, now. I need to figure out who has been investigating her, and what options they can offer. Surely, they won't arrest her. She's already emotionally frail, and the loss of anything else may destroy her.

I won't go to Ft. Collins for the car just yet. It's Thursday and the public health offices will be open in Pueblo, the closest big city. And although I'm in no hurry to head for Ohio, I can't leave my grandmother behind. She isn't at all what I expected, but she's mine.

-25-

I find the Pueblo County Department of Public Health without issue, but it takes me ten minutes to get the courage to walk through the glass doors. After washing up in the public bathroom, I head to the office. I don't want to add more negative information about my grandmother to the authorities, but I can't see the solution to helping her without getting them involved.

Fears that they might harshly brand her are put to rest when a middle-aged woman whose badge says Melinda returns with the preliminary paperwork. She wears large earrings—the big clattery kind with metal stars hanging down—and clearly does not understand why any of this should be my business. She holds it away from me, so I don't catch the name on the label.

"I want to help her out of this bad situation." I say the words preemptively, not ready to confess to this stranger about my possible familial connection.

Melinda scowls. What should look like random kindness is not enough to soften her heart. I push on, "She has a compulsion—it's a known mental disorder and she's had a hard life. She said she can't let more belongings go."

"We see a lot of this kind of thing in this county." Her voice sounds bored, even though she's shaking her head like she's sorry. "It seems the poorer people get to be, the harder it is for them to part with their *prosperity*." The last word is loaded with sarcasm.

"That's exactly what's going on with her." I lean toward the file. "What's happened so far? She said someone came by and gave her a warning?"

Melinda moves papers around and flips through several stapled together before she reads from one. Melinda is a woman who does not discuss ideas, she states facts. "We've made our first visit out there. At that time, she was given a warning. She has one month to get rid of the cats and clean out the house." She raises her eyebrows. "Has she made any progress toward that?"

"The cat population may have lessened." I didn't want to think about how many have probably died in the house. She joins me in pretending this is good progress.

"And she can't do this by herself," I say. "Who can help her?"

"Of course she can't." Melinda looks offended. "We'll put together a task force to provide the assistance and resources she needs to improve her quality of life."

Will she ever have a quality life? As is always the case with hoarding, there is more going on than the cats and the stacks of papers and old photos. No amount of scrubbing or sanitizing will replace all that she's lost.

She continues, "We try to keep people independent if we can. We'll get everyone involved—Behavioral Health, Adult Protective Services, Environmental Health, law enforcement, the fire department, waste facilities." Melinda is leafing through the paperwork again when she stalls on a form, frowning. "Does she have any family?"

"Did she list anyone?" I pretend to peek into the notes.

"No. She told the officers she has no one." Her forehead bunches as she studies me. "Didn't you say you are related?"

My dad always said, if you're being chased by a bear with a friend, shoot the friend first, then run like hell. It was one of his favorite lines.

I know before I say the next words that I'm about to do just that—shoot my grandmother, as I leave the area. "It's a convoluted family connection that breaks down somewhere over the years." I draw in a long breath. "I'm her grandson, but she wouldn't know about me." I pause. "She may have a daughter somewhere, but I'm not sure they're in touch either or that her daughter is even alive."

Melinda scribbles in the chart.

"Patricia Powell," I say. "Or she could go by Dardin."

Melinda writes some more and then looks up. "Yup. Got it." She closes the file. "Here's the hard news. Because you aren't *technically* related to her, I've already told you too much."

She waits as I wrestle with my conscience and the dilemma this presents. I can stay in Colorado for the next few days to help. I can push back the soft deadlines for the new art project I had in mind. My dogs? Greta is there. The junkyard is busy this time of year, but again, people will wait, and I have no appointments scheduled.

She presses on. "The task force will act on what you've told us, and she'll get help."

"If she has valuables? You'll respect that, right?"

Melinda squints her eyes. "Anything of value is rarely the case. But if something looks promising, an auction is usually in order."

I shove my hands under my armpits because suddenly they're cold. Was I doing the right thing? I try to picture Cleone living at the junk-yard with me, and I can't make that work. Sunset Ridge is a top-rated nursing home near my house. I can afford paying for her to live there, and the structure and routine would be healthy. Plus they have a pet limit.

Melinda stares at me, waiting.

"What's the next step?"

She taps the file on the counter. "The process is slow, though. There's a lot of steps involved. It could be three to four weeks."

Weeks? I'm going to have to come back. "Okay. As long as you're gentle with her."

Her mouth sets in a flat line, as if I've offended her again. She changes the subject, and it feels like an offer for me to leave. "Hopefully her daughter can be found. Mrs. Powell may need a place to live soon."

Her words push me out into the early afternoon. Cleone is in good physical health even if her mental state is questionable. She gets around her place and isn't in danger of falling.

My sense of smell is finally recovered from the acidic scouring in Cleone's house. I lean against the side of the building, suddenly exhausted. My grandmother's life will get better, but she is going to hate the process she's about to go through to arrive there.

Melinda wrote my home phone number in the file, but it's doubtful they'll call me first.

"Because you aren't technically related to her…"

The social workers will be challenged enough working with her without insisting she has a grandson that she fiercely denies.

I make a vow to return when she's healthier, and then we can start over.

Five hours later, clouds blow in and conspire with dusk to drain all color from the landscape. The new gloom and a hefty dose of guilt force me to pull off I-25 just north of Ft. Collins to call Victoria from a Texaco station hooked to a massive truck stop. I'm towing a car I bought an hour ago from a burly guy wearing a short-sleeved shirt, like a farmer wears to church.

I went with something more modern, something a bit faster than the models I usually favor. A change for the better. It's a 1980 Lotus Esprit, finished in Carnival Red with a tan interior. Although it's in immaculate condition, I'm sure I got robbed on the price, but I couldn't come home empty-handed after being gone for so long, so I made the deal. The last time I splurged like this was when I gave up my commission in trade for the dogs.

Look at me changing things up like an Indy pitstop mechanic.

I'd promised to call Victoria after visiting Cleone. I won't blame her if she's perturbed with me since most of the day has passed.

Just as I drop the coins in the phone, I glance at my watch. Victoria was going to a fundraising planning meeting around this time. I nearly replace the phone receiver into its finger-smudged hook when I heard a tinny-sounding, "Hello?"

"Oh. Hi. You're there." I'm sure it sounds as lame to her as it does to me. Why else would I call if I don't think I'll reach her?

"I am." She sounds out of breath. "I decided not to go to that fundraiser dinner. It's no fun to go alone, and I didn't want to take anyone else. I'm still doing the race Saturday though." I can hear her drinking something. I know she isn't being passive-aggressive about having to go alone; she's being honest. She's direct like that. It's one of the qualities I love most about her, and it's probably what makes our relationship work.

"I just pulled off the road after driving all day. I bought an extra cool car though."

"You know I only give half a shit about cars." She laughs. There's that honesty again. "So, what did you find out when you went to the family homestead. Were they happy to meet you? Do they have an address for your mother? You're killing me here."

"There isn't much to tell you, so I got back on the road."

That isn't completely a lie. I have nothing I *want* to tell her. Now is not the time to introduce my half-crazed grandmother to my insanely normal girlfriend.

"How could you have nothing to report?" She lets out an exasperated breath. "What were they like?"

"Not they. My grandfather is dead; the mailman hinted at that. And the woman in the house is recluse, and I didn't get much out of her. It's really not much of a mansion either."

After ten seconds of dead silence, she says, "Well, that makes complete sense, Wyatt."

It's my turn to be confused. "What does?"

"Don't get mad. I didn't do any *new* research after we talked last night, but something I was looking into yesterday still bugged me. It was the part about the house being a Collyer's Mansion. I tried to find out who the Collyers were."

"I can assure you the mansion information is completely wrong." I snort. "Who are they?"

"Not who but what. I'm not sure what you saw because a Collyer's Mansion is, and I'm quoting here, 'a modern firefighting term for a house of hoarders so filled with trash and debris it becomes a serious danger to the occupants and emergency responders.'" She pauses for effect. "The name comes from brothers who were infamous hoarders in Manhattan. They were discovered dead in 1947 surrounded by one hundred and forty tons of junk they'd collected." Her voice goes higher with disbelief. "It wasn't that bad, was it?"

I compare the brothers' tonnage to what I observed in Cleone's house.

I can't guess what a house full of photos and furniture would weigh, but it has to be right up there.

I'm suddenly irritated by this description. The stacks in the house are what my grandmother deemed keepsakes, and even though it's mostly junk, it's her only legacy.

I listen to trucks pulling in and out of the plaza, the angry growl of their gears as they downshift, their rumble matching a similar sensation growing inside of me. I'm not angry with Victoria, but rather at my own selfishness, the insecurity that prevents me from telling her too much about Cleone, about the hoarding, the potential cat abuse.

"Wow, those brothers," I say, "what a crazy story." I pause and then push a lie through the telephone wire. "I'll have to keep looking for relatives, I guess."

"When you eventually find someone from your mother's family, it will be amazing. Give it time."

"Always a positive attitude. I like that about you." The phone gives me the wrap-it-up warning. I talk fast. "I'm going to stay in Wyoming tonight and come back along I-80. Different scenery than the way out here."

"You'll be home by Saturday night?"

"I should be. I'll let you know, and we'll figure out when I can stop by."

"Maybe I should come by your place. It's not—"

The phone goes to dead air before she finishes.

A quick rapping on the booth snaps me back from my place in Ohio to the blurry image of myself in the metal phone plate.

A woman glowers at me, then makes a rolling signal with her index finger that can only mean, "Get going, buster." Her frazzled black hair is white at the roots for over two inches, and she looks like she can clean and jerk four hundred pounds of dead weight.

I take her cue and leave.

Back on the road, the day slips into night. I try to recall the faded picture I have of my mother. She read a lot, and we often met the bookmobile driver at the end of a long logging road once a month like it was our lifeline. For my mother, I suppose it was.

My mom helped me nurse a chipmunk back to health; it was bitten by something bigger, with one back leg torn up. We kept this a secret from Dad because he would have killed her if he found out. We named the chipmunk Shirley Doolittle because my mom would say, "she surely does little around here except eat and sleep."

The night lowers itself, black and velvety, on the open road. Most drivers have left the interstate, so for long periods at a time it's just my headlights slicing through the dark veil ahead.

This is my kind of driving.

I've crossed the Wyoming border and am east of Cheyenne on I-80 when I start looking for a hotel. A strong wind hits out of nowhere, blasting sand and pebbles against the sides of the truck. The Lotus sways back and forth on the tow bar behind me. I worry it's getting damaged. I'm looking forward to driving it, to opening it up on some flat stretch of road.

I've not been thinking clearly. I should be driving it already. Taking the truck back to the junkyard is risky if someone wants to compare its worn-out tire tread to that at Foster's farm. With all the unclaimed wilderness along my return trip home, I can park it in some woods or swamp and it will rot away over time.

I tap my fingers on the steering wheel. I'll be in my sports car sooner than I planned. I slow down and aim for the faint glow of civilization on the far horizon where I'll spend the night.

Once I'm off the interstate, I turn into a parking lot for the Cowboy Ranch Inn. A giant cowboy boot slowly pivots back and forth above the two-story building, white lights outlining it against the night. A cheesy tribute to Las Vegas.

A few minutes later in the motel room, I step out from under the elephant-force showerhead, then towel dry and sit on the edge of the bed, clicking through the TV channels. I slip under the thin covers and settle for reruns of *Knight Rider* from the mid-'80s. I was obsessed with this show during my teens, right after I arrived at the junkyard. Michael Knight, always on a crusade to champion the innocent, fighting in a world full of criminals who operated above the law.

This episode is aptly named "The Final Verdict."

I drift off, vowing that I'm done killing, on purpose or by accident. Let gossip and fear keep the VAPPA mystique alive.

I did my part.

Now I can return to the life I had before Jasper arrived in my art class with a broken arm.

-26-

Friday's dawn pushes anemic beams through an overcast sky. The air is cool and thick with wood smoke, ripe weeds, and stagnant water. Finishing my morning run, I pound my way back toward the motel, running hard on a trail that follows a drainage ditch off into what looked like the edge of the earth. The forty-minute run releases pent-up stress; three days without an endorphin surge was way too long. I miss running with my dogs, and with the way Greta is feeding them, they'll be too fat to waddle if I don't get home soon.

Running has always come easy for me. It was my only mode of transportation when I was a kid. If you walked to the lake to fish, you used up half of the day just getting to the water. Old logging trails, deer paths, fire tower roads—I got to know all the shortcuts with Keesha by my side, but never once did I think to walk. I don't know if I was built to run, but I do know running surely built me. Now I use long runs to think, to problem solve, and to design art projects. Today is a problem-solving day, and I've come up with several clear decisions.

I'm still settled on my resolution from the night before—let the idea of a violent vigilante group named VAPPA play on pet-abuser's fears and not go after anyone else.

My neck bruises are clearing, so I should be okay to get home tomorrow. I have to get preliminary sketches of a relief requested by a Cincinnati law firm by Monday, as promised. The firm deals with construction accidents, and I've been playing around with ideas of the law firm's name rising from a pile of rubble.

I'll call Melinda in Pueblo once I get home and tell her that I want to pay for anything Cleone needs. Immediate professional attention, help with cleaning out the house, and any medical visits. Everything that happens after her arrest and the task force taking over, I'll be involved in.

I shower and pack, then leave everything in the motel room and cross the parking lot to the train boxcar transformed into Betty and Bud's Diner. I'm starving; my appetite is back for the first time in days.

I hold the door until an elderly couple enters the small foyer. While I'm waiting for them to move forward, someone taps my shoulder.

My adrenaline surges, and I'm certain it's the police. I've been tracked here, and the jig is up.

I release the door and turn so I'm outside with my back to the red wooden wall, my hands tightly fisted at my sides. "What's up?" The startled tone in my voice carries.

If ferrets wear hunting hats with earflaps, that's what's standing in front of me. The man is about five feet eight, thin but sinewy and tough-looking, with a hawkish nose and a tattoo covering one whole side of his face. He's wearing grimy jeans and a T-shirt that was once black but now is faded to a pewter tone. His crooked smile pulls toward the side of his face with the tattoo.

"You dropped your keys." They dangle from his outstretched hand.

Is he a pickpocket? I didn't hear them drop. "Hey, thanks." I accept them and push them deeper into my jeans.

"Can you spare some change, you know, being a local boy like me?" His face falls and I want to hand him an Oscar for the poor-beggar look he's perfected. The olive backpack he carries is an old military issue.

I study him for a few seconds. "I'm not from around here."

He circles his hand in the air and then points to my truck, as if he's showcasing a prize on a game show. "That your rig?"

I chuckle. "Do we call pickup trucks 'rigs' now?"

His face bunches into a scowl. "You got something rigged to it, so yeah, it's a rig. With Wyoming plates. That almost makes you kin."

Now there's a scary thought.

His amber eyes narrow to slits.

I scan the parking area. Almost all the vehicles have plates with the cowboy on the bucking horse. "You just liked my truck the best?"

"No. You just looked like you might have money."

Am I about to get rolled? He's no physical threat; I'd drop him in a second. "Well, I'll say this, your honesty is refreshing. Join me for break-fast?" I can't say why I make the offer, but curiosity plays into my invitation.

His head swivels from side to side, suspicious, as if he's being set up. The marks and lines on the right side of his face fall into place, and I make out a tattoo of an eagle's head, its curved beak perfectly aligning with his hooked nose.

Nothing will stop me from hearing this guy's story. I sweep my hand toward the diner. "C'mon. Let's eat."

Inside, he follows me to a booth along the back wall, where we're handed menus and have coffee poured before we speak. The waitress's eyelids perfectly match her blue fingernails.

"How are you today?" I smile toward her.

"Just dandy." Her questioning stare lingers on Eagle Man before she leaves.

Not a full minute passes before she's back with her pad and pen. "What'll it be?"

The scrawny guy orders big, going for the Hungry Man's Feast. He meets my gaze, his stare a prickly challenge to see if I'll deny him.

"Good choice." I nod, then hand her my menu. "I'll take the Denver omelet with a side of bacon."

After the waitress leaves, I pretend to check out the restaurant as my booth mate stares at me.

The place is packed. Short-order cooks weave around each other behind the stainless steel prep area, and steam rising in front of them is infused with the heavy smell of grease. The steady staticky sound of meat sizzling behind conversations fills the room.

I reach for my coffee and turn to my breakfast companion. "How are you?"

He nods. "Good. Doing my time."

He sounds like an inmate. "I'm Wyatt." I unwrap my silverware from a paper napkin. "Do you have a name?"

"Got the one I was born with and the one I go by." He drains his coffee and analyzes the bottom of the cup. "Cory Speers by birth. Kaw by rebirth."

I snort and quickly cover it by following it with another as if I have a tick. "Kaw? Like the sound an eagle makes?"

His stained smile says he has no dental insurance. "Right." He turns his face to show the markings as if they aren't already evident. "My animal totem."

"Are you part Native American?"

"Indian? No, but I'm from Chugwater, northwest of here. That used to be Indian territory, but nothing dark like that in my blood."

I flinch at the casual racism while stirring more cream into the cup of rocket fuel. "So what do you do, Mr. Kaw?"

"Just Kaw." His face sets into a serious mask as if he's now at a job interview. "I'm engaged in life's movements and, really, those seem to fill up my day."

The waitress returns and unloads plates and side dishes on the Formica tabletop. She refills our coffee fast, like she may implode if she's stuck there one more second.

"Do you know her?" I point in the direction she's gone.

"I hang outside once in a while, so she's seen me around." Kaw continues as if I've encouraged him to explain more about himself. "But as far as my life, I'm very fluctuant, you know, always on the move. It keeps me ahead of all the prying eyes."

I've never reached the prying-eyes stage, but with the gas receipt fiasco back at Foster's, I was within jumping range of being paranoid.

He falls into his food, and it appears a fork and his fingers are all the utensils he requires. I pass him a paper napkin from the metal box against the diner wall, and he swipes it across his mouth.

I cut into my omelet. "You have people watching you?"

"Everything is bugged with worms."

"Really? Everything?" I pause and study him. "I hope that's not true."

"I wouldn't shit'cha." He speaks around a mouthful of potatoes, "I don't like TVs or computers because people can watch you through them. I mean how can you stop them?"

We're both quiet, and I realize he's waiting for my answer. "I don't know. Do you?" I know I'm digging through an insane person's psyche, but I'm interested in what it's like in there. If this is what true insanity looks and sounds like, then my grandmother doesn't fall into this category. She's lonely, confused, but not this delusional.

His fork stalls in midair and his eyes pierce mine. "I stay in fear mode all the time. It's arduous at the very least."

We eat in silence for a few moments. His elevated vocabulary surprises me. "I'm wondering. What makes you scared?"

"The government, mostly. I'm really trying to follow the new state rules but…" He looks as unsure as his sentence sounds. "I'm afraid they'll eventually get me."

"What rules?"

He wipes his mouth with his sleeve, the napkin crumpled beside his plate.

I snap another from the metal container and hand it to him.

"Like right here. Wyoming has shit-for-brain laws. I can't use a firearm to fish. Strictly fucking forbidden." He shakes his head as if to say breathing air has been declared illegal.

I nearly spit out my coffee. A smile tugs at my mouth but I keep it from spreading, wanting to avoid angering him. "You usually use a gun to fish?"

"No, but I might desire to someday. You know a man has got to have alternatives."

My turn to nod. "I agree with that one."

Kaw leans into this conversation, having found someone to listen to his ramblings. "The worst is at night when my bed is saturated."

"Saturated? With…?"

"With time, man. Saturated with too much time. It presses in, and down, I got whole hours I can't breathe. That's when I hear the jibber jabber of those dead soldiers. The silhouettes get marching around." His hand holding the fork flies in circles above the table. "There's noise and then too much quiet. I tell you; my head gets too full."

"Do you take drugs, Cory?" I keep my tone nonaccusatory.

"No sir, I am not a frequent user of hard drugs."

"Infrequent user?"

"Well, that is closer to the honest-to-ghost truth."

"Honest-to-God, I believe you." I smile. "You should probably cut them out altogether. It sounds like they are contraindicated for someone with all, uh...the worries you have."

He acts like I haven't lectured him and charges ahead. "I might move to Utah. Did you know that in Utah, birds have the right of way on all the highways?"

I shake my head, although I'm not sure he needs my attention. "You're a bird advocate?"

"I'm a bird *protector*." He mops at a sunny-side egg with a slice of toast and holds it over the plate as the yolk drips like a melting Goldenrod Crayola crayon. "But then there's a downside to Utah."

"Ah, the strict religious culture." Having never been, I've heard drinking coffee begins the slippery slope to hell.

"Nope. I'm referencing boxing matches. You don't get to bite your opponent. It's completely illegal there." He truly looks puzzled. "How does that even work, I ask you?"

I raise my hand and stop him. "Do you have any family around here?"

"That's a big zero. I'm on my own now. Out looking for a major purpose." He uses the napkin this time to get a glob of ketchup off his mouth.

He's growing on me. I feel for him. He's frayed some very strong tethers to reality and dealing with it must have left him on his own. "I hope you find a purpose because everybody needs one."

He finishes his meal before mine's half done. He signals for more coffee by waving his cup around in a figure eight pattern in the air. This time our waitress puts all the distance she can between herself and Kaw, as she stands as far away as she possibly can while still pouring the steaming liquid.

"Anything else?" she asks, looking my way.

"Just the check. Thanks."

She pulls a sheath of order slips from her pocket and flips through them before handing me one. "Thanks for coming," she says, but I'm sure she's happier we're leaving.

I study Kaw as he stuffs sugar packets into his backpack. As long as he doesn't reach for the big stuff like the napkin holder and salt and pepper shakers, I won't stop him. And this eagle tattoo, I'm curious. When does a person wake up and decide to do something like that?

I stick my hand out. "Well, Cory Kaw Speers, it's been a pleasure meeting you."

His eyes spring open and he looks like a shocked lemur. "You're leaving already?"

Whatever he expected from our time together, this is not it. I say, "Well, we're done eating and there's a long line waiting for tables."

He surveys the front door then jumps to his feet. "I want to see your truck." He heads for the entrance.

I drop cash on the table and follow. He's standing by my vehicle when I reach his side. In the light of day, the pale, uncommanding fuzz on his chin stands out, and he seems much younger than I first thought. "How old are you?"

He raises his chin a fraction of an inch. "Old enough to know I've died five times and to remember what each time felt like." He scratches at his chest. "It's not good."

"I can only imagine." How to ease my way into leaving?

Kaw runs a hand along the truck's fender. "You ever want to sell this beauty, give me a call."

The new Lotus catches my attention. An idea is forming.

He continues and points a finger my way. "But remember, I won't do a criminal background check." He pushes dirt around with the toe of his hiking boot.

"Do you have a criminal background worth checking?" If he's arrest-free, I'll sell my hands to science.

"No, but I got a background that's bigger than most people could handle." He walks to the other side of the vehicle.

Don't we all?

"If I had a truck, this truck, I could get a job or at least try to find my major purpose."

Jesus. What are the pros and cons of unloading my truck right here and now? Maybe this is why we met. He needs a truck and I'm not keeping this one.

"Shit." I slowly exhale before coming to a decision. "I guess this is your lucky day. How much money have you got?"

He raises his hands. "$4.50, but I usually end up with $15.00 by the end of my time here requesting a little help."

I pull out my wallet. "Here you go, Cory. I mean Kaw." I push four fifties into his hand.

He holds the money flat on his outstretched hand as if it's a gold bar. Then he smiles, his face pulling toward the eagle side again. "How much for the truck?" He fans the bills out and flaps them back and forth, a man with the pride of real ownership. "Here's two hundred clams."

"The truck's only worth a hundred." I accept two of my fifties back. "You'll need the rest for fuel with gas prices running up around a buck thirty these days." I pause. "Oil companies. That's a group you should fear."

"Oh, I do. I highly do." He nods solemnly.

"Do you live far from here? I need to write out a bill of sale." I want to leave him in a place where he'll not be inclined to follow me once he gets the keys. Ever. I haven't been able to comfortably calculate his mood swings or danger rating.

"Just about half an hour. But we don't need to go there. I'll take that documentation right here." He extends his palm.

I pause, then create an answer he'll understand. I point to the lampposts bordering the parking lot. "See those? All the lights have cameras. The watchers will see you getting this fine truck and then they'll be able to follow you."

His eyes dart from one light to another, then he hunches over defensively, pulling his ear flaps lower.

"We'll slowly drive away,"—I point to the road—"head to your house, and make a private exchange."

"Deal." He's in the cab before I open my door.

I lean in the driver's side. "Wait here and keep your head down." I jog back across the motel lot to my room and grab my things, leaving the room key on the nightstand. Whatever guilt still lingered inside me after what happened to Randall and Foster, it seems Karma is firmly on my side today. The truck will have a new owner whose conspiracy theories make him cop-suspicious and hard to locate, should the evidence left at Foster's ever actually lead back to the truck.

Back outside, I load my stuff into the car and lock it before I hop into the truck and turn it over.

"I like the sound of them horses," Kaw says, his face lighting up with an innocent expectation.

A sudden buoyancy in my chest justifies my reason for giving him the truck. It is a win for us both. He apparently hasn't had any good luck, especially since he's prone to beg regularly at a diner. Maybe the truck will give him new opportunities.

He directs me along a two-lane paved road, then onto a lesser, more disparaging piece of tarmac that runs through the hilly grassland. He solves the problem of what we'll talk about while trapped together in the cab by launching into more free-flowing musings.

"Did you know that some government groups are trying to modify the weather to control us? You ever see ball lightning?"

"I have not. Is it real?"

"Fuck a duck, yeah. It'll chase you down. Got a mind of its own, I hear. And nothing can stop it. I'm even afraid to open my letters and shit."

He's lost me. "Because of...lightning?"

His glare says I'm quickly losing his respect. "No. Because of the two trillion spores of old dried-out nerve gas that's still missing. The FBI is putting it in envelopes of people with higher thinking skills."

The day takes on a gloomy feel. This poor guy is struggling with paranoia, and I suppose this is also the voice of schizophrenia, although I'm no psychologist. "Do you really think they are targeting you? You live out here in nowheresville. Why would they want to kill you?"

His face reddens. "They know I'm solving mysteries they've tried to keep hidden."

I back off, reminding myself he's a textbook case for the term *unstable*. He doesn't need to sense that I'm his enemy, especially since he's within arm's length of punching me in the throat or worse. "You know, you're right. It's better to be safe than sorry." I point my finger his way. "My grandfather used to say that." It was one of many of Gramps's sayings.

We bounce along and I find I won't miss this old Ford. It's been loyal when I needed it, but now I can easily let it go. If it helps Kaw get a job, then it really is a win-win exchange.

Kaw is animated. "My father used to say, 'Stop blowing up seagulls or I'll turn you into one.'"

What hell has he been through that's left him at this rickety level of sanity?

"Take the next left." He points to a cutout ahead in the hay field that leads down a sloped road to a knot of trees in the distance.

He prattles on. "I don't know if this happens to you, but sometimes I got body parts talking to me. I'm terrified of being alone 'cause of that. Suppose that and the money is why I like the diner parking lot so much. And I looked up the other thing I have. Trypanophobia. I got that one real bad." He's talking fast, all nervous and jumpy.

It never crossed my mind he may be carrying a weapon. I force calmness into my voice. "I have no idea what that is."

"I'm scared to death of injections and needles."

We're pulling up to a lopsided shack, a squat building of old lumber and tin, more of a lean-to than a whole structure. The roof is battered metal with a chimney pushing out of the top. The whole place puts off several notes of despair.

I park the truck so I can easily unhook the car and drive away. But one burning question comes first. "How did you get through all of that tattoo work if you hate needles?"

As we face each other in the hot cab, I try to guess where the conversation is going.

Kaw becomes animated. "My dad caught me blowing up seagulls that I fed Alka-Seltzer to. We lived near Reno and the birds were everywhere. And you know kids." He raises his shoulders in a whatcha-gonna-do gesture. "We were bored. I was eleven when my old man held me down and tattooed my face. He learned how to do it in the navy."

Stop blowing up seagulls or I'll turn you into one. Not just disconnected ramblings from a paranoid mind. He's paid a hell of a price at the hands of a cruel father.

"My old man was smart." Kaw touches his inked cheek thoughtfully. "I've never forgotten people and animals are connected. He taught me that."

And your dad fried your wiring. Good God.

Victoria has a favorite Zen quote. *Perspective and enlightenment—the teacher and the pupil in the school of life.* Never made much sense before but now I get it.

As we walk to his house, I'm at a loss for words. There should be calliope music and sad clowns standing around. That tattoo would have taken a long time to complete. I picture Kaw screaming, blood running into his other eye as he's held sideways. And what's a good reply? He's not the least bit upset in the retelling, while my breakfast is souring in my stomach.

I don't say anything.

The shack is one large room, dark and cluttered, where fruit crates double as chairs and an old computer sits on a coffee table. The wood-burning stove is missing its front door, and logs sag from the opening onto the littered linoleum floor.

"My old man, huh?" He moves magazines off a folding chair and motions for me to sit. The periodical slides to the floor. *Shooter's Survival Guide* is across the top.

The hair raises at the back of my neck, and I slowly turn and take in the room, looking for guns. I don't see any. Appeasing him seems like the best choice but I'm stuck on what to say. I go with, "I guess it's a good thing you've stopped killing birds. There's a new group out there called VAPPA. They're hunting down people who abuse people or pets."

He pauses then says, "Then, I am one lucky bastard that my dad thought to put me right when he did." He turns on a pole lamp beside the door. "What does the VAPER group do when they find someone?"

"V-A-P-P-A." I spell it out. "From what I read, one guy disappeared so nobody knows what happened to him, but this last guy was killed near his farm for hurting his horses."

He considers this. "This group must have spies listening to the news, then they go looking for the bad people?"

"Might be they do." I shrug, then for some reason I don't drop the subject. I want to share how I found information about abusers because who else can I tell without raising suspicion. "I hear there are databases on the Internet that list abusers, but I don't own a computer yet so that might not be true."

"Bet it's true. But *Wired Magazine* said the Internet is only a few years from collapsing."

"That won't change my life," I say. "And it's probably here to stay."

"The *Wired* guy says we gotta retrain two hundred and fifty million people in order to make it last."

I shrug. I turn the conversation around and let it roll away from me. "Hey, I thought you didn't like computers?" I point to his older model on the low table.

"That one's scrubbed clean. Got no spy bugs or worms in there anymore, and it's protected with that bug bouncer I built." He jabs a finger toward a wooden, folding clothes rack that stands over the computer, tin foil completely wrapped around its bars. "Nothing can penetrate this device. The spy waves just bounce off and go to the next house." He starts pacing. "I'm thinking of manufacturing them. Selling them. Now that I have wheels, this can be my new purpose."

"Well, stuff like that takes a while to catch on." I bob my head since arguing the viability of his Bug Bouncer will do no good. "I'll write up a bill of sale and let you get to that." I open the portfolio I carry, holding all my legal papers. The truck was last registered to a Harold Smythe and since I've never registered it, the bill of sale will show Kaw purchasing it from the long-dead Harold. The junkyard address and phone number are stamped at the top. "I'm going to put the document in your birth name though, not your nickname. Is that alright?"

His eyebrows knit together. "Okay, but can you say I bought it two months ago?"

I stop writing. "Uh, why is that?"

"I owed somebody money awhile back and told them I didn't have it. This way they'll know I had a virtuous reason—I bought a truck. Might not beat me up when they see me."

There are legal ramifications of falsifying the bill of sale, but I can't come up with any negatives in this situation. This truck hasn't been registered for eight years and sat unused at the yard for all that time. This will also show proof that it was under his ownership the day Foster was run over. "Sure."

I scribble April 12, 1998, on the form and add the selling price of $100. "You need to get it registered in your name within the next month, and you'll pay just a small sales tax on the hundred bucks."

He scrubs his hands up and down the sides of his head, hard enough to turn his ears red. A high keening sound emanates from him.

"Hey. Hey. Calm down." Who was I kidding? Cory Kaw Speers wasn't going into any government agency without handcuffs on, and nothing I say would change that. "I'm required to tell you that. Do what you want with the information."

He drops his hands and paces the small room. "You got me all spiraled up there, Wyatt."

"Didn't mean to." I toss him the keys. "It's all yours. Let me clean a few things out of it."

He follows me outside where I lean in and unhook the CB radio. I grab my sunglasses and a pair of work gloves and then clear out the papers from the glove box.

Around the back, I drop those items through the car's window and grab a small toolbox and my tire iron from the truck bed. Next, I crank the sports car off the tow bar and dismantle and put the towing equipment and the items from my truck bed in the car's tiny trunk.

I slap dust from my hands and turn to face the craziest guy I've ever met. "You take care, Kaw, and it's been, well...very interesting to have met you."

He thumps the roof of the truck. "This truck is going to help me outrun some of my periods of pausation, you know when the common day starts moving in?" He halts, then offers a crooked smile. "Looks like I picked a grand day to go meeting people outside the diner."

I shake his hand before slipping into the tiny car. It fits like a comfortable baseball glove. The engine rumbles as I urge it to life, and I ramp the RPMs to 3000 to blow out the pipes. I wave, and the last image I have of Cory Kaw is his shrinking, hawkish face, growing smaller and smaller in the side mirror, like a branded bird, broken yet hopeful.

-27-

L iquid night falls somewhere on the east side of Omaha, Nebraska. Plastered around on the inky backdrop, the stars look carefree, much brighter than usual.

I decide to give the CB a try tonight, sick of hearing the same songs on the radio or driving in silence. The chatter turns extra lively tonight when a fight breaks out because one guy is hogging the airwaves. Big R is driving a Roadway Truck and calls the blabbermouth a ratchet jaw and asks him to stay off the mic for two seconds so others can talk. Ratchet Jaw threatens to meet him at the next pressure check—weigh station—along Big Road 80 to have a meetup.

I participate in the call to key up so that when blabbermouth starts talking again, we all repeatedly hit the transmission key on our mics, which shuts him out for over a minute. He disappears after that.

Ah, the power of a convoy.

Normal chatter prevails again. Weather, radar-free roads, good gas prices.

Then it changes.

"Breaker, one-nine. I'm driving a Wally World"—*a Walmart truck*— "toward Des Moines. Looking for a good lot lizard location."

"Wally World driver, what's your handle? Over."

"Back Row Bob." He laughs and it's a nasty sound.

Over-the-road-sex must go on all the time, but I hate that young girls are the target.

"Back Row Bob. You got sleeper creepers in Shelby." This guy's new. He has a nasal quality to his voice.

"Bed Bugger here." This new guy's driving a household moving van. "I'm at lollipop 34"—*mile marker 34*—"and you've got flashers and bears all over that area."

"Come back, Bed Bugger." Back Row Bob, more nasal than before, wants it repeated.

"Avoid Shelby stop. Got a car greasy side up in the hammer lane. Nothing but Christmas lights everywhere."

Ha! Back Row Bob got shut down for finding innocent girls at that stop. Keep driving, horn dog.

"Breaker, one-nine. This is Dr. Yes." Another man with a strong voice, authoritarian. "Head east to Walnut."

Chills race up my back. Dr. Yes? Could Dr. No, the suspected killer of nine young women working from Ohio truck stops, have a new handle? He sounds informed about which truck stops have prostitutes.

I can't help myself. "Breaker, one-nine. This is Dobie Dad. You in that area now, Dr. Yes? Over." I'm less than an hour from Walnut. Might check out the son of a bitch.

"Negatory, Dobie Dad. I hit Davenport and am having shutter problems. Gonna get my nightgown on and call it a day. What you looking for? Over."

"Was hoping to hear the fare they're serving in the back lot at Walnut. You seem to be the man in the know. Over."

"They're peaches and cream. Over." Dr. Yes chuckles.

"I'm moving on now," I say. "Maybe on the flip side I'll check in again when I need good info."

"You got it, good buddy. Over and out."

What if this is the serial killer? I should have asked what he's driving. Several dozen trucks lay over at truck stops at a time. Asking each of them to chat searching for a nasal tone would get me punched in the face.

My imagination may be way off this time. Dr. Yes might be a single guy who lives on the road and has his favorite place to get a quickie.

Shaking away those thoughts, I stop for food and coffee at the next off ramp and walk around the service center, working blood back into my legs and the crick out of my neck. I've had a lot of open road to think about Mark Foster, my grandmother and the mess she's in, and the mentally ill Eagle Man Kaw. I couldn't have predicted meeting any of these people when I left home.

I circle the service plaza until I spot a pay phone, and dial Victoria.

She's excited to hear I'll be home by tomorrow night.

"Should I plan on Sunday night?" I can hear flirtiness in her voice, and in my mind I see her in bed, a sheet barely covering my favorite parts of her.

"Sure." That gives me a day to rest up, and the bruises on my neck are light enough to be explained away if she notices them at all.

"What's your day been like?"

"Just a lot of driving. I sold the old truck and I'm driving the sports car back."

I change the subject before I spill that I was out in the boonies with a crazy guy. "Hey Vic. I was going to ask you yesterday, something about the old mansion. When you read through the story about the house in Manzanola, did they say who was living there?"

She's quiet for a moment. "It was a weird name. Nothing with Powell or Dardin, I checked that. Something strange like Sally Poodledoo."

"Really? Poodledoo?" I laugh. "This is what you're remembering?"

"Yeah. I thought it sounded made up. I'll try to find the name again."

"Good. I'm curious."

We say good night. I replace the receiver.

Maybe the cat hoarder in the old house was a complete stranger. But the mailman said the mail going in there was addressed to a Powell and the mailbox once had that name on it even though it's now missing. And the old woman answered all the questions about her parents and responded to the name Mrs. Powell. Something didn't add up.

But it can wait. I need to get home.

I hit the toilet one more time, and at the stained sink, I splash cold water on my face. I return through the small grocery store. The lights inside are too bright and they flicker as I search the shelves for a box of caffeine pills. They worked when I crammed for tests in college, so anticipating my long night on the road, I pile those, some snacks, and a Perrier water on the counter and pay with cash.

Near the front door, a picture on the front page of a paper in the newsstand catches my eye. The headline reads, "A Break In The VAPPA Case?"

The newspaper shows a grainy picture of the rear of an old truck filling up with gas. My truck. The truck I sold to Kaw.

I casually reach for the paper and throw a dollar on the counter, steadying the shake in my hand. As I push through the doors, the cashier says, "Here's your change." I wave him off.

With blood pounding in my ears, I move my car to the far end of the plaza under a lamppost. In the garish glow, I read how the cash receipt found near Mark Foster's property was traced to the gas station in Kansas where I filled up—one of the few service stations in the country to install security cameras in the last few months.

Well, hell.

I sink back into the soft leather. The car suddenly feels more like a coffin than a luxury ride.

A camera. There are pictures.

Reality charges right up to my face, and I don't like the looks of it at all. The police were able to check out which vehicles had been in that station and at what time from the receipt? Did they have my picture too?

I shake my head. They'd have my face plastered on the front page if they had a shot of me.

A damn security camera at the pumps. Why didn't I throw the receipt away? Why carry it with me just to have it fall out when my wallet fell?

Everything had been lining up so well. Was this the beginning of it crumbling like a tower built of sand?

I get gas, pay cash, and sit for a quick bite.

The truck stop and service center are suddenly eerie. There are certainly signs of life on this warm summer night—lights flickering on the highway above, distant sounds from the gas station behind me—but in this corner of the parking lot, there's nothing, not a sound or movement, only hushed time and space. I wipe my hands on my pants.

Who saw me with the truck and what could that mean? Greta didn't know which vehicle I drove away from the junkyard because I left after she took my dogs to her house. No one in Kansas recognized it or they wouldn't make such a deal about the gas receipt. I registered at the motel in Colorado with bogus information. A truck sitting in the parking lot all night in ranch country isn't so unusual, and other guests wouldn't have given it a second glance. The woman I suspect is my grandmother probably didn't notice what I drove, and the postal worker in Manzanola hadn't looked past his double door once he closed it on me. The caseworker in Pueblo was a no. I had to park two blocks away. The guy I bought the Lotus Esprit from in Ft. Collins was waiting on two of us at the same time, and the other guy was doing a lot of haggling. I was easily dismissible, and though I was miffed about it at the time, it turns out to be a lucky break.

Then there's Cory Kaw Speers. He might recognize this picture if he sees it. Hopefully with his level of paranoia, he avoids newspapers, thinking they can read back or do some sort of a mind meld that sucks out his soul.

Once again, I study the article and the fuzzy picture. One small corner of the license plate is barely visible. Neither the plate numbers nor the bucking bronco motto of Wyoming shows. Ford made a boatload of the white pickup trucks in 1971, a universal color.

The better news is no part of me is in the photo. It looks like the camera takes snapshots rather than video.

I draw in a long breath. The only loose end points back to Kaw. If there is more information than the newspaper article lets on, then he might become a person of interest as soon as he registers the truck. Not that I think he'll do that. If, by some miracle, the cops track the truck down and point the finger at him, he'll rave so long and hard about conspiracy that he's sure to get an insanity plea. Then he might even get the help he very well needs. It's an unsettling justification, but I've set up the cards, it's time to let them fall where they may. More importantly, it's time to go home.

I head east again, but with a veil of foreboding pressing in on all sides. What am I worried about? My left leg bounces up and down. Are these my last free hours before the police show up? It will be the FBI involved now, with similarity in murders found across state lines.

I'll soon find out if my fears are because of nerves or if they're grounded in reality.

–28–

I arrive at Greta's an hour after sunrise and the dogs are over-the-top-crazy to see me. I feel the same way as I give them each a good scratching.

"You look tired," Greta says. She's in a fuzzy blue bathrobe and slippers. She points to the bandanna around my neck. "You get cowboy boots to go with that?"

I touch the scarf, not ready to remove it in case the faint bruises garner attention. "Naw. Those suckers are uncomfortable." The dogs are plastered one on each side of me, and I keep a hand on their backs. "Thanks for taking good care of these rascals."

"You know I love having them." She yawns. "When you're rested, I need to hear what you found out about your mother's family."

It seems like weeks since I was at the ruined mansion and met the woman who must be my grandmother, but it's only been a mere three days. "There's a lot to tell you." I turn to go but snap my fingers. "I saw a license plate that beats all." We've always enjoyed the times we've been together in a car, trying to decipher the meaning behind the letters and numbers on some plates.

"Tell me." Her face lights up anticipating another puzzle.

"I'll spell it. A-N-U-S-H-O-R-E." I raise my eyebrows. "Gross, huh?"

Her forehead knits together and she narrows her eyes. "A new shore?"

"What? Wait." I run through the letters again. God, I have such a filthy mind. "Very good. Not what I came up with, but now you see why I need sleep."

She's still laughing as I lead the dogs to the sports car. I put Rome in the front seat and pack Florence in the smaller back area. I only have a half-mile drive to get their bewildered faces home since they're used to bigger seating.

Once we arrive, I wander the property, checking to make sure it's as I left it. I drink in the humid morning air, remembering the unpleasant scrape of dry air at the back of my throat in Colorado. I'll take this any day.

As I pass the metal barrel where I burn the house trash, I pull out the index card where I scribbled Kaw's phone number before leaving him with the truck. I wish Cory Kaw Speers luck, and heaven knows he needs more than that, but I also hope to never see him again.

Striking a match, I light the paper, and the flame eating away at the card is satisfying.

I feed the dogs and scramble two eggs and fry a piece of ham for me.

I head to the bedroom and almost pass out immediately but not before my mind runs through all the things connecting me to Foster. I assume I've tied them all up. But as I've learned, assumptions in life are often bulldozed under by the truth.

After I awaken, I make a pot of extra strong coffee and plan to spend most of the day on the preliminary sketches for the lawyer's office.

I clean up the kitchen and settle into my studio and immerse myself in the new project. Sketching isn't my favorite part of the job, but later, when those ideas come alive and grow three-dimensionally, that's the payoff for me. Not exactly a phoenix rising from its ashes, but almost.

The law office in Cincinnati has a large open foyer with enough skylights, wood molding, and chrome to look like they can rescue your estate and then keep it for themselves. All they lack is a centerpiece inside the glass doors that makes a statement. For twenty thousand big ones, I'll build that declaration for them over the next two months.

When I stagger upstairs to the bedroom, the dogs follow. I don't bother undressing as I fall face-first onto the bed and drop off into the void that invites an exhausted mind.

Sunday, I work nonstop for two hours and finish the sketches. I call Victoria to let her know I need to move our date to the next evening, and that I will come to her place. "How was the race yesterday?" She doesn't run that often, but she's no sloth on the pavement.

"I took twelfth in the overall women's. Really had a good run."

Whoa. I feel a kind of happy sadness well up in me. I realize that I really miss her. "I'm sorry I wasn't there to see that. Congrats."

"Thanks." There's pride in her voice.

A bride-to-be and her photographer are coming soon. What they eventually figure out as backdrops with the old cars is always entertaining.

Greta's up front running the store, so when a guy and his daughter come looking for a bumper for her Ford Tempo, I lead them to where they can find one.

Locusts are buzzing for all they're worth in the trees, a cyclical song that will last for a few weeks. Their energy enlivens me, but their constant noise bothered Gram. Her usual saying was, "Silence is golden. The mouthy brats should just eat the crops and shut their yaps."

The father is clean-shaven, in plaid Bermuda shorts and a T-shirt with Jesus peeking around a door frame. "I saw that" is across the front in large lettering. And it doesn't take long for me to learn he's upset with his daughter.

"Her friend broke the bumper of her car, so she's paying for this one." He lets out an impatient huff. "Don't do her any favors."

She's in wide-legged jeans and her T-shirt reads, "Hi. Not interested. Thanks." Her long dark hair is clipped away from her face with tiny butterfly clips. Two long strands hang down, framing her face, a style I've always thought of as noncommittal. *I pull my long hair back to keep it out of the way but leave these two pieces to hang free.*

"He's my *boyfriend*, Dad." She's clutching a handheld purse against her chest like a shield.

"Yeah." The man ignores her and turns to me. "She's seventeen, and he's twenty-two, a drunk, and chafes my backside every time I think about him."

"Then stop doing it." Her face reddens.

He opens his mouth to argue but stops. "My name's Nolan Hard and this is Abigail."

"Nice to meet you." I'm all for changing the subject. "I can grab some tools if you didn't bring any."

"He's the only tool." Abigail tugs at her shirt sleeve and smiles, seeming to savor the insult.

Nolan offers a quick, false smile. "She's just getting warmed up. I'll take a wrench."

"Be right back." Once I turn, I let loose a repressed smile. That guy's gonna have scabby knees if he's petitioning the Lord on her behalf.

I return with the wrench. "Want me to get it for you?"

"That'd be dandy." He rubs his hands down the front of his shorts. "Then I can get Miss Sassymouth home."

She groans and it's a theatrical marvel. "If you're name calling, then use my handle, Mary Magdalene."

That stops me. "You use a CB radio?"

She gives me a hesitant nod.

"Her friend gave her one so he can always check up on her." Nolan rubs the back of his neck. "Those CBs are gonna be the death of our youth, you watch. Talking and driving, spoiled rotten. Just pick up the phone when you get home, I say."

"I want that bumper." Abigail points to another Ford, three cars over.

Nolan and I turn and almost in unison say, "No."

It has a bright green bumper sticker that says *Honk if You're Horny.*

"Whatever," she says.

I crawl under the car in front of us and loosen bolts. Nolan holds the bumper as it comes loose.

Once it's off, I stick the wrench in my back pocket.

"How much?" Nolan wipes dust from his hands.

"Let's do fifty." I weigh my next words before I offer them to her. "Not trying to judge you, but a single girl chatting on a CB is dangerous." I think of the chatter I overheard while on the road. Dr. Yes or Dr. No, there are some sickos out there.

She briefly closes her eyes and takes a deep breath. "We're just having fun with truckers. They don't know who we are." She digs through her purse and pulls out two twenties and a ten.

"Thanks." I fold the money and push it into my other pocket. "Just be careful."

"I swear. Kids." Nolan nudges a small stone around with the toe of his shoe. He turns to me. "Do you have any?"

"Got a couple of four-legged ones. That's about all I can handle."

Abigail, a.k.a. Mary Magdalene, is already stalking back to the pickup truck they arrived in.

"I hear ya." Nolan nods a goodbye, hefts the bumper, and follows behind her. He's got his hands full, but I'm worried for her. She has no idea what messing around on the radio can do. Breaking FTC regulations is the first problem. They will come after you and fine you for bad behavior. The bigger problem is pissing off a trucker who's driving a fully loaded semi weighing seventy thousand pounds, no match for her bitsy Ford Tempo. A little nudge and she'll be off the road.

She needs to watch the movie *Duel,* starring Dennis Weaver. That would scare the bell-bottoms right off her.

I push through the store door. Greta is in a rocking chair working on a cross-stitch.

"Who were they?" she asks.

"A poor sucker who would have an easier time taming a mountain lion than that daughter." I open the cooler and take out a Pepsi then use the bottle opener to pop off the cap. "Sounded like you had some customers earlier. I heard car doors when I was in the studio."

"Six people." She sets the needlework on the small table next to the chair. The design is a 1920s steam train she's making for a nephew who's obsessed. "I sold two jugs of my maple syrup. We still have thirteen jugs in inventory. One lady bought a pickle crock, and a family passing through had a couple kids, so we moved some of those Hacky Sacks to the boys, and the girl bought the stick-on earrings." She rolls her eyes. "You know how I feel about those."

She's voiced her opinion of the temporariness of possessions. Girls buying star- or heart-shaped stick-ons that they'll discard later that day.

"I do." I shrug. "It's a different world now. Everyone's in a hurry."

"The girl also wanted one of those Tamagotchis. I told her we don't have any. She acted like I cut off the air supply in the room."

"I don't know what that is." As far as toys go, I'm still in the land of the Magic 8 Ball.

"It's called a digital pet. But it sounds like a pain in the arse."

"Like a robot dog or cat?"

"No. It's on a key ring and is a square device with buttons. The kid has to attend to it when it's hungry or has to poop. It grows up through different stages, I guess, and it can even be so neglected it dies."

"What ever happened to dolls and toy soldiers?" I shake my head. "I sound so old."

"It's supposed to teach kids how to care for something."

"A real pet would do that." My mind snaps to Jasper and Marcus. Those boys have learned compassion with Millie, now that the ogre in the family is gone.

She points me to the other rocker. "Tell me what you found in Colorado."

I take the seat, sipping the drink before I start. Greta has never judged me about my life's choices, about remaining single, about hating my father. But when she hears I left my grandmother behind, will that all change?

I rub one hand back and forth along the rocker's arm. "I went to the house and the woman there is a hoarder, keeping everything her parents passed down and more. It's a bad situation with too many cats, most of whom are sick."

"Oh, dear," Greta says, putting a hand to her neck. "Who's living there?"

"My grandmother, Cleone Powell, but at first, I couldn't believe it. The more we talked, I realized it was her, although some of her answers didn't make sense." I remember how physically she was doing fine, not feeble in the least. "She's isolated, confused. I left her to the care of Social Services in Pueblo, who already had a case file opened on her."

"Oh, the poor woman. Did you get to ask about your mother?"

"She got upset when I told her I was her grandson. Really upset, started throwing things, yelling."

"She must not know about you." Greta tsks. "Maybe it's for the best right now. What will Pueblo do for her?"

"Clean up the place, make it less of a fire hazard, get her counseling." I pause. "I found a nice surprise though. My mom named me after her only brother. He died on the property that Cleone still owns, from what I read in an old newspaper."

"Well, that's something." She smiles. "Your mother was secretive from what your grandmother said."

"Yeah. Gram never mentioned I had an uncle named Wyatt." I take another sip. "And I have a new license plate for you to figure out. It took me over an hour."

"Let's hear it."

I write it down. JK MNO.

"Oh, dear." She turns the paper to study it. "This could take me awhile."

The tiny bells over the door jingle and an older woman enters. "I'm looking for press-on earrings."

Greta faces me and raises her eyebrows before taking on her shop-keeper mode. "You're in luck. We have quite a variety."

"Yes, you are," I say to the woman, standing. To Greta, I say, "Let me know when you've figured it out."

Ten minutes later, the bride-to-be, Marissa Stowe, arrives. The photographer, Grayson, has cameras hanging off him in every direction and carries a folded tripod.

"I can get you to the woods and then it's just a short walk up the path to the car you picked out." I lead them to a golf cart I use to navigate the narrow paths between the cars.

She lifts the hem of her full dress as she tries to climb in the front.

"I'll help you." I gather possibly a thousand dollars' worth of silk and satin and once she's seated, lay it across her lap. She nearly disappears behind a cloud of white.

Grayson clatters his way onto the rear-facing seat and adjusts his equipment. "All set," he calls.

The ride isn't terribly bumpy as we stop short of the woods. I get out and help her out of the cart.

"This way," I say, heading off on a path into the older trees that have reclaimed the vehicles abandoned there.

She oohs and aahs over a pink VW Bus, which is lifted about eight inches in the air by a tree growing out of the front wheel well.

"That one's rad." She points to a '57 Ford truck with an oak rising through the bed, its gnarly branches forming a ghoulish green umbrella over the whole vehicle.

I nod. "Or if you can climb, there's always that." A 1962 Triumph three-cylinder motorcycle is wedged in the arms of a maple. This year it's suspended eighteen feet in the air...next year it will be a few inches higher.

She laughs. "I'm cool with all the ones down here."

We arrive in the white birch section. "There's your 1940 Caddy, but use any of these cars out here." I point to a blue '63 Lincoln with a hood so big you could hold a church service on it. "You could spread that beautiful dress out on that one and still show off that Acapulco blue color."

"Wicked." She wanders to the car and studies the moss and ferns in the open trunk.

"Remember," I say. "The floorboards are almost always gone or unreliable, so stay on the seats or the frames."

I wait in the cart as Grayson takes over sixty shots, some of them downright suggestive. Should a future bride be shown straddling thick branches, glee painted on her face? He took some shots that will be stunning, with the multicolored forest, the white of her dress, and the unusual cars.

She chatters about the many options all the way back to the house, where I accept her check and wish her good luck.

The fact that someone else finds the same beauty in these old things is always satisfying. It says I'm not a weirdo. It's the permanence of the place that is comforting, yet during the year, it's also ever-changing. Dusted in snow, or with a fresh crown of orange and gold leaves—it's never the same.

My heart jumps as a car backfires somewhere along the road. It doesn't make logical sense, but something inside me is still unsettled over the smallest possibility of being arrested. But what happened with Foster, certainly with Randall, was the thing that felt right in the moment. And now that it's done, justice is served.

As a reward, the dogs and I will go for a nice long run.

– 29 –

I overnight the sketches for the law firm to Cincinnati from a shipping store on the way to the Boys and Girls Club the next day, satisfied that I've pulled off a good design in a short time. It's an origami day at the club with no mess to clean up after. I'm always happy to see Jasper, and now his younger brother, Marcus, attends as well. Their stories about Millie send a shiver of joy through me. She's learned six commands and sleeps on their bed. A happy household.

I head toward Victoria's, our first face-to-face since my run-in with Foster. I checked my neck earlier, ensuring the bruises from Foster's fingers are gone.

At Victoria's house in Ovid, I knock but she doesn't answer, so I find the spare key under a god-awful monkey statue she bought last year at an art show. It's a scrawny, three-foot clay figure painted in African green, with a maniacal grin. I offered to make something elegant for her front stoop, but she likes Zeke—her name for the hateful thing.

Once I let myself in, I'm thrilled to find Vic stepping out of the shower. Our reunion is wet, warm, and a doubleheader.

An hour later we lean against the couch, comfortable in our underwear, eating a fully loaded meat pizza. A tumbler of red wine on the coffee table catches the sunset and throws rosy bands across the white leather couch.

"Do you think we can try a short vacation together?" She tilts her head, studying me.

"What are you thinking?" I'm not sure what's changed for her since I got back, but I'm fine with the not-many-sleepovers-status of our relationship. What would going on a trip together mean?

"I've been invited to share how I started the nonprofit at an East Coast fundraiser, in Ocean City."

My smile feels like an eel trying to wiggle off my face. I fight to hold eye contact. "When is it?"

"We would go this weekend, and I was thinking we could stay a few days."

The crowds. It will be wall-to-wall people. "Do you think we can pull this off?" I rub her neck and leave my hand there. "I mean last time in Cleveland we didn't get much sleep."

"I slept great. You were the one who was up all night." Her shoulders slump. "I'd like to give it another try."

I picture the packed town, the hybrid scents of Coppertone and hamburgers everywhere. And one bed. She looks so hopeful. She's one of the few special people in my life, and I want to keep her around, but with everything going on the last month, I feel like my life is unsettled. In flux. I want to spend time with Victoria, but I don't want to promise any more of me. I don't have pieces to give right now. I raise my hands. "Is there any way we can rent a two bedroom?" It's a weird ask, I know, especially since we are still in the afterglow of having sex. But if we share space on vacation, will she ask for that and more when we get back?

She pauses, her eyes narrowed. "If that's what you need, um…want."

"Just in case." I shrug. "I'm willing to try. And if it becomes uncomfortable, I give you permission to send me home." I don't look at her, worried that I'm forecasting my concerns. I really care about Victoria, maybe I even love her. But I can't do any more change in my life right now.

"Well, I can't imagine that will happen, but okay." She shakes her head. Then she snaps her fingers and brightens. "I have something for you."

"So many surprises." I'm worried about what's next.

She crosses to her desk. The item she lifts from the drawer is the size of a shoe box. When she sets it on the table in front of me, my shoulders sag.

It's a Nokia GSM phone. Even though I told her I'd get one, I really don't want a cellular phone of any size or shape, but according to the box, here's a 187-gram lightweight model staring my way. It might as well be a ten-pound albatross.

"Nice, huh?" She tears into the box, unwraps the plastic packaging and sticks it in my hand. She launches into all the features. The front with the full number pad right there, the fact that this smaller, six-inch model fits easily in my hand, making it more portable than last year's model. The menu button, the back button, the terms are all so foreign, she may as well be speaking Swahili.

"Wow." I turn it over, studying it, wondering how they make it this small while keeping all the necessary parts. "Amazing," I mumble.

"I know. After this last road trip, I'll bet you realize how much you need one." She's so proud of her gift. "No more searching for dirty pay phones."

A mobile phone? Not being inconveniently found when I was on the road worked out for me this last trip, especially on my unplanned stop outside Halsom, Kansas. I know Victoria only cares about me, worries about me, but can someone like me—someone who has done the things I've done—risk having someone so close to them?

"Thank you," I whisper into her hair. "I'll need your help learning what all the buttons are for, but I'm sure I'll figure it out."

"Good." She pulls back and her eyes meet mine. "You want to practice pushing my buttons again?"

I feign exhaustion, which isn't difficult. Round three will have to wait. "You taking some new vitamins or something?"

"No, it's you." She nudges my shoulder with hers. "You've got an edge, something primal I haven't noticed before. I like it."

My heart kicks up a notch. Am I putting off some new animalistic aura and my pores are bleeding testosterone? "Maybe I need to investigate my bleak genealogy more often." I hope my reply sounds flirty and not laden with the guilt and worry that has been nagging at my thoughts since leaving Cleone and her photo piles and her cats.

She gathers the plates and moves to the kitchen. "Maybe. You're less guarded now, and I like getting a peek inside."

She might like these new film clips, but I bet she'd hate Wyatt the movie. If I seem like a different person to her, do others notice? Greta hasn't said anything. I review our conversation at the store, but remember no side glances or puzzled looks from her.

I miss what Victoria says next. "Sorry?"

She laughs. "You looked so far away just then. Like a little boy."

I'm not sure what broken and trapped looks like, because that would have been me as a child, but a flush of humiliation races through me at the thought of those things showing in my face. I force levity into my words. "Did I look cuter than hell?"

"You did." She comes back and drops next to me on the couch, throwing her legs over my lap. "We don't have to mess around again if you're ready to leave."

"No way." She likes the primal me, so maybe I should give in to it. Plus, our conversation has felt awkward, and I don't want to leave things that way. I fall backward on the couch, pulling her with me. "I'm not sure how long this new primal thing will last, but I'm willing to keep testing it out."

We've dozed for forty-five minutes according to her alarm clock. My arm is asleep under Victoria's head. When the couch proved too uncomfortable, we made a stumbling migration into her bedroom.

I roll toward her and gently run my hand down her stomach and hips.

A smile touches her lips and her eyes slowly open.

"Hey, Gorgeous. Can I have my arm back?" I wiggle my shoulder to try to free myself. "I'll need it tomorrow to paint."

She lifts her head. "It's all yours."

A prickle of blood rushes to my lower arm and hand, and I sit up, trying to shake feeling into them.

"What time is it?" Her voice is sleepy.

"1:00 a.m. Time for me to skedaddle." I slap her butt as I leave the bed and go in search of my clothes.

As I dress, I review what I need to do later today. I'll call the lawyers about the preliminary sketches, which should arrive my midmorning. And I need to ask Greta if she can watch the dogs this weekend when we go to the beach.

Vic stands in the bedroom doorway, buttoning the top two buttons on white silk PJs. "Hey, I remember the weird name of the lady in the old house in Colorado."

I nod and raise my eyebrows, preparing myself to hear the name Cleone Powell. "What was it?"

"Shirley Doolittle." She chuckles. "I told you the name was something silly."

I flinch and the hair rises on my arms. *Shirley Doolittle.* The name my mother and I gave the chipmunk we rescued and nursed back to health. The name no one knows but us.

"You okay?" she asks.

"Fine," I mumble, staring off in space. Victoria couldn't have known the effect the words would have, but they cut, hard and quick. I fight to breathe, and when air finally fills my lungs again, I feel the empty hollow the words made.

My vision blurs. Shirley Doolittle. I try to stand dominoes of possibilities end-to-end in my mind—my mother returned home after leaving Montana and told her mother, Cleone, the name of the chipmunk. That must be it. But one logical domino falls against the next, creating blackened steppes off into the distance, a path of truth.

Her apparent physical health. She looked elderly, but if her hair had been kept up, her clothing fit her, she could be in her fifties rather than her seventies.

The fact she said she had no daughter and denied having a grandson.

A sinking truth fills the pit of my stomach. That poor woman is my mother!

Somehow over the next five minutes, I finish dressing. "I'll call you tomorrow." I kiss Victoria and hurry out the door.

I have the car on the road and pointed toward the openness of the backcountry before I allow my emotions to hit, like holding back vomit until an appropriate place can be found to let it fly.

I jerk the car to the side of the road and stop.

My mother? The old woman living in squalor in the mansion, the cat hoarder, is my mother? I'm lost, like a blind guy running my fingers over a smooth map, trying to figure out what this all means.

Shirley Doolittle.

My grandmother's face morphs into my mother's, from the younger version I remember.

Add years of hard living and sixty pounds and it could be her. The green eyes. The stacks of books that go along with her love of reading. Her arm when I touched it was firmer than I expected—younger muscles, not those of an elderly lady.

And when she said, "Wyatt," my grown-up brain hadn't registered her voice, but my nine-year-old mind made the memory connection, and I was frozen in time for a moment.

Not my grandmother. My mother.

"Shit." I shake my head. When I was in her house, and we talked about her family, she said her father had a hard time as a teenager during the Dust Bowl years and later, she added he married and had two kids. I knew something was wrong. My Grandmother Powell would have raised three kids. My mother only had one sibling, my uncle Wyatt. She said, *"My mother worked hard around here, went to raising two kids for all she was worth. Didn't do her much good in the end."*

She was talking about her dead brother, Wyatt, and herself. She'd run away and her mom was left with no children in the end.

I start driving again. The wind blows, and bits of dirt and debris swirl across the road, forming into circular patterns.

The person I desperately wanted to find, I had so easily abandoned because she hadn't fit the image I carried in my head? Another mistake to tattoo on my soul.

When had my mother moved back into the family house? Were her parents alive when she returned? Was it right after leaving Montana, or had she come back later? I have so many questions.

"This is my house. These are my parents' possessions," she said.

That meant Ralph and Cleone's house, *their* photos and furniture from the Dust Bowl years. My mom must have inherited the unusable house, yet hadn't changed anything, only making it worse by hoarding cats instead of possessions.

I park in my driveway and greet the dogs. As I pet their wiggly flanks, I'm more fucked-up than I've been for a long time. Just when I figured I have control over my life and nothing unforeseen will ever blindside me again, my book of life has been tossed in the air, its pages separated and scattered, never to be put back in the same order again.

My mother is alive and she needs help. Fingers of fog wrap around my brain and squeeze. As I crawl into bed, knowing I probably won't be able to sleep, I fight the guilt. *You left her behind.*

This same numbness overwhelmed me when I learned my grandparents had died.

Most of the images I stored away from those days are caught in time, like movie clips or old photographs. The first time I walked through the kitchen after the funeral. It was so empty, instantly devoid of recognizable smells that came with the house. The meals cooked in that room for the many years I lived there were swept away in an instant.

At night, sleep wouldn't come. I felt eyes on me even when no one was looking.

Greta made all the funeral arrangements. I have very little memory of being asked to do anything during that period, although I was thirty-one years old. I was an artist, could drink a beer, and legally gamble. A therapist once warned me that an emotional shock could spiral me back to my childhood, and in this case it did.

Confusion and anxiety arrived through the door with the layer cakes and tuna casseroles, but those two emotions were slathered over with grief, deep and penetrating.

I'd never felt so alone.

Even when I ran to the woods after Mom left, I knew I wasn't alone. I always had Keesha by my side until my father shot her. There was a person to talk to back at the cabin, even though I hated him. But, again, like people who cling to each other on a sinking ship, there was someone there even more fucked-up than I was.

When the sheriff pulled away after delivering the ghastly news—the drunk driver was a power company worker, it was a head-on, they died instantly—I was struck with disbelief. My grandparents were too damn alive to be dead.

The emptiness haunted me. After two months of doing nothing but painting like a druggie on speed, I bought the Doberman pups and the earth tilted just a hair toward hopeful. Everything less flat and devastated. Not quite two years after my grandparents' deaths, I met Victoria.

But now, I'm hollowed out again with something that's my fault this time. True, I found my mother and she'll be getting help, but I should have done much more when I was there, even with the supposition she was my grandmother.

It's more pressing now that I call the caseworker in Pueblo and let her know I want to be involved.

I painted so many images of what my mom would look like now, both on canvas and in my head. They were all wrong. Who stole the happy fifty-six-year-old woman I imagined was out there living her life, involved in cookie exchanges, playing tennis, doing great things? I wanted to think my mother left me behind because something important called her away. Perhaps a life experience she craved to fulfill. Not the run-down mansion full of sick cats, a muddled mind, and despair. I want to be worth more than that.

Back at the house, I strip and slide into bed. The dogs join me. I sling an arm over Florence who is curled into my chest with Rome pressed against my back. Bookended by their warm bodies, I match my breathing to their calming breaths and soon drift off to sleep.

After the sun has risen, I change my clothes and hit the wooded trails with the dogs at my side. I push farther and longer than I usually do, finishing in just over an hour. The dog's tongues hang out like those on worn down shoes. They drink long and deep from the gallon buckets I fill beside the house.

I cook eggs and sausage for the three of us, clean the dishes and then give the dogs each a long brushing. Rome endures the brush because he likes the attention, but Florence would let me groom her for hours. She licks my hand as I pass near her head.

"I love you, too, sweet girl."

After I shower, I dig in my wallet for the card Melinda gave me at the Pueblo Department of Public Health. It's barely nine a.m. Colorado time. Seven rings later, someone answers.

"I need to speak to Melinda, please."

There are beeps and clicks before Melinda picks up. I swear I can hear her dangly earrings over the phone.

I identify myself.

"I was just thinking about you," she says.

"Really? Why's that?"

"We arrested your, uh, maybe-she-is or maybe-she-isn't grandmother on the animal hoarding charges yesterday. She was processed and taken back home last night. A case worker is out there today with animal control."

My pulse quickens. "I thought you said the process would take weeks."

"Her case came up and the officers were free, so we went for it." Her voice holds a challenging edge. "And it's a mess out there. Not just the cats, but the sheer amount of piled stuff. It'll take weeks to get through the front room let alone the attic and basement."

"Is she alright? She seemed quite fragile."

Melinda is momentarily gone as she answers a question in the background. "I'm back. She's fine. I've already told you too much since you *aren't* related. Is this what you called to find out?"

"No. I discovered she's my mother."

A snort comes through the phone. "Is this the complicated-family-tree-that-wouldn't-hold-up-legally story?" She laughs. "Now you are the long-lost son? You said she had a long-lost daughter!"

I can waste time trying to explain the whole scenario or attempt another route. "I called to get her phone number. I want to talk to her."

She clears her throat. "We can ask her permission to give you the number, but that's all I can do since you said she technically wasn't family only a few days ago."

I swear and shake my head. I give her my name and home phone number again and ask her to call me back as soon as she's reached my mother. Melinda is already talking to someone else as she hangs up.

Hours pass and I try to keep busy updating the store, the junkyard, and my art sales profit and loss statements. Quarterly taxes come around again next month, and I've learned to never wait until the last minute.

Victoria calls to find out how the new mobile phone is working. I sag in the office chair realizing I left it on her coffee table.

"Damn." She knows I don't have it. "I'm sorry. I'm not used to carrying it yet. Besides, I need you to show me how to put phone numbers in and all of that." I uncoil the phone cord so I can push the chair farther back and prop my feet on the desk. I see where there'd be a benefit to walking around and talking at the same time.

"Okay, I'll show you the next time you're over." She pauses. "Also, I have more trip details if you still want to go to Ocean City like I mentioned."

"Sure." I scratch at a mosquito bite on my calf. "What are we doing?"

I let her talk about a travel agent who got us into a higher end condo on the beach as I contemplate what to do next. My mother is alive. She's been arrested because of me. Her home and life are being torn apart, because of me. Victoria's voice continues, mentioning something called Assateague Island where wild ponies live. Half of me wants to blurt out that I've found my mother. She would celebrate that with me, I think. But it feels too big to admit to, and she'll want me to discuss it, but I'm not ready to conjure the reality of it with open conversation.

"We'd plan the other two days once we get there," she concludes.

"Good enough." I can't fully wrap my mind around a trip right now. I need to manage her expectations. "Can we make a deal that no one's feelings are hurt if it feels too cramped?"

"Like I said before. If that feels best to you."

"I don't want to ruin anything between us." Maybe this won't be all that bad. Separate bedrooms and she has the conference she's speaking at to fill her time. It might do me, and us, good to get away. Take a breather from everything happening right now. "I've never been there, have you?"

"Nope. But I hear it's pretty." I hear the smile in her voice. "See you Friday."

We say goodbye. Not wanting to dwell on my thoughts, I move down my to-do list. I call the Cincinnati lawyers. They received the sketches and have some changes. Overall, they're excited.

Out in the lime shack, I check the lime putty temperature. All good. I have enough slack lime, but the lawyer's foyer will take up most of that. Randall is down the drain, and once I wash the last of leftovers from this batch down, he'll be spread even thinner.

I barely step foot into the house when I hear the phone. I charge into the office, catching it on the last ring.

Melinda, from Colorado. She's straightforward, skipping the polite greeting. "I might get fired for saying this, but I like you less and less. Your request for that phone number sent our client into a tailspin."

My heart thumped faster. "What happened?"

"The case worker went out there and let her know her son was trying to reach her. Gave her your name." Her voice is laced with something ugly. "The worker said Mrs. Powell ran into her house and started screaming and dumping boxes over."

"Oh, God." That's the opposite reaction I wanted to hear.

Pages are turning on her end of the line. "There's more. In her rant she said her son is dead and how dare we bring this subject up. She had to be sedated and taken to the hospital."

A dull ache fills my chest. I picture my mother losing it, screaming, and clawing at the heaps of pictures. I should have stayed.

"Our question is, what do you want with this woman?" Her voice is rife with accusation.

I draw a long breath. "She *is* my mother. I haven't seen her since I was nine. I'm not surprised she believes I'm dead. I didn't know if she was alive or not until I found her last week."

I wait to see how that plays out. How can they argue the logic of a sane man over a woman who is clearly out of touch with reality?

The silence spreads out. Melinda finally speaks. "Tell you what. Get me a birth certificate that proves she's your mother and we can move forward. Right now, I have a sick woman I'm trying to help."

The phone goes dead in my ear, and a tiny part of me dies inside.

I bite the inside of my cheek and roll my neck from side to side.

Even if I present a birth certificate, will it help my mother heal from all she has suffered? Can she accept that I'm alive and be ready to make us a family again?

A piece of paper is just that if mentally she's too far gone.

My throat tightens and tears slide down my cheeks for the first time in years.

-30-

"Hey, Wyatt," Greta says as I enter the store. "I brought you a couple slices of vinegar pie."

"You baked it?" The name is all wrong for the delicious egg, brown sugar, and butter dessert. It's one of my favorites.

"Yup. Used your grandmother's recipe but I added a titch more apple-cider vinegar." She pulls out a plastic wrap-covered plate from under the counter. "Here you go. And I figured out the license plate."

"I knew you would."

"JK MNO." She laughs. "There's no L. So it's a name, Noel."

"Tough one, right?" I eye the dessert. "You've made my day." I accept the pie. "Seriously. I'm going upstairs at the house to dig through my dad's boxes before we leave for Ocean City, and this will help take the edge off." I explain what happened with the phone call to my mother and the need to find my original birth certificate. I had a copy but that's missing, too. Makes me wonder if the CIA doesn't still have it at Langley, the last place I needed to prove my citizenship.

It's good to have someone I can discuss my mother with. And when Victoria and I get to Ocean City I'll tell her the latest news. That feels like a better way to do it rather than over the phone. She'll have ideas about how to help Mom. Her nonprofit focuses on poor and abused women, and my mother fits both categories.

"Did you check the wall safe?" Greta knows where my Gram and Gramps kept important papers because she dealt with everything after their deaths.

"I checked. It wasn't there." I shrug. "Wish me luck and don't work too hard."

She laughs knowing she's mostly paid to read trashy novels and help the few customers who wander in.

At the house, I let the dogs run the yard for half an hour then I settle them inside. I pour a shot of tequila and get my feet moving toward my father's bedroom, the one room I avoid as much as possible. I dust and throw a vacuum around in there a few times a year, but that's about it.

After he died in Montana, I arrived here with a suitcase of clothes and a few personal belongings. A forest ranger's son has the whole outdoors as a playground, and I owned very few toys or trinkets. The trunk of my grandparent's car held three cartons of my father's belongings, which went directly into his childhood room at the end of the upstairs hallway.

I flip on the light switch, and the overhead light-and-fan combo moves the stuffy air around. My birth certificate must be in one of the boxes. They sit in a row at the foot of the bed, which is covered with a Workman's Quilt made from old shirts Dad and Gramps owned. Gram explained it's an Irish tradition from her side of the family, and she made it after my dad died.

Kneeling in front of the first box, I open the flaps. A smell rises from inside, triggering a memory, my dad's scent locked away all these years, a spicy cologne that reminds me of him.

I rock back on my heels and force my eyes closed as images of our cabin flash in my mind. The blackened woodstove against the north wall. The swing on the porch, the ground around the cabin padded with inches of thick pine needles, the sharp scent of wood smoke and pine sap, riding high in the clear morning breeze before the sun pressed it closer to the ground.

And the tiny desk my father built so I could do my schooling. I was clueless that other children rode buses to large buildings where they were taught in an orderly fashion. My schooling was a stack of encyclopedias, a book of maps to teach me mathematical concepts—"if it's three miles to the fire tower and you can walk seven miles per hour…"

There were writing tablets, and I recall printing letters over and over again, perfecting my penmanship.

I return to my task, pawing through the pieces of a life my father determined to mean the most to him.

Army memorabilia fills the first box. I hold up my father's dog tags, the ones he often wore when he got drunk, the rubber around their edges a silencer so the enemy couldn't hear the jingling. The imprint stamped in the aluminum shows my father's name, serial number, blood type, and the letters stamped PROT, for his religion. They should have spelled, REM for Remington, the only God Dad really followed.

A pouch of tobacco. A couple of Elvis tapes. Flannel shirts.

The next box holds only clothes, so I push it aside and reach for the third. This one is heavier. It reveals books and stacks of papers. I lift out two books by Kurt Vonnegut, *Welcome to the Monkey House* and *Cat's Cradle*. The third book is Joseph Heller's *Catch-22*. These were probably Mom's. There had been a bookshelf by their bedside that held dozens of paperbacks, yet he burned those and kept only these few. *Catch-22* was one of my favorite books at Ohio State. Heller asks, "What will a sane man do to survive in an insane society?" I relate to that question.

I stack the books on the tan tweed carpet and reach for the flat piece of cardboard below. My heart jolts. It's a sketch of Mom, exactly as I remember her in my dreams.

Done in charcoal, some of it has smeared, but it shows her looking off to the side, a small, secretive smile on her lips. I turn it over to find the artist's signature, but there's nothing. Then on the front, small initials near my mother's collarbone—PPD. Patricia Powell Dardin.

My mother drew a damned good self-portrait. I had no idea she could sketch. Means my genetic pool isn't completely polluted and I inherited my mother's skill. Tears prick my eyes and I flash to the old house in Manzanola. The youthful woman in this drawing was beaten down by life. No drawings on her walls, no paintings. How does complete degeneration happen in a mere twenty-six years?

This will hang in the living room, I decide as I set it aside. I pull out their marriage certificate, two strong signatures at the bottom promising hopefulness. In the end, were they officially divorced? Maybe not, and if after she left, she never filed, she has money coming to her. There's $40,000 and change available in my father's bank account I gained access to when I turned eighteen. I never touched the money, wanting no part of his legacy.

I sift through more papers, some military, some letters from his army buddies after he was sent home. Then I spot Mom's familiar handwriting.

Postmarked October 20th, 1973, when I was ten. I open the brittle page of blue stationery. My heart pounds as I read her words from back then.

"I can't believe you waited this long to tell me. He's my son too. I've rented an apartment big enough for us and now you say he's not coming? I never want to see or hear from you again. When I leave Modesto, I'm dropping "off the map" as you would say. As far as you and your family are concerned, I never existed. You've ruined my life and your son's life and I hope you roast in hell."

I hear something nearly imperceptible from the hallway behind me, almost a stalling of air. I turn in that direction, but nothing is there. Then the sound of the fan returns.

"You've ruined my life and your son's life and I hope you roast in hell."

I freeze and rub my eyes. What had my dad said or done to get this reaction? I try to remember what happened before she left, but nothing surfaces. My mind races through possibilities. Had I said something unkind about Mom and Dad put it in a letter? Early on, I was so angry at her for leaving.

Now you tell me he's not coming.

Is this why my mother told the social workers her son was dead? Had she written me off?

This gives me pause. What did a kid know about the world? But maybe it was the opposite of that. My father may have made up something hurtful I was *supposed* to have said, maybe adding that his whole family felt that way about her.

I hope to hear her side of the story soon. My parents fought a lot before she left, but it still never explained why she hadn't taken me.

I put the letter aside with the sketch and reach the bottom of the box.

No birth certificate.

It has to exist. But why isn't it in the office safe where everything else of importance is stored?

I'll look again. Waiting for a new one could take months, and I want to talk to Mom before that.

I stand and kick at the dusty boxes. My father's life came down to three boxes and me in the end. That's one sorry legacy.

In my bedroom, I start packing for the beach. My new cellular phone is charging on top of my scarred bureau. Victoria was kind enough to drop it off last night. I push the green button and dial a number.

Victoria picks up on the fourth ring.

"Do I sound different to you?" I ask.

"Is this the voice of a mobile phone owner?" She laughs. "Have you packed?"

"Just starting," I say. "I wasted a bunch of time trying to find my birth certificate."

"What do you need that for?" There's a tiny bit of reproach in her voice.

"I'll tell you when we're at the beach."

"If you knocked somebody up, I hope you have quintuplets."

I snort. "That would serve me right." I pause. "See you soon." The red button on the device disconnects us. Very slick.

Punching in another sequence of numbers, the phone downstairs jangles, then the answering machine comes on. Gramps's famous last words float upward to me, "You've reached the Dardin home. Thomas Dardin here. Sure sorry we missed you but we should be right back to you soon." I could never bring myself to erase the message and replace it with my own. A twinge of pain races through me now at hearing his voice. It exemplifies everything he was—kind, gracious, funny. I redial and listen two more times.

Moments later, I have my clothes and toiletries in a small suitcase. I bound down the stairs and leave the phone on the cracked surface of the pine dining table. On winter nights we all lived within ten feet of that table—reading the paper, doing homework, Gram's mending.

I miss my grandparents daily, more than I miss my mother or father. I hardly knew Mom, and at this point, the woman in Manzanola is a stranger. My father, I knew all too well. But there's a strong bond created when people step in to save you, and save me is what my grandparents did.

The dogs are on alert, giving me their needy eye gaze. "Do you want to go for a run?" Their reaction is always the same as they jump skyward as if a puppeteer yanks them to life.

Within five minutes the dogs and I crest the rise and I stand near my grandparents' headstone, my labored breathing cutting the silence into sections. The dogs sniff at the other gravestones and at the edges of the weeds.

"Guess who I met last week?" I pause. What if they can hear me from beyond? "Patricia Dardin. Your daughter-in-law is alive."

I turn to my father's grave. "Alive and ruined because of you."

Spinning back to my grandparents, I pluck a weed from the side of their headstone. "She's not in great shape. I don't know what happened after she left Montana, but something bad went down by the looks of her."

Then to my Dad. "I'm blaming you. You must have told her lies about me."

The dogs continue sniffing around the old gravestones.

Then to my grandparents. "Oh. Any idea where we put my birth certificate? I'm going to need it so I can talk to her again."

A twig snaps behind me. I spin around and my heart almost stops. Why do I always expect the dead at times like this?

The dogs charge past me to circle Lloyd Barney, who scratches their flanks, talking baby talk to them.

Lloyd, the sixty-year-old farmer to the south of me, stands ten feet away in bib overalls and a Buckeye's logo on his ball cap. "You up here robbing graves?" He belly laughs then spits a brown stream of tobacco chew on the ground.

"You almost scared the life out of me, Lloyd."

"Everything going okay with you over here?" He moves a wad of tobacco to the other side of his mouth, and that cheek bulges.

He's been a good neighbor since my grandparents passed, especially since he's not a nuisance.

"Can't complain," I say.

"I hear ya." He offers a rusty chuckle honed over the years from Lucky Strikes. "And if we did, got nobody to listen."

"You got Velma." She matches Lloyd in his smoking habit and raises the ante on cancer by getting the darkest tan she can, spending sunny days in a plastic lawn chair slathered in baby oil.

"Well, thirty years of marriage seems to have worn her listening skills away, if you know what I mean." There's that rumbling laugh again.

He turns his eyes to me. "What *her* are you trying to contact?" His speech is a bit slurred, indicating he's had some time with his friend Pabst Blue Ribbon today.

My throat freezes, refusing to let words pass. I shrug and manage to keep a weak smile afloat. "I like talking to my grandparents."

The skin is loose around his eyes, and his double chin protrudes past his jaw. When he swallows, a lot of movement takes place. "Greta mentioned you're leaving town soon. Do you need me to watch the house while you're gone?"

"Sure, thanks." Gramps was a good neighbor, and I'm still reaping the benefits of his kindness from people like Greta and Lloyd. "I'm back in four days."

"No problem." His gaze follows the dogs as they sniff and dig. "Have a good time."

"I'll try. The kids and I are off to Hidden Lake. Always good to see you." He raises a hand in farewell and begins to turn.

"Lloyd, wait a second. I have a mobile phone now. I'll leave my number inside in case you need to reach me. You still have a key?"

"I do." He leaves, waving and whistling a Disney tune.

I motion the dogs forward, and we hit the trail leading deeper into the forest. We weave through the trees and up and down hills for twenty minutes, then I slow when the footpath runs another fifty yards to a clearing.

Hidden Lake is more of a large pond full of trout and frogs, and it runs clear. It's stream fed from higher up. Large flat stones frame around the edges, one of my favorite places to sit. Today, I stretch out on my stomach on the biggest rock, with my head on my hands, and peer over the edge into the pond. The water is clear and calm, and the bottom plants looked like a diorama of a tiny forest, covered in nonglare glass, only the occasional water skater breaking the illusion. It's a whole other world down there. A minnow squirms around the grassy roots, and the sun touches the hills and slopes of the muddy bottom. I spent many hours here in my teens. I build my paintings in 3D all the time but here is a nature-made three-dimensional picture.

I round up the dogs and we head back to the house on a different trail. I shower and dress, looking forward to the trip. Beach running is physically harder than trail running, and I'm a glutton for that kind of punishment. Fresh seafood, sun, and wine on the deck at sunset. And sometime during the next few days, I'll bounce ideas off Victoria about my mother.

With everything planned, I'm not sure why but I have an uneasy sense about me that I have difficulty shaking.

-31-

Victoria slowly spins the flute of champagne, holding it up to the night sky, capturing the shimmering moon in her glass. She's a little drunk, a rarity for her. Earlier, we finished off great Italian fare at Da Vinci's by the Sea and walked back to our condo along the wide boardwalk.

Around us are pairings of other couples enjoying an evening stroll. The high winds from earlier in the day subsided, and the full moon is a bright orb suspended above us.

"I'm staying here forever," she says, sighing for about the eighteenth time since we settled onto the padded deck chairs that face a view of the sea.

"Okay." I smile, pretending to agree. The ocean surf rumbles and crashes in soothing, rhythmic murmurs, as the salty-water scent swirls around us. I make a move to get up, ready to pack us up and move us here. "I'll go get the dogs. They'll love it here." I watch her face to see her reaction to my joke.

She turns her sleepy eyes my way. We've had a full day—an afternoon flight to Baltimore, rental car to the beach. Hours in the water, sex before dinner, a long walk. A perfect day. So why am I making a joke of it?

I settle back into the chair, laughing at my own joke but realizing it might be insensitive. I've made such a big deal of not sharing rooms on this trip, and now I'm joking about moving us here? Together? I'm sending mixed signals and I need to cool it.

All evening I've waited to tell her about my mother, to carefully explain the hoarding, to retell the details in her final letter to my dad, but it feels intrusive and out of place right now. Tomorrow, I'll bring it up. Or perhaps never.

"It's so peaceful here." She slurs the next words a bit. "Not a care in the world."

I nod, trying to push away the meddling worries bubbling up in my head.

"It's the waves. All of that breaking, washing up on shore, then disappearing. Takes them all away." It's a nice thought, but not true. Even on vacation, you bring your worries with you. Is Mom being cared for or is she being treated like a forgotten old lady with no one in the world to check on her? There have been no updates in the news about VAPPA or Kaw and the truck. Either those investigations have finally run cold, or they're keeping things out of the papers until they gather enough evidence that finally leads to me.

"Hmmm," is all she manages.

Five minutes later, she's snoring softly. I remove the glass from her hand then carry her to her bedroom, undress her enough to be comfortable, and pull the covers over her. She's lovely as she sleeps, and I try to imagine a life together. I could update Gram and Gramps's house, make it a place she would enjoy coming home to every day, though that would increase her commute. But that isn't the real issue. Not really.

I'm edgy. I wander through the condo, not ready to go to my own room yet. I look for something to read. I brought a Grisham novel, but I'm too wound up to focus. Things are too uncertain right now. That's why I don't want to promise anything more to Victoria. Or maybe I'm worried that if I tie her too close to me, the complications in my life, the things I've done, will bring her down too. If everything comes to light, I'll lose the life I've built. I can't risk destroying hers as well.

Victoria's laptop sits on the kitchen counter, AOL news blurbs on the home screen. Maybe if I plan a great day for us tomorrow, it will mask the awkwardness of tonight. I decide to use my simplistic search skills to see what I can find out about Assateague Island. I can plan a hike for us, or maybe some kayaking. I start to close the main page when my finger stalls; one headline grips me by the throat.

Horrific Animal Torture Goes Unpunished.

I drop onto the barstool and lean into the screen, compelled to click and scroll to read more. The story details a rich kid, Harrison Fields II from Fenwick Island, which is over the Delaware border about eight miles north. My palms start to sweat. This happened right here? He tried to kill his girlfriend's chocolate Lab puppy by putting drain cleaner in its food. The caustic toxin burned the puppy's mouth while the girlfriend raced to the vet with the screaming animal. Surgery saved the poor little guy, but the story reported he has a long road to full recovery, possibly requiring tube feeding for the rest of his life. This was two weeks ago, but the article reiterates Harrison's final verdict in the case. A whopping $250 fine and three months of probation. He's prevented from owning a pet for a year.

A year! My stomach clenches and my dinner threatens at the back of my throat. Drawing in a long cooling breath, I concentrate on not puking.

How fucking tragic for him. No pets for a year? Should be no freedom for him forever and a drain cleaner enema.

His father, Harrison the first, is a mega real estate broker renting out half of the beach properties along this northern Maryland coast and up into Delaware toward Rehoboth Beach. His dad's influence clearly helped his twenty-eight-year-old son's case. When Harrison II was asked if he worried about vigilantes coming for him, in particular VAPPA, he reportedly laughed and said, "No one's going to get me."

Prick.

I pace the floor and wander out to the deck, facing the ocean again. I picture the puppy and what it went through in that awful stretch of time when it almost died.

"No one's going to get me."

It's a challenge I can almost taste. That call resonates inside me again, almost moving me into action, but no, I need to leave this alone. I can't go after *every* abuser, even though I wish I could make it all stop. How will things ever progress the way Victoria wants if I continue as VAPPA? I've saved some animals, and that has to be enough.

My hands contract against my jeans and I bang my fist on my thigh. My head fills with images that jump from this chocolate Lab to a real estate sign in the article with the Fields company name emblazoned on it.

Moonlight twitches and sparkles on the surface of the unstoppable sea.

The longer I think about Harrison, the more I side with the other opinion floating around in my head, the one that whispers, "But you're already here."

I've been running along the beach for over an hour, the sand silvery in the moonbeams. My destination is a boat harbor on Assawoman Bay, eight miles north of the condo. I asked directions at an all-night gas station moments ago, so I know I'm close to the marina where Harrison keeps his yacht.

If Victoria awakens, she'll find my note about going for a run, not an unheard-of activity for me. But with all that champagne on board, I bet she'll sleep through the night.

The news article gave the marina's name where Harrison lives and stated that Beachcomber Marina security was called in to keep picketers in line who were marching in front of Harrison II's yacht after the news broke about what he did.

I trot along the sidewalk that edges the marina, not sure what I'm looking for. Without a boat slip number, I have no idea what his yacht looks like. The smaller cruisers can be ruled out since he's from big money and it must be spacious enough to live on. Even at this late hour, people are out, walking along the moonlit harbor path. I hope I blend in with my gray athletic T-shirt and running shorts.

My plan isn't to hurt Harrison, but he needs to understand that what he did was awful. He should do more with his resources to make up for his actions. I want a glimpse of where he lives and to talk to him, maybe encourage him to donate some big money to an animal shelter or do something that will actually make a difference.

I walk the marina looking for *"Sunny" Fields*. A play on the fact that he's the *son* of the senior Fields. Except there's nothing sunny about this guy. I change directions when the line of boats ends and I head back the way I'd come. Then I see the name emblazoned on the side of a medium-sized yacht.

I stop and stretch out my quads, pulling my foot up to my butt, studying the abuser's home. It's outfitted with all the toys of the rich—a small motorboat on a winch, fishing gear big enough for marlin, plenty of sunning decks. And a security guard. A burly man steps from the shadow of a roof, which overhangs the main cabin door. Gun belt, night stick, and arms that can tear a door from its hinges.

Of course, he has a guard. It's why he bragged no one would be getting to him.

The guard is studying me about as hard as I'm watching him. I break into a limping jog as if I have a charley horse I'm working out.

I'd like to get a glimpse of the asshole, but the guard will get suspicious if I linger for too long, so I leave. During the run back to the condo, I plot ways to get past Harrison's protection, like swimming to the boat from out in the harbor, knife in my mouth. A scene from a movie for sure.

But that isn't going to happen. I hate the fact that he has gotten away with such an awful act and there's so little I can do about it.

On the way back, I abandon the beach and rip up the streets, sprinting the last mile, reaching the condo spent and hurting. Almost sixteen miles, a new first for me. The run did some good, though. I tear up my note to Victoria. As anticipated, she's in the same position as when I left her. It's well past midnight when I shower and slip into bed in the second bedroom, falling asleep immediately.

$-32-$

E arly the next morning, Victoria and I sit on a beach wall overlooking Assateague State Park, swatting away mosquitoes and flies. The island is divided, separating Chincoteague Island, a Virginia property, from Assateague Island, a holding of the state of Maryland. We are near the end of a self-guided walk through the bird refuge. The lush trees above are filled with various colorful birds, some with long feathered tails, others so small they flit around in a blur. I smile and follow Victoria's finger as she points some out, but my mind keeps returning to Harrison. How many others like him get away with terrible acts with little more than a slap on the wrist?

The thoughts are making me gloomy and poor company. I look over at Victoria, who is taking in the sanctuary with her usual cheeriness. A sudden need to confide in her washes over me. There is so much to share, but much of it is too dangerous to say.

We stop by a plaster wall that serves as a resting place and viewing area. I join her next to the wall and nudge her with my shoulder. "If you're interested, I have news about my mother."

"What?" Her eyes fly open. "When did you get an update?" She's off the wall and, in one movement, drums out a beat on my chest with her palms. "Shut up! Wyatt! Really?"

I grin. I knew she'd be excited, but this reaction is amusing. She cares so much. I really don't deserve her. "Okay, okay." I laugh, hands up in surrender. "The story doesn't come all nicely packaged in a Tiffany's box. She's had a tough life."

Victoria is still nodding, but her smile changes to a sympathetic look. "Tell me everything."

There in the refuge, with the sounds of chirping and trilling all around us, I tell her about my stop in Pueblo. "I met with a social worker, Melinda.

She told me the woman I thought was my grandmother living at the old house has a legal case opened against her for cat hoarding."

"What?" Her brows knit together. "How many cats does she have?"

I shake my head. "Hard to say." I refuse to mention that many were sick, as the truth of that still makes me feel uneasy. "Melinda mentioned dozens."

Victoria lets out a low whistle. "Hefty Friskies tab." She touches my hand. "Sorry, that was insensitive."

I nod, wanting to move on from that point. "And she lives alone."

"What happened to your grandparents?" She pauses. "Wait, is this the fire hazard house?"

"Yeah. My mother must have moved back in. I don't know what happened to my grandmother. The county records don't have her listed as deceased."

A family walks by us on the way to the viewing area for some wild ponies. One of the small boys is skipping and chanting, "I'm going to ride a horsey!" The kid is about to get a taste of disappointment. No one rides these free-spirit horses.

"I told the county worker that I was related. Things went downhill from there."

We sit on the little bench in silence for a moment. The family has moved on and for now we are alone on this part of the path.

"Social services told me there's nothing I could do for her until the arrest, which is a formality and it already happened. Now, to prove who I am and before I go back, I need to find my birth certificate." I explain the chipmunk story, how my mom and I named the injured creature Shirley Doolittle. I squeeze her leg. "Imagine my shock when you said that name."

She laughs. "No wonder you fled the house quicker than usual."

"I don't flee." It comes out too harshly, but she just looks back at me with her soft brown eyes.

"Yes, you do." She smiles knowingly. "How was the extra bedroom last night, anyway?"

A flush rises up my neck and my face feels hot. Well, damn. This woman sees right through me. And I thought I was managing it all so fucking well.

She's giving me a way in as she leans into me. Her eyes beg me to take this chance to be vulnerable, to tell her my fears, but even forming the words in my mind is too much, too big, so I put my arm around her and put a little levity in my voice, pretending I don't know how accurately she's seen me. "Even better knowing you're in the next room."

"Maybe one day we'll figure out the sharing a bed thing." She hugs me tighter. "Lots of people do it." So unendingly patient, but for how long?

"Lots of people do many things we don't do." I move her away a foot and study her face. "We're okay, don't you think?"

"So far, so good." But she breaks eye contact. She's been patient, is willing to be patient for a little longer, but time is running out. "What's next for your mom?"

I let her change the subject. We'll have to circle back to our relationship health another time. "I need to write to Montana and get a copy of my birth certificate."

"That could take a while." Her shoulders drop.

I brush hair out of her eyes. "Maybe a few weeks."

We begin walking back to the trailhead. I'd hoped that during this tour my worries would dissipate, but they haven't. It's almost a relief to let my mind think about Harrison again, visualize the boat, review what I witnessed for any security weaknesses.

Victoria nudges me. "Hey. I'm talking to you."

I sling my arm around her back and pull her to me. "I'm sorry, just running through ideas. What'd you say?"

"Do you wonder what your mom will think of you? I mean, she's got a big surprise coming if she thinks you're dead."

That shock, I relate to now. I had the younger version of her stuck in my head, and the older version was unexpected. "She does. Not much left of the nine-year-old she last saw."

"Want me to go with you?"

"That's nice." I squeeze her hand. "I'll keep that in mind." But it isn't something I can see or believe in. I'll never have the "bring your girlfriend to meet your parents" moment, not like others have, so why even let myself imagine it?

We spend the next hour walking the Lighthouse Trail and then waiting at another viewing area to see the two separate herds of wild horses—ponies as the state park calls them. I recall Foster and the terrible injuries to the young colt he dragged. Shooting one of his horses. The fear in the other horses' eyes as he raised the gun again.

He deserved what he got.

We leave and drive back along the Coastal Highway and stop at a pub just shy of Ocean City for a plate of blue crabs and a couple of beers.

"Remember I need to check you for ticks," I say once we're seated at the plank table on the patio. Beach Boys surfer hits are the jaunty background rhythm playing above the ocean's surf.

Victoria laughs. "That *is* what the state park flyer advised."

"A thorough inspection."

She plays along, a flirty smirk on her lips. "Inside and out."

I raise my eyebrows. "You keep talking like that, it'll be right here."

She laughs, and I'm glad we at least have this. Flirting and fun. I push away the nagging worry that I'll never be ready for anything more.

Once we stuff ourselves with crabs, we drive north again. Victoria is dozing when I suck in a sharp breath.

A large home on the bayside of the coastal highway is for lease. The sign says I should call Harrison Fields II to see it. There's a phone number with a lot of fives, easy enough to memorize.

A new idea is forming, one I refuse to stop mulling over. My only decision so far is to find a library while I'm here. It wouldn't do to use Victoria's computer to search for answers to the questions I have about drain cleaners and other lye-based products. The harder part is how to deal with Fields and still leave no trace. I don't have the safety of back woods or a remote farm. This will be the trick. How not to be seen.

At the condo, Victoria pads to the kitchen to review her talk at her event later today. I grab a sketchpad and colored pencils and head to the shaded porch to do some sketching. I draw the ocean, then a lady with a large, floppy red hat. Since she looks like a flower, I cover the beach in a garden of floppy hats. Chewing the end of the pencil, I ponder the endless cycle of water coming in this direction. I pick out three blue colors and draw the ocean going away from the shore, building into waves the farther they get from the edge of land. The idea that at some point, there will be a collision of walls of water, is exciting. My cell phone rings, yanking me back to dry land.

My heart skips a beat—only three people have this number and one of them is with me. This is Lloyd which means something has happened at home. "Hello?"

"Wyatt? Lloyd here."

"Hey. What's going on?" I try for casual but say it too fast to be anything but nervous. I try not to envision five police cars surrounding my property, cops banging down the door, then going over to my neighbor to find out where I am.

"I was in your kitchen when I heard your phone ring like five different times. Hope you don't mind but I grabbed the call."

What's so important he's calling today? Surely it can't be about a person needing a headlight.

"No problem, Lloyd. Who was it?" My two guesses—either the police from Kansas or Melinda from Pueblo.

"A guy named Karl Speers. Or something like that."

Aw hell. Kaw Speers. It had to be. Why did that crazy motherfucker keep my phone number?

"What did he want?"

Lloyd clears his throat. "He said a bunch of crazy shit…"

I'm sure he did.

"…but he said to tell you to call him right away because he took your advice."

I frown. I didn't give him any advice except to not register the truck. "That's it? Just that he took my advice?"

"About—and these are his exact words—about 'getting out on the road to find his major purpose.' He left his number. You want it?"

Is he headed my way? I do not need any connection to Cory Kaw Speers in my life. "Yeah, let me have it." I scribble the number on the sketch of waves rolling away. I thank Lloyd and hang up.

I hope Kaw did find his purpose, but why did he feel the need to call and tell me about it? I start to dial his number on my mobile phone then stop. There'd be a record of the call, and a record is not anything I want. He has the truck and that's connection enough.

I leave my sketches, all except the one with Kaw's number written on it that I stuff into my pocket. I wander back into the kitchen and find Victoria typing away at the counter.

"I'm going to walk to the liquor store and grab some wine for later." I kiss her forehead.

"Perfect," she says, never looking up.

Ten minutes later I find a phone booth, drop in some coins, and dial Kaw's number from the crinkled paper.

As it rings, I picture the shed-like structure he lives in, his scrawny build, yellow teeth, and tarnished mind. I disconnect after twenty rings. Should I be worried that I can't reach him?

I'm sick of worrying. There's a knot of a hundred threads tangled in my mind, and if I pull on any of them, it only makes the tangles worse. I have to do something. I need a task. My mind shifts to Harrison Fields II. I'm working on a plan, but it's still shoddy, full of holes. The CIA job that seems a lifetime ago would have rejected such lousy planning in a second. But if I don't act, I'll be forced to keep pulling on the worried mess even more.

I dial Kaw once more, hoping to put at least one thread to rest, but as before, there's no answer. I'll be home in two days, and I hope to God I don't find my old truck parked there.

-33-

"You've been quiet all afternoon," Victoria says, setting aside her computer on the patio table. She's reviewing her notes and is ready to leave for the event. She looks smart in a pleather skirt and a flowy white top.

I'm beyond preoccupied. My whole body feels like a cocked fist, ready to fly in any direction. Twice I've left the condo and called Kaw, along with other errands, but he never answers. And my attention is divided with watching the clock and making sure Victoria gets ready so she'll be gone before I head out on my mission.

I've enacted the beginnings of my unsteady plan. In forty minutes, Harrison Fields is going to show me the big house we drove by after lunch today. During my "wine run," I went out to the residence, to make sure there are no cameras this time, like the gas station.

"I have another book, if that's no good," she offers.

Clearly, she's noticed I'm not turning any pages in the one on my lap.

"No, it's fine." I roll my shoulders back. "I'm designing that law firm project in here." I point to my head.

She sips her iced tea. "You can change your mind and come to the talk."

I stretch, imitating what I hope looks like a guy with no worries, no hurries, no plans to teach an abusive asshole that he can't hurt animals without consequences. Thirty-seven minutes to showtime. "You said earlier I'd make you nervous. You go dazzle them, and we'll celebrate later. How long will you be gone?"

"About two hours, I think."

After I kiss her and wish her luck, I wait ten minutes. I leave the condo, the warm salty air a welcome scent. I'm wearing an extra-large blue button-down shirt and black slacks. Earlier at a Goodwill store, I paid cash for these and added a Cardinals ball cap, a sandy blond wig, and a pair of reading glasses. I also pick up a bath towel and two Ace bandages, and I've wrapped the Ace bandages around towels to invent an oversized middle. Disguise complete.

At a bike rental, I choose an orange bike from the long rack, take a ticket from a kid that smells like weed, and push off toward the pavilion.

I debated all afternoon how to get rid of the security guard, knowing I had no interest in hurting him. My plan will either work and I'll have Fields alone, or I'll merely be another guy looking at a house. Counselors say disappointment builds character, but in this case, if I don't succeed, the hot coal burning inside me might kill me. If someone did to my dogs what this guy had done to his girlfriend's—the screaming puppy, the traumatized owner, the emotional scars—I'd have tortured him to death already.

Thirty minutes later, I arrive near the two-story house, which is set up on a hillside at the end of a steep driveway. I leave the bike out of sight and walk up the drive.

Something inside me knows that what I'm doing is a whole new ballpark. Every other time it was the animal I'd gone to help, but this bastard needs payback for the horrific abuse he got away with.

I'm playing this by ear.

A black Mercedes is parked at the top, and the front door is just closing as I reach the steps. Breathing hard and sweating, I barely need to act out the part of the overweight guy I'm trying to portray. A writhing nest of snakes is crawling around inside—old nerves and new nerves firing together, slipping around each other.

Shit, Dardin. You can walk away right now, you know.

I picture Florence and Rome in excruciating pain, caustic poison burning their gums and tongues, and it presses me forward, stoking the rage.

I rap on the door and then push the ornate entry inward and force my voice much higher than my natural tone. "Hello?"

The light inside the expansive room is lazy and diffused and would certainly set a homeowner at ease. I pull the baseball cap lower over my eyes. Although the heavy-rimmed reading glasses keep slipping down my nose, they're a great distraction. The visual correction in the lenses was the smallest I could find, but my vision still warps, creating a surreal world.

Voices come from another room, discussing something. Harry didn't come alone. Option two, I'll play the part of a simple house hunter. I would have rather had him to myself, but at least I'd considered this possibility.

I call out again, pleased that my voice sounds steady to me.

Fields, the puppy torturer, walks through an arched doorway, matching his billboard photo. His mugshot wouldn't have shown this side of him—clean, rich, entitled.

He sticks out his hand. "David?" He's wearing a smile, but it looks rotten.

"Yes." I cross the few steps to the center of the room and reach for his hand. "Harrison, right?"

The burly bald guy I saw at the boat walks into view. He squints my way and then moves to the front window and faces out. "Where'd you park?" There's an edge in his voice.

I hook a thumb over my shoulder. "I hiked up from the Edgewater Hotel. This looks a helluva lot closer than it really is." I wipe my brow. "But I'm never going to lose weight if I don't keep at it." I stroke my huge belly, hoping I won't be going through a pat down. "This is what a month on the Riviera does to you."

Fields studies me, still smiling. "Haven't been to France yet."

And if things work out the way I hope, he never will.

"Oh, the missus and I. Marseille is our favorite spot on earth." I gesture toward the ceiling. "But this. This house will be a birthday present for her if I'm taken with it. What say you show me around?" In my black slacks and brown shoes, my hope is I look like a guy who bumbled into some bucks. No one they should worry about.

The security guard and Fields exchange looks.

"I'll be outside," the guard says. He pulls a cigarette pack from his pocket and moves toward the back door, the opposite of where I want him to go.

I clasp my hands behind my back to keep them from shaking.

I follow Fields, barely listening to details about the weatherboard and stone construction, the 3,800 square feet, the four bedrooms and three baths, and the wrap-around porch with 260 degrees of views. As nice as that is, it's the other hundred feet of porch I'm interested in.

He doesn't know that I've already looked through the property, the outside at least, this afternoon when I staked out the place and left a few items to execute my plan today.

We move through the top floor and return to the kitchen when I ask, "Is the neighborhood safe?"

He looks surprised. "Yeah. Why?"

"You have a bodyguard." My heart picks up its pace. Maybe I can ask to see the backyard, then ask for the guard to give us a little space. I keep my tone light. "We don't need them in Milwaukee."

He pauses then says, "I had a bit of trouble a few weeks back, so Bart tags along once in a while." He twists a large gold ring on his right hand, something with a college insignia. Daddy probably paid his way through that institution.

"You're not mob, are you?" I hold my hands up and step back.

He shakes his head, and a genuine smile appears. "No. Just a stupid girlfriend problem." He raises his hands as if to say, "you know how that is."

"Been married too long, I guess." I pause as if I've remembered something, then snap my fingers. "Wait a ding dong second. Weren't you just on the news?" Maybe I should keep it cool, not bring it up, but I need to see his reaction. If I read guilt on his overindulgent face, maybe I'll leave. Walk away and let his conscience do the job of corroding his self-assured ego.

He looks away and heads out to the back deck. He feels shame, but not guilt. He just wants it to blow over so he can move on with his life. I follow in the heated waves of anger trailing behind him. I can feel the cords in my neck stand out. I'll never get him alone with his guard dog here.

The deck is long and sturdy and gives a lovely view of the other wealthy homes here with their tall trees and manicured yards, and beyond them is the wide expanse of the ocean. Fields studies the water in silence.

Bart paces and smokes, pretending we aren't there, but his sidelong glances say he's fully on alert.

Shit. There's no good way for me to step off the porch and pull the items I stashed there. My fingers twitch, but I try to follow what he's saying.

"My girlfriend's dog got sick on my watch. That's what you heard."

Is he fucking kidding? Got sick?

Then he laughs. "Ex-girlfriend. I gotta stop dating stupid girls."

Heat rises in every pore on my body. My fists clench. I want to run for the turkey baster hidden under the porch and push the plunger full of drain cleaner down his throat the way I planned. But it won't work. The guard will stop me before I leave the deck.

"You don't sound too smart yourself." I move closer.

My words have their effect. Fields stiffens and the guard turns our way. "Who the hell do you think you are?" His friendly pretense is gone. His eyes are drilling mine, and I'm thankful for the thick glasses.

"There's a vigilante group out there taking out assholes like you." I chuckle, a forced, crackling noise. My hand stiffens in preparation for plan B. "Sounds like you'll spend your days watching your back."

"You need to leave," he snarls.

The guard is behind him, turned our way, sensing the tone between us has changed, but he hasn't yet moved.

"Yes, I do. And I need a real estate agent who will be alive by the time the house closes." The flicker of worry I see in his eyes is satisfying. "I'll let myself down these stairs." I pass by him and although he gives me a wide berth, I lunge. With one hand, I jam stiff fingers into his windpipe at the same time I plant my fist below his ear feeling the satisfying snap of his jaw hinge. The CIA taught me a few good moves.

His eyes say "Motherfucker!" but only choking sounds come out as he drops to his knees.

The guard is already moving so I don't wait around. I sprint down the steps and run around the house. Out in front, I jump a neighboring hedge, barely clearing it, and charge down that driveway.

At the beach access alley, I change in the beach pavilion, unwrap the padding and remove the hat and wig. I drop those in a can outside a food stand, where they'll be lost in the sandwich parts and wrappers. The clothes and towels go into a big Goodwill bin near the showers. I pull the bike from the rack and pedal toward the rental shop. I never look back.

I pedal for several blocks before finally slowing down a bit. I escaped capture, but the relief is barely a salve on the ulcer burning inside me. I failed the mission.

I scared the shit out of him, that's something. But once again, he will get off without any permanent change to his life. He could forget today and continue on with no repercussions.

I wander the streets. My stomach is an acid bath, so I look around for a sandwich shop or some place to disrupt the churning bile with some carbs. Frank's Hotdog Hut offers a pastrami on rye. I eat it at one of the small picnic tables and watch the steady stream of beachgoers, keeping an eye out for the bald bodyguard, but of course I don't see him.

The whole thing had been an iffy plan to begin with. What had happened to the neatly arranged pieces I'd imagined earlier? Get him alone, hit him with the cleaner. Watch his eyes as he feels the very pain he put that dog through.

I crumble up the sandwich wrapper and toss it in the trash, having eaten the sandwich without really tasting it. I could try again tomorrow—we have the condo for another day and a half before we fly back, but if he has one guard today, he'll have ten tomorrow. Maybe getting to his boat would have been the better plan, but that fucking guard made it nearly impossible.

Deep inside, I know all I gave the guy was a busted jaw and weeks of eating with a wired mouth. The failure still makes my stomach churn, but it could have gone worse. The guard could have caught me, turned me over to the authorities. It is time to call it quits on Harrison Fields II.

After another hour, I return to the condo hot and frustrated. Victoria is in the kitchen making Long Island iced teas when I walk in.

"Just in time," she says, flush with excitement. "I was hoping you'd be back soon."

"How did it go?"

The grin on her face looks permanent. "Spectacular. They want me to create a website with them so we can share information."

"Do you know how to do that?" The computer stuff is Martian-speak to me.

"They'll train me." She hands me the drink and clinks my glass. "Here's to expanding into other states."

The drink is cold, strong, and burns a path inside me. "I'm so proud of you."

"Thanks. Oh, you might like to see this." She pulls me to her computer, to the headlines. "Look. That vigilante group killed someone else out west."

My mind cartwheels through the idea that VAPPA made the national news without me doing anything.

But there it is in bold typeface—Vigilante Group Strikes Again.

Fear flies around me in rough circles. I imagine I hear beating wings, but it's my heart pounding in my ears. Victoria's next statement sounds muffled, but I catch the word "puppy."

"In Kansas again?" No need to pretend—I'm genuinely confused.

I wait for the reply, although I have no idea what is coming.

"No." She shakes her head and scrolls down the article. "A place called Sandy, Utah. A guy beat a rottweiler puppy so badly it nearly died at the vet's."

Although my head nods, nothing inside of me feels agreeable. Utah? What the hell?

"The dead guy, Jeremy Smathers, threw the dog in the ditch behind the house, and his girlfriend took it to the vet. Locals have been holding a protest all week because he only received a fifty-dollar fine. Seems someone took it a step further."

"In Utah?" A copy-cat killer. "Was there a note?" is all I manage since she's waiting for my reaction.

"Yeah. The story said it's somewhat different from the first."

I'll bet.

She leans toward the article and reads, "In quotes it reads, 'this man has been VAPPA-ized. It's our major purpose.'" She looks at me. "Weird, huh?"

I nod because I've forgotten how to breathe.

Major purpose.

My time with Kaw rises up to engulf me, like a filthy tsunami wave, filling my ears with an ocean roar. Kaw's message to Lloyd said he was "getting out on the road to find his major purpose." Literally.

Driving my old truck.

I take a long swallow from the drink while I sort through the possible consequences. This is bad. I need to get to Kaw. I mentioned VAPPA one damn time. He's mentally intact enough to have read this story from Utah and acted on it. I misjudged him. I need to talk him out of doing this again.

"Did the story say how this guy was killed?"

"He was run off a back road…"

Once again, my truck.

"…and beaten to death. He works at a big copper mine on the west side of the city and someone found him dead on one of the empty stretches of road out there."

Too many connections. "That's crazy," I mutter.

"The FBI has formed a special investigative team." Victoria closes her laptop. "Let's go for a swim."

My legs are unsteady enough I'm not sure I'd make it to the shoreline. The FBI. Maybe that's why they shared this note but not the previous ones. They have a different tactic than the local police. They want to give enough information to the public so that they get curious. Start looking at their neighbors, their cousins, that weird guy at work. I bet their tip line is going crazy.

I pull her into a warm embrace and say into her hair, "I'm not feeling that great. I grabbed a couple of raw oysters while I was out. Stomach's flipping around right now."

She looks a little disappointed but doesn't say so. Instead, she pats my shoulder. "Maybe tomorrow."

The thought of one more day here is nothing short of claustrophobic. Kaw was the link between Foster and me. If he got arrested, would he turn me in? Mention me? The bill of sale is backdated; I sell used cars all the time. My mind is already constructing its defense in case Kaw keeps at this. He will get caught, and he'll eventually mention me. I'm certain of it.

"Yeah, tomorrow." I finish the drink and toss the napkin in the trash under the sink. "If I go to bed, do you have something to do?"

"Not a problem." She kisses my chin and turns to the deck. "I'll read."

That'll keep her off the computer and away from any new headlines. I need time to think about what to do.

I barely slept all night, but finally came to a decision before dawn. I've just gotten off the phone with the airlines and made the change.

I step out of my room and see that Vic is already out on the deck with a coffee. I debate the pros and cons of the conversation I'm about to have with her. I have two special people in my life, and she is one of them. I don't want to hurt her feelings or make her angry enough to be done with me. But I can't stop what I'm about to do.

She turns as I drag the deck's sliding door open. The ocean breeze carries a heavy mix of salt water and sunscreen. Seagulls circle overhead, their cries lost across the wilderness of dark-blue water.

"Good morning." She sets the cup down, and her eyebrows lift to match her smile. "I was just about to come in to see if you'd died."

I sit sideways on the chaise next to her so I'm facing her way. "I had a rough night but I'm still here."

"I'm sorry you didn't feel well." She touches my hand. "We can just be lazy today."

I set my face into what I hope is an apologetic look. "I'm sorry but for lots of reasons, I have to fly home early."

The waves murmur disapproval in the background. I study the line where the ocean and the sky meet, and it suddenly calls to me. A place to disappear, a peaceful end. I could walk straight out there and let it take me away.

She blinks and then sits up and swings her tanned legs so they're touching mine. Her eyes search my face as she seems to digest this information.

"Too much togetherness?" She nods. "I get it."

"That's not it." I take her hand. "This weekend has been great. I'll do it again if you're willing."

"I'm feeling discarded." Her eyes narrow. "You can't even stay one more night?"

How can I do this to her? She's an amazing girlfriend—nonclingy, sexy, intelligent.

"It's Rome," I lie. "Lloyd wasn't specific but said he's acting funny."

"Oh, no." She stands. "I hope he's okay."

"That's what I need to go deal with." I lead her into the condo. My bag is packed and waiting by the door. "I've called a cab so you can use the rental car through tomorrow."

She cocks her head and frowns. "Seriously? You just decide to leave without discussing this?" She chuffs, an exasperated sound I rarely hear from her. "I would have gone back today with you, Wyatt. My event is over."

"I didn't want to take you away from this great place. You never get to relax like this. And we agreed to not finish out the weekend together if one of us needed to leave."

Tears prick her eyes. "And clearly you can't stand to stay another day and half with me."

I reach for her, but she steps away. I can't blame her.

"I'm sorry, Vic. It's not about you. I love our time together."

She crosses her arms. "Yeah. Give me a call when you find out what's the matter with Rome."

"I will." The kiss I intend for her lips lands on her cheek as she turns her head. There's disappointment in the set of her chin.

"I'll pick you up when you land in Cleveland."

"Well, let me know if that works." She shrugs. "I can get a ride."

"Nonsense. I'll be there." Have I ruined us? I avoid eye contact as I grab my bag and turn to leave. I'm desperate to get home, but a veil of gloominess drops over me. I do love her. This weekend solidified that for me. She's perfect in every way, and more than that, she puts up with me.

But she absolutely can't learn of my connection to Kaw, to VAPPA.

That would be the absolute end.

~34~

Back at the junkyard, the day feels long and bleak for several reasons. A summer storm comes out of nowhere, carting the heat of the season up against an expected downpour. Rain falls in sheets from the quilted gray expanse as the sky loses its customary good charm. Pissy. The sky and I are both responding the same way.

I stop at Greta's, barely, and tell her I'm back early. I give her the "long story" excuse and make it into the house with the dogs in tow before the deluge starts and the temperature drops.

As the dogs settle in around me, I call Victoria's phone from my cellular and it goes to voicemail. I leave a message saying all is well with Rome and it was a false alarm. I ask her to call me back.

To stay busy, I'm filling out paperwork for my business license renewal when the home phone rings.

"Wyatt. Where are you?" Cory Kaw Speers. He acts like I've stood him up for a prearranged event.

"Hey, Kaw." I fight to keep my tone casual. "I was on vacation. Just found out you called."

"Hey, I'm sleeping great, and those dead soldiers have stopped marching around at night." Apparently, he didn't need a reply from me as he charges on. "I joined the group that's rescuing pets."

I picture him pacing, his speech matching a pattern of stop-and-turn movements.

My pulse quickens. "Is there a group doing that?" I feign surprise.

"You told me about them."

I clear my throat. Could his phone be bugged? I doubt it. "I told you about a vigilante group that is killing pet abusers. I didn't say they were rescuing any pets."

"VAPPA in Kansas took those horses. Now I'm on board in their western division." Across the thousand or so miles, pride is evident in his voice.

Hail spatters against the roof, like buckshot on tin, and I flinch at the first volley. "Then I'm glad you called. You probably haven't heard, but now there's a huge government group looking into those killings. They're everywhere and they *will* find the members."

"They will?" Pride shifts to paranoia.

"Yup. All of them. You can't hide from the FBI, Kaw. Get another purpose. Something under the radar, but not this VAPPA deal."

He's silent, then says. "Shit. Just when the truck was working for me. That investment sure isn't paying off, and that's the honest to gooseneck truth."

I shake my head at his word choice. My mind sifts through new ideas to send him in another direction. "How about cutting and hauling wood for the locals? Or garbage. Old people need garbage carted away."

The phone goes quiet. Do I hear crickets in the background?

"That's a lot of insignificance. I'm not wrapping my head around any of that at all."

Poor guy. His crazy switch is stuck in the on position. He probably isn't wrapping his head around much of anything. I need to get that old truck back so I can destroy it. I could trade him for another from the yard if he'd drive it to me. It's a risk, but it feels better than just waiting around for the cops to figure out the connection between Kaw, the truck, and me.

"Hey, Kaw. You thinking about upgrading that truck anytime soon? I have another one that's a whole lot better. Same price." I pause, then add, "And it'd be a vehicle that you didn't actually drive to Utah."

Distrust bleeds through his next words. "How do you know that was me?"

"I'm only guessing." I have to stay on good terms with him until he agrees to bring the truck back. I'll crush it and that will be the end of that.

"Maybe I'm not done, and I'll go after that guy in Maryland," he snaps.

A vein pulses in my forehead. An hour ago, Harrison Fields II hit the national news; some wacko tried to hurt him and his security guard stopped the attack. The article hadn't included details about the attack, and it said he'd been released from the hospital. Interestingly, it was Fields who believed that VAPPA came after him disguised as a house hunter.

"VAPPA is everywhere, Wyatt," Kaw says with increased vehemence. "We're on the West Coast, East Coast, and all the hellish plateaus in between."

"You really have to stop, Kaw. You'll get arrested and lose that truck if you don't."

"I might unjoin that group"—his words are short and angry—"but I'm keeping the truck."

"Well, if you change your mind, I'm only a couple of days' drive away."

"I won't." It's nearly a scream, then the line goes dead.

Did I scare him enough so he'd lay off the vigilantism? He is like a fire that starts after the tornado rips apart the town—a disaster inside of a disaster.

While I wait for the evening news—something I've watched more in the last month than in the last four years—I write a letter to the State of Montana and ask for a copy of my birth certificate.

I grab a pad and start to sketch new ideas for another project. Elaborate treehouses that I dreamed of living in as a child. After forty-five minutes my concentration fades as Kaw's words blink off and on in my head.

Before I left Maryland, I had the cab stop a block from the house for sale and grabbed the items I'd stashed under the back deck. The fact that an investigative team was assigned to the VAPPA killings truly means I'm done with that vendetta. Now I need to make sure Kaw is done. If he's caught, even a rookie cop will see the flashing red arrow pointing my way.

The dogs are pacing inside, but the ground is too soggy to go for a run so I snatch the radio control car from the cupboard in the mudroom and we do the next best thing.

The junkyard property claims the belly of a wide valley, with the main road dropping down from a hilltop about a quarter mile in each direction. If sixteen cars pass in a twenty-four-hour period, it's a banner day or a funeral out at the old Belton cemetery, and with a clear view in either direction, I know what's coming long before anything reaches the house, so that makes it perfectly safe to let the dogs get their energy out on some solid pavement.

Once we're on the side of the road, the dogs get excited. We haven't played "cars" for a while. I send the small car bouncing off on its big rubbery tires to the east ten seconds before I give them the command, "Bambi."

They turn into black-and-brown torpedoes as they launch themselves after it, scratching for toeholds on the wet blacktop. Once they reach the car, I skid it in the other direction, and they head back my way, trained to not actually bite the toy. That action requires the command, "grizzly bear."

They run themselves out in fifteen minutes. The day is crawling toward evening as I pack the toy car away and settle the dogs with dinner. I pour a whiskey, neat, and sink into Gramps's living room chair.

The dogs drop on the braided rug in front of me.

"You know, I'll bet that crazy guy goes into hiding." Sometimes a guy just needs a sounding board, and for me it has always been my dogs. Keesha, until she died, and now these two.

The dogs look my way then slump their heads on their paws, eyes still lifted toward me. If there was a dialogue bubble over their head it would say, "Here we go again. This is going to take a while."

I sip the drink, relishing the burn as it heads to my stomach. "He'll hide out, afraid of the government finding him." I pause. "You two wouldn't have liked him. He's unpredictable, for one. And he never said he likes dogs, but I know he's a fan of birds."

I'm in their western division now.

Who am I kidding? Kaw has never had this kind of power. He's not going to stop looking for other vigilante opportunities, and God knows the world wide web has a thousand to offer.

Trickles of fear run down my back. The second he's caught and questioned, I'm done for. I need to think of a better way to stop him, short of killing him, which I have no interest in doing. He's a broken bird. I need to convince him there's a better nest of opportunities out there waiting for him.

How could I have been so stupid to tell him about VAPPA? Not in a hundred years did I imagine he'd process and act on that information.

The news is full of vigilante killers, pluralized now because of the cross-country incidents. Ohio, Kansas, and Utah. I almost put a pushpin in

Ocean City, Maryland. As much as I hate Fields, I'm glad I walked away on that one. The FBI would be tracing travel between the West and the East Coasts. They announced they are looking for multiple offenders. They have that part right. I suppose I can thank Kaw for that, since the FBI task force won't be looking for a single perpetrator.

I check my watch; eight p.m. and Victoria hasn't called. Has she caught on to my lies about Rome? Or is she miffed I left her? I don't blame her there. I'm a terrible partner when it comes to spending long hours together.

But I'm confident our relationship is solid. We've established a year-long pattern, and it's working fine. She stated early on that she didn't want someone who hooks onto her and is there all the time. She said she doesn't like nice boys. She wants someone who is emotionally roughed up.

She got that with me.

Now if she'd just call, my confidence will return that she's still happy with her choice.

The next morning, I awaken early, blurry-eyed and exhausted from a restless sleep. The whiskey last night had the opposite effect on my nerves and wasn't the liquid anesthesia I expected. I might as well have slugged down a gallon of espresso before bed, I was that wired.

As soon as the junkyard opens for the day, I sell some engine parts to a guy for an old Malibu he's rehabbing for his son, and an older gentleman comes by for a windshield out of a Volvo. None of it helps distract me for long. I try Victoria's phone again. She must be enjoying her last morning at the beach before leaving for the airport.

I receive the lawyers' okay about the mural in the form of a manila folder stuffed with a thick contract. Demanding lawyers. I sign the many pages marked with small tabs then stick it in the return envelope to send back. It will be nice to bury myself in the new project.

I walk the property edge before stopping by the slack-lime shed to check the mixture in the troughs. It'll be perfect for the big horizontal relief of a lateral phoenix rising out from the lobby wall.

I throw balls to the dogs and watch two hawks wheeling overhead, enemies by nature, now in a slow dance against a backdrop of bunching white clouds.

The phone jangles, but I don't make it to the office in time to answer it. The machine offers Gramps's cheery message, and then comes a click of a hang up. I need caller ID.

I check my watch. Five hours to go before I leave for the airport to pick up Victoria. I hope to talk to her before she gets on the plane, but the flight is only an hour and a half, and she probably figures we'll see each other soon enough.

I retreat to my studio, pull out my sketchpad, the one reserved for my mother. Flipping through all the versions I've drawn over the years, I stop on the one most like my mom, right before she left Montana. She has the start of a smile like she has a secret to share. Her long, brown hair is parted in the middle, and a thin, paisley-patterned headband crosses her forehead and holds her hair back. I drew her in wide leg jeans and a peasant blouse, sitting on a log, relaxed, one hand holding a cowbell. We carried the bells to scare off the black bears when we headed into the forest to pick blackberries.

I flip to a fresh page. Sketching a few lines, I try to capture the visage of my mother, twenty-six years later. Soon, I've drafted an old woman and it's obvious all joy is bleached out of her life, leaving her slouched and waiting for the end. Hard-shelled, clinging to a dried-out routine, no reason to change anything.

Tearing the page out, I crumple it. I'll hold on to the happier version for now.

My leg bounces as I anticipate seeing her again. As soon as I can get legal access to my mom, I'll go to Manzanola to pack up her sad life and move her near me. I can't imagine she'll want to live here in my dad's childhood home. She clearly seemed to hate him in that letter I found.

The phone rings, and this time I dash from the studio into the office and snag the phone on the fifth ring.

"Hi there," I say, a bit out of breath, assuming it's Victoria calling me on her way to the airport.

"I'm looking at hours of pure ugly driving."

The earth tilts for a second as I register Kaw's voice. I hoped to hell he'd disappear like dandelion fuzz in a gale. Migrate to a new piece of ground, put down a withered seed, and start over. I didn't want him casually dialing me up.

"Kaw. What's up?" I tie a towel around my waist, hoping for a short talk.

"Sometimes a soul gets all occupied, all full of conflagration."

Here we go again with him sharing the disjointed ribbons of thoughts swirling in his head.

He continues, "I got a burning and it's feeling deep-seated indeed."

There's no way to know what he's talking about. He probably doesn't know either. "Are you worried about something, Kaw?"

"I've got preoccupations now." His voice holds an edge of blame. "Ever since we talked."

My palms start to sweat. "About the FBI looking into the VAPPA group? Is that what you mean?" I fist pump the air. I've scared him off the vigilante path.

"Yeah. I'm seeing eyes everywhere."

My next words spool out with the calmness of a counselor. "You don't have to worry about them as long as you don't do anything like that again."

He's silent for a second. Then he says, "What if they get to you? Ask you questions? I mean, you know all about Utah. You're the weakest link in our cross-country chain."

Rivulets of panic rise in me. I don't like him using *our* as if we're a team. This guy is dangerous, having gone off the rails of logic and reasoning a long time ago. "Well, you don't have to worry about me. I like you."

"Hmmm. I thought so, but I don't always know. Can't always catch on to the emotional signs and signalations." He burps, but it's not followed by an apology. "Like when you asked for the truck back. That spooked me."

I drop into the office chair, the conversation going on longer than I want. "I only want to upgrade your truck, no extra cost to you. No hidden agenda." And in that second, I hope he refuses. I don't want to see him, don't want him here.

"Why would you do that?"

"Well, when I met you, I thought you needed a break. Something good should come from that bleak childhood of yours." I pause. "But, like you say, it's a great vehicle. Just park it for a few weeks and don't draw any attention to yourself."

Silence fills the earpiece. I wait him out.

"Okay." He pauses. "You're a rare bird. I'll keep you."

"Mutual respect is good." Will that make him happy?

"I'll bring the truck back tomorrow night. Or the next day. Sometime."

Fuck.

"Yup. But first, late tonight I'm heading out on one last VAPPA mission. Been on the interwebs looking for new arrests. Found one that's round about on my way to you." He pauses. "Gotta visit Colorado. A police report says an old lady pet hoarder there is killing cats."

Electricity shoots through my body as the room spins. I rapidly blink to bring the office back in focus, but by then the hum from the receiver tells me he's hung up.

-35-

I take small steps as I dress and gather a change of clothes. My mind says that if I take my time, I'm not really putting something in motion I might regret.

Once the ricocheting thoughts stop banging around in my head, I have a few definite ideas strapped to a chair that I can focus on. Kaw is without a doubt talking about my mother. With her recent arrest record posted online, it must be her. My rage duels with the need to get to him, but I'm also angry with myself. By visiting my mother's house, getting the authorities involved in Pueblo to help her, I'm probably the one who set Kaw in her direction.

It's time to go plead with Melinda and take Mom back with me.

Kaw said he was leaving Wyoming tonight, after dark I suppose, and then he has over a four-hour drive. I'm leaving Belton in five minutes and I have nineteen hours ahead of me, eighteen if I push it. Her address should be hard for him to find since the house is registered to a Shirley Doolittle. I half expect he'll never locate it at all, but I can't take that chance.

Flying to Denver and renting a car is out. In case this turns ugly, I can't have any paper trails. And I don't anticipate this going smoothly, especially since he's nearly impossible to reason with.

I move the dogs to their house and climb into a black '83 Trans Am. Although the Lotus is faster, Kaw would recognize it. I point the car west, knowing there will be lots of uncluttered highway where I can open it up. I haven't decided how I'll stop Kaw, but in my duffle bag are two vials of fast-acting insulin and a syringe. No bleach and no damn turkey baster this time. Gram was diabetic and I never threw her medications out. Determining what the shelf life of insulin is, I have no time for. If I inject someone I've knocked out, I'm sure it will kill them soon.

Hours later at a rest stop, I decide to get Melinda involved. I use a pay phone to call the Pueblo office. It's three in the afternoon Colorado time. When she answers, I jam my finger into my other ear to block out traffic noise near me on I-70.

I tell her who I am then add, "I'm worried about my mother's safety. Could you check on her for me?"

Her voice, rancorous at best, responds to my question with her own inquiry. "And how do you know she's unsafe?"

Because the guy who's going to kill her told me so. "I have a bad feeling, and I'm usually right about them."

"Sure," she chuffs. "Any tips or bad feelings concerning the stock market you want to share while I have you on the horn?"

"It's not a joke, Melinda."

She releases an exasperated burst of air. Then she queries, "Any luck on getting your birth certificate?"

"I've written to Montana. It's on its way to me."

"Huhn." She pauses. "We just got Patricia settled back home after she was so upset. I'm not going to frighten her again unless you can tell me something definitive."

I debate my choices. I can alert the state police, saying Kaw has stolen a truck from my yard. I can tell them the bill of sale is forged or something—if he was smart enough to hang on to it. The problem is Cory Kaw Speers isn't entirely crazy. In his lucid moments, Speers could convince someone of our association then trace the truck back to the photo from the gas station in Kansas.

"I'm telling you about a gut feeling. All you'd need to do is call her." I silently curse. "I'm heading her way right now, but I'll arrive late tonight."

"Well, my gut feeling tells me that you don't have her best interests in mind." The phone clicks off.

My only choice is to drive faster.

As evening drops in, my head is screaming with the uncertainty of what I might find. Schizophrenic weather is the order at sundown, from a sullen wind that suddenly turns into gale, followed by a volley of water.

What if Kaw does find my mother's house? Would he really kill a woman? He said pet hoarder, and he would know her name from the police report but as I found out, it's not that easy finding her house. He could ask for Cleone and my mother would deny that was her. Best-case scenario—he never finds the house in the first place.

My phone rings and I flinch. I haven't set up caller ID so I take my chances.

"Hello?"

"You on your way?" Victoria's voice is peppy. "I can't see where you parked."

My eyes cut to the clock in the car. Shit. "Oh my God. You're at the airport."

"Of course I am." She pauses. "Let me guess, you're not."

"I'm so sorry." I talk fast. "I got a call about my mother. I'm on my way to Colorado."

"Seriously?" She snorts. "I would have called a friend if I'd known."

She's perturbed, a rarity for her.

"You're upset and I don't blame you. I was prepared to pick you up when the call came in." How could I have forgotten her? Greta could have gone to the airport if I'd asked.

"I'll be able to hear all about it later. Right now, I'm tired and have to inconvenience someone to come get me." The click in my ear sounds like a small explosion.

The fact that everyone is hanging up on me should tell me something. Everything is circling back to bite me in the ass.

It was only a matter of time, I guess.

Fear seeps around the edges of my vision. My mother *is* in danger. The FBI has VAPPA as a pet project, which means they may be zeroing in on me, and now I have to figure out how to make Kaw stay quiet.

My orderly world is corkscrewing down a dark rabbit hole.

I jam the accelerator to the floor. Maybe by morning, I can solve at least one of those problems.

At one a.m. I cross the Kansas border into Colorado, with about two hours to go to get to Manzanola. Flashes of doing this same drive come back to me from nearly two weeks ago, after my second kill. With all that's happened, it's hard to believe it's only been that long. And what a disaster this whole thing has become.

As the next two hours pass, I play with a scenario of how I'll rescue my mom, pack her in the car, and get her out of there. She'll believe that I'm her son once I reminisce about our clandestine chipmunk rescue, all the days we spent picking berries, how she taught me to swim in an ice-cold lake. Melinda can't stop my mother from moving to Ohio. The cats most likely were removed during their last visit, the junk in the house supposedly will be cleaned up soon. My mother doesn't need to be stuck in that old, dirty house, her tiny room no more than a goiter attached to the side of a crumbling wooden beast.

I try to visualize the property. Woods in the back, dead trees out front, a long driveway to announce my arrival. I'll park down the road and approach the house through the cornfields next to it, on the chance that Kaw beat me there.

I enter the outskirts of Manzanola again, passing by dismal blocks of cheap housing, signifying that neither the owners nor renters care.

Passing the post office, I make the final turn toward the country road and my mother. I've no reason for the swell of happiness inside, but it's there anyway. I pull my foot from the accelerator, excited I'm returning now and not in a few weeks.

When I see a glowing light on the horizon ahead, I'm confused. I must have made a wrong turn, because I'm heading toward the brightness of another town and not the open flat land surrounding my mother's house. It's in that moment that the wailing of sirens cuts the peaceful night in half and I glance ahead again.

The terrible truth descends. No city lies ahead. The old mansion is engulfed in a massive fire.

My chest tightens, my heartbeat repeating the phrase *I'm too late. I'm too late*.

Flashing lights fill the road behind me, and I yank the car onto the grassy shoulder. Two fire trucks, a police car, and an ambulance scream by, rocking my car in their after-surge. Energy bleeds from my arms and legs and for a moment I'm paralyzed.

Then I shift the car and hurry after the vehicles.

She may be fine after all. I need to see the mansion for myself.

A lane parallels this road and I take it, my lights off as I near the house. The fire consumes the darkness around the building and the huge blaze lights the entire scene like a gigantic theatrical production, with harsh lights in the center, diffusing to gray in the wings. Silhouettes of actors running in front of the light take on a theatrical atmosphere. I stop as the flickering brightness pulses into my car, and a sick feeling rises in my gut.

The small shed is gone, a smoldering pile of debris, the first building the fire hoses reached.

No one could have survived this inferno.

In my mind, I see a horrifying image of my mother burned alive, asleep in her makeshift slouchy chair and ottoman bed, well past midnight, believing everything is all right in the world.

Tears fall down my cheeks. I'm a terrible person.

In the mirror, the dashboard lights illuminate my face. It's mask-like, hollowed out and frozen in place. I no longer recognize myself.

Minutes pass. The blaze grows and shrinks against the black canvas of night, a demon's laughter, if that's even possible.

Tendrils of smoke reach the car, toxic, full of poisonous fumes from thousands of melting photos, plastic, and paint.

The fumes burn my eyes. There's nothing I can do here. The realization sits heavy and rancid in my stomach. I was never meant to have a mother; the message is clear. This is my punishment for waiting so long to do anything about helping her.

Suddenly, I have an all-consuming need to get home to my dogs, to hold them close, to curl up in my bed with them.

Like so many other desperate times in my life, I flee.

-36-

Two hours later, close to the Kansas border, I pull into an all-night diner, shutting down the engine and stopping the car on the busted-up cement pad that serves as a parking lot. The place is proudly unrefined, not giving in to any push to remodel or remake itself in the last four decades.

At the red Formica counter, I take a seat. It's five a.m. and there's one other person in the place, a guy hunched over a table, with a scruffy beard, distracted, holding a cigarette with a half inch of ash at the tip.

A waitress slides a single-sided plastic menu in front of me. She flips a cup over and pours coffee without asking if I want any. Her face is weathered, and any negotiation she made with youth is long gone. Peach-brown lipstick settles in the cracks around her lips, and her eyes have dark rings under them.

The night shift must be hell.

Her voice, smoky and abused, reaches me. "I'm having trouble reading your mind, buddy." She taps a fingernail on her order pad.

I point to an item and push the menu away, willing my brain to stop seeing the burning house. I focus on the waitress, her competent hands and her fluid movements from gripping the coffee pot to juggling plates, to working her pen across the order slip. This rehearsed dance becomes the most important thing in my life, and the distraction works for all of five minutes. Then, the truth takes over.

I'm a terrible son. I shot my father. I abandoned my mother to a fiery hell. My world is small, and not because it's always been my comfort zone. I don't invite in many relationships. Today, I may have lost another one that I cherish. Victoria is independent, but she doesn't need a forgetful, inattentive guy in her life.

I'm numb inside. My mother was right there in my life. I'd found her after all these years. As soon as Victoria said Shirley Doolittle, I should have raced back to my mother's house and convinced her of who I am. She'd be alive now.

My chin trembles and my throat aches.

I push the pancakes and eggs around after they arrive, their taste as questionable as my future.

Shock slows my thoughts, and my mind begins a sluggish crawl through options that I need to consider.

Heading home to my dogs is all I have. To my art career, to running the junkyard, to the warmth of Greta's companionship. Hopefully, Victoria will be there in the mix, but that isn't a given.

And to wait for Kaw.

He said he might be at the junkyard tomorrow, which now means today. In that case, I need to arrive home before him.

I shove the meal away, just as the diner door opens. A pair of state troopers swagger in and claim two stools at the counter, ten feet away. The guy nearest to me has hound dog side jowls, his dark hair swept back, shiny as if wet. The other Statey has a bulbous nose and eyes that go stony the second he looks my way.

My coffee cup commands my complete focus as I remember to breathe. Are they here for me? This will probably be the first question to pop in my head from now on when cops show up.

"Hey, Eve," the hound dog says to the waitress. "The usual for us." His thick thumb jerks back and forth between his buddy and him.

I hadn't noticed the waitress's name on her tag. What a cruel joke to be named Eve as she slaves away in a dump that's the antithesis of the Garden of Eden. She makes a clucking sound by sucking the side of one cheek away from her teeth. "Rough night, boys?"

Stony gaze says, "Been running between here and the Colorado border most the night. Got a firebug over in Manzanola with an APB out on his ass."

They know about Kaw. He may not make it to Ohio after all.

The one nearest me swallows his coffee fast, then stifles a belch by banging one fist on his chest. He smiles at Eve as if to showcase his good manners.

I've always been highly competitive, and right now that urge rises to the surface. I don't want these guys to find Kaw first. He's mine. That maniacal mess of sinewy muscles and fibers needs to die by my hand, and not be arrested and locked away by these cops. It was my mother he burned up.

"I've been through Manzanola," Eve says. "Kind of a sleepy place if you ask me. What'd he burn down?"

Bulbous nose complies. "A huge house outside town. A goddamn nightmare, we hear. About seventy years of papers and junk inside."

Pulling the bill toward me, I fish my wallet out of my back pocket.

The trooper next to me turns my way to follow my movement but keeps talking to Eve. "Going to be days before that blaze is completely knocked down."

Eve seems to have perked up with this newsworthy story. "Anybody inside?"

Stony again. "An old woman. The neighbors say she never leaves."

My chest constricts and my legs nearly buckle.

The jowly guy speaks. "We're getting conflicting reports about whether it was spontaneous combustion or an arsonist. Someone in town said a scrawny guy with his face all tattooed up with a bird. An eagle, I think they said." His partner nodded to confirm. Jowls continued. "He asked for directions about forty minutes before the fire started."

In my mind, I see Kaw's awful tat. The one his father pinned him to the floor and forced on him as a child.

"A stranger?" Eve shakes her head and wipes at an invisible spill with a plaid rag. "I don't like to hear a guy comes into town and torches something. Scary."

Eve has no worries from Kaw unless she's hiding a rap sheet for abuse.

The cop next to me wipes his mouth with his napkin and says, "That's the conflict. A county worker suspects the woman's son. He called to say he was on his way. Seems like he had some grudge or financial motive."

An angry flush rushes through me. How had Melinda gotten that nonsense from my call, pleading that someone check on my mother? It's right then, staring down at the bill, that I realize I need to leave before anyone runs my plates. This time the car I'm driving has my name on the registration, which Melinda would have shared with the authorities.

I stand, drop cash on the bill and set a saltshaker on top.

I'm almost to the door when I change my mind and turn to the lawmen. "Excuse me."

Everyone in the diner turns my way. The quiet that follows is as distressing as if I entered the building naked.

I raise my hands. "Sorry, I overheard your conversation. I'm traveling east from Nevada. I saw a guy like you described. At a gas station in Richfield, Utah. He freaked everybody out with that eagle face tattoo."

Stony stares hard, and I fight to keep my face relaxed.

He said, "What's he driving?"

I pretend to think hard. "Old truck, dark color. Didn't look at it too hard."

"You see which way he was heading?" The cop with the stare hops off his stool and pulls a phone from his belt.

"South. I remember thinking that if he's heading to Vegas, he looks like one unlucky bastard and he hasn't even hit the tables yet."

They nod and the lone guy at the table chuckles. I raise my hand again and head out the door, thankful that I'm a guy that looks like everybody's brother or neighbor.

Forcing myself to not look back over my shoulder, I face the diner again when I slip into the car. The police are still inside, talking on the phone, and no one is looking my way. I ease the car into reverse and don't stop until I'm out of the spill of lights. It's not until I pull onto the freeway that I hit the headlights.

Once I let a quarter mile disappear under the tires, I punch it, and other headlights dwindle behind me. I need to be at the junkyard before the Colorado sheriff department contacts my local sheriff's department and they come looking for Wyatt Dardin from Ohio who said he had a bad feeling about his mother's safety.

Now that I think back on it, I can't blame Melinda. First, I insisted Patricia wasn't my grandmother, then I called, contending she is my mother. Again, a call from me, crazy with fear that something bad was about to happen but offering no details as to how I knew that. Melinda has my home phone number. Police can easily stick a pin in an Ohio map and nail the junkyard to a wall.

I blow by Kansas City. The lights of that metropolis turn the sky to a muted shade of amber.

My mom is dead, and I was too late in helping her. I store those emotions away, push them way down, knowing all of them will take up much more room in my chest later.

The road blurs as I pull into the back lot of a Howard Johnsons so I can sleep for a few hours. I need to get home before the cops arrive. To get there to meet Kaw.

He's heading my way and I have to be ready for him.

-37-

The next morning, I shake away the trailing fingers from a terrible dream, sitting up sweaty and trembling in my bed. The bad images are the kind you tell yourself can't be real, that it doesn't mean anything.

In the dream, I'm back in Montana. It is too bright to actually be the homestead because there the pines lean in and shade the place most of the day, and it never got this light. My feet are tangled in vines, twenty feet from a cabin that's engulfed in flames. My mother screams for help from inside, but I can't move. As much as I tear the plants away from my legs, they instantly grow back.

Sitting up, I scrub my hand across my face and cut my eyes to the alarm clock. Midmorning. I've slept three hours.

Forcing the images away, I roll out of bed. After my two-hour nap in the back lot of Howard Johnson's, I finally reached the junkyard after sunup, relieved to find no FBI command post set up on my property. I called the dogs inside, locked all the doors, and with my buddies asleep on the rug, I passed out on top of my quilted bed.

I wander into the kitchen in my boxers and produce a pot of coffee. While the dogs eat, I explain my night to them. "Honestly, Florence. Rome. It was a shit show. I had so many plans. Now, I'm the number one suspect in that fire, and my mom's dead…"

I choke on the last words. That jagged pain needs to stay locked deep down inside for now, until I'm officially *informed* of her death. Feigned surprise and raw grief is what I'll show in that moment. "I can handle the police. But you know what I'm worried about? What happens when Kaw shows up here?"

The dog's quizzical faces tilt sideways, watching my eyes. "Oh, you'll meet him. As sure as hell, he'll find his way here. Like an idiot, I gave him a bill of sale with this address on it." I put fresh water down for them, and they start lapping it up. "He's flip city, but believe me, the lid sometimes snaps in place long enough for him to make sense. We can't let him talk to anyone."

I pause. "And he killed my mother, a woman who had already lost so much. This was to be her new start—she was getting help, and we'd be a family." I bite into a piece of wheat toast smeared with Greta's homemade quince jam. "You know, killing her goes against the VAPPA rules." I chew some more as I consider these words. A chuckle escapes my throat, but it holds no levity. "Not that there are any hard and fast rules."

Carrying my coffee to the backyard, I settle into a lawn chair where I flick balls to the dogs between sips.

Thoughts from my dream remind me of the good years before my mother left. The bookmobile guy was our lifeline to the real world. Jimmy Snarr drove a van full of books in the good-weather months and a Sno-Cat with a few crates of novels in the winter. Jimmy would ruffle my hair and usually brought me a Sugar Daddy sucker or a paper sack full of jelly beans. Mom always laughed and was full of life when he was around.

After Mom left, we stopped going to meet Jimmy because Dad said it was too much effort. Dad mail-ordered my books for school and they came to a PO Box in Missoula.

Jimmy was killed six months after Mom left us, struck by lightning while fishing on Lake Como. Dad told the story of his death with no sadness, just his famous smirk. "That man was burned to a crisp. But he served a good purpose."

A vision of my bookmobile friend, all blackened with blistered skin hanging from his face in rags, haunted me for months.

How cruel to be so cavalier. And what purpose did my father think Jimmy served?

Back inside, I refill my coffee.

No cops yet. No Kaw.

In lieu of sitting and waiting for the inevitable visits, I go with being proactive. I'm convinced my birth certificate is in the house. More than ever, I need to hold the evidence of my birth now that the two names on the document are deceased.

I sit back in the office chair and let chambers open and close in my chest. Who am I is a good question. An artist. Close that valve. A son. *Bang,* that one slams shut. A killer. Another door of certainty. But the fourth chamber? Not a father, not a husband. Not even a good boyfriend. I'm an animal lover. Greta is like a grandmother to me. Neighbor Lloyd mentions that he thinks I'm weird, but I know he likes me. The kids at the Boys and Girls Club seem to idolize me.

But do I like me?

My conscience feels rumpled, like an unpaid lawyer with big rent and no one to sue. I'm in a foul mood for many reasons. Even though I would most certainly have been caught, I hate that I didn't take care of Fields in Ocean City.

I wander the house. I want to call Victoria, but I'm afraid of that conversation. She'd fare better without me in her life, with all the uncertainty swirling my way.

The dogs stay on my heels as I take the stairs two at a time, heading to Dad's old room, the one he had as a kid. A powerful, empty feeling is in the air.

I unload all my father's army mementos. I'll burn them later.

At the bottom of the musty box, I spot a piece of paper under one of the cardboard flaps, the corner barely visible. I carefully pull it free. Once unfolded, I smile when the word "certificate" comes into focus on the face of the paper. Finally. Proof of my birth.

"The hell?"

This is a death certificate. Within seconds I've moved from elation to shock as if I've been shoved into an entirely new room. Blaming lack of sleep on what I think I see, I hold it away from my face for a few seconds, then pull it close and squint harder.

Name: Wyatt H. Dardin.
Date of death: October 11, 1973.

I'm ten that fall, but apparently, I died. Cause of death? Lightning strike.

I slump back against the bed frame, forcing my eyes shut against the room's tilt, and fight to breathe in the room's stale air.

My face feels so rigid one harsh word would break it to pieces.

At least he served a purpose. My father's words about Jimmy Snarr. Dad must have bribed one of his coroner or sheriff buddies to dummy up the original record and change Jimmy's name to mine.

My mother's words in the letter she'd sent my father now have some context. *I just found an apartment for us and now you tell me he's not coming. I hate you and your family.* This and other letters must have gone back and forth between my parents, a tug-of-war about where I would live. With the pressure of losing me to her, my father brought out the big gun and shot my mom's dream to pieces with this death certificate. My father's cruel and final blow to the woman who dared to leave him.

My father never sent in an official report or I never would have been able to get a driver's license or join the CIA if I was registered as dead. He must have found a way to copy Jimmy's death certificate, then change it to my name. I guess that was easier than just making a fake one from scratch. Or maybe the idea only occurred to him when Jimmy died. Either way, it was dummied up for my mother's eyes and never made official. Still, Dad went to a lot of trouble to put together something that looked legit enough to keep my mother away.

I push away the temporary shock of yet another reason to despise my father and instead allow a ripple of elation to run through me. My mother wanted me to live with her. She pulled something together, an apartment, some sort of life just for us. Then she learned her only son was dead and gave up on life. Returned to the ruined family mansion and let it crumble around her.

I wish I could reach back through time and follow my mom out of those woods when I was nine. All my stored hate and anger may never have existed.

No. That's a cop-out. Does anyone ever have what he or she needs?

A faded echo of Gram's voice dances through my brain. "If wishes were horses, beggars would ride." A childish saying, probably passed on from her Depression-era parents.

I stand and stomp the box of memories and documents flat. "I didn't want horses," I growl. "I just wanted normal." The dogs cower, unsure of the direction of my anger. I should have tried to kill him way earlier.

The dogs' ears swivel backward, then they're on their feet and charging down the hallway.

I take in a sharp breath. My heart jackhammers as I get to my feet, then a scrape of a foot on the floor in the hall downstairs sends it into overdrive.

Christ. Kaw is inside the house.

I rush down the stairs, trying to decide between talking to him or jumping straight into a tackle then tying that crazy bastard to a chair and making a plan that will keep us both free from the law.

Instead, Victoria tentatively steps around the corner just as I pounce on the landing.

"Hey, Wyatt."

Once the shock of seeing her wears off, my past and present collide. "Oh my God. It's you." I consider how much to share with her and in what order to spill it. I speak with the caution of a guilty teenager, stammering, placing each word safely out in front before venturing to offer the next word. "Victoria. So much has happened."

She nods but doesn't smile. "I can imagine. I wanted to see you up close because you sounded a bit out of control on the phone."

"My father." I hold up my faked death certificate. "I can't believe what a horrible thing he did to my mother."

"You're putting yourself through *that* ordeal again?" She tilts her head to the ceiling and lets out a long sigh. "And upstairs, I heard you. You were talking to…?"

"The dogs." I shrug. "They're great listeners."

The entryway is small, and she is within arm's reach in four steps, but she only leans closer, studying my face. "I have to know you're going to be okay."

I run a hand through my hair, realizing I must look terrible. "I'm dealing with some things. And I'm such a flake. Who picked you up at the airport?"

"John Pike."

Her last boyfriend. "Okay." It's impossible to keep jealousy out of my tone. "Hopefully you didn't wait too long."

"Nope."

"Are we okay?" I need to prepare for how alone I may be if she's done with me.

"I'm going to let you sort out whatever is going on." She crosses her arms. "If you bring your mom here, I want to involve her in my program."

I teeter dangerously on the edge of telling her my mother is dead, but I couldn't know this fact yet without having been there.

"This will sound awful, Wyatt, but the things you've been saying lately. The way you've been following that VAPPA case. I don't know…do you have something to tell me?" She jams her hands into the pockets of her hoodie, but they continue to point and gesture, like two ferrets struggling to get out. "The kid at the Boys and Girls Club, his dad disappears. This VAPPA is blamed. Then you leave on a road trip through Kansas and sure enough, VAPPA pops up again at some guy's horse ranch."

How has she been holding this all inside? I force a laugh. "I guess that could be me. And I made it to Utah and killed that guy the night we slept in Ocean City, right? They say VAPPA did that too, you know."

She pushes ahead, her voice steady. "I know how much you love animals, even over people sometimes." She pauses. "I'm not sure I'd be upset if it's you." She rubs her temples. "Call me amoral, but I'm leaning toward supporting this group, or this person, or you."

"Victoria," I say. Her suspicion sends a jolt through me. She would be okay learning I'm a killer? That stops me for a moment. I want to tell her everything, to confess. But can anyone accept that their partner can kill, cover his tracks, and above all lie about it straight to their face? I smile. "I'm not that guy. We can talk through all of this, just not right now." Kaw could be parking outside as we speak. He'll verify what she suspects, and she'll see the truck. I have to get her out of here.

She eyes me carefully and I see that she's very serious. "You have secrets. You've always had them, and I've accepted that. I just want you to let me in. Know that I'll try to understand; I'll hear your side." Her eye contact intensifies, and I can't look away. "Let me know when you're ready to share. You know where to find me." She turns and waves goodbye, her hand fluttering over her head.

One minute later, I hear her car door open and close.

She surprises me. What was I thinking? She's smart, so of course her mind would look at every angle. All those weeks ago, I had clearly been overly interested in new updates about Randall. And during my road trip, it wouldn't take much to wonder if I'd taken a slight detour in Kansas on the way to Colorado. Would she really not care that I can kill and act like nothing happened? She says that now, but we all think we can handle the truth until we find out we can't.

I know I should work on my treehouse idea and get another trough of putty ready, but the thought of going to the lime shack and remembering what I dissolved there is more than my psyche can handle. Instead, I grab the leashes and call the dogs for a run. A little exercise has always helped me clear my mind.

The dogs jump up before I can attach their leashes, their short brittle barks pointed toward the front of the house. My heart kicks into defensive mode, knowing that whatever has them on alert probably isn't someone buying metal since I have no appointments for today.

My work boots crunch on the gravel as I walk to meet the sheriff's cruiser pulling up alongside the house. I wave, recognizing the deputies from their visit a month earlier. Breathe, dammit. I can handle these guys.

Bobby Neat Guy exits the car first, looking a bit broader than before. Once Doug Poole is out, he pulls at his belt, his stomach hanging like a lip of snow over a roofline. He carries a manila envelope.

"Welcome back." Whole chunks of my life seem to have fallen into disrepair in these last weeks since they were here. I will my heart to slow down. This is a much-needed visit. Someone has to inform me that my mother is dead before I can tell everyone and then plan a funeral.

"Afternoon." Bobby sticks out his hand. "You remember us?"

"Of course." I accept, knowing he's checking for sweaty palms. He'll get none of that from me. "You're Bobby Smith."

Bobby arranges his mouth into something short of pissed off. Not the reaction I expected; maybe this isn't about my mother. Or he's terrible at delivering tragic news. He points to the road where another car is pulling in. "We brought friends this time." His smile is more of a gloat.

The two men step out of the deluxe Pontiac in suits, and I don't need to see their proffered badges to know they're federal. They're introduced as O'Conner and Peck.

I shake their hands, keeping my face neutral and friendly, if a little puzzled. "Nice to meet you."

"Can we go inside?" Bobby asks. "We have a few more questions."

I give the dogs the stay sign and motion the men to lead the way. "Can I get you a cup of my so-so coffee?" We're all passing through the kitchen.

Their mutual grunts sound like four affirmatives.

Once we're seated around the table with filled mugs, Doug pulls out a police sketch and hands it to me.

It's supposed to be Cory Kaw Speers, but it hardly looks like him. The tattoo resembles a smashed chicken, the lines forming nothing even close to an eagle on the side of his face. I frown and turn the page to a diagonal, squinting as if trying to identify what the tattoo could be.

Peck speaks, his voice precise and polished; I'll bet he got all As in FBI school. "Do you know this man?" he asks, pointing at the sketch.

I shake my head, deciding to say little and keep things simple. I hand the paper back. "Who is it?"

Bobby produces a pocket-sized notebook and opens it. "We hope you can tell us." His eyes never leave my face as he flicks a pen and writes something on the page. "You got any friends that look like this?"

I sip my coffee and add a loud swallow, never breaking eye contact, moving my gaze from one to the next. What has connected Kaw to me? "I don't have many friends, so I'd remember this guy for sure."

"We know," Bobby says, a smirk splitting his broad face for the first time. Of course, they've investigated me. And Bobby doesn't like me much. What does he think he knows?

"I have two neighbors I'm chummy with, I occasionally see my girl-friend, and I have no relatives nearby. And none with a tattoo like that, whatever that is." I raise my mug to my lips. "Other than that, my parents are gone, and my grandparents died several years ago. Maybe I'm one of those odd types that raises suspicion?" I sip the coffee again, even though the jolt is the last thing I need right now.

O'Conner leans forward. "Your parents. Where are they?"

They regard me unemotionally, but I keep my face arranged to look what I think is the normal amount of somber for this subject, though my gut fills with spiky burrs. "My dad died in an accidental shooting when I was eleven, and recently I discovered my mom lives in Colorado. She left when I was a kid." I look back and forth between Bobby and Doug, the local guys. "I've been in contact with a social worker out there. We're trying to put together a plan to help her with her mental illness."

"Monday, you called that social worker," Bobby says. "Reported something bad was about to happen to this woman in Manzanola. What was that all about?"

"A bad feeling." I look away and stand, as if the feeling still weighs on me and I'm not ready to talk about it. I cross to the sink and dump my coffee then lean against the counter, my hands in my pockets. "After all these years of knowing nothing about her, I finally found my mother. It feels like, I don't know, Karma or fate or some shit is going to keep us from truly reuniting." My heart lurches as I process my own words. There will be no reunion. I shrug it off. "I got off on the wrong foot with Melinda. I understand that she protects her clients, and she's right, I need to produce a birth certificate before she'll let me legally help. Then I started getting that feeling, so I asked her to send someone to check on her. That's all." I raise my hands in surrender, then rebury them in my pockets.

Their faces say they know this. I hope this confession short-circuits their questions.

Peck this time. "Where were you Monday night?" He slides the sketch of Kaw back into the folder.

Here it comes. I raise one eyebrow. "Here, working on a big project I have coming up. If I'm not at Victoria's, this is where you'll find me."

More scribbling on the notepad. Bobby squints my way. "Anybody vouch for that?"

"All of my friends." I shrug.

They stare. Not even a chuckle. I'm not sure why I taunt them except it calms my nerves in a strange way. I relent. "Next neighbor over, Lloyd Barney, keeps a close eye on me. He watches the place while I'm away." Lloyd drinks from noon on and enjoys his blurry evening TV viewing. I doubt he'd see aliens land at my place once the sun has set.

I nod toward their sketch of Kaw. "Besides showing me the guy with the circus face, what else brings you here?" I struggle to form the next set of words. "What happened Monday night?"

Peck pushes the chair back and stands, an obvious move to be at my level. The others follow his lead. I try to judge Peck's age. His eyes say he's grown weary of the hunt while his face holds onto its youth. It's the deep creases at the back of his neck that peg him around middle age.

His smile doesn't suit me at all. I want to punch him for being so smug. And Bobby seems equally willing to share the bad news they've come to tell. There's a twitch on his lips.

I use my hands to steady myself as I press into the counter and wait for the words. A flicker of hope flashes through my chest that the cops at the diner heard wrong. Melinda might have heeded my call and gotten my mother out. There's been no news about a murder or arson. Surely a story like that would be headlines.

"Somebody burned your mother's house to the ground," Bobby says.

Hazy evening sun filters through the blousy kitchen windows, but it doesn't soften the blow. I grip the counter and flinch, surprised at my own reaction to the old news. "What? Was she hurt?"

Please, tell me she wasn't there. My inner voice sounds like a childish plea.

O'Conner brushes something from his sleeve. "One person was found inside. In the basement. The coroner's working on the identification since the fire was a complete inferno."

An uncontrollable shiver races through me. I don't even know what my face is doing, but if it's responding to my feelings, it must telegraph my grief. Mom lived alone. If there was one body, it had to have been hers.

"Sorry," Bobby and Doug add almost at the same time.

The feds offer no condolences.

I draw in a ragged breath, and it's no act this time. The full weight of her death blankets me, depleting any childish hope that she's fine. She died a horrifying death, trapped in a basement. Was she cowering there, in an area of the house I never even saw, a dank, cluttered area, balled tightly in fear, shielding some cats, as smoke filled the room?

Tears run down my cheeks, and I palm them away.

I close my eyes and picture Cory Kaw Speers. Why had I told him about VAPPA? As much as I'm to blame, my inclination to kill him is raw and personal.

"Hey." Doug moves next to me and drops a hand on my shoulder. "You going to be okay?"

Numb, wordless, I nod.

The silence that follows offers a reverent feel, nearly taking shape as it fills the space between us. I bob my head again. "Yeah. I'll make it." My voice sounds rough and alien.

Before they leave, Bobby turns back toward me. "As much as we like your coffee, I hope we don't need to come back here a third time."

He doesn't seem to expect an answer and I don't offer one. Maybe I'll never learn why he doesn't like me, but that's the last of my concerns now.

Outside, I make sure the officers get past my dogs. I can't tolerate anything else going wrong.

The cops and the FBI fall into a conversation next to the cruiser. I walk to the side of the drive and call the dogs. They lean against me, and I press their heads into the sides of my thighs, more for my comfort than for theirs.

I scan the long sloping hill to the right, leading to the west, to the ashes of my youth.

The hair rises at the back of my neck. On the horizon, the beater truck I sold Kaw lazes its way down into the valley. My valley. He will be at the wheel and arrive in a minute and a half, and the cops can't leave as he's pulling in.

He'll confirm that I recently sold him the truck in Wyoming and that I told him about VAPPA.

I shoot a look toward the police cruiser and the Pontiac behind it. The Feds are in the Pontiac and closing the doors. I stay the dogs and jog to the car, knocking on the hood as it eases backward. They stop. I make a rolling motion with my finger, and Peck's window hums lower. Bobby and Doug walk back and gather around the window, puzzled looks on their faces. I stand to the front of the side mirror, so the men are facing forward as I talk. I need to keep them here just a bit longer.

Forty-five seconds until Kaw arrives.

"Sorry. I'm starting to think of things I need to do. Just wondering who I call about my mother's remains? Not sure what happens in a case like this. I want to make arrangements to have her buried in our family plot up there." I point to the forest, another angle to keep their view off the road behind them.

Thirty seconds.

The men look toward the forest.

O'Conner speaks, all business, a practiced answer from years of delivering bad news. "You'll have to wait until the coroner makes the identification and this is no longer deemed a criminal case."

I slowly nod. "Any idea how long that can take?"

Twenty seconds.

O'Conner lowers the volume on the police scanner before he says, "Honestly, it could be a while. We've got leads we're following. That takes time."

Ten seconds.

I pray Kaw doesn't find the driveway on the first try. I'm screwed if he pulls in behind these cars. I said I didn't know the guy in the police sketch yet he's about to sail into my drive like an old friend.

Doug adjusts the watch on his meaty arm as if it's uncomfortable. "The county knows about your cemetery?" His head flicks indicating the tree line.

Out of the corner of my eye the old truck passes slowly by the front of the entryway, then it picks up speed and keeps going. I sag in relief. Kaw saw the lawmen. His paranoid thoughts must be slamming from side to side in his mind right about now.

They're waiting for my answer. O'Conner glances in the rearview mirror, but the road is empty.

Now I want them out of here as fast as possible.

"The cemetery is listed as a historical site. The county mapped out all the cemeteries dating back to the 1700s. It's that old." My insides squirm like I ate a plate of live eels.

Doug again. "Call the county, make your burial plans, and we'll let you know when this can be wrapped up."

I tap the hood as I step back. "I'm not going to go as far as saying I'm glad you came by, but thank you for giving me the awful news about my mother." My voice breaks and I swallow hard.

Both cars back out and head to the west after they pull through the front gate.

I head inside and work on sketching out a new art project, but after an hour, I can't focus so I head out into the fading daylight, waiting to see if Kaw returns. My feet are too heavy to pick up and move. My life unfolds in film snippets around me, a slow carousel of visions. My childhood with the initial loss of my mother, then Keesha's death, my father's death, the years of regrouping that covered my late teens to age twenty-two—when I discovered working for the CIA, organizing and protecting dark secrets, healed me—then more loss with Gramps and Gram passing. Now my mother.

My last conversation with Victoria makes me nervous. She says she wants to listen, but what if she's tired of my antics? I should call her.

One task at a time. I need to look up the local mortuary's number. Figure out the preparations, then how best to honor my mother's choices of services. I shove the horrible image away of my mother's body burned to death. It will be a closed coffin.

I don't do either of those things. Deadened with indecision, all I'm focused on is killing Kaw in spite of my mental exhaustion. He burned my mother alive. He is a monster, and he needs to be stopped.

Until he's gone, my world is like a garbage bag pinned to a nail on a pole, rioting against the wind but stuck there until some big solution comes along.

Up until just over a month ago, I hadn't touched a rifle since my childhood. I head inside to the gun safe.

-38-

The next morning, I work the stiffness out of my neck, having fallen asleep in the armchair with the gun across my lap.

Where the hell is fucking Kaw? I thought he would come right back, give me the opportunity to get rid of him and move on to the next set of tasks filling my brain, but he never did. This throws off making any plans for today.

I drive a short distance into Belton, buy groceries and dog food and plug a few coins into the pay phone. Kaw doesn't answer his phone and I don't leave a message. Was he spooked enough by the cops in my driveway to return to Wyoming?

My need to kill him hasn't passed; I'm like a starving man chasing a sandwich. I've nearly worn a path in the wooden floor, pacing from the kitchen to the front room to check the road and back. His demise is all I can think of.

I try Victoria's number. I want to offer to be at her house at eight o'clock tonight. To talk. Her phone rings but her voicemail doesn't come on. I didn't know that was a possibility. If she turned it off on purpose, then I've taken too long to call her back and tell her my secrets or whatever. This may be the answer to the status of our relationship.

With a growing sense of feeling trapped, I walk the road in front of the junkyard and chuck rocks at car shells. I throw with everything I have—the louder the *twang*, the better it resonates inside me. I want life to be fair. I want kids to not feel pain like I have. It's why I love volunteering at the Boys and Girls Club.

But I've changed. When I killed Randall, I had to deal with the guilt and then the reasoning. I had to accept my calling to help those weaker than myself. Foster nearly strangled me to death and was willing to shoot all of his horses to prove his point. He had to be stopped.

I killed people and I'm okay with it. I can't be the only one who thinks about taking out child rapists and pet torturers.

A car pulls into the drive, and I stop midthrow. My heart throbs with an ancient warrior rhythm until I spot the words "courier service" on the side of the vehicle. Not Kaw, unless he's stolen a car.

Where in God's name is he?

A young guy jumps out and hands me a thick envelope.

I rip it open to find the first deposit for the lawyers' project. "Thanks," I say, signing the delivery confirmation.

The driver looks around the junkyard. His upper lip and chin sprout blond fuzz, but I'll bet he's not yet acquainted with a daily shave. "Cool stuff. Where'd you get it all?"

"Inherited it." I tuck the envelope under my arm and study him. Tall and lanky, he'd make a great center for a small-town basketball team. "You like old cars?"

"I do. I want a Corvette, something prime." He shakes his head. "I inherited a big Buick when my dad died. Might as well have left me a blinking 'nerd' sign."

Mine left me three boxes of memories and a warehouse of emotional baggage.

I laugh. I like this kid. "I've got twenty or more Corvettes here. You know where I am. Come back sometime. and I'll show you around."

As he slides into the truck's seat, he says, "You live in nowhere, man. If it weren't for the undercover cops parked up the road,"—he points in the direction away from Belton—"I'd still be driving around."

Swallowing hard, I fight to stay composed. "Accident or speed trap this time?" I know it's neither. They're watching me, or someone spotted Kaw's truck. Both options are a problem.

"Couldn't tell. They're just parked along the road in a plain car, but they reek of NARC." He laughs. "Probably sneaking a doobie."

"I wouldn't be surprised." I chuckle but it's more of a choking sound. I'm being watched.

After he pulls away, I study the empty road. No wonder Kaw hasn't come back. I have the FBI playing guard dog to the entrance of my valley, messing up my chance to get rid of him. I don't relish the idea of returning to Wyoming to do that, but I see no reason why he'd stick around here.

I place the envelope on my desk, adding the need to deposit the check into my account to the ever-growing list of tasks filling my head. But I don't want to leave the house, pass the cops, or give them any more reasons to be curious about me.

So I clear everything out of my studio and set up an extra-large table in the center, settling in for a few hours of layering slack-lime putty on the board. The activity banishes all thoughts of Victoria, my mother, and Kaw. The logo of the law firm's name rising from a crumbled building will be seven feet tall and five feet wide.

Three hours pass before I stop and grab a sandwich from the store and exchange a quick greeting with Greta. Thankfully, she left before the cops arrived yesterday, so I don't have to field any questions, and I'm not in the mood today for one of our usual friendly chats. I finish the sandwiches off with a beer and wave goodbye since it's midafternoon and has been a slow day. I head back to my studio, excusing my brusqueness with being mid-project. I'm making great progress, not only on the artwork, but at pretending Kaw has left the area and my property is safe.

Before getting my hands dirty again, I grab my mobile phone and dial Victoria. I wait through the ringing, hoping for her upbeat voice to ask me to leave a message. No voicemail again. I frown. I haven't talked to her since she left here yesterday. She uses this phone to run her company, so how is she getting messages?

She must really be pissed.

I change clothes and take the dogs for a long run. It barely stems the anxiety coursing through me, but the dogs are happy and tired when we return.

"It's just us right now," I say, kneeling between them in the backyard, pulling their heads to my chest. "We're going to be all right. I can pull out of this deep hole I've dug." I squeeze them some more and Rome licks my chin. I want to lick back, I'm that grateful for these two.

Inside, I grill chicken for all of us and try to stay busy. I check the cell phone for messages a hundred times. My breathing stops every time there's a creak in the house. Why haven't I noticed how noisy this old place is?

Stop overreacting.

The house is confining, so I head outside. The dogs chase the ball in the backyard as night slowly drops in, its ghostly gray fingers pulling their way across my grass, stealing the color from the trees and the stacks of cars.

When night has erased every last bit of light, we go inside and I lock the house up tight.

If there is an indication of things to come, the weather is delivering it. Wind arrives and strong-arms the trees and roofline only moments before rain pounds the world into submission.

When the phone rings, I flinch, and my roller chair jerks backward a few inches. I stare at the rotary dial, willing for it to tell me who is on the other end. The police? Cory? Victoria?

I'm wrong on all accounts. It's Greta.

"Wyatt. Something weird is going on."

"Are you okay?" I sweep a shaky hand across my forehead. Kaw could easily have stopped at her place.

"I'm hunky-dory, but some cops came by my house asking about you." She pauses. "Are *you* okay?"

"Oh yeah," I say. "They came by yesterday and brought the FBI. In fact, I think they're still up the road." Maybe I should have mentioned something to her earlier, but I had no idea the cops would start investigating my life like this.

"It's crazy, but they seem to think you have something to do with an arson incident in Colorado. Is this about your trip there a couple of weeks ago?"

My chest constricts. My mother is dead. "They've got some ugly guy pinned to that." After I take in a slow breath, I bring out the big guns. "The truth is it's not just arson now. It's murder. My mother was in that house."

She gasps. "Oh my stars! When did you learn this?"

"When they came yesterday."

"You didn't tell me?" She sounds hurt, and she's right. I should have said something, but I wasn't ready to tell anyone yet. "This is terrible news."

"I haven't been able to talk to anyone about it, so I'm glad you called."

"Wyatt, I'm not sure what the Sam Hill is going on, but the cops I talked to were thinking about coming back to your place with a search warrant."

The pockmarked ceiling tiles shape-shift in the glow of the tiny desk lamp. I've run through everything I've done since I killed Randall. The police won't find the old Firenza I smashed, but the cemetery is flashing a beacon for someone looking for dead bodies. I might as well have posted a sign that reads, "Fresh kill located here." I don't want my grandparents' resting place disturbed.

If they talk to Lloyd about the graveyard, he always jokes it would be a great place to hide a dead person.

I should pack up the dogs, buy a motorhome, and haul it to a remote place in the middle of Montana. Back to my roots. It probably wouldn't stop my ultimate arrest, but I'll get to see the old cabin once more, and from a grown-up perspective, maybe let go of some of my childhood demons before I head to prison.

Greta could run the store and raise my dogs.

Victoria would find a normal boyfriend.

But that's not me. I'm a runner, but I always circle back home. I have to decide what to do about Randall's DNA in the leach lines below the lime drains. If there is anything to be done. That's the only incriminating evidence on my property, but final reports from the field years ago clarified nothing much was left of a person after the same technique I used on Randall.

I'll sit tight and not dig anything up for now.

My mind made up, I head outside, the dogs at my heels for their last outing before bed. The sky has cleared, and the crickets are back at it, playing a high-pitched symphony.

I'm almost back inside the door as headlights sweep across the junkyard gate, preceded by the rumble of the old truck's engine long before it creeps up the drive.

Kaw has arrived.

-39-

K aw and I sit in the same dining chairs the cops vacated the day before. I've been able to keep my hands from shaking, but I have an eye twitch I can't control. It bangs out "Camp Town Races."

Greta warned me about a search warrant for my place, but the police won't need to look beyond the Eagle Man in my kitchen if they show up now.

"You got any booze?" Kaw asks around a mouthful of leftover chicken.

I wonder how he knew the cops were away from their post, visiting with Greta. Had he been watching them in the trees? Biding his time?

Kaw sits at my table and finishes off a half a loaf of sourdough bread and a jug of orange juice. His face looks worse than I remember. He pushes grubby fingers through his matted hair, and he smells like he hasn't bathed in a week—probably hasn't. He looks like a frayed rope.

"Sorry." I lie so easily these days. "Drunk driver killed my grandparents. No booze here."

"You're not much of a man then, are you?" He squints and the eagle on his face moves. "You gotta get over crap like that. I did."

I'm dumbfounded by his lack of insight, but I guess that's the reality of living with mental illness and past trauma without proper help. When I first met him, I was empathetic because he came across as an injured animal. Now, I can't excuse his failings. He killed my mother.

"Where have you been since we talked?" I sit across from him, maintaining eye contact. I need him to admit what he did.

He points a fork at me. "I went to Colorado. I told you about the lady killing cats there."

My hands remain fisted and pressed so hard into the underside of the table that it may start to lift. "Why her? There are hundreds of people arrested every day for pet abuse."

He stops eating and analyzes me. He's on alert, from something in my voice, I suppose. "She's one of the newest people listed out on that inter-web place you told me about. And it was close to my house."

Fuck fuck fuck. I really did just hand my mother to him. My fists con-tract tighter and I can feel them grow cold from lack of blood flow.

My silence spooks him because he's on his feet and yelling, "I knew it. You're in thick with the cops!"

I stand and raise my hands in front of me, a signal to calm down. "I most certainly am not." I want to hear what he knows—in particular, are the police still on the roads around my place? "Where did you see cops?"

"In your driveway yesterday." Pieces of bread spray down his shirt, and his face bunches in rage. "You brought them here to talk about me."

"Nope." I shake my head hard. "They buy junkers for their demolition derby from the yard." I cross my arms and pretend I hadn't seen him drive into the valley. "You've been in the area since yesterday? What've you been doing?"

"Hiding in the woods. Watching. Getting an insurance policy in place."

The hair on my arms stands up. I'm up in those woods most days with my dogs. There are only so many spots where you could see my place, none of them far from the trails I run.

I force a smile. "I'm glad you came here. You need to dump that truck and get another one. I'll give you a newer one, no extra cost." This sounds generous, but he isn't going to be driving anything new or old away from here.

His face forms a sneer, which also might be a smile. "Free *gratis*?" He sits again.

Nodding, I start to clear the plates, never completely turning my back on him. "Any vehicle that runs. We'll find a good one."

"Where'd you put your dogs?" His head swivels back and forth. "Nice specimens. Lots of potential seriousness there."

When he pulled in, I locked the dogs in their pen and quieted them. They will not be getting friendly with Cory.

"They're locked up for the night. Junkyard dogs, you know, kept dan-gerous for a reason."

I need to accomplish two things. The first is hiding the truck, and the second is a bit harder—I need to kill Kaw and get rid of his body. This won't be happening tonight. A new trough of slack-lime putty will take all night to drain. Then in the morning, more hydrochloric acid and he will disappear down the drain like Randall.

I have eighty pounds and five inches on him; he shouldn't be too hard to tackle.

"Let's hide that truck of yours," I say. "Then you can have a shower. I'll put you in the guest room for the night. You'll be on your way before dawn in a new ride."

He stuffs the heel of the bread in his jacket pocket, a vagrant squirreling away food for lean times.

Do not feel sorry for him. He killed your mom.

"Yeah. I got to leave and spread the causation some more," he says. "A son of a bitch in Kentucky cut off his dog's ears 'cause it wouldn't listen. Almost bled out in front of his kids."

My stomach turns and at the same time my interest piques. Kentucky wouldn't be that far of a drive.

I shake my head. I don't need a new problem in Kentucky. And I can't have Kaw leaving here with a new vehicle that can be traced back to me and connect me to another killing.

I motion him outside, following the bouncing circle of the flashlight I hold as we walk toward the truck. When we reach the back, I say, "I'll take it from here. I know where I'm going." I hop in the driver's seat, and Kaw protests for a second but climbs in the passenger's side. When I fire up the engine, I pull ahead. The feel of Foster's body rolling under the wheels comes back to crawl through my system.

It's no longer unpleasant.

I leave the headlights off and weave around the ghostly stacks of metal, finding my way to the back edge of the lot where several large willow trees hang low and heavy over a culvert—another teenage secret hiding place when I wanted a safe haven. It wouldn't survive a search warrant, but I'll have the truck cut up into scrap by noon tomorrow.

"Smart thinking," Kaw says, scrambling out of the cab.

"You have anything in here?" I look around the cab's interior.

"Always got stealth on my side." He taps his head, the movement barely visible in the moon's pale glow. "Bring nothing. Leave nothing."

I glimpse the sanity in his madness, and it's too lucid for my liking.

We walk back toward my machine shop. I need him to follow me inside. "How did you burn down that house in Manzanola if you didn't take anything with you?"

"I always carry matches. Smoker, you know. But there were drums of gas around the back of that dump. Easy to conflagrate."

The bastard and his incorrect use of big words. I want to drop him right here.

Twenty more steps to the machine shop.

"Did you see the woman in the house before you torched it?"

He stops in a circle of light from the shop's sensor. Confusion knits his brow. "I checked. Pissed me off I couldn't see inside too good."

I keep my voice steady. "The news said her body was in the basement."

"The news?" When he shakes his head, his hair swings back and forth, like dirty strings on a mop. "I walked through that dump. Crowded with shit, but it looked as empty as a hatchling's shell. Must have been hiding, a woman with guilty genes. I sure as shooting sent a message with the fire—'don't mess with animals.'"

I choke back anger. Five steps to the door. "You leave a VAPPA note?"

"Didn't have time. Place went up like Hiroshima." His hands mimic a mushroom cloud. "They know it's us. Got vengeance written all over it."

I roll the large doors open and flick on an overhead bulb. Once we cross the threshold, I shut the doors again. "You fucked up."

Confusion bunches his eyebrows when he realizes what I've said. "What?"

Taking a step away from him, I say. "You're a royal screwup. That was my mother in that house. You killed her."

He glances around the room, a rabbit planning his escape. "It wasn't your mother. It was some old lady on the arrest list from the interwebs."

"She was cleaning up her life; the cats were gone. She didn't deserve to die."

I can't say the words without a shiver of pain coursing through me.

He pauses and puffs out his chest. "Even so. You know the VAPPA rules. She had to be punished."

"*You* don't know the rules, asshole," I spit. I point to him, "And punishment? Like your dad did to you? You are batshit crazy because of it, my man."

Unconsciously, I slowly circle him.

His face goes flaccid, like someone unplugged him. If it weren't for the pulse of one vein in his forehead, he could be dead.

Kaw nods. He realizes we're no longer on the same side, but for some reason he smiles. "You did this on purpose. You are government issue, through and through."

"Not true. Back at the diner, I *wanted* to help you. Then, I tried to protect you by telling you to bring the truck here and I'd get rid of it. But hell no. You had to drive to Colorado first."

"I found a major purpose like I told you."

My laugh is a bitter sound to match the taste in my mouth. "West Coast division of VAPPA, right?"

He stands straighter. "Yes. And if you hurt me, VAPPA'll hunt your ass down."

"Unlikely." I move toward a table where I keep duct tape and rope. I need to subdue him. "There's no *they*, you know." I hook a thumb toward my chest. "You're looking at the entire group of VAPPA." I'm not worried about sharing this—he won't live to spread the word.

His eyes dart around, and he licks his lips. He's working hard to process that news.

My gaze moves to look at the table, and he uses that moment to knock me to the concrete floor, and my head bounces once. Lights flash in the back of my eyes. I roll out from under him and find my footing, although it's unsteady as I stagger away from his reach.

I've misjudged him. He's scrawny but tough.

"I knew you were bad news." Breathing hard, he spits the words my way.

"I was on your side until you started killing people." I don't like the ragged sound of my voice. A crowbar leans against the door. I judge the distance and leap for it.

He grabs the back of my shirt before I reach the bar. Our shoes scrape on the floor as we both fight for a toehold, throwing punches at each other. I push him away, and he staggers against a workbench. As I dive for the bar again, he's on me, and he swings a long wrench, connecting with my left forearm. The bone gives way with a crack and the skin lays open in a large flap. Blood flies.

Pain tears through my arm and rages on razor-sharp teeth upward to my neck and back. My legs abandon me, and I buckle.

I'm about to die, yet all my fear has flown. I accept this is the way my life wraps up.

Cory circles me. "I'm the kingpin now, motherfucker. I get to carry on the VAPPA name."

"Screw you." My words are on shaky ground like me.

He kicks my legs. "And I'm taking those dogs. I'm going to need protection out on the road."

My mind is far from clear, and the swirling fog striped with red pain makes him hard to hear, but his reference to my dogs wipes it all away. "Never," is all I say.

With newfound rage, I swipe his legs out from under him and clamber to a standing position, cradling my broken arm. He goes down with a satisfying thud.

"And your girlfriend…"

With the strength I have left, I kick him in the side of his head, not letting him finish any more threats to those I love.

He lies still, the rise and fall of his chest the only indication we aren't done yet.

Every movement sends a riptide of fire up my arm. I pull my bleeding arm through the arm hole of my T-shirt, then tuck the shirt into my jeans to create some stability against my body. Then with my good hand, I wind the rope around Kaw's arms pulled behind his back and tug him toward the giant magnet of the crane. Grateful for years of rope tying under Gramps's tutelage, it isn't as difficult as I expect to create a knot one-handed, though

I have to bend down and use my teeth to pull the other end to tighten it. That done, I step back, trying to ignore the jagged pain of my bleeding arm.

Kaw is still out, and his unwashed head hangs with his arms pulled behind him. The rope hugs him around the middle, lashing him to one of the three chains that hold the magnet. His legs are bent beneath him and will probably lose circulation after a while in this position. But I'll be back after I can fix myself up, and pins and needles will be the least of his worries then.

Working the duct tape is harder. Ignoring the grating pain of my arm that has bled through my T-shirt and created a warm, wet heat against my body, I wedge the roll between my knees and draw out a length, attaching the sticky end to the floor, then use my teeth to tear it. I wrap that across Kaw's mouth.

My vision wavering, I look down at the blood now dripping from my jeans. I must be losing blood faster than I thought. I turn out the lights and stagger to the dogs' pen. I hear Rome and Florence sniffing, waiting for me to release them. I open their door and let them push me up the steps of the porch, then into the house. They smell the blood, and they post up like guards around me, on high alert.

Once we're in the house, I lock up.

First things first, I need to get the pain under control, then stabilize the arm. I don't have time to run to an ER and get it looked at. Finally, I'll need to find a more permanent solution to getting rid of Kaw. Even though he's locked inside the machine shop, I'm not certain police agencies don't serve search warrants at night.

"*And your girlfriend...* " His words come back to me.

How does he know about Victoria? It doesn't occur to me to question that until now, but he must have seen her when he was watching from the woods. Victoria left not long before the cops showed up yesterday.

Rummaging through the medicine cabinet, I find half a bottle of morphine tablets. The dose says one, so I palm two and throw them back, chasing them with water. Searching for gauze and hydrogen peroxide—Gram's solution to cleaning every wound—I push aside her various prescriptions before pulling out the bandages.

I'll have to go to a hospital sooner than later, since my arm points a few degrees in the wrong direction and I have no idea how to correct that. The bleeding seems to be from a gash caused by the impact, not from the bone sticking out of the wound, so at least I don't need to worry about compound fracture.

My body movements follow the short phrases ricocheting in my head.

Clean off the blood.

Pour peroxide.

Apply antibacterial ointment.

Wrap it, tape it.

The room spins with each step; only the sink keeps me upright. Blood is on every surface I touch. I'll need to clean up the trail leading from the shed to the house too.

The dogs stand in the doorway, ears pricked on alert. "It's okay," I mutter. "He's not getting you two."

The process takes a lifetime to complete. Beads of sweat pop out on my face. How much time has passed?

To the dogs I say, "I'm going back out there to get rid of him."

I brush by them, cradling my arm. Folding a flowered twin sheet from the linen closet, I make a hasty sling, tying a knot with my right hand and my teeth. I duck my head under the knot and as I ease my arm into the sling, a scream flies from my throat. I grab the closet door for support and wait for my vision to clear.

The dogs hover and whine. I pat their heads and call them to the bedroom. The movement is too much for me. The room spins to gray.

It isn't morning, but it's too close to dawn to feel anything but abject fear, knowing how the light will soon warm the eastern sky.

"Dammit." I sit up from the bedroom floor where I'd fallen. The pain medication worked too well because I passed out all night. My arm has a dull throb, a deep and permanent feeling.

I wobble into the bathroom. My face in the mirror tells the story of my physical state. My skin has a whitish hue, graying almost, speckled with blood, grizzled with day-old facial hair. "You're a fucking mess, Dardin."

With my uninjured arm, I reach for the bottle of morphine tabs again and dissolve ten in a small amount of warm water then pull out one of my grandmother's syringes. Drawing up the liquid from the glass is tricky without the use of my broken arm, but I manage. My theory—and I'm winging it here—is that the entire amount will certainly kill Kaw since two tablets knocked me out for hours.

He'll slip away.

I leave the dogs inside and return to the shed carrying the capped syringe in my back pocket. Before I pull the door aside, I draw in a deep breath, then yank the door sideways and rush inside. Hopefully he's asleep so I can sneak up and plunge the syringe into his neck, leave, and let the morphine do the work. Then I'll have to figure out what to do with the body. Being injured, I can't imagine trying to lift or dig, but that's a problem for later. I flick on the overhead lights.

All the air in my lungs escapes.

He's gone.

The ropes lie in a pile at the base of the machine's step, the duct tape curled like discarded snakeskin. I spin in all directions, my eyes boring into every shadowy corner, trying to discern human from equipment.

At the steps of the machine, I grab the ropes. He gnawed through them like a goddamn beaver. Somehow, he got his hands in front of him and chewed through the cords?

Shit shit shit.

I cradle my throbbing arm, the sling doing very little to stop the pain as I scan the interior. He busted out the back window. Fuck.

My head swivels from side to side as I dash for the house. The morning is still somber gray, but my eyes adjust to the shadows. Where would he go? To the road? Flag down the rare car that comes this way? Would he be desperate enough to run to the undercover cops, assuming they're still out there keeping an eye on me?

Back inside, I debate going upstairs for my Glock, but I have no time.

I reach the gun cabinet, unlock it, and choose my grandfather's 30-30. It feels right in my hand.

At the door to the back porch, I call the dogs. Once we're outside, I lead them to the shed and let them sniff the rope that held Kaw. Outside the window, they turn in circles, picking up his scent on the dirt path leading off toward the junkyard. Thank God it isn't toward the highway.

"Bambi," I command, and the Dobermans take off.

I run as fast as I can, keeping my feet low to the ground, ignoring the excruciating shards of pain raking my arm as I push forward.

Rounding a row of cars, I find the dogs jumping up and down, circling a gold-colored Porsche. I raise the gun, approaching from the side, a clear shot at the sleeping person inside the driver's window.

This is too easy. Even out here, someone might hear a gunshot, so I set the rifle down and pull out the syringe. I'll shoot him full of morphine, get a slurry trough ready, immerse and wait.

One step closer and the image isn't right. The hair is too full, the shoulders too narrow. I stuff the syringe back into my pocket and yank the door open. Victoria tumbles out of the car to the ground, a limp rag of a woman, no sign of life.

A silent scream bangs around in my chest but refuses to exit my mouth. *"And your girlfriend..."*

Kaw had already taken her when he said those words last night. We drove near here when I parked the old truck, but I had the headlights off and was so preoccupied with getting Kaw in the shed, I hadn't looked this way.

"...putting an insurance policy in place."

An ocean's roar of hate fills my head. He'd already done this while I was plotting how to get rid of him.

I touch her neck. She isn't the icy cold I expect, but then again the inside of the car would be warm from the morning sun. She has a huge cut on the side of her head. Dark blood has run down her face and neck and soaks her clothes. It's dried, so he must have done this before he showed up at my house last night.

My hands shake as I gently lift her head into my lap to feel for her carotid. Do I feel a pulse or is it my heartbeat in my own fingertips? I'm afraid to move my hands to try another vein. What if I don't find a pulse there either? A sob breaks free from my throat. "No no no."

How long has she been injured? She left here a day and a half ago, but he could have kept her tied somewhere before hurting her.

Her cell phone rings from within her pocket. I grab it. The name of a guy I usually wouldn't want to appear is on her caller ID. Her old boyfriend.

"John!" I scream. "This is Wyatt. Victoria's been hurt at my place on Old Farm Road. Get an ambulance out here now."

I don't wait for a response, I don't care if he thinks it's a joke—any moron will hear the fear and panic in my voice. I hang up, then hear a twig snap in the distance.

I whirl in that direction and my dogs, who'd been sitting near me, clearly aware of my shock, now point their noses toward the noise and whine.

Kaw.

Pure rage fills every nerve, every cell in my body. "I will kill you!" My words bounce around the car husks and trees.

I gently lay Victoria's head on the ground and straighten her on her back. I can do nothing to medically help her. I kiss her. "Help is coming," I whisper. Waves of nausea sweep over me, but I regain my focus to my new plan of murdering Kaw.

The dogs are off toward the woods, not on the dirt road but in the weeds to the left side of it, leading up to the cemetery. I stumble to my feet, grabbing the gun, and follow the rustling sounds ahead of me as best I can, panting, stumbling, catching myself, almost dropping the gun.

I can't see him, and I know Kaw could hide in these woods for days. But this is my home, my land. My hand grips the gun. My aim will be off trying to shoot one-handed, and I didn't bring extra ammo, so I'll need to be close to get him.

The dogs lead as I cross into the high weeds. Within seconds my jeans are wet from the knees down. I duck under branches, moving without hesitation, following the swishing sound of the dogs in front of me. These dogs are nearly silent hunters, no baying to alert any prey that something is tight on their heels. The only indication they're moving is the ripple of grasses flowing past their bodies.

Walking forward in the gray morning light in a spastic dance, I push my right leg in front of me like a blind man's cane, then my left. My nylon jacket rustles, and I curse its noise, but it keeps my poorly bandaged arm from getting wet, so I ignore it.

I stop climbing, trying to get a feel for the direction the dogs are headed. I cross the dried creek and am in the trees now, navigating the steep side of the hill. Still lightheaded from the pain and what's happened to Victoria, I lean into the slope, finding footholds in the roots and branches to continue the climb upward toward the family graveyard.

The dogs stop moving. They've either lost his scent or they have him cornered. My hand tightens on the gun, finger ready to place on the trigger.

I crest the slope, entering the cemetery in the old section, away from the graves of my grandparents and Dad. The dogs stand in front of me, bristled, noses extended, bodies flexed to launch themselves. One command will do it. I hold off for the moment. I want him for myself.

Kaw is there, arms and feet apart, waiting. He holds a shovel over his shoulder in a baseball-player stance, looking as tightly wound as a rookie during spring training. My shovel, stolen from the machine shop perhaps.

His hands are covered in dried blood. His mouth looks torn and raw from gnawing the ropes, the dark wounds blending nicely with the ugly eagle tattoo spread across his jawline.

I stop. Here is the silence again, the morning's somber tones winning over the dark entrails from the night before. We study each other. He flinches as he spots the rifle, and waves of hatred roll my way.

I push them back with a question. "What're you digging?"

He must have broken ground a while ago. A foot of dirt has already been moved off to the side.

He smirks. "Something for you."

The gun hangs to my side, and I lift it a bit and let it drop down, like a shrug. "Really?" I ask. The question sounds as delirious as my thoughts. "You're the one not leaving this hill."

He laughs. "You shoot much with one arm?"

I rock my neck from side to side as if working out a crick. "I don't shoot much at all." Why aren't I panicked? Instead, I can see everything happening in front of me like a chess match, pieces of a carefully laid plan. This is where we would always end up, he and I. And today would be checkmate.

I raise the rifle this time, I let my finger rest on the trigger. "Carry on. You gotta go a lot deeper than that or animals will dig me up."

His face doesn't change, but he leans back as though he's taking punches. "Bastard. You were going to kill me." Spikes fly with his words.

"Yup." I nod pleasantly. "You killed my mother. And now I find my girlfriend half dead."

"Nope. She's all the way a goner." He shrugs. "She was pretty though." His voice is high-pitched, edgy.

My heart freezes at his declaration that Victoria is dead. That can't be right. I felt a pulse. But was it mine or hers? Pain rips through me. Almost everyone I love is gone. Maybe the bullet should be for me.

I glance at my beautiful dogs. My salvations during the lost years. Kaw will take them the second I'm gone, and that horrifies me.

I edge closer to him. I need something to steady the barrel on before I can take a shot. "Maybe you're right."

"I am." Hope flickers across his face for a second, then that thought seems to dissolve. "She's dead."

I gesture with the gun. "Dig."

Kaw punches the shovel into the dirt and digs a scoop of earth. He piles it to the side and buries the shovel again. In a flash, he flings the contents my way.

I turn as dirt rains down on my head and back.

He bolts for the trees, taking the shovel with him. I raise the gun but he's already disappeared into the forest.

I have no choice.

"Grizzly bear!" I shout to the dogs, their command to attack. It sends them charging after him. I follow the thrashing sounds and hear Kaw yell out. My dogs have never attacked a person, and I hate that it has come to this.

As I get closer, more growling noises arise and Kaw shrieks again.

Then my heart stops at the sound of one of my dogs screaming, a pitiful wail that hurts more than my broken arm. I fight the tightness in my throat and gather the raw pain inside and rush into the small clearing. Florence lies on the ground in front of Kaw, her chest hitching up and down, her front legs scrambling to move, her hindquarters motionless. Has he broken her back with the shovel? Her crying alternates, whimpers between yelps.

Rome circles Kaw. Kaw has blood running from his arms and neck, and I hope Florence got a good chunk of him before he did that to her.

Like a cobra, Kaw strikes with the point of the shovel, sending Rome sprawling at his feet. He lets out a sharp bark, then staggers back up, teeth bared and snapping at Kaw.

We're near the newer section where my grandparents' and father's markers stand.

I raise the gun, honing it in on a clear shot, but the barrel wobbles around even as I try to balance it on my broken arm.

Dropping to the ground, Kaw grabs Rome and drags the stunned dog a few feet. Rome growls but cannot turn to bite him.

I struggle to find a clear shot, helpless to do anything. "Let my dog go!" My scream bounces off the trees surrounding the graveyard.

Kaw laughs and holds Rome in front of him, a shield, balancing the dog on his haunches. Rome tries to squirm out of his arms. Cory Kaw Speers might be crazy, but he's also wily. He knows I'll never shoot if Rome is in the way.

How he has the strength to hold a thrashing ninety-pound dog in place, I have no time to consider. I scan the area in front and find my solution. There's one small spot behind Rome where Cory's head is barely visible. In my younger days I was a crack shot even while running. Do I still have it?

That's when a strange image flies through my mind from decades earlier. I'm in Montana, in the clearing. My father is half turned. He spots the bear coming up beside him. He yells, "Shoot it, Wyatt!" My hands are shaking as I raise the rifle. "Don't you fuck up, son!"

I see myself pointing the gun toward the bear's chest, and I know it might take all six slugs to knock him down. But a bizarre thing happens. I inch the barrel a millimeter to the left, putting the first bullet through my dad's head, then back to the right, I bull's-eye the next five into the bear's heart and the animal falls.

The instantaneous rage of an eleven-year-old who saw his dog shot to death just days before.

That truth is finally freed.

I drop to my knees behind my father's headstone, balance the rifle on the granite top and yell, "Setz!" the command that makes Rome freeze at the same time as I steady my breath, focus on the target behind Rome, and pull the trigger.

Kaw flies backward, his forehead and skull catapulting behind him. Acrid gunpowder burns my nose. The forest embraces the boom of the shot, sending it echoing off into the depths.

Rome tumbles to the ground, and I rush to him, dropping the gun in the scattered leaves and dirt. He jumps and licks at me, and I relish his gratitude, knowing I did it even more for me than for him.

I stand to see what's left of Kaw. He lies on his back, body crumpled, eyes staring upward. Where there should be relief I only feel regret. It all went on too long. He stole three loved ones from my life, and even if Victoria or Florence survive their attacks, our lives are forever changed.

I lead Rome to Florence, who nuzzles her as she lets out a small whine. I kneel next to her, trying to assess her injury. My voice breaks at her sounds of pain. "No. My beautiful girl," I mutter, "I can't lose you."

I sit that way for several moments, Rome glued to my side but shifting anxiously, obviously recognizing his sister is hurt.

The forest birds go quiet, and it's clear I'm not alone. I turn to see the blurry image of four policemen with pistols drawn and pointed coming my way.

"Don't move!" the command ricochets in the stillness, but by then the morning light, now eerily yellow, leaves me illuminated in a cone of pain, all from my own making.

~ 40 ~

The month has flown by since I shot Kaw, and there have been several surprises. The biggest one was a call from Melinda. Something in my voice urged her to heed my plea, and she got my mother out of the house hours before Kaw torched it. She and the police kept it to themselves, trying to flush out the arsonist.

The body in the cellar of the house was identified as Cleone, my grandmother. She'd been dead for over two decades, dying three years after my mother had returned to her family home and had received my father's letter saying I'd been killed by a lightning strike.

When the social workers asked my mother why she'd left her dead mother in the basement, Mom replied she couldn't let anyone take her or then she'd be alone. Whether her mental illness had begun to show itself all those years ago, or if this was the revision of that history through her current mental state isn't clear. But after that she moved into the little room at the front of the house, leaving the mansion as a shrine. With so much clutter, no one had been in the basement in all that time.

When the police showed up, I made one of them stay with Florence and call someone to come help her while I led the others to Victoria. Thank God and any other creator, Kaw had been wrong. She was alive, though she'd lost a good amount of blood and had a serious concussion that kept her in a coma for two days until the swelling in her brain went down.

I paced the halls of the hospital the entirety of that time, reviewing how I'd treated her these past few months. She wanted me to let her in, and sure, I had a lot of history to keep me from letting anyone close. But I also had Gram, and Gramps, and Greta. People who cared about me. And I was gonna lose Victoria for good if I didn't finally let her see the real me. Even the dark parts.

My arm was set and casted. I got news from the animal surgeon that

Florence's back wasn't broken, though the injury created swelling that affected the nerves. It will be a long recovery, and she may never be able to run as fast as she once had, but I will happily exchange walks for our daily runs if it means I can hold on to her a few years longer.

Greta cared for a very anxious Rome while I stayed with Victoria. He refused to eat and paced Greta's front hall until she finally took him to see Florence at the animal hospital. As soon as Rome saw her, he jumped onto the little bed, lay next to her, and refused to move.

The dogs will be home tomorrow, but until then, I've packed some things and am staying at Victoria's house where we share a room and a bed.

We've finished takeout from our favorite Thai place, and sounds of a late night talk show are our background noise as I pull Victoria close with my good arm, careful not to bump her too hard with my cast, which she signed in really big letters so no one else would have room.

The scar on her head where Kaw hit her with the wrench is starting to fade. It's a constant reminder of how I nearly got my loved ones killed by telling Kaw too much. Seems the CIA taught me nothing. Kaw followed her car when she left my house and ran it off the road. He hid it down a dirt road and kept her tied up in the woods for one night before walking her to the junk car on my property and knocking her out. She told me all of it when she woke up from her coma. Thankfully, she didn't have any major cognitive losses, though she seems to struggle at times with the names of things. My relief at her surviving Kaw hasn't dulled, and even as I sit next to her on the sofa, savoring the soft, sweet scent of her shampoo, the perfect way she fits next to me, I know that whatever our future looks like, my stupid hesitation to commit to us won't get in the way of our relationship again.

"And your mother. Will she be okay?" she asks, snuggling into me, her eyes on the TV but not really watching it.

"She isn't completely healthy." I sigh. "Her mind is full of shifting sand. We had a good talk this morning. Yesterday she blamed me for taking her cats away and burning down her house."

"But she's in your life again." Victoria puts a hand on my leg. "Something you've dreamed of."

I have a hundred questions for my mother, but all in good time. I bought a condo for her in a gated community ten miles from the junkyard. I gave her the inheritance my father's will left to me, now well over forty grand, and found a caregiver to check in on her daily to cook meals and monitor her health. I also gifted her a sweet-tempered tabby kitten, which she named Sammy. I made sure the cleaner who goes in three times a week is fine with pets and doesn't mind changing the litter box.

She and Greta have started to bond. Sometimes Greta brings her to the store and I find them laughing or talking about TV shows they watch, and they both like dime-store romance novels. It feels like the woman I met months ago, living in garbage and ruin, is barely related to the woman my mother is now. Her hair is cut short, revealing lovely eyes that squint when she smiles. She's still quiet, but when she talks her mind is focused and lucid. Turns out most of us can only be our best when we have a reason to live and someone to love.

One room in Mom's condo holds a growing miniature dollhouse collection, an activity she spends most of her time on. I've been supplying her with miniature objects that she paints and adds to the house. It's becoming quite intricate. Turns out, I get my artistic side from her.

Sammy is growing fast, and has the loudest purr I've ever heard from a cat. The cat was spayed when I bought her, and Mom has gotten tired of my reminding her that she can only have one cat in the condo. It's the limit.

It's become very clear that we all need limits.

"I still find it funny my mom had an affair with Jimmy, the bookmobile guy we met each month. No wonder my dad said she was too wild for the woods."

Victoria laughs. "I can't get the image out of my head that they did it in a Sno-Cat. That's dedication."

"Or desperation." I chuckle. "I'm erasing that from my head. But I know why my father used Jimmy Snarr's death by lightning as payback, dummying up his death certificate with my name, hurting the woman who burned him."

"Creatively cruel." Victoria shakes her head.

"Have I said how sorry I am yet today?" I whisper into Victoria's hair.

I've been apologizing since she left the hospital and I don't plan to stop. But a few layers of doubt slough off as she presses against me.

"It was awful. But I'm glad we're both alive," she says softly. "I've always said that junkyard was dangerous."

I squeeze her a little closer.

Once the police and news teams had their way with the property, I packed up the house and locked it up. I plan to move the dogs' house to Victoria's backyard in a few weeks—still working out the logistics of that. The junkyard with my studio will be my place of work. I'll still use Gramps's office, and if I have to meet someone late, I can do the rare sleepover there, but it's time for me to separate myself from my old life and embrace something new with Victoria.

Victoria clears her throat and turns to meet my eyes. "You ready to answer some questions?" The topic of VAPPA and what happened in Kansas has hung over us since she woke up. If I'm fully committing, it's time to prove it. I reach for the remote and turn the sound down to almost nothing.

I can't look at her, so I withdraw my arm from her shoulders and let my fingers clasp and unclasp as I search for where to start. Do I talk about Jasper coming into the club hurt and crying over his puppy? Or how things just went terribly wrong when I went to confront Randall? Or how all I wanted to do was help those poor horses at Foster's ranch, and ended up running him over?

"Who is VAPPA?" she asks, giving me an opening.

I look up at her. "Me." The truth is simple when you commit to just saying it.

Her mouth crooks a bit and I'm not sure if she's disturbed or upset so I continue. I tell her all of it, starting with Jasper, then Randall. I tell her about the police scanner and the call I felt to do more to help children and animals who weren't being cared for.

She nods and lets me continue as I get to the story of Foster in Kansas. I see horror in her eyes as I talk about Foster killing his horse and how I backed over him to stop him from killing the other two.

When I get to meeting Kaw and giving him the truck, I see hurt there and I can't keep going with the story.

"I'm so sorry, Vic." My fingers are red with how much I'm rubbing them. "I should have seen how mentally unstable he was. I told him too much; I manipulated him. I did." And this is where my guilt really lies. I'm the planner, and even though I didn't think I was setting it all up, that's exactly what I was doing when I filled out that bill of sale, when I told Kaw about VAPPA, when I tried to get him to come to the yard to switch out the truck for another one. Anything to keep the eye of the law from targeting me. Instead, I turned my loved ones into the targets.

"I'm just so sorry." A weighty pain fills me.

She lets the tears fall down my cheeks, lets me hunch over and feel the full weight of my actions. Then I can feel her hand on my back in small, comforting circles. She keeps that up for a while until I finally sit up, wiping my face.

Her face has sadness in it, but not anger. I know I'm asking too much of her to say something, to give me words of comfort.

"I killed my dad."

Her eyes shift sharply to me, and I see confusion there. When we were getting to know each other, I told her my dad died in a hunting accident and that's why I moved in with my grandparents. I tell everyone that. Now, in a jumble of words that I can't stop, I tell her the real story. About Keesha, about the years of abuse before that, about lifting the rifle and pulling the trigger. How lost and confused and out of control I felt, and how it was a secret buried so deep inside that no one knew about it.

We sit like that until I realize the only thing that needs to be answered for me.

"Can you live with someone who has done all this? Can you still be with me?"

I'm not good at vulnerable. Not good at being open and holding myself bare, but there is no other question in the world that is more important. I hold my breath as she looks up at me.

Then her face softens, and she nods. "Thank you for telling me, babe."

I pull her toward me, and I bury my face in her soft neck.

She holds me and I'm afraid to break the moment. Afraid that it's a dream.

"I now know why you've seemed different these last few months. I told you whatever you were doing, not to change." She laughs. "Hearing all these stories, little did I know I was encouraging a serial killer."

"Can we just say vigilante?"

She gives me a good long stare and nods. "Believe me. I won't be saying either of those words to anyone."

-41-

The Feds ask to meet me at Gram and Gramps's place. I've already stopped thinking about it as my home.

Victoria and I stayed up most of the night talking more. She needed to know all the details, and I saw her watching my face to catch the hint of a lie. Did I want to hurt these people or was it all happenstance? I had to admit to Harrison Fields II. She got angry with me when I told her what he did to his girlfriend's dog. I had to admit to the premeditation of this attack, and I saw her displeasure as I told her about the hidden bleach syringe and drain cleaner turkey baster. I realized that I was glad that whole scheme had failed, and that I finally understood revenge and justice are two different things, although at the time they felt very much the same.

We slept in each other's arms for a few hours. In the morning, I kept watching for a change in her, a hesitation to let me touch her, a flinch when I spoke. Instead, she talked about when the dogs would be here and how happy she was we are all together. She talked about our future. Damn, but I'm a lucky man.

As I drive the distance to the junkyard and house, I realize that she wasn't just okay with everything. She'd been disturbed by what I shared, but instead of judging the actions, she chose to see me. The whole me. The hurt little boy, the lover and defender of animals, the crusader desiring to make the world a less shitty place. It will take more discussions, I'm sure, but having someone really see me for me? That is a precious thing I know I need to earn and not lose.

The Feds and I settle into the living room with lemonade I grabbed from the store on the way here. I pour them each a glass then sit sipping my own, letting them go first.

Peck has lightened up a bit over the month, but he suspects things about me, and I can tell it bugs him. "Your mother settling in okay over at Aspen Hills?"

"It's been an adjustment. One day at a time, I guess." I smile. The small talk is bullshit but it's a part of our dance.

They've already combed through my home phone and cell phone records, and thank goodness the only two calls from Kaw included the one Lloyd took while I was at the beach and the last one when Kaw said he was bringing the truck back. Pay phones saved my ass. Lloyd backed me up, said that Kaw sounded crazier than a loon on the phone, ranting on and on about a "major purpose."

"So when Mr. Speers called you again in June," O'Conner asks, "he wanted to buy another vehicle from you?"

"That's what he told Lloyd on the phone. I was still at the beach." Kaw would have been proud of the title of *Mister* Speers. "When I rang him back, he said he was unsure what he planned to do. I told him he knew where I lived, not really believing he would come."

Peck leans forward. "Funny. We showed you his picture not long after that, and you said you'd never seen him before."

I clear my throat, hoping to sound contrite. "The tattoo on the guy you showed me looked all wrong. But I should have thought about Mr. Speers. He wasn't here very long in May when he bought that truck off me, but he was one strange ranger."

"How'd he find you in the first place?" O'Conner rocks his head from side to side, stretching his neck.

I shrug. "Like anyone else, I guess. Phone book. Drive by." I pause. "Could have been camping out in the back of my woods all spring for all I know."

They found evidence that he was staying up there right before he took Victoria and came to the house. Or as I explained it, right before he attacked me. When they removed the old truck parked under the willow tree, I justified my prints on the wheel because I was forced to drive it there. The soot on the truck matched ash from my mother's house. And in the bed of the truck they found three empty gas cans.

I lean back into the couch. During past visits, I've had to watch my words, my facial expressions, all to keep them off my trail. But I don't feel that anymore. Victoria loves me for me, Kaw is gone, my mother is alive, and though Florence will have a long and painful recovery, at least she's still with us. I sip my lemonade and wait for whatever they want to talk about next.

"You made an impossible shot," O'Conner says. "Most police departments could use a sharpshooter if you get bored selling car parts and painting."

"I'll keep that in mind." I've celebrated that shot over and over in my mind. If I'd missed it things could have been so much worse.

They stand and tip their hats again, and I lead them to the door.

"You know we still don't completely believe your story," Peck says, but his face shows he's ribbing me a bit.

O'Conner squints my way. I've learned this is his agreeable look.

"What can I say?" I raise my good arm. "I come off as that kind of guy, I guess."

"Keep this in mind." Pecks taps his hat against his leg, a little more serious now. "We'll be watching you. You so much as take a piss in the woods, and we'll know about it. Another person goes missing, you're our first stop."

"Anytime you're in the area." I smile.

I'm not worried. If I go hunting again, it won't be in my own back yard.

Machiavelli said that if you need to injure someone, it should be so severe you don't have to fear their vengeance. I have nothing to fear from Randall, Foster, or Kaw.

When a story of child or animal abuse hits the news, people ask if VAPPA was really a crazy guy from Wyoming. All in due time, people. All in due time.

There's a push for stiffer laws for abusers, but that's like cold molasses moving through Congress.

I lock up the house and turn my latest ride, a blue 1979 Volvo with Idaho plates, toward the highway. Victoria's been listening to the CB and heard about a puppy farm a little over four hours' drive from here. They keep the ones they think can be sold for thousands and drown the others. It's worth a look-see.

Today is as good as any day to go for a drive.

THE END

ACKNOWLEDGEMENTS

Thank you to my beta readers for your insights, your story tweaks, and your detailed reviews. As always, it takes many sets of eyes to make a book ready to be birthed into the world. I need you every time! A hearty hug to Lynda-Smart Brown, Jeff Lowder, Linda Orvis, Dennis Miller, and Rick Christensen.

To my story editors at The Manuscript Dr. Thank you for driving the story deeper than I imagined, especially as I needed to create a likeable vigilante.

Thank you to Ann Riza and Ann Suhs for your professional edits and for catching timeline issues and so much more.

Emma Faith Mayo. You are an amazing artist and you've once again created a beautiful, yet meaningful cover that captures the essence of the novel. I appreciate your years of making me look better in all ways and for your loyalty to my writing journey.

To John Hardy, who is my husband, friend, and non-stop cheerleader. Thanks for remaining a great sounding board as we talk through the murkier parts of the plot. You encouraged me to pull this old manuscript out of the recesses of the computer and get it out into the world. I'm glad you did.

A final thank-you to everyone who adopts rescued pets or works in the pet-saving, pet nurturing business. You are the heroes.

"We can judge the heart of a man by his treatment of animals."
— Immanuel Kant

AUTHOR'S NOTE

I first wrote this manuscript in 2005 after a story of a man in my city who beat his puppy in front of his kids hit the news. People stood vigil around his property, not allowed to step onto it, shouting that he should have received a harsher sentence. But he didn't and the protestors went home. But my mind asked, "What if a vigilante decided to take this guy's punishment one step further?"

I wrote the book in eight months, had beta readers who loved it, and was ready to send it out into the world. Then *Dexter* started streaming on HBO and it took the wind out of my sails.

All these years later, people are more pet-obsessed than ever. Animals are our family members. Stories of animal rescues make the evening news right alongside hurricane and political stories. We dress our dogs and cats up for Halloween, buy them Valentine's Day treats, and call them Service Pets so we can take them everywhere. Airports have convenient pet lounges; restaurants accept our furry children inside.

And above all, we won't tolerate abuse when we see it.

If you bought this book, an animal thanks you because a portion of your purchase price went to the ASPCA. If you enjoyed this book, please consider leaving a review on sites where other readers may also discover this story.

And if nothing else, whether person or animal, always be kind to the unsheltered.

Now for what's true and not true. There was a serial killer who was dubbed Dr. No who killed over nine women working at truck stops in Ohio between 1981-1990. He was never caught.

The town of Manzanola is real but the town hall is not as I described.

Many junkyard owners are rich, a fact I wouldn't have known, and there is a giant junkyard in Georgia that rents out for photo opportunities like Wyatt does in the story.

The larger cities in the book are real but the small towns are made up.

The CB radio chatter was fun to write and taken from old CB sites.

AUTHOR BIO

Karla M. Jay writes about injustice. From the holocaust to women joining the ranks of the KKK, her goal is to tell little-remembered stories (or those not yet heard) that we should never forget about. She lives in Utah with her husband and one very large gray dog. When she's not writing, she's reading, gardening, or traveling to a place she has yet to visit, in hopes of discovering another story begging to see the light of day.

Follow her at https://www.karlajay.com

Check out Karla's award-winning novel, *It Happened in Silence set in Georgia, 1921.*

Amazon Link

Goodreads Link

Read Chapter 1 now

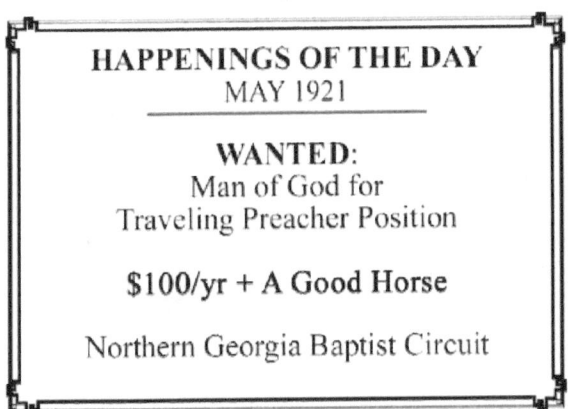

HAPPENINGS OF THE DAY
MAY 1921

WANTED:
Man of God for
Traveling Preacher Position

$100/yr + A Good Horse

Northern Georgia Baptist Circuit

Stewart Mountain, Georgia. May 1921
Chapter 1
Willow Stewart

Our ancient rooster, Cockle, splits the morning calm with his scratchy crowing and rips me from an eddy of a daydream I prayed I could hold on to. That bird has been irritating since he hatched, but today he sounds worse than a metal scoop scraping the insides of an empty cookpot. I'm fully awake now, reality reaching into my chest and squeezing my heart. I fight my bucking chin, trying to hold back tears, although I know they have a mind of their own and can't be intimidated. I was dreaming of Mama. She wore her playful smile, and her bubbly laugh filled my ears. Then Cockle ruined it all. My insides and outsides hurt as if I've been tumbled in a rockslide, though nothing the likes of that happened. But the notion that death isn't fully done hunting my family is pounding me from all sides.

I've a long day before me, heading off our mountaintop to find a traveling preacher. The baby's birth went bad, and Mama is laid up inside, doing poorly. On this sad morning, I'm angry at the birds for singing their fresh tunes, for welcoming the spill of warm sun across our rocky peak.

My one wish is to hear Mama say my name again. Soft, like a breeze through tree boughs. *Willow.* People's voices create colors in my mind, and Mama's is creamy peach. I want her to tell me everything will be fine, that she is just worn out and resting. Sorrowfully, she stopped talking hours ago.

My sister Ruthy, to be married after she turns eighteen in three months, enters the kitchen from the parlor. The blue of her eyes stands out against the bloodshot white, whether from the constant irritation of crying or the long sleepless nights. She has our Poppy's brown hair, but it's a messy bird's nest this morning. I inherited Mama's Scottish red mane and managed it into a braid last night or I'd look the same mess. She catches me staring at her hair and runs her fingers through it.

Ruthy reaches for my hand and gives it a quick squeeze. "You go sit with Mama, Willow."

I nod. Born mute, I sign my question to her. *"Has she talked again?"*

"She's still unconscious"—she straightens her flowered shift—"but breathing regular."

My heart thuds as I push into the sitting room where we spend most evenings in the fall and winter. The oil-fired heaters that will warm the room again wait in the barn for the first cold snap. They've barely been packed away. Two windows are open. A spring breeze sweeps in the smooth lemony fragrance of magnolias mingling with drying mud and the biting scent of newly sawn wood. The neighbor men worked through the night building the coffin in case it's necessary. It waits alongside the cabin, next to another smaller one. I used to love fresh-cut pine scent but now it's ruined. I jump ahead in my mind and see Mama's burying box, decades from now under the cover of moss, rotting there, never needed. I pray God is listening to our prayers and deciding that fate for the box. That we won't need it. Calling home one Stewart kin member this day is pain enough.

In the center of the room, Mama lies on a single bed. A ray of sun strikes the ornate oil lamp hanging from the center beam above her. It casts a rosy glow through its hand-painted floral glass shade. Mama looks at peace, her folded arms rising and falling on the white sheet covering her. Her pale hands like two sleeping doves.

The menfolk moved great-grandmother's Colonial-style cedar chest from the center of the room to the far wall next to Mama's favorite padded chair and sewing stand. The stitching hoop still holds the last of the pillow-cases she's embroidering for Ruthy's wedding to Leeman Castlelaw.

I sit in the spindle chair next to her bed and hope Mama knows it's me. Her "silent gift" as she calls me. When it was clear as moonshine I'd never speak, she and I created a hand signaling language that works well. My older brother Briar caught on and was often my translator, especially if we ever found ourselves in unfamiliar company. But that was a rare event due to how far up in the hollow we live. Poppy, Ruthy, and my little brother, Billy Leo, understand me sometimes—but only basic ideas. If my thoughts are simple enough, like following water skeeters across a pond's surface, they understand me. But for my below-the-surface opinions, I need Mama or Briar.

My eyes move to the three-shelf bookcase below the window. The top shelf holds one of Mama's favorite books, *Black Beauty*. A tale about a horse's early years and what his doting mother teaches him. The binding is worn from all the times she read it to us. When I recite the whole story in my head, word for word, it's my mother's voice I hear. I'm lucky that way. Most folks must hear their own voice when they think or have an inside-the-head conversation. Since I've never made even a squeak, I have mama's speech tone in there, especially when I'm reading.

I study her hands and picture her fingers flying over the piano keys, my Poppy slapping his knee and saying, "Della Rae, you play like an angel in a vaudeville show."

Those fingers. They braid my unruly red hair and tickle the backs of my legs. And Mama is a hand-holder. She always says holding hands is a promise between two people, a way to speak without words.

Reaching for her now, I wedge my fingers under her palm. The coolness surprises me and races straight to my throat, threatening to stop my breath. Why have I not held her hand more often? Spent more time in the house with her and less time in the forest? *I'm sorry, Mama*, I scream in my head. *I'll be around more. Just as soon as I get back from fetching a preacher. And trying to coax Briar home.* I sob and choke and cry some more. My stomach tightens, and silence twists through the room, snakelike, burrowing through my fifteen years of happiness. If Mama passes, I wouldn't care if I follow her into the next world because I don't know if anything can fill the holes if I remain behind.

Ruthy enters with my youngest brother, Billy Leo, twelve, groggy and clinging to her side. She's going to marry in a few months. Appears to me Ruthy doesn't mind that Leeman reeks of the wild onion sulfur-like stink from digging the rare bulbs he sells to lowlanders at the Broken Fork Country Store. I know for sure I'll be giving any future husband a good sniff before I ever agree to marry. That is if anyone will have me. At fifteen, it's looking mighty doubtful.

"You best get going, Willow. I packed you a food parcel by the door. Poppy's waiting on you outside."

When I lean closer and kiss Mama, my tears splash her cool, dry cheek. *I'll be back tomorrow. Please be here when I get home.* I wipe the moisture from her face, then turn to my sister, wrap my arms around her for a hard squeeze, and accept her kiss atop my head. Billy Leo lets me run my hand through his messy hair. The smile I try to form jitters around on my lips. Seems I know I've failed at offering a spark of optimism.

I leave the room, but Ruthy's voice, with its scarlet-red cheeriness, pokes at my heart as she tells Mama that Billy Leo has come to sit a spell. When Ruthy marries off, I'll be Mama and Poppy's main helper, cooking and tending the gardens, working the old mule with Poppy in the fields. Ruthy won't be but five miles away, though in the dark surrender of winter's reach, distance increases tenfold.

I open the screen door and cut my eyes to the left.

Lucille and Everett Tate sit in rockers on our wide porch, sipping sassafras tea. The soft blue-green color of the porch ceiling reflects onto Everett's white shirt. Although the paint color keeps the evil haint spirits from crossing our threshold, it can't shoo away folks like these two. Mama and Poppy welcome everyone to our house, but some folks they're less enthused about. The Tates are kinfolk. Cousins on Poppy's side. But so far removed it would take exploring the family Bible back to when his relations first reached these mountains to figure how they fit in with our Scottish kin. Poppy likes to say if Everett ever had the notion to work his own crops, that notion would die of loneliness. Instead of being self-reliant farmers like the rest of the folks in our community, the Tates pester the circuit preacher to point them toward the next deathwatch or funeral where food is abundant, and gossip, singing, and a secret mug of liquor fill an evening.

"Sorry about your baby brother, Willow." Lucille Tate is taller than her husband with a scowl between her eyebrows that ofttimes smooths out when her hair is pulled into a tight bun. Today is a loose-hair day, and her scowl's so deep it looks likely to sing if handed a hymnal.

"We attended the four-county revival meeting just last week," Missus Tate goes on to mention. Her voice swirls like gray ashes in my mind. "Reverend Cox done a bold meeting. Dozens of folks walked the aisle and was saved."

The Tates believe they praise God's glory more than the rest of us. Poppy says truth be told, they do seem busy in the eyes of the Lord, following His word to every pic-a-nic and church supper they catch wind of.

"We did an altar call in your name, Willow, asking the Lord to heal your affliction." Lucille smiles. "You just wait, child. One day, He will answer."

I sign, *"Thank you,"* but feel like a traitor, and heat flares in my neck. There are more important prayers that need to be sent heavenward than that of me talking someday.

My hand is clenched on the wooden railing. I release it and exhale as I walk down the three steps to stand by Poppy. He's tall and solid, with bushy eyebrows, the left one cocked higher than the right, as if to say he is wise to the ways of the world. His fair skin, permanently seamed with wrinkles and laugh lines, will be bronze by summer's end. He generally wears his whiskers only in the winter, but a two-days' growth now spikes his chin and cheeks.

"They're here," he says, his usual hazel-blue voice a threadbare version of itself, worn thin from greeting everyone while under such strain. He points a knuckled finger toward our last kinfolk to arrive on our side of the Stewart mountain. Uncle Virgil with his crooked leg from the world war, and Auntie Effie with plum-size eyes that say she is stuffed full of more sadness than she knows what to do with.

They are my favorite relations.

Auntie and Uncle lead their horses to the crowded corral. I study the yard full of folks gathered round the makeshift tables of old wooden doors set across sawhorses. An hour ago, Ruthy and I served up fried rabbit and squirrel with wild horseradish pulp and early lettuce from the garden. Thirty-eight people have arrived for Mama's deathwatch. Pans of corn-bread drizzled with bacon grease and honey disappeared in one passing.

Poppy reaches for my hand.

"C'mere, Pumpkin." He pulls me closer, then slowly rubs my arm, wrist to elbow and back. He wasn't a hugger, but his calming way of smooth-ing out the wild side in our livestock works on us children too. Affection from him is rare. He's done become a hardened man these past few years. Tragedy has nearabout wrung the happiness out of him.

My nervous insides feel as if they might burst out like a bottle of shook-up pop. I lean into his warm hands and enjoy the moment.

"You'll soon be on your way, Willow." His voice sounds full of tiny river pebbles, stonier today than usual. He returned from the war with a lower, crackling voice, surviving a mustard-gas attack that killed many a soldier. Now, like the rest of us, he hasn't slept since Baby Luther died yesterday. "Just to the church in Helen and back. You remember my directions?"

I nod. The church is the easy part of my trip. Finding my twenty-year-old brother, Briar, might take me longer. He needs to come home. Fifteen months is long enough to heal old wounds.

Cornhusk mattresses and extra chairs cover our grassy yard. Past that is the corral where my horse Jacca, a ten-year-old red roan with black points, mingles with the guests' horses. His name means God's Gift. Poppy bought him off the local Cherokee chief two years ago for a handmade chest of drawers. My pa is a right good furniture maker and Briar was taking an interest before he left home. The chief said Jacca was terrible for hunting because he was the talkingest horse they ever heard. Nickering and snorting, always trying to get his way. I smile. He's at it again in the enclosure, trying to push his way around a huge draft horse to make eye contact and beg oats from the big guy. It surely is a gift from God that a mute girl should own a horse that's pert and pushy.

Aunt Effie reaches my side and pulls me into a full-chested hug. My aunt and uncle would have arrived yesterday with the other relations and neighbors after Poppy rang the large dinner bell. Five quick clangs meaning our family needed help, and then after a moment's pause, he added one more for Baby Luther's passing. It was right then, before the startled birds returned to their morning song, a heavy rain broke loose and stayed hard at it most of the day. The river swelled, forcing my aunt and uncle the long way up Stewart Mountain to reach our cabin.

I breathe in Auntie's lavender soap scent. A warm memory sweeps through me. Mama and my aunt sitting out on our front porch in the slant of the evening sun, breaking apart dried lavender heads into a pot of warm lard and lye and laughing about menfolk or family antics as they make enough soap to last the winter.

Uncle Virgil steps to Poppy and shakes his hand, then leans in to give me a quick squeeze. He and Aunt Effie treat me good, like nothing's wrong with me. When I was younger and my cousin Len was still alive, I spent a lot of time at their house. They live right in our holler across the ravine. In late fall after the hickory oaks drop their leaves, their house and butcher shed peek through the scattered pines. With Aunt Effie being Mama's sister and all, she and Ruthy will take over organizing the household duties while Mama is getting better.

My plan is to follow the old road off our mountain, make a left at the Chattahoochee River, and parallel it all the way to the lumber town of Helen pitched along the big river. Never been there before, but it isn't more than eighteen miles away.

Poppy rubs my back as he speaks to my aunt and uncle.

"Willow is about to get busier than a moth in a mitten, but she's up to it."

Warmth moves through me at his praise. He's been afeared that Mama might follow Baby Luther into the grave, and this has softened him.

"You travel safe," Aunt Effie speaks into my hair, "and come back right quick."

I try not to feel too proudful that Poppy asked me to ride out to fetch a pastor. God will easily slap down a person chock-full of pride as easy as batting a fat tick. It comes down to the fact that I'm good on a horse. I'm also the best reader and writer in the family and at the right age to be off on my own. I'll find the first Protestant church I come across and hand them a note, asking for the next traveling preacher to offer a respectable funeral at our mountainside cemetery. Poppy said it don't make no never mind which religion shows up. The pastors all know how to wrestle God's attention for a time. Then on to a post office to get a message to Briar explaining the baby he knew nothing about died, and Mama is in a bad way. That's the secret part of my journey.

"You don't have a care now, Willow," Aunt Effie says. "I'll spend time with your ma and help the other womenfolk with chores."

I squeeze my hands together over my heart. My sign for thank you.

Without a voice, I use hundreds of homemade hand signs, but my relatives understand very little. It isn't their problem and it doesn't bother me. At age ten, I shed my ill feelings about not being able to make a sound. Mama read the story from the *Atlanta Constitution* about a woman who has it worse off than me. That Miss Helen Keller can't see or hear, but she gave a talk in a meeting hall. She said the greatest gifts in her life were curiosity and imagination. Mama said Miss Keller might as well be mountain folk with her message that the only excuse for being in this world is doing things to help one another. That's how we live.

"Don't you let folks get ugly to you out there." Uncle Virgil's brows knit together.

I nod and try to force a smile, but I've got no happy in me, just a stomach full of wriggling worries. I reach for the charm string round my neck. My fingers move across the four buttons there, finding the pink mother-of-pearl from Mama's wedding dress. I rub the raised floral pattern between my thumb and forefinger, and my body eases. Mama called it a forever charm, passed down from her own mother's wedding dress bought from a fancy store in Paris, France. It's left over after making Ruthy's bridal dress and my first happy ornament. The other three buttons are for remembering people who passed.

A pressed pewter button from Uncle Stewart's Civil War uniform, a burnished brown one from older brother Luther Junior's only suit coat, and a wooden one from my cousin Len's hunting jacket.

Ray Finch, the holler veterinarian, walks by carrying a heavy burlap poke, darker at the bottom where it's wet.

"Virgil. Effie," Mr. Finch says. "Good to see you, although the circumstances are a cryin' shame."

Mr. Finch brought ice from his cave deep in Gumlog Gulch, and extra camphor. Baby Luther's body has been kept cold in his tiny coffin with camphor cloths placed over his face to keep his skin from turning black.

Mr. Finch turns to Poppy. "How's Della Rae doing, Luther?"

Poppy is the first Luther in our family. My older brother Luther Junior died in a mining accident on Pigeon Mountain fifteen months ago. He was barely twenty. The explosion happened only six months after Poppy returned from France, sick and dog-tired. Those days after Luther Junior was killed were a blur. All-day crying, no one able to believe Luther Junior was really gone. Poppy fighting with Briar over what had happened. The sharpest image I hold from that day are the shiny nailheads in the wood, where someone overdone the hammering to shut the wood-slat crate they sent my brother home in. A note came attached, stiff with condolences from Mr. Mercer, the Estelle Mining owner. Other scrawled words said the company believed they'd recovered most of my brother from the explosion but warned us not to open the lid and check.

After he was buried in the family cemetery on a high knob, the neighbor men left their handmade leather boots outside the cabin, covered with fresh earth from Luther Junior's grave. I studied that dark dirt, stuck on the notion that it unfairly exchanged places with my brother. The black soil was free to watch the sunshine poke daggers of light through the morning fog while my brother was destined to darkness. I was only fourteen but learned an oak-size life lesson that day. In order to pack down the pain of losing a loved one, adults turn their talk to everyday concerns, such as how months of foggy mornings could rot through a birch outhouse faster than one bad winter.

Now our new Baby Luther isn't with us anymore. Appears as if God wants only one Luther in this family.

"Willow will be back tomorrow." Poppy squeezes my arm and his eyes squint, a move I know dams back tears. "God hasn't called Della Rae home yet, and she's a strong woman. In all her years of healing everyone else, she's taught Ruthy how to help her now."

He swipes the back of his hand across his eyes where it comes away wet. His next words are nothing more than choked sounds, and I hardly recognize his voice.

"Better she's here if she passes."

Hearing Poppy admit Mama may be dying sets me to crying big silent sobs. Snot running down the back of my throat threatens to suffocate me. Not only am I mute, but the airway parts in my throat don't work like they do for other people. I have room for either phlegm or air but not both at the same time. "Narrow tubes," the visiting doctor told Mama when I was four.

Poppy gently pounds my back and my breath returns.

Before Mama weakened and stopped talking, she asked me to be strong. I can do that.

"Let's get you going, Willow. Do you have your whistle?"

I pat my dress pocket and nod.

He picks up my burlap sack with the food Ruthy packed. Before he takes a step, he says, "I have something for you." Secretive-like, Poppy reaches into his pocket and pulls out a square wrapped in cloth.

I feel my eyes go wide at seeing the peanuts through the cloth. Mama's skillet-made peanut brittle.

Poppy must see the surprise on my face.

"Ruthy insisted you have a special treat for the ride." He tucks them inside my burlap sack and tightens the drawstring. "You enjoy this during your travels."

I swallow hard. Poppy always says, *"If you light a lamp for somebody, it will also brighten your path."* This treat cheers me for the moment and puts a tiny rip into the uncertain veil of death hanging over the day.

Poppy's face is full of emotion as he lays a hand across my back and plays with my braid. "Jacca looks ready."

We walk across the yard toward the corral, so filled with dandelions the ground might as well be a soft buttery blanket. It begs me to lie down on top to let its velvet yellow petals tickle my arms. I'd pour out my pain into their simple cheery stamina. That's the thing I like about dandelions. They're strong, all busting out from cold earth the moment the spring sun chases off winter's icy fingers. And then overnight, the dandelion turns to a white puff ball, and the first time a holler wind reaches up the mountainside, it blows the puff to pieces, sending the bits traveling to places far afield never to return.

Today I'm like that puff ball, except I'll be back to my home in no time.

Poppy is no hand-holder, but our arms touch on purpose as we cross the yard. Everywhere I look reminds me of Mama. The yellow roses she's trained to climb a fence. The newly planted vegetable garden. Her favorite chair on the porch, with its slightly crooked rocker and pleasant *creak creak* on the old boards early in the mornings when she's shucking something or knitting. Her hands always busy. Sassy, the goat Mama bottle-fed when Poppy told her to let it die, stands below the clothesline looking lost and confused. Where's her morning scratch behind the ears? Mama's blue gingham dress, the last one she wore before giving birth, hangs empty over the poor critter's head.

I'm feeling as hollowed out as that piece of clothing.

The guests sit on their thin mattresses, spread out like horizontal headstones in the yard. Some folks are asleep. Others are smoking corncob pipes and trading stories. The woven scents of honeysuckle, fresh churned dirt, and cherry tobacco make me dizzy, and for a moment, the world blurs at the edges. I sense the guests' eyes following me as I open the gate and coax out Jacca. They all know my purpose in leaving. To find a preacher to give Baby Luther a Christian send-off. But they don't hear the prayer playing through my head.

I pray that if I ride fast enough, using one of the skills God granted me, nothing will happen to Mama while I'm gone. Burrowed deep inside my heart, a tiny voice, one I don't recognize, speaks in golden tones. It says Mama won't pass with all of her children home and by her side. It's why I've secretly vowed to find Briar, even though his parting words to Poppy were that he'd never set foot on our homestead again. Perhaps time has picked away his feeling of scorn.

Slipping the sack's long drawstring over my head and across one shoulder, I climb onto Jacca's back. I touch my necklace, return Poppy's wink, and head off Moss Lick Knob, or as our kinfolk call it, Stewart Mountain.

www.ingramcontent.com/pod-product-compliance
Lightning Source LLC
Chambersburg PA
CBHW020408260626
47156CB00007B/2286